Praise fo

"What at first seems like a teenage beach read turns into a tribute to art's place in a young woman's life. It reveals Stacey's crumpled self-image in the face of the unattainable expectations she's up against. The book's portrait of teenage angst works as catharsis and creative release. Ska, grunge, and 1990s indie-rock music references are a vibrant backdrop to Stacey's concerns. Stacey changes from the inside out. Her artistic development, resulting in song lyrics and paintings, is a story within a story. What she learns and applies in her life about perspective, expression, and letting go inspires the book's audience, too."

—Mari Carlson, US Review of Books

"Few novels make me stay up late to read and also have me thinking about them when I wake up, but with Absorbed I wanted to know what happens next…I highly recommend this book for teens and their parents to heighten their awareness of how alone kids feel and ways to support them through the tumultuous high school years."

—Barbara Farrell

"Absorbed is one of those rare novels that doesn't just tell a story; it takes you back in time. It's perfect for anyone looking to revisit the magic and messiness of late-90s youth, as well as for younger readers curious about what life felt like before the digital age truly took over. It's a captivating story about growth, self-discovery, and the universal challenge of finding your place in the world."

—Jacqueline Asbury

"The title says it all! I was one hundred percent absorbed in this story from the start and absolutely loved it. The characters are fantastic and the writing is superb. Loved it!"

—Jill Marie

"Absorbed magnificently pairs the excitement of teenage life with the bittersweet consequences that are often out of a young adult's control. The arc of a group of teens who work together at a pool intertwine inextricably with the universal angst that plays, sometimes heartlessly, with the songs, emotions, and consequences of lives barely lived. This first book by Jaime Townzen does not disappoint. It is a must-read for young adults and their parents alike."

—Angela Sager

"This was everything that I wanted from this type of book, it had that concept that I was looking for from the description and enjoyed the characters and how they developed from it. Jaime Townzen has a strong style for this genre and that the characters worked overall in this story."

—Kathryn McLeer

"This story takes the reader to a very real place which is realistic for a teen but would also appeal for many adults... She deals with some very adult issues, which once again I think reflects some of the struggles we still face or may reflect on when growing up. "

—Meryl Soh, Librarian

"This book is a great way to begin conversations with your own teens or loved ones as it shows that honest discussions can lead to healing and reconciliation."

—Elizabeth Apkarian

"When you reach the end of the book you may find it hard to believe that only a summer has passed because of all the things the main character has had to go and grow through. For the reader, this translates into a story that keeps moving and evolving…with plenty of surprises along the way!"

—Andrea Zonneveld

"The author's words seemed to flow effortlessly, and my interest in the story grew stronger as the story progressed. I found it hard to put down. Most readers will connect with their own awkward moments…of being a teen, and trying to figure out where they fit in."

—Jeri Knickelbein

"Such a nostalgic read for me. I graduated high school in 1996 so the song references got me! I liked the characters and the lifeguarding aspect along with the self-discovery and friendship aspect."

—Kelly Pramberger

"I couldn't stop reading this book and I really didn't want it to come to an end…I really enjoyed Stacey's character and how confident she was even if she didn't feel confident herself. The ending was a surprise to me but a GREAT surprise."

—Lisa Kontny

"This novel, set in the summer of 1996, beautifully captures the intense, emotional turbulence of coming of age. The characters are incredibly relatable, especially Stacey, who struggles with identity, self-esteem, and the pressure to fit in. Her journey is both raw and real. This is a fun and nostalgic read for anyone who remembers the emotional rollercoaster of being a teen in the 90s and is interested in the timeless story of self-discovery."

—Nicole Dragoo

"It just goes to show, no matter where you were raised, we all experience similar growing pains! This book is so relevant, whether you are 16, 36 or 56, there is something so identifiable in every chapter! Be prepared to be taken back with music references you may have forgotten…to relive those teenage moments and be thankful we've all turned out just fine! Be prepared to read one of the best stories you'll ever come across."

—Louise Hutten

"Jaime Townzen's focus on a girl who is entering the complex realm of becoming a new adult… uses evocative, descriptive language that draws readers into her thought processes and motivations. Libraries will find it easy to point reading groups and patrons in the direction of Absorbed, which might initially seem like a fine beach read, but proves to contain scenarios of impact that encourage readers to draw better connections between thought, direction, and the consequences of infatuation… A thoroughly engrossing story, full of book club discussion material about coming of age, growth and transformation…"

—Diane Donovan, Midwest Book Review

Absorbed

JAIME TOWNZEN

Palm
Tree
PRESS

Palm
Tree
PRESS

Palm Tree Press Books, LLC
P.O. Box 178
Los Alamitos, CA 90720

First published by Palm Tree Press January 2025

Palm Tree Press Books can arrange live events with authors. For more information or to book an event, contact the Palm Tree Press Books publicity coordinator at 562-294-1624 or email palmtreepressbooks@gmail.com.

Interior design by Jaime Townzen.
Cover design by Mary Ann Smith.
Cover artwork collaboration Jaime Townzen, Mary Ann Smith, Canva.

Manufactured in the United States of America.

Library of Congress Cataloging-in-Publication Data is available.

ISBN (eBook): 979-8-218-51359-7
ISBN (paperback): 979-8-218-51358-0
ISBN (hardcover): 9798218516178

For every girl who underestimated herself or
people-pleased her dreams away.
You are more than enough.
There's no timeline to meet or mold to fit into.
Your passion is your power. Be true to you.

For Dani and Kara. You are stronger, kinder, and wiser than
I've ever been, and I couldn't be prouder to be your mom.
And for Patrick, my best friend, greatest champion, and truest
love. Thank you for believing in me, even when I struggled to
believe in myself.

PART ONE

Wading In

Chapter One

Stacey drifted along the stucco wall in the science wing, hoping to spot Gabe in the passing mob of students. Her Doc Martens crushed Doritos bags and Pop Rocks pouches littering the sweltering hallway. Emptied of the comforting weight of her textbooks, her backpack hung limp on her shoulder. With only a few days left of school, Stacey needed reassurance this summer wouldn't be as lonely and lame as last year. Her heart sank. No Gabe. She took a long gulp of her warm Dr. Pepper, then turned toward art.

Stacey navigated around cliques of FFA students, athletes, and drama kids as laughter echoed off open metal lockers along the breezeway. Several basketball players were huddled across the quad. Gabe, in his signature plain white T-shirt, had his back to her. She squeezed excitedly through a cluster of underclassmen, rushing toward him, squinting in the bright sunlight. The hollow whir of skateboard wheels and the blur of a body rushed at her.

"Holy shnikes!" the skater shouted, colliding into Stacey's left shoulder. The board rammed her ankle.

She stumbled, banged into a bank of lockers and landed hard on her butt on the hot concrete. "Ow!" she shrieked.

Students clapped and cheered.

"Gnarly," said a boy with a backward ball cap.

Stacey fought back the sting of tears.

"Sick crash, Jess!" someone called out.

Jess? When he bent to pick up his board, Stacey's mouth fell open. Jessie Thomas turned toward her practically in slow-motion, his sun-bleached hair swinging away from his face. Golden rays reflected off his perfect, glistening teeth. Sexy, guitar-strumming, graduating-senior Jessie Thomas. The boy she'd stalked all year in Christian Club, even though she'd never belonged to a church.

"You okay?" he asked, extending his hand. His WWJD charm shone among the dozen bracelets tied round his wrist. "You came out of nowhere!"

Stacey tucked her hand into his, staring into Jessie's crystal blue eyes. He heaved her to her feet. She sucked in her stomach and tugged her shirt down, embarrassed.

Jessie brushed a hand through his hair. "Hey, you're…"

"Stacey," she said. She bit her bottom lip.

"Wet." Jessie pointed downward to the brown stain blooming across the front of her jeans. He plucked the empty Dr. Pepper bottle from the ground and pushed it at her.

Stacey felt her face flush. She opened her palm to grab it, but fumbled. The bottle fell back to the ground.

"Sorry, Stephanie. Gotta jam. I'm totally late!" Jessie bolted toward the football field, his board in his hand. Turning the corner, he waved a shaka, then disappeared.

"Stace!" Gabe jogged up, his loose Levi's hanging low on his hips. He grasped her shoulders, scanning her up and down. "What happened? Are you hurt?"

Stacey hung her head, humiliated. "I stepped in front of him." She dusted the back of her pants and flinched, feeling the tenderness of a bruise forming.

"I saw. You sure you're okay? Need me to grab spare gym shorts from my locker?"

"With Docs? That'd be hilarious." Stacey tucked her long blonde hair behind her ear. "I'm alright. I only have art left. Thanks for coming to my rescue."

"Jessie's a dipshit. I could beat his ass if you want me to." Gabe palmed his fist, flexing his broad shoulders while making a goofy, menacing expression. His snug tee stretched across his pecs. Stacey felt her cheeks flush again and looked away.

Gabe picked up her backpack and handed it to her. She held it in front of her wet pants. He shot the empty Dr. Pepper bottle at a trash can 15 feet away, and it disappeared noiselessly. "Nothin' but net."

"Nice shot."

The warning bell rang.

"Shit, we better go. Call me later," he hollered over his shoulder, jogging toward his chemistry final.

The art room was loud with chatter. While Stacey focused on shading the veins of a leaf with her pencil, the other students signed yearbooks with colorful pens. Stacey's knees were pulled up against the edge of the desk, a graphite sunflower blossoming over the sketch paper pad covering the stain on her jeans. Someone nudged her elbow and the pencil scratched across the page.

Beside her, Amanda's freckled nose bobbed upward, directing Stacey to the front of the room.

Ms. Moreno was striking a colorful, wooden instrument, her signal all year to get the class's attention. She was in her mid-twenties, perpetually wearing splattered jeans and an apron, with a paintbrush shoved through the lopsided mass of tight curls atop her head.

While the other students took their seats, Stacey continued shielding her stain and lowered her knees to skootch her chair under the table. She folded her hands over the drawing and flashed her most innocent smile toward their art teacher.

"Brown-noser," Amanda said out of the side of her mouth.

"Takes one to know one," Stacey whispered.

Ms. Moreno set down the guiro. "I'm sure with school ending you all have a lot going on." Her words rolled out melodically, rounding the edges off hard consonants. "Don't forget to collect your pottery from the shelves and grab your portfolios before you go. Anything left over summer will be thrown out."

The only artwork remaining on the classroom's peeling ecru walls were the bright Clara Ledesma and Frida Khalo prints, along with an "Immigrant Rights = Human Rights, STOP PROP 187" sign beside the American flag.

Ms. Moreno waved a stack of blue flyers. "Also, I'll have Art Lab open Monday and Wednesday nights…" The bell announcing the end of the day echoed across the ceiling tiles, and was immediately drowned out by metal stool legs scraping across the concrete floor. Ms. Moreno sighed, dropping the stack of flyers on the overhead projector. "Have a great summer!"

Stacey waited out the crowd. Art class was officially over, and soon enough her junior year would be also. Just two days to go. She shoved her portfolio and sketchbook into her backpack, then looked toward the pottery shelves, wrinkling her nose. Stacey pulled her shoulder through the strap of her backpack and started toward the open door.

"Stacey, wait," Ms. Moreno called. "Your self-portrait..."

Turning slowly, Stacey winced. Ms. Moreno approached, holding up the large white frame, and Stacey checked over her shoulder that the other students had really gone.

The misshapen body and blurred features of the painting belonged in the garbage where Stacey originally tossed it, not flattened behind plexiglass with a blue and gold ribbon. Stacey still resented Ms. Moreno for entering it in the regional art competition in the first place. At least the label said the artist and the title were both "ANONYMOUS."

Stacey accepted the frame, but clutched the image firmly to her chest, hiding it from sight. Will this day ever end?

"I'm sure your family will be so proud of you! But why isn't your name on the list for advance art next year?" She stilled her fluttering hands on her hips. Staring at Stacey, she awaited an explanation.

Stacey shrugged. "I have a really full schedule. All AP and honors classes."

"Exactly! It would be a good outlet for you, and it's only for students up to the challenge. I hope you'll reconsider." She held out her flyer. "And I'd love to see you at Art Escape this summer. I'm focusing the workshops on watercolor."

"Sounds fun, but I got a job," Stacey lied. She hadn't heard yet whether she would be lifeguarding at the community pool, but the idea of spending any part of her summer at school depressed her. She wanted something more than always hiding in classrooms and behind books. She accepted the blue paper, tucking it between her fingers and the back of the frame. "I really need to head home."

Ms. Moreno grabbed a doubled paper grocery bag from beside the door. Whatever was inside clanked as she handed it to Stacey. "This is yours, too. You left almost all of your pottery on the shelves."

"I thought you said you would throw it all away."

"I'm glad I don't have to."

"Yeah. Thanks. Well, have a good summer, Ms. Moreno," she said, forcing a smile.

Stacey trudged down the stairs to the lower parking lot and she breathed a sigh of relief that most of campus was deserted. The last few cars streamed out at the stoplight, beeping at one another, arms waving out of windows.

Heat waves rippled off the asphalt as Stacey unlocked the Silver Bullet, her '87 hatchback Civic. She popped the driver's seat forward and wedged the frame into the back, laying it face down with her backpack on top. She dumped the bag of pottery on the floor and pushed the seat back into place.

Without getting in, she turned the key in the ignition to get the AC going. She slipped her Dookie CD into the slot on the stereo, and turned up the volume. "Welcome to Paradise" blared out of the speakers while she waited for the car to cool down. Stacey turned back to look at the high school perched on the dusty hillside.

Her stomach dropped. For better or worse, Mesa Valley High was the only place she knew what was expected of her. And in two days, a whole summer of unknowns would begin.

Chapter Two

Stacey set her backpack on the kitchen counter, beside the blinking answering machine. She palmed a handful of Corn Pops straight from the box and pressed play.

"This message is for Miss Stacey Chapman. Congratulations! You've been hired for the 1996 summer season. Please attend orientation at 8 am on Saturday at the facility on Seventh Street."

Stacey dropped the box of cereal and squealed, pulling the beige phone cord across the speckled Formica. Round yellow puffs scattered across the linoleum. Her golden retriever, Murphy Brown, wagged her tail as she devoured them. Stacey dialed Gabe's number, wrapping the twisted cord around her index finger and bouncing on the heels of her feet.

"I got the job!" she squealed when he answered.

"No way? That's awesome!"

"I start Saturday!"

"We'll still hit the beach at least a few times this summer, right?"

"Of course!" she said, then caught her reflection in the oven door. Her face fell and she dropped back onto flat feet, slumping forward. "Shit…I'm going to have to wear a bathing suit…like…all the time!"

"Duh…"

"The other guards are going to look like Pamela Anderson." Stacey groaned, lifting her tank top and turning sideways to take in the full glory of her pale belly rolls. She grimaced and looked away.

"You've gotta be kidding. Pamela Anderson paid a plastic surgeon to look like Pamela Anderson," Gabe said, laughing. "Don't sweat it. You're gonna make so much money. Way more than I do bussing tables."

"Where can I get a red swimsuit?" Stacey pulled the empty cereal box away from Murphy's muzzle and shoved it in the garbage.

"The mall?"

"Worth a try. Up for a road trip?"

"Can't." He sighed. "Algebra 2 final tomorrow."

Stacey did her best nasally-imitation of Nelson from the Simpsons. "Ha, ha!"

"Jerk," Gabe teased.

"I can help you study," she offered, holding the phone close and biting her bottom lip. Please, please, please say yes.

"Jenny's coming over."

Disappointment washed over her. "Oh…" Jenny, the prom date. She hadn't realized he and Jenny were still a thing. "That's cool." Stacey threw her head back and searched the ceiling for answers.

Over the line, she could hear Gabe's mom's voice in the distance. "Hang on," Gabe said to Stacey, and muffled the mouthpiece.

Stacey overheard Gabe's mom say something about taking out the garbage. Stacey pulled the stash of Nutter Butters from the cabinet above the fridge and gnawed on one while looking out the window. A mobile home park backed up to the backyard fence, and Stacey's gaze caught on the glint of sun reflecting off aluminum foil in a trailer's windows.

"Hey," Gabe huffed into the phone. "I gotta go. Call you later?"

"Mmm hmmm," she managed through her peanut butter coated mouth, doing her best to swallow.

"Congrats again on the job, Stace. It'll be great."

"Thanks," she garbled as Gabe hung up.

Murphy laid on the brown floral linoleum by Stacey's feet. "I've gotta get out of Mesa Valley, Murph," she said, sliding down the cabinets to slump onto the floor. "Ow! Shit!" She rubbed the tender spot on her butt, a reminder of her fall at school, and leaned back, letting Murphy lick the crumbs from her hand. Stacey tugged at the dried stain on her pants. "Why am I so lame? No one will ever fall in love with me like this."

Murphy wriggled onto her lap. Stacey scratched her fingers through her dog's mane, grateful for the brief cuddle before Murphy started licking her cheek. "Okay, okay. I know, YOU love me. That's enough!" Stacey shielded her face and scrambled back to standing. "Let's call Mom."

After the salon receptionist put her on hold, Stacey's mom answered. "This is Sharon."

"Mom, I have good news! I got the lifeguard job."

"That's great, Doodle Bug! I knew you would."

Stacey hated that nickname, a holdout from years spent coloring in her room alone. Her tone became clipped. "I need to buy a red swimsuit."

"Okay. Maybe from Lands' End? Or Speedo? Can we talk about it when I get home? My client's under the dryer."

"But Saturd—"

"Also, can you start dinner?" Her mom raised her voice over the whizz of a blow dryer. "My last appointment's running late. It's a full perm. I got stuff for Veggie-Roni bowls."

"Sure," Stacey replied. She robotically grabbed the boxed rice and canned vegetables from the cupboard and set them on the counter.

"See you after six." The line dropped.

"Bye," Stacey muttered. Returning the phone to its cradle, she added bitterly, "Love you, too."

It was still early to start dinner. She wanted to figure out the swimsuit situation. But shopping in Mesa Valley was complicated. Other than thrift stores, the nearest mall was over thirty miles away, and people got stabbed and mugged there a few times a year. Without Gabe, she was too afraid to go. Especially without knowing if the trip would even be worthwhile.

Crossing to the living room Stacey grabbed her mom's stack of catalogs and turned on MTV.

"Now up two spots from last week," Daisy Fuentes' voice filled the room, "our favorite band from across the Atlantic, Oasis, with 'Don't Look Back in Anger.'"

Stacey flopped onto the orange corduroy couch. Envying Daisy's shaggy bangs, she contemplated cutting her own with a spare pair of her mom's professional scissors, then thought better of it.

With the catalogs stacked in her lap, she started flipping through them, talking to herself. "Spiegel? No. JC Penney? No. Sears? Definitely not." Piling at least a dozen rejected home and linen catalogs next to her, she began losing faith.

"Victoria's Secret? That's promising…" Stacey flipped past Wonderbras and thong underwear, and found three pages of swimsuits. Lean, tan models stared seductively in barely-there bikinis. White sand clung to the smooth curve of their hips. A suit like that would get Gabe's attention. Or Jessie's.

Then her heart sank. Each piece cost $65! Her mom would freak. Plus, the only red suit was plaid, which wouldn't work. It had to be solid red. So much for that.

She slapped Victoria's Secret onto her discard pile, promising herself she'd buy one to wear to the beach after her first paycheck.

The final catalog was the Land's End swimsuit sale edition. Boring, solid, one-piece swimsuits filled every page. The same thin model appeared in every suit in the same pose, even the ones with "tummy control panels," whatever that meant. All for the "Season's Lowest Price: $39.99!"

Stacey called the 800 number. The woman on the other end of the line assured her the expedited shipping fee would get her the cardinal red "waist shaping" suit before Saturday. Using the emergency credit card her mom kept in her underwear drawer, Stacey ordered the suit, feeling proud she'd solved the problem on her own.

The stench of manure from the chicken ranch at the end of their street wafted through the screen door. Stacey held her breath and pulled the sliding door closed. Her mom had rules about using the air conditioner when it was under 85 in the house. But 83 was close enough. Stacey hated the way their neighborhood reeked, and she worried people could smell it on her clothes. Outside, it was a boiling 95 degrees with no breeze.

"This is borderline abusive, Murphy," she muttered, and flipped on the AC.

Stacey measured the butter and set it to melt on the stove, then started opening cans: black beans, stewed tomatoes, mixed vegetables. After making this meal at least once a week the past three years, she could have prepared it blindfolded. Stacey stirred the Rice-a-Roni into the saucepan, then added the stewed tomatoes. Her mom loved this dish because it made four servings for less than $5 total and it had all the food groups. Once the ingredients were combined it was a salty, colorful sludge Stacey regretted ever saying she liked.

"Why can't we have TV dinners like normal people?" she asked Murphy, and switched off the stove. She filled her bowl and plopped on the couch, eating mindlessly while watching a rerun of Real World San Francisco.

At 6:30, her mother barreled through the front door, swatting at a cloud of flies swarming in around her.

"Hey, Mom..." Stacey said, turning off the TV and peeling herself from the couch. "Your food's on the stove." She set her empty bowl in the sink and sat on a barstool.

"Thanks, Bug." Her mom set her purse down and took a bottle of cheap wine from a paper bag.

"Stopped at the liquor store?" Stacey's voice was heavy with criticism.

"Long day. Don't judge me," her mom said, grabbing a mug. "How are you?" She took a sip of wine, then took a fork from the drawer.

Stacey shrugged. "I ordered the Lands' End suit."

"What? Why didn't you wait?"

"I need it by Saturday. You always forget."

Mom clenched her teeth. "How much?"

"Fifty bucks, including tax and shipping."

"You can't spend $50 without talking to me first."

"You told me you want me to take more responsibility. I dealt with it."

Her mother took a large gulp, her eyes on Stacey over the rim of her mug. "Maybe we can get your dad to pay for it."

"Yeah…right. Good luck with that."

"Stacey, I'm doing the best I can. I hope you never have to find out what it's like to raise a kid on your own."

"Dad bought my car. He's paying my insurance. There's no way I'm calling to ask for a swimsuit, too."

"You're going to need more than one suit to lifeguard the whole summer. The card you used is almost maxed out. Call your stepmother. She'll give you the money." Her mom set her fork in the sink, put the leftovers in the fridge and refilled her mug.

Stacey snorted. "No way am I asking Jackie. I'll buy it myself."

"Don't go spending your money before you earn it. You need to pay for gas, too."

"Whatever," Stacey said, picking up her backpack. "I need to study. More finals tomorrow."

"Open your window," her mom called after her. "I'm turning the AC off."

Stacey waved a thumbs-up over her shoulder without turning back around. Murphy trotted after her, and once they'd both slipped into her bedroom, Stacey slammed the door. The full-length mirror hanging on the back rattled. She turned on her stereo, letting Jewel's "Pieces of You" saturate the room, and fell onto the bed. Stacey dialed Gabe's number, biting the inside of her cheek. Busy. She let the handset roll onto her pillow.

"Nothing's ever good enough, Murph." She buried her face in the dog's neck. "I made dinner, found the swimsuit. I'm a straight-A student, and never get into trouble! But that's not enough, is it? I'm too fat. Too ugly. A total dork. I'm so sick of it!"

Tacked to the wall above her dresser was an ad for Eternity perfume. A beautiful couple rolled in the sand, so clearly in love. That's what she wanted: for Gabe to take her in his arms and confess he was crazy about her. Or Jessie to even acknowledge her existence. Anyone to ask her out. Kiss her. They'd fall madly in love. Get away from Mesa Valley. Together. Forever.

Then she could stop feeling so alone.

For that, Stacey would do almost anything.

Chapter Three

Standing in her underwear, Stacey checked the number on the scale. Ten pounds heavier than she thought. And only three days before she was supposed to start at the pool. She kicked the scale back under her bed and stood in front of the mirror, pinching her belly fat and groaning at her thighs.

"I look like the Blind Melon Bee Girl," Stacey whimpered.

Murphy raised one eyebrow, but didn't lift her muzzle from her paws at the end of the bed.

At ten that night, done studying, Stacey started exercising frantically. She was determined to have an hourglass waist and supermodel thighs before morning. She rotated sit ups, leg lifts, and crunches, ignoring the acid lump her dinner formed in the back of her throat. Digging through the entryway coat closet, she pulled out her mother's ThighMaster triumphantly.

With Nirvana Unplugged in the background and the soft glow from her lava lamp, Stacey laid on the carpet on her right side, Suzanne-Somers-style. She started squeezing the royal blue foam-wrapped bars between her knees. After twenty squeezes, her inner thighs started to burn. The ground was hard under her hip, so she switched to the left, getting winded around fifty reps, then flipped again. With both hips aching and beads of sweat on her forehead, Stacey grunted her way to eighty, then laid back to catch her breath.

Checking the clock on her nightstand, Stacey dropped her head in defeat; she'd only exercised for fifteen minutes. Accepting she wouldn't be able to pull an all-nighter, she hoped she could at least manage two hundred reps. Stacey repositioned herself to sit on the edge of the bed, and turned the direction of the ThighMaster to face outward.

Her inner thighs were sweaty and sore. Her legs struggled to grip the ThighMaster in the new position. It slipped multiple times, and her knees quivered. Then, on squeeze one hundred and twenty-six, the boomerang-shaped torture device launched like a missile across the room, onto her desk. It flew straight into her lava lamp. The glass broke, along with the internal lightbulb. The room was instantly dark.

Murphy sat up on the bed and barked.

"What was that?" her mom yelled from her bedroom.

Stacey stood and pulled on the ceiling fan light to survey the damage. The mix of water, glass and pink goo dripped and pooled on the carpet.

Her mom threw open the door wearing a threadbare nightgown and waving a fireplace poker.

"It's only me!" Stacey hovered over the mess, attempting to block her mother's view of the hot pink stain forming.

Her mom hit the power button on the stereo, silencing "All Apologies." "Why didn't you answer me?"

"Get Murphy out. There's broken glass!"

"What the hell happened?" Her mom tugged the dog by her collar into the hall, then closed the door.

"I need a towel or something."

"What broke? It's water, right?" She handed Stacey the towel that was draped over the corner of a drawer. "Is that the ThighMaster?"

"Yeah," Stacey responded with a rude lilt. "So?"

"You know, young lady…," her mother said curtly. She huffed air out her nose and shook her head. "Nevermind. I have an eight a.m. client. Clean it up on your own. I'm going back to bed."

Stacey sat back on her haunches and waited for the sound of the door clicking closed. After scooping up as much of the goo and glass as possible, she threw the mess in the outside garbage can along with the towel. She pulled the desk over to hide the stain, and shoved the ThighMaster back in the coat closet.

She needed a new plan.

Her mom was always telling her that "grapefruit juice makes the fat melt off of you," so Stacey figured she could consume nothing else for the next few days.

By the time the swimsuit arrived Friday night, Stacey had lost six pounds, and was feeling proud of herself. But when she tried the swimsuit on and looked in the mirror, any shred of confidence she had found was lost.

"No!" Stacey shrieked from down the hall. "Mom!" She threw open her mother's bedroom door and ran to her, Stacey's face drained of color.

"What's wrong?" Stacey's mom stood in front of her mirror applying make-up, but spun around quickly, mascara wand held high.

"I can't wear this! It's too tight, and looks like Cabbage Patch granny-panties." Stacey faced the mirror, and tugged at the leg openings. "It cuts off the top of my legs like they're giant sausages, and makes my butt and thighs look enormous!"

"THAT'S what you're screaming about? You cannot be serious, Stacey." Her mom turned back to her mirror and took a deep breath, then resumed applying her mascara. "You look fine. You spent 50 bucks on that suit; you're wearing it!"

"YOU can't be serious, Mom!" She stood behind her mother, pulling at the suit and scowling at her reflection.

"Tough luck. There's no other option right now. And I have a date." She blotted her lipstick on a tissue while side-eyeing her daughter.

With fists clenched, Stacey screamed in defeat, then slapped her thighs. She stormed out, slamming her mother's bedroom door behind her, and then her own, before throwing herself face first onto her pillow. She screamed long and loud, her voice reverberating off the mattress springs.

After the front door closed, and Stacey heard her mother's car back out of the driveway, she sat on her bed, holding her head.

It was the end of Stacey's first official day of summer, and this was a bad sign. There were only fifteen hours before her orientation at the pool. She considered begging Gabe to go with her to search the sketchy mall for a solution, but its biggest department stores— Gottschalks and Mervyn's—probably wouldn't carry anything close to a lifeguard suit. She had no choice but to make this swimsuit work.

Stacey peeled it off, and–standing completely naked–stepped into the shoulder straps, pulling up on the suit's crotch until she heard the elastic begin to snap. Next she put a foot in the crotch, and pulled each of the leg elastics as hard as she could.

"Don't look at me like I'm crazy," she said to Murphy as she tugged. The dog laid on the bed, her head hanging off the side, watching Stacey's every move.

Finally, Stacey put her heels in the chest area, and pulled the rest of the suit around her feet, tugging for every millimeter of give possible.

Trying the suit on again, Stacey looked in the mirror, mumbling to herself. "Zero improvement. What kind of anorexic geriatrics wear Lands End suits, anyway?"

Fed up, Stacey peeled the offensive fabric from her body and threw it on the floor. She pulled on oversized boxers and a tank top, then flopped on her back on the comforter beside Murphy. "Maybe I don't actually have to wear the suit to orientation. Better to postpone my public humiliation as long as possible, right?"

Murphy thumped her tail.

Stacey curled around her golden dog, rubbing Murphy's white belly, desperate to ease the butterflies in her own stomach before morning.

"Please tell me this is actually going to be a good summer, Murph."

The dog rolled onto her back and looked at Stacey upside down, her tongue lolling out of her mouth.

"Well, that's reassuring." Stacey snorted.

Chapter Four

The Plunge? The pool's nickname reminded Stacey of toilets. Urinal cakes and chlorine muted only by mildew. The stench burned Stacey's nostrils when she pulled open the squeaky lobby door. The lights were off. She hoped she hadn't written down the wrong time.

Stacey peeked through a small window in a door to her right. Nothing in the girl's locker room had changed since she'd last been there several years before. The cracked cement floors were covered in standing puddles of water. There were no doors on any changing stalls and the cinder block walls were peeling. An identical door across the lobby said BOYS, but before she could see what that locker room looked like, she heard someone whistling.

Stacey turned to look through the plate glass window into the dim interior of the main pool office. The guard shack. Coach Bob entered through the back door and the bright sunlight from the outdoor pool deck flooded the dark office interior. Bob Smith was a PE teacher, the varsity baseball coach, and he ran the pool every summer. The deck door banged closed behind him and the space was again shrouded in darkness.

Bob flipped on the guard shack lights, then noticed Stacey waiting in the lobby. He smiled and opened the door for her. Wearing his standard Mesa Valley High School T-shirt and ball-cap uniform, Bob's permanent farmer's tan peeked out from navy athletic shorts.

"Hey, Stacey! Early-bird gets first pick."

"First pick of…what?" Stacey asked.

Other voices boomed into the lobby. There were bursts of laughter and a big guy with shaggy, sun-bleached hair and a goatee yelled out, "I call hosing the deck!" The group filed past Stacey without acknowledging her.

Stacey slithered into the room behind everyone else and shrank against the wall.

When she was a kid, the guard shack seemed like a secret haven where mysterious, cool lifeguards ate take-out and were the gatekeepers of band-aids and lost goggles. Now, she wouldn't want to walk barefoot on the filthy, threadbare carpet. A few of the plywood locker doors hung crooked, and the beige and brown plaid couch looked like it had been pulled from a dumpster.

"Every morning, we divvy up the jobs before we open the pool," Bob told the group as they settled into seats. "Today you learn what those jobs are. Mark, you have seniority; sure, you can hose the deck. But first you've gotta show 'em how to get the covers off, and lane lines in and out."

Mark, the big guy with the goatee, was nodding, his sunglasses still on. He wore a faded and stained City of Mesa Valley logo T-shirt and a large-brimmed thatched hat hung down his back. He wore red trunks. Panicking, Stacey looked around the room. Only one other guard seemed to be wearing a red swimsuit. Fortunately, she wasn't the only one in street clothes.

"No way am I cleaning bathrooms," a lean brunette girl said, crossing her arms. Perched on the edge of the couch cushion, she looked as though she was posing for a magazine, and above menial labor. Stacey recognized her. She'd just graduated and ran track. She had thighs with huge oval muscles on top that created perfect definition along the side, like racing stripes.

The lobby door swung open. "I'm here!" a voice yelled out. Jessie entered the guard shack panting and leaned his skateboard against the desk. Stacey's stomach flipped.

"Thank you for joining us, Jessie," Bob said. "Have a seat." Bob turned his attention back to the track star on the couch. "Melissa, all the guards take turns cleaning the bathrooms. Taking care of this place is part of your responsibility."

Jessie crossed to the other side of the room, flipped a folding chair around and sat down backwards. Stacey sunk further into the corner, hoping she was out of his line of sight.

"It's not so bad. We mostly only hose it out and take out the trash," Mark said. "Don't forget your flip flops and rubber gloves."

Melissa narrowed her dark, stormy eyes, sneering at him.

"This is as good a time as any to establish the most important aspect of working here," Coach Bob said, standing in the center of the room. "I expect you all to work as a team to keep our facility clean and safe. If anyone isn't pulling their weight, you will address that as a team as well. That includes ALL cleaning duties," he said, looking in Melissa's direction. Then he turned toward Jessie. "And being on time for each shift." He moved to stand beside the desk. "Now, let's go around and introduce ourselves. I'm Bob. I've coached and taught at the high school for twenty-five years and been pool manager during the summers for the last ten. This is Mark, assistant pool manager. You're up, Sport."

"Yup, I'm Mark," he said, moving the sunglasses to the back of his neck. "This is my third year at The Plunge and I'm lucky enough to work here year-round. Just think, if you become a college dropout, you too could be living the dream like me."

Everyone else laughed. Stacey nervously chuckled along. Is he serious?

"Funny guy," Coach Bob said, clapping Mark on the shoulder. "Mark handles pool maintenance for the swim team September through May. If I'm called away, Mark's in charge."

Mark pulled the straw hat onto his head and slumped back into the office chair, both feet up on the desk. He aimed finger guns at a petite girl in a red athletic two-piece.

"Hi, I'm Tiffany!" She bounced on her heels and smiled brightly, her short, white-blonde curls swaying. She was like a Drew Barrymore clone. "I know most of you, but…" Tiffany looked at Stacey.

The other guards gazed in Stacey's direction. She stood taller and sucked in her stomach.

Tiffany went on. "I've been swimming at The Plunge my entire life. I was varsity swim captain and this is my second-year lifeguarding." Tiffany looked around the room. "It's going to be such a great summer!" she added, like she was the official Plunge mascot.

Stacey wondered what brand Tiffany's bathing suit was and whether the other girls would also be in bikinis. Before she went home, she needed to find a way to ask Tiffany about where she'd bought it.

"Mark and Tiffany will be training the rest of you over the first week, until you're all up to speed," Bob said. "And of course, if there's anything these two veterans can't answer, then come to me."

Melissa stood, pursing her lips. She had glowing skin the color of damp sand and her long dark hair reached almost to her waist. "I'm Melissa Phillips. I'm attending ASU in September on a full track scholarship. I'll study business and in four years I'm going to law school to become a private practice corporate lawyer." Her tone was serious and she lifted one eyebrow as she spoke. With her hands on her hips, her cropped tank and micro denim shorts revealed her taut abs. "I've never been a lifeguard before, but the past two summers, I worked at Baskin Robbins. I can still use my discount, if anyone's interested."

Stacey wished she liked running if it meant she could eat Baskin Robbins regularly and still have zero body fat, like Melissa. She figured the running and the perfect body must be genetic anomalies.

"Are your parents those Pakistanis who work at the Baskin Robbins in Red Hills?" the guy seated on the couch asked.

Melissa glared at him. "We're NOT from Pakistan," she hissed through clenched teeth. "We're Indian, you dumbass. And we OWN three stores, actually." She kept her eyes locked on his as she sat back down.

"That's a very generous offer, Melissa. Thank you," Bob said before he waved his hand to the guy seated next to Melissa on the couch.

The guy cleared his throat, then leaned back and pulled on the end of his shorts. "Hey, I'm Chad," he said without getting up. He had a dimple in his right cheek and a crooked smile. He reminded Stacey of Christian Slater. "I play soccer. I was in ASB. I'm going to Cal State in the fall. It's my first summer guarding and it's great to be here."

Despite how friendly and easygoing Chad seemed, the girl on his other side was leaning away from him onto the arm of the couch. She was petite, busty, and biting the inside of her cheek, looking up at the ceiling. Her nose and cheeks were covered in faint freckles. She looked almost as uncomfortable as Stacey felt. Chad put his hand on the girl's thigh, saying, "And this is Desiree."

Desiree flared her nostrils. Whatever was going on, there was some serious sexual tension between them. Desiree stood, unsuccessfully tugging up on the spaghetti strap of her babydoll dress, which emphasized her significant cleavage and thin legs. Stacey found herself panicking on Desiree's behalf that one of her straps could break, which the guys in the room were probably attempting to cause through Jedi mind-tricks.

Crossing her arm over her waist, she held her strap with her other hand. "I'm Desiree," she snapped at Chad, then blinked several times and smiled around the room. "I also just graduated and this is my first summer lifeguarding as well. I was in ASB with Chad and I'm going to USC." Desiree sat, pulling her dress under her, and smiled sweetly. When Chad reached for her thigh again, she swatted his hand away, then crossed her arms, leaning back into her corner of the couch.

Everyone's attention shifted to Jessie.

He'd been held back at some point early on, so he was almost nineteen. A bicep tribal tattoo peeked out from under his T-shirt. Stacey had heard a rumor that he referred to it as his crown of thorns.

"Hi! I'm Jessie," he said, flipping his wavy, sun-bleached hair out of his face. "I'm finished with high school now, too. I actually guarded last summer at the Y in Red Hills, but that's an indoor pool. It totally sucked being inside all summer, so it's awesome being here. I really don't know what I'm doing this fall, but it will for sure involve a half-pipe and my guitar."

Stacey fixated on how Jessie's folded arms made his triceps stand out, and how the hairs on his forearm were golden from hours in the sun. Her eyes traveled up and found Jessie grinning, staring directly at her. Stacey jerked her gaze away.

Six more pairs of eyes watched Stacey expectantly.

"Batter up, Chapman," Bob said.

Stacey sucked air through her teeth and pushed away from the wall. Pulling her long blonde hair to the front on one side, she combed through it with all ten fingers. "Uh… hi. I'm Stacey. Um… I'm a junio… sorry, I mean… I guess, I'm a…senior…now. And, yeah, this is my…first time, too." She could feel her whole face flush bright red, and felt like there was a giant boulder in her stomach. "My… my first-time lifeguarding, I mean."

The expressions of the other guards ranged from dumbfounded shock to pure pity given the level of loser Stacey had exposed herself to be. She wanted to crawl under a rock and die.

"Okay," Bob said, in a gameshow-host voice, clapping his hands together without skipping a beat. "Let's start learning the ropes!"

Bob played the Beach Boys over the PA's tinny speakers through a dusty old stereo. The crew took turns pulling the covers off the pool, put a few lane lines in, and learned how the valves in the equipment room worked. They used metal grabbers and buckets to collect Hubba Bubba wrappers and soggy socks from under the bleachers. Then Mark showed them the bottles in the chemical closet for the pool and a pink powder antibacterial substance to shake across the floor of the bathrooms to supposedly disinfect them.

"Never get this crap in your eyes," Mark said, tapping the side of the bottle. "It burns like a mother!"

Stacey tried to imagine how Mark found that out, and she instinctively backed away. They all left the chemical room and Bob handed his keys to Tiffany to lock the door.

"Finally, before we open each day," Bob said, leaning against the railing of the diving board and pointing toward the water, "someone has to dive down to the deep-end drain and clear it of any debris."

Stacey peered over the edge of the pool and grimaced at a messy pile stuck at the bottom of the deep end.

Jessie, in board shorts and a puka-shell necklace, kicked off his flip-flops and threw his T-shirt aside, saying, "I got this."

Stacey surged with excitement seeing Jessie's bare chest for the first time, and the way his shorts hung just low enough to reveal where his tan ended.

Running off the edge of the pool, Jessie kicked his feet into a gainer flip, arching his back and grabbing his ankles behind him. His body rotated in a full circle before entering the water feet first, and he immediately dropped to the bottom of the pool.

His small splash sprinkled water onto Stacey's shins and feet. She was in awe of his confidence and how perfectly he executed the flip without even using the diving board.

A few seconds later Jessie came up with a fistful of leaves, strands of long dark hair, and a couple of Band-Aids. He dropped the mess on the side of the deck in front of Melissa's feet like a cat's hairball and she leaped back from the pile, disgusted.

Every muscle in Jessie's arms flexed as he pushed himself out of the water, and Stacey's heart raced. Oh. My. God. With her hand at her mouth and a fingernail between her teeth, her gaze followed droplets sliding over goosebumps on his torso and clinging to the fine hairs forming a trail above his drawstring. Holding her breath, with her little finger touching the tip of her tongue, she focused on the tight nubs of his small, purplish-red nipples, and she felt overwhelmed by a desire to reach out and touch them.

"Whew," Jessie said, shaking his hair out and pulling his shorts away from his skin. "Chilly!"

Stacey didn't even blink as the water from his hair sprinkled her cheeks. Then he caught her staring at him. Quickly, she turned away, pulling her hand from her mouth, and reached behind her back to grab hold of her other arm.

"Impressive," Bob said, laughing. He picked up the pile with a trash grabber and dropped it into a bucket. "But next time use gloves, okay, Jess? We've pulled some pretty nasty things out over the years."

Mark tossed Jessie's T-shirt at him and shook his head.

The crew returned to the guard shack and went over the first week's schedule. Tiffany and Mark were working practically non-stop, with the rest of the guards filling in the second and third posts until everyone was trained. Melissa was up first, and removed her tank top and shorts without hesitation, revealing her miniscule red two piece beneath. She's got a red bikini, too?

Stacey didn't want to admit to Gabe how right she'd been about the fit-ness of the other guards. Tiffany and Melissa had perfect bodies. And Desiree appeared to have curves in all the right places. Stacey's first shift would be the next afternoon, so she was grateful she had another day to resolve her swimsuit worries. She felt giddy, though, when she saw her name next to Jessie's on the schedule for Tuesday's night swim.

"That reminds me," Bob said, clearing his throat and turning to grab a stack of flyers on the desk. "Anyone in need of appropriate lifeguard gear, a warehouse in Riverside is offering a 30% discount."

Relieved, Stacey took a flyer. Chad, Desiree, and Jessie each grabbed one as well. From the address and hours listed in the corner, Stacey figured it was about twenty-five miles away, and only open on weekdays. She folded the paper into a square and shoved it in her back pocket.

"Jess," Bob said. "Your shift starts at one this afternoon. Don't be late again."

"Yes sir!" Jessie said, holding his folded flyer to his forehead and saluting Bob. Stacey couldn't imagine anyone staying angry with Jessie when he flashed his beautiful smile like that.

Jessie pushed the flyer into his pocket, grabbed his skateboard, and headed out the back door. Stacey quickly followed, hopeful for an excuse to talk to him.

As soon as he got outside, though, Jessie set his board down and started toward the boulevard. Stacey stopped, slumping her shoulders. Bummer.

She wondered if he had a car. They rode the same bus in middle school. She knew he lived in the Desert Oasis apartment complex, two blocks from her house. She saw him doing tricks in the parking lot sometimes. But they lived more than three miles from The Plunge, on the other side of town. There were massive hills between the pool and their neighborhood, and most roads didn't have sidewalks. Is that why he was late? Would he ride his skateboard back and forth every day, in hundred-degree weather? How would he get to Riverside? Would it seem creepy to offer Jessie a ride?

Desiree threw open the door behind Stacey, then stomped passed with Chad trailing after her. He grabbed Desiree around the waist and she pushed him off, storming over to a small white pickup in the parking lot that said "Toy" on the tailgate. Chad caught up to her again, whispering too softly for Stacey to hear.

Despite Desiree's crossed arms, Chad put his hands on her hips and leaned down to look into her furious eyes. Even from her vantage point, Stacey could see the moment Desiree's defenses melted away. Within seconds, Chad was kissing her cheek, then her mouth, then Desiree's arms were around his neck. He lifted her off the ground, her short dress revealing lace panties beneath.

Stacey hadn't known what to expect from her first job, or what it would be like to work at the pool. But thinking about Jessie in his dripping wet shorts, she felt a surge of desire rush throughout her whole body. And while watching Desiree and Chad's passionate parking lot make-out session, she began to imagine a summer romance that would put any Eternity ad to shame.

Chapter Five

Stacey stood in front of her mirror Sunday morning, attempting to look cute and casual while remaining as covered as possible. Since the swimsuit outlet wasn't open until Monday, she had no choice but to wear the horrendous Lands End one-piece for her first shift. But all she could think of was Tiffany and Melissa's perfect bodies in their tiny two pieces. Every time she looked at her own reflection in this suit, she envisioned herself on a platter with an apple in her mouth.

For the past couple of years, Stacey's wardrobe had been prep-school-girl-grunge. She'd doubled down on plaid skirts with knee socks and platform Mary Janes, or Levi's with buttoned collared shirts over lacy camisoles. None of that paired well with what was basically was a red leotard, and it was too hot out to hide under a flannel.

She settled on wearing loose overalls with no shirt and Birkenstocks. As Steven Tyler screamed out of her stereo, Stacey acknowledged that her hair was finally long enough to resemble Alicia Silverstone's. At least my hair covers my back-fat.

Back in the guard shack in time for her shift, Stacey was surprised to find Mark snoring on the couch. He had one arm over his eyes, his other hand holding a half-eaten burrito in his lap.

Bob's attention was on the sports pages while a baseball play-by-play came from a transistor radio on the desk. He barely glanced up to take the money from arriving swimmers, let alone acknowledge Stacey as she came in.

"Is there a certain locker I should use?" Stacey asked.

"Whichever one is free," Bob said without looking at her.

The only unclaimed locker had an unidentifiable reddish-black furry residue in the base. Stacey hung her backpack from the hook at the top and made a mental note to find out if the pink powder antibacterial stuff could clean that mess up, too.

Chad was already outside on his tower, in red trunks and aviators, applying sunscreen, and the first couple of swimmers were slithering into the water. She grabbed the doorknob and was about to head out to the pool when Bob stopped her.

"You can't wear those overalls," he said.

"Oh…" Stacey's heart sunk. "Yeah. Right. Of course not." She went back to her locker and started unhooking her straps.

Stacey peeked over her shoulder. Mark still hadn't moved. Once she was sure Bob wasn't looking her way, she wrapped her towel around herself, up high under her arms, letting the overalls drop to the ground. She quickly shoved them into her backpack and hustled out the door.

Scanning the pool deck for anyone she knew, Stacey headed for the far lifeguard tower. She climbed the ladder one-handed while the towel was secured with the other, then slumped into the chair. Chad smiled and waved across the pool and she timidly waved back. She squinted in the white light of the sun reflecting off the water. Forgetting her sunglasses was another rookie mistake she'd never make again.

After all her worry, Stacey didn't see anyone she knew. At one o'clock on the first Sunday in summer, the last thing anyone going into their senior year would want to do is hang out at the community pool. With only a chain link fence separating the pool from the outside world, she'd felt like every cheerleader and star-pitcher would be laughing at her, a fat dork up there posing as a lifeguard in an old lady leotard. She couldn't get that fear out of her mind.

In reality, the pool was occupied by a dozen little kids, most around six to eight years old, with their parents and grandparents. They didn't care who the lifeguards were. It was summer, it was hot, and The Plunge offered cheap entertainment.

Lifeguarding got really boring, really quickly. And hot. Really hot. Hiding inside her towel, Stacey curled under the minimal shade provided by the ancient, dusty umbrella, fanning herself in an unsuccessful attempt to minimize boob and butt sweat marks. What she hadn't expected, though, was how quickly she would embrace her newfound power.

All afternoon, Stacey blew her whistle, yelling, "No running!"

She knew the concrete was about a thousand degrees and kids were running to avoid second degree burns, but that didn't matter. Stacey was a lifeguard now, and she loved the authority that gave her.

Within her first ten minutes, a scrawny boy with eyes red from the chlorine stood at the base of her tower shuffling from foot to foot. "Will the water actually change colors if someone pees in the pool?" he asked.

"Do you want to find out?" Stacey replied. "If I see it happen, I have to announce to the whole pool who peed and make everyone get out."

The kid's eyes grew wide, and he ran in the direction of the boy's locker room.

Stacey blew her whistle at him and yelled "Walk!"

Every thirty minutes the guards rotated. After he awoke from his food-coma, Mark took over Stacey's post in the deep-end tower and Chad went inside.

Mark wore only his red trunks and large-brimmed hat with sunglasses. His belly hung over his waistband, but he didn't seem self-conscious. Once Chad was inside, Stacey lowered her towel to around her waist.

"Check this out," Mark said, as Stacey climbed down so he could take over her position. He pointed out a large, fully-clothed family walking over to the bleachers without towels or a bag. They started taking off their shoes. The dad removed his belt, took his wallet out of his pocket and hid it in his shoe, and everyone piled their items in a small heap under the bleachers. Then all six family members climbed into the pool with all their clothes on. They wore pants, T-shirts, even socks. Some had on multiple layers. And they attempted to swim.

While the majority of the family members stuck to the shallowest parts of the pool, two of the fully clothed kids got the wild idea that they were ready for more of a challenge. Holding onto the side, they inched their way around the edge and pulled themselves up the ladder, their heavy clothes weighing them down.

When the older kid—about nine years old—headed for the diving board, Mark hopped down, grabbed the shepherd's crook from the wall and leaned it against his tower.

Back in February, the Red Cross instructor had shown Stacey's class what to do with the giant metal hook, but she thought it would only be used as a last resort. She was surprised to see Mark using it her first day on the job.

Standing with his toes hanging off the end of the diving board, the kid held the waist of his pants up with one hand, then flopped down into the water. After resurfacing, he clearly struggled to keep his face up as he doggy-paddled toward the side.

Stacey stood on her platform and let her towel fall, ready to jump in. She was afraid the boy would never make it to the ledge.

Mark blew his whistle. Yawning, he reached the pole down and told the kid to grab on, then swung the pole over to where the kid could grab the ladder. Once the kid climbed out, Mark motioned for the two boys to talk to him. Whatever he said, the boys seemed genuinely afraid to go off the diving board again.

Stacey was amazed. Mark actually seemed pretty good at lifeguarding.

"The city won't let us make rules about what clothes people swim in," Mark told her. "If someone's fully dressed, I usually make them take a swim test. That weeds most of 'em out. And don't dive in to help them! I learned that the hard way my first summer rescuing a lady in a parka."

"A parka?"

"Don't ask."

"When do you dive in?" Stacey asked.

"Almost never. Except to cool off. Someone needs to be on the bottom of the pool, not moving, before we get in the water with them. Otherwise, fish 'em out with the pole."

Stacey could see why Bob wasn't lenient about the overalls. Even dealing with her towel wrapped too tightly would have gotten in the way if she'd had to quickly pull someone out of the water.

The rest of the afternoon, Stacey left her towel on the seat, and started demanding swim tests for any kid she suspected would be problematic. It put her mind at ease and also helped pass the time. If she said they weren't ready to go off the board yet, the kids would mope away, only to return twenty minutes later begging to be retested.

What Stacey struggled most with was parents attempting to toss in their toddlers from the diving board. At seventeen, Stacey knew it wasn't her place to advise those adults on their parenting strategy, but she was fairly certain they were doing irreversible psychological damage.

When one father walked to the end of the board and dropped his terrified little girl in, she screamed from the time he let go until her head sunk beneath the water, and both floaties popped off her arms. Fortunately, the child's mother was already in the water and grabbed her quickly. But the toddler came up coughing and gasping for air. There was immense fear in the small child's huge eyes and the way she gripped her mother's arms until her fingers were white. Stacey wanted to scream at those parents on the little girl's behalf: who could she ever trust if her parents would do that to her?

From then on, Stacey began barking out rules over the megaphone against more than one person on the diving board and anyone jumping off with floaties. She whistled and shouted and announced her rules to regulate the chaos across the pool all afternoon.

And each time she did, it gave her a little thrill.

If someone asked her that first day, Stacey would have said the diving board seemed like the most dangerous aspect of the job.

Lifeguarding was about preventing accidents. The guards said "no running," because kids slipped, skinned knees, stubbed toes—even fell on their faces and smacked their heads.

But the worst accidents were the ones no one would have predicted.

Chapter Six

On Monday morning, Stacey grabbed her mom's emergency credit card from the dresser drawer and drove to Riverside. She knew she should have asked permission, but figured it was better to apologize later than be told no. She needed to be ready to buy something at the warehouse sale.

Three freeways and a maze of industrial parks later, she arrived at a nondescript large white building. There was a black glass door with the words "The Outlet" in white lettering. If there hadn't been a rack of colorful swimsuits out front, she might have questioned whether she was in the right place.

Inside, the well-lit retail store had at least twenty round racks of swimsuits for men, women, and children, and glass displays full of aquatic accessories.

"Hi there," a friendly woman's voice called out from behind the register. She was a little older than Stacey's mom, she guessed, with short curly brown hair and droopy cheeks. "How can I help you?" She had a twangy accent from somewhere in the south. It seemed too big for her small mouth.

"I need a swimsuit. For lifeguarding," Stacey said.

The woman came around from behind the counter and motioned for Stacey to follow her toward the back of the store. "Are you about five foot ten?"

Stacey nodded. As they walked, the woman pulled solid red swim suits from various racks.

"I don't like to ask girls their size. Too many lie and most don't actually know what would fit them best. But trust me, because I do!"

By the time they reached the dressing room, the sales clerk had selected eight different suits for Stacey to try on. After pulling back the curtain, she hung them inside.

"My name's Rosie. Give these a try, but leave your underpants on, and holler if you need anything."

"Thanks," Stacey said. She pulled the curtain closed, wishing she'd known about this store before the whole Lands End situation. With so many suits to choose from, at least one had to fit.

Each suit was more comfortable than the last, and they all fit Stacey better than any suit she had ever worn. The one pieces were long enough and flattered her waist and chest. Even though she still hated her thighs, the suits were cut to highlight her long legs, and somehow made her backside look smaller. The bikinis were designed for athletes, and made Stacey feel like she could pass as one. She struggled to decide which she liked best, wishing she could have them all. She knew she should choose by price.

The least expensive suit was eighty dollars. The two-pieces cost a hundred and ten. Even with the thirty percent discount flyer, she couldn't afford more than one suit. She'd have a huge fight with her mom about it no matter what. But she'd already driven all the way there, and there was no way she was going home empty-handed.

Stacey stood in front of the mirror again in a red bikini and imagined herself at the pool. Jessie would walk in. She'd drop her towel. He'd see her and... She didn't finish the thought. Without removing the bikini, Stacey reached for her T-shirt and pulled it over her head. She stepped into her shorts, zipped and buttoned them, and slid her feet into her flip-flops.

"You doing okay in there?" Rosie called through the curtain.

"I'm good. Thanks," Stacey said, then bit her bottom lip. The sales lady was so nice. Stacey started to feel sick. She avoided looking at herself in the mirror. She took a deep breath, grabbed the cheapest one piece, and pulled back the curtain.

"How'd we do?" Rosie asked. She was straightening the hangers on a nearby clothing rack.

"They all fit great. Thanks so much for your help. I can only afford this one, though," Stacey said, handing over the suit.

They walked together to the register at the front of the store. Stacey tried to stay a half-step behind, hoping the woman wouldn't notice the bikini beneath her clothing.

Stacey clamped her arms to her ribs to stop her hand from shaking as she offered her mother's credit card. "And I have this flyer," she said, pulling the folded piece of paper from her pocket.

Rosie took it and looked up smiling. "Oh, you're from Mesa Valley!" She began ringing up the purchase. "Coach Bob's an old friend."

Stacey's heart was racing. Rosie is friends with Bob?

"You know, you remind me of my daughter. She's tall, like you. She's older now, but she was a swimmer in her high school days and hated searching for the right swimsuits."

Stacey softened. "I wish you could do all my shopping for me," she said quietly, surprised by the affection she felt for Rosie. "Your daughter's lucky."

"Well, bless your heart. What a nice thing to say!" Rosie winked at her. "Too bad you didn't buy two suits."

Stacey felt her face flush. Was Rosie hinting that she knew?

"Yeaaahhh." Stacey forced a shaky chuckle. Sweat formed on her brow. If Rosie knew, would she call the police? Or Coach Bob? Or her mother? She felt like she was going to throw up.

"Here ya go, darlin'," Rosie said, handing Stacey the swimsuit in a bag, with the receipt wrapped around her mother's credit card. "I'm so glad you came in today."

"Uh, thanks. Me too," Stacey said, gripping the bag to her belly. "Actually...I need to, um... go straight to work," she lied. "Is it okay if I change into my new suit here?"

"Sure, sweetheart. Go on ahead," Rosie said, nodding back toward the dressing room.

Stacey maneuvered through the racks as coolly as she could. Holding her breath, she pulled the curtain closed behind her, eager to strip off her clothes. Stacey hung the bikini back on the hanger, and shoved it behind the other suits on the wall. Only then could she fully exhale.

After she put on the suit she'd purchased and was fully dressed again, Stacey finally looked at her reflection. She was disgusted with herself and couldn't believe what she'd almost done. She leaned her head back against the back of the changing stall and waited for her pulse to slow.

On her way out of the store, Stacey waved at Rosie, but didn't stop until she was back in her car. She unlocked the door and tossed the bag with her underwear and the credit card behind her into the back seat.

The sound of the bag hitting something solid made her turn in the driver's seat. It had landed on her awful self-portrait from Ms. Moreno's class, the one she desperately wished she'd never created.

The painting that won first prize. Stacey had completely forgotten about it. She was grateful she hadn't given Jessie a ride yet, or he might have seen the pile of art junk. She needed to take it into the house before she forgot again.

That evening after her shift at the pool, Stacey walked into the kitchen hoping to find her mom making dinner. Stacey had dumped the pile from the car into the entryway that morning, and her mom had strewn it across the counter like an investigation. Stacey's self-portrait was face up, its ribbon still attached.

"Why didn't you tell me about this?" her mother demanded, her hand slicing through the air toward the mess. It knocked into her wine bottle, but she grabbed it just before it toppled over.

Stacey shrugged. "Why are you making it such a big deal?"

"Because I almost broke my neck tripping over it on my way into the house tonight. And it is a big deal! A first-place award from an art contest you never mentioned? And–" she waved the receipt between them, "sixty dollars you charged to my credit card without asking? Again!"

Stacey sucked in her cheeks and inhaled sharply. Her eyes flashed to the painting she hated, to her mother's furious expression, then back again. She felt like throwing something at both of them. Through clenched teeth she said, "I needed another suit. You even said I did."

"I told you to wear the one you bought before! You were supposed to ask your father for the money—"

"You never listen to me!"

"You stole my credit card! Twice!"

"I didn't steal anything!" Stacey screamed, blinking back hot tears. "I told you I would pay for it!" She balled her hands into fists.

Her mom crossed her arms and flared her nostrils. "Fine. Give me your paycheck!"

"I've only worked two days!"

"Exactly!" Her mom slapped the counter and the stacked art-class pottery rattled.

"You don't get it!" Stacey grabbed her keys and stomped to pull open the front door. "No one understands what my life is like!" She slammed the door behind her.

She collapsed into the driver's seat and turned up the radio. She whipped the car out of the driveway, finally allowing the hot tears to fall as she turned out of the neighborhood.

She drove past Gabe's house. His car wasn't there. She thought about going to his work, but reconsidered. What if he got in trouble for talking to her when he was supposed to be bussing tables? What if someone else was already there visiting him? Like Jenny?

She drove toward the center of town, unsure where she was headed. It had to be anywhere but home. With the windows down, she wiped at her cheeks. She squeezed her jaw to avoid screaming and her breaths skipped frantically behind her ribs.

Stacey turned right and headed down the boulevard. She heard a flapping sound and noticed a blue piece of paper flying around the backseat. It fluttered into Stacey's face, then at the front windshield. Shit, she thought, swerving, and tried to grab it. She pulled to the side of the road, put the car in park, and grabbed the paper off the dash. It was Ms. Moreno's Art lab flier. When Stacey took the self-portrait and pottery inside, the flier must have slipped beneath the seat.

She was about to crumple the paper when she read: "Escape on an ART adventure this summer." It was super cheesy, and so typical Ms. Moreno. She probably hung travel posters all over the walls, too. Stacey grinned, imagining the colorful classroom. Ms.

Moreno's gentleness appealed more to Stacey than being alone. She filled her lungs with a gulp of air, exhaled slowly, then pulled back onto the road, and drove to campus.

The lights for the Art Studio were on. In the parking lot behind the art building, there was only one other car. A small, boxy VW with Ricky Martin, Shakira, and Selena stickers on the back windshield. Definitely Ms. Moreno's.

Stacey turned off her car and sat for a minute, chewing her left thumbnail. She looked at her reflection in the rearview mirror, relieved that the short drive had helped the redness fade from her eyes and cheeks. She could hear Vanessa Williams's soulful voice rang out from the classroom.

Ms. Moreno sat with her back to the door. She was the only person in the Art Studio. The music was loud enough to drown out Stacey's footsteps, so she didn't think Ms. Moreno noticed when she entered. There was a strong smell of rubbing alcohol that Stacey recognized from cleaning acrylic paint off brushes in class. Over that, she smelled the patchouli incense that was burning on the overhead projector.

Taped to the butcher block table was a plain sheet of paper, and in front of Ms. Moreno were mason jars of water, several brushes, a rag, and a small tin beside a large white ceramic plate. Stacey approached on her teacher's right quietly, not wanting to startle her.

Ms. Moreno's long, creamy brown fingers gripped a broad paintbrush, coating her paper with clean water until it reflected the fluorescent lights. Curious, Stacey inched closer, watching over her teacher's shoulder as she used a smaller brush dipped in what looked like a pool of black ink, and touched it to the edges of the paper. It was more of a navy color that diffused to a bluish-purplygray as it combined with the water and spread across the surface of the paper.

It was mesmerizing to watch the color move and fade. Ms. Moreno re-dipped the brush in the water and the paint, and again touched the paper's corners. From the edges reaching inward, the blue seeped into itself, becoming darker and deeper and richer, while the center of the page stayed a watery white.

"Hi," Ms. Moreno said without turning.

Stacey gasped. "Sorry, I didn't want to interrupt you."

"You didn't." Ms. Moreno looked at Stacey out of the corner of her eye and grinned. "I saw your car lights through the windows." She nodded toward the row of panes at the top of the wall. Then she eased more dark paint onto the corners of the soaked surface and Stacey watched as it blended into the rest. "I'm glad you're here. Pull up a stool."

"What are you painting?" The metal feet of the stool dragged on the concrete.

"Aurora borealis."

"You mean that northern lights thing that happens in Alaska?" Stacey lowered herself onto the stool. "We studied it in science."

"It happens in a lot of places the closer you get to the North Pole. Canada, Iceland, Russia…. Have you ever seen it?"

Stacey shook her head.

"Me either. But I've always wanted to. It was so hot today, I felt like a colder climate would be nice tonight."

Stacey stifled a laugh. Despite the late hour, it was still about ninety degrees in the classroom. Stacey held her arms away from her body to keep the sweat from dripping down her sides. The scent of sweet jasmine emanated from her teacher, and Stacey hoped it was enough to mask her own odor.

Ms. Moreno rinsed her brush in the dirty water and dipped it in the clean water again, then re-wet the center of the page. This time the water pushed the navy paint back onto itself. Swirling the tip of her brush in a green puddle on the plate, Ms. Moreno barely grazed the paper's wet surface with a ribbon of sea green that arched and wove its way across the diagonal of the page, diffusing at its edges into the blue.

It was magical how the clear water could both blend and separate the colors, moving like the lights in the sky, just as Stacey had imagined back when she was a freshman.

Within seconds, Ms. Moreno created two green flashes of color that danced over the darkness, then cleaned her brush and added a brighter blue hue that curved upward between them like fingers, and magenta streaks that eased downward along the edges of the inky sky.

Stacey was in awe of the scene appearing before her, and the ease of Ms. Moreno's movements. Her teacher's serene expression as she painted inspired a lighter feeling in Stacey as well.

With the narrowest brush, Ms. Moreno pulled rivers of navy between the bright aurora borealis streaks. The colors began blending at their blurry edges, while unifying into one picturesque night scene. Each color stretched and moved harmoniously with the others, but remained individual and pure. It was like watching a ballet of paint. Stacey was hypnotized by the paint's flow on the page under the iridescent lights.

"Now we've seen it," Ms. Moreno said. Stacey turned to look at her, and her teacher lifted her eyebrows. "Ready to try?" She motioned toward another piece of paper taped to the table.

Stacey tilted back, both hands up. "Uh uh. There's no way I could do that."

"Why not try? It's only a piece of paper."

Stacey shrugged, rocking back on the legs of the stool.

"You're here. What else did you plan to do?" Ms. Moreno smiled. "Give it a shot."

Stacey shrugged again, then pulled the stool up to the table. She used a large brush to coat the paper with water.

"Now, mix equal parts azure and amethyst on your palette. Add a tiny bit of black," Ms. Moreno instructed.

Stacey combined the colors as directed and noted how they blended first to electric blue, then the addition of black turned it to the midnight color Ms. Moreno had used. She dragged the large brush across the top of the blank white page, creating an inky streak of sky.

"Before you put any more paint down, decide in your mind how you want your composition to look. Art should be approached with intention, but be flexible with how it wants to turn out. If you cover the paper with all that darkness, there won't be space for the light to show. Leave breathing room."

Stacey remembered the way Ms. Moreno only touched the very edges of the page at first, reapplying the paint there multiple times, and using clean water to push the color outward and keep the center mostly white. Stacey did the same. The night sky deepened into itself as she added more of the dark tones along the top edge. Her composition wouldn't have the bright colors drifting off the top of the sheet like Ms. Moreno's. Stacey's own northern lights would be smaller, a flash in the distance.

Ms. Moreno explained the rest of the process again step-by-step. Stacey traded out the large brush for smaller ones, alternating the dark and vibrant hues. She imitated Ms. Moreno's way of holding her elbow out, her finger-grip loose on the brush. Along with the smooth swipe of the bristles across the grain of the paper,

Stacey felt a gentle wave passing through her own body, as though the day's worries had been washed away.

Minutes later, Stacey's aurora borealis appeared before her. Without knowing it, the world around her had evaporated, and she'd managed to escape to this magical place, at least for twenty minutes or so.

Ms. Moreno stood next to her. "Hermosa," she said.

Stacey eased back on the stool and grinned. "Thank you."

"Ready for the fun part?" Her teacher held up two old toothbrushes with a mischievous smile.

Stacey cocked her head, skeptical of Ms. Moreno's enthusiasm.

Ms. Moreno poured a puddle of white onto a plate. She handed Stacey a toothbrush, and dipped her own toothbrush into the water, then into the paint. "Don't forget to tap it on the side of the plate to get the excess off," she said, demonstrating. She aligned her toothbrush with the ribbons of color on the paper and pulled her finger up the bristles. A faint spray of stars flicked across the scene. She did it again and again, angling the toothbrush to scatter the stars across the paper. At one end, the tiny stars were smaller and closer. On the other side, they were spread apart, giving the night sky a natural curvature.

Ms. Moreno rinsed the toothbrush, wiped it on the rag, then dipped her fingers in the water and did the same. Her dark fingers were coated in chalky white paint that pooled under her fingernails, but she didn't seem to care. She nodded in Stacey's direction, encouraging her to try.

Stacey didn't tap off enough paint or angle her toothbrush the right way. Her first spray of scattered stars was chaotic; some were too large, and they all fell across the bottom of the paper.

"Damnit," Stacey said, dropping the toothbrush on the table and grabbing the rag.

"Wait!"

"They're too big! I need to—"

"If you wipe them away, you'll lift off all the beautiful color you laid down beneath it. Just wait, Stacey."

"But I totally messed up."

"No, you didn't. There are no mistakes in art."

Stacey rolled her eyes. "I remember. Only lessons."

"Well, sure, that's true. But sometimes we have to let the painting tell us what it wants to be."

"Should I start over?" Stacey stood up and reached for a new piece of paper from the center of the table.

"No," Ms. Moreno said, gently putting her hand on Stacey's shoulder. "Stop trying to control every detail. Wait and see what happens." She stared at Stacey's paper.

Stacey plopped back down on the stool and tried to see what Ms. Moreno was looking at. Her paper was still damp, and the white splatters had already begun to bleed into the wet page. A misty aura formed along the bottom of the composition.

"Do you think you can replicate that coming from the other direction?"

Without a word, convinced the painting was a lost cause anyway, Stacey dipped her toothbrush in the water and the paint. She angled the toothbrush, and used her opposite finger to pull the bristles. Across the bottom of the page, another layer of misty white bled into the original splatters.

Stacey looked up at the ceiling tiles, and tossed the toothbrush aside. "They don't look anything like stars!"

"Stand up and step back," Ms. Moreno said calmly.

Stacey fought the urge to dump the mason jar of filthy water on her painting.

Ms. Moreno stood about three feet from the table. "Stacey, stand here with me, and squint your eyes."

Chewing the inside of her cheek, Stacey obeyed. The legs of the stool scraped the concrete floor as she pushed away from the butcher block. She took the spot next to her teacher.

Softly, Ms. Moreno said, "When things don't go the way we want them to, we can learn not to make the same mistake. Or, we can learn how to make something new, and be open to appreciating the unexpected."

Stacey squinted at her painting. Suddenly, the white mist formed by the splatters made sense. Approaching the table again, Stacey grabbed a paintbrush, wet it, and dipped it in the white paint, not bothering to sit. She spread the paint across the bottom of the page, rinsing and adding water so it became milky. She added hints of blue, keeping her eyes narrowed. She grabbed the toothbrush again, tapping it until almost no paint remained, then flicked it more gently. She went back and forth between the brushes, tilting her head this way and that.

Stacey worked in silence, not noticing any smells in the room, or the song being played, or the ticking of the classroom clock. When she put down her brush and stepped back, Ms. Moreno joined her. Standing side-by-side, they assessed their paintings.

While Stacey was occupied, Ms. Moreno had added the tops of dark trees to the bottom of her painting. Stacey's was now a serene snowy landscape. The paintings both started the same way, and complemented one another, but each finished scene was an entirely unique version of the northern lights.

Stacey felt something release–as though the tension across her shoulders dissolved–as she realized what she was capable of creating. She never would have painted anything like this on her own.

"Seems like a change of perspective was all you needed," Ms. Moreno said.

"Maybe." Stacey nodded. "I'm glad I came."

"You did a great job. Why don't you take some paper and that small palette of watercolors with you?" Ms. Moreno told her. "You can practice at home and show me when you come back."

"Oh, I don't think…"

Ms. Moreno pushed the tin into Stacey's hand and shrugged. "Either way, take it."

"Thanks," Stacey said, accepting the paints and stack of paper.

"I'm really glad you came tonight."

As she drove home, Stacey kept mumbling Ms. Moreno's words. Approach with intention. Be flexible with how it turns out.

The two-lane road had no street lamps, and the silver bullet's headlights cut through the blackness. She thought of being in the art room, the water diffusing the darkness into shades of blue and gray and purple on the page, and how the brightness of the northern lights could only be visible when she left room for it. She thought of how she had screamed at her mom earlier. They'd both been so angry. So dark.

In the sky to the east, a full moon was rising. As she drove, the pale blue glow of the moonlight fell on the dark foothills and grassy fields giving the appearance of rolling waves. Stacey remembered the peaceful wave that passed through her as she painted. She wanted to hold tight to that feeling when she walked in the door at home.

Pulling into the dark driveway, the only light in the house was shining from her mom's bedroom window. She put the car in park and grabbed the pile of paints and paper from the seat beside her. Even though it felt a little childish, she thought about giving her mom the aurora borealis painting as a sort of peace offering. This particular artwork was one she didn't want to hide away. She hoped it could bring a little light back for them both.

Chapter Seven

Stacey showed up at the pool at 6:25 pm the next day, Tuesday, to work her first night swim. She was freshly showered, with her hair done and makeup on. Jessie Thomas was also on the schedule, and it was their first shift working together. Wearing her new swimsuit with cut-offs, she practiced plastering a smile on her face in the mirror at home, and pushing out her chest, hoping it would make her look more attractive. All day she'd run through possible topics to talk to Jessie about: What church do you go to? When did you start skateboarding? Were you born in Mesa Valley? She desperately wanted it to sound natural when she offered to give him a ride home.

When she got to the pool, though, the door was locked. She leaned against the painted cinderblock wall facing the parking lot, hoping Jessie would walk up and see her looking cool and casual. She sucked in her stomach, and propped her right foot up like Julia Roberts on the Pretty Woman movie poster. But after ten minutes, her standing leg was sore. When she shifted her weight, she realized her left Birkenstock was stuck to gum. She was leaning over, scraping the gum off with a stick into the planter when Mark finally pulled into the parking lot.

Stacey stood back up, scowling at him with her arms crossed as Mark approached with his Carl's Jr. dinner in hand. She salivated at the smell of the greasy fries, her mother's bland turkey meatloaf turning over in her stomach. Mark's shaggy hair and wrinkled T-shirt looked like he'd just rolled out of bed.

"Look who's here! It's Miiiiiiss Punctuality. And, tell her what she's won, Johnny!" Mark said, pushing his cup and bag into Stacey's hands so he could unlock the door. Stacey uncrossed her arms, taking the bundle and a deep inhale of the fried food smell. She considered reaching in the bag to steal some fries.

"Bob said we always need to be on time," she reminded Mark.

"For him, you do. For me..." He took the food back and looked in her eyes. "...you should chill."

Stacey followed Mark into the guard shack, flipping on the lights, and set her bag in her locker. He sat at the desk and began eating his burger.

"Don't we need to clean the bathrooms?" Stacey asked.

"Be my guest," Mark replied through a full mouth without turning around.

Seriously? He'd better not be expecting me to clean this place by myself. Night swim starts in a few minutes. Where's Jessie?

The lobby door swung open with a loud squeak. Jessie held the door as he and Melissa came into the guard shack. They both had bags of Del Taco and Macho 44 cups. With a nod to Mark, who nodded back in response, the pair flopped onto the couch beside one another, deep in conversation about the last episode of 90210, grabbing food from each other's bags.

Stacey stood next to her locker feeling invisible. What the...doesn't anyone realize I am standing right here? Did Melissa give Jessie a ride to work? Are they together now? She shook her head and rolled her eyes, then threw open the door to the pool deck and started emptying the overflowing trash cans. Jessie and Melissa could deal with the bathrooms.

At 6:59 she slumped into the furthest lifeguard chair, next to the deep end, and Mark opened the doors to the public.

About fifty people came to the pool that night, the most Stacey had seen so far. There were even a few skater kids she recognized who were a couple of years behind her in school. They did tricks off the diving board while Jessie teased them from his tower opposite her.

"Real men aren't afraid to eat it doing tricks," Jessie told them through his megaphone. "I'll give a dollar to whoever lands the loudest belly flop."

One after another, the skater kids ran off the end of the board and landed with a loud smack on the water. They climbed the ladder out of the pool, their bellies splotched red, and looked to Jessie for their score.

Stacey was embarrassed on their behalf, torturing themselves for his entertainment. After watching the fully-clothed kids and the toddlers in floaties nearly drown in the deep end over the weekend, Stacey was even more afraid of what accident might occur because of the diving board that summer. She was fairly certain they'd end up having to backboard one of these skater kids if Jessie kept egging them on. But it did help pass the time, and strangely the sound of their skin slapping the water actually cheered her up.

After thirty minutes, they rotated their lifeguarding positions, and it was Jessie's turn for the first break. Stacey took over his position watching the shallow end, and Melissa was on duty to watch the deep end. But, rather than go inside as they usually did on breaks, Jessie went to the diving board to show the hot-dogging skaters how to land back-flips and gainers. Stacey was supposed to be focused on the shallow end, but it was impossible for her not to look over her shoulder in his direction. She was intoxicated watching every muscle in his lean body engage as he flipped off the board. It was like he moved in slow motion. And his teeth somehow glowed whiter at night.

Then Melissa's voice came over the megaphone. "Is that the best you can do, JT?" she said after he'd executed a perfect back flip and landed feet first. "If you're such a stud, why don't you show us your belly flop?" Over the megaphone, Melissa gave Jessie her "judge's score," and the sound of her voice grated on Stacey's nerves.

After thirty minutes of listening to Melissa's sassy flirting with Jessie, it was Stacey's turn for a break, and all she wanted was to get as far from both of them as possible. She held her towel tight and walked into the guard shack. Mark was dozing in the chair, his feet on the desk. She grabbed her book from her locker and stormed out, winding through the lobby to the front of the facility, slamming doors behind her. The glass in the metal frame of the cashier's window rattled. Stacey leaned against the outside wall of the building and slid down to the concrete, tossing her copy of Animal Farm beside her. She closed her eyes and collapsed against the warm cinder block.

The door inched open a few minutes later and Stacey looked up to see Mark peeking out, then down at her. "What are you doing?" he asked, a spot of what looked like ranch dressing crusted in his goatee.

"Reading," she sneered.

"Doesn't look like it."

"Whatever."

"You look miserable," he said.

"I'm not miserable!" But even Stacey could hear how pathetic she sounded.

"If there's an accident, I need you in the guard shack so you're ready to respond," he said, but Stacey didn't move. "Like, NOW."

Stacey rolled her eyes. Now he wants to act responsible? She grabbed her book and followed him back inside.

From the couch, she could hear Melissa and Jessie's megaphone banter through the closed door. She wished she had headphones.

"As if they would even notice if someone was drowning out there," she said to Mark, who had returned to his seat at the desk but kept his back turned, ignoring her.

Stacey stomped over and turned on the stereo. She felt Mark watching her out of the corner of his eye. She fiddled with the dial trying to find the Ska Parade until she heard the familiar sound of the Reel Big Fish trombone tooting "Everything Sucks." The song made her smile to herself. She turned the volume up until she could barely hear any noise from the pool area. She saw Mark watching her and erased her grin, then flopped back onto the couch, crossing her arms and glaring across the office at Mark.

Mark lifted his eyebrows, shook his head and exhaled, then walked out to the deck.

Stacey was throwing a tantrum and she knew it. But everything about the night totally sucked. After all her anticipation about working with Jessie, he hadn't even acknowledged her existence. No one had, except Mark, who clearly couldn't stand her. She sat alone in the guard shack, rereading the same page three times, wondering what she could do to make any of it better. The final shift needed to end so she could go home.

For the last thirty minutes of night swim, Stacey had to go back out to watch the deep end again. It was Melissa's break, but when Jessie took over her position watching the shallow end of the pool,

Melissa sat on the railing of Jessie's guard tower talking to him for the whole thirty minutes, directly in Stacey's line of sight.

Jessie would say something that made Melissa laugh, then she'd throw her head back like it was the funniest thing she'd ever heard, elongating her golden neck. Arching her back, Melissa would pushed her narrow chest out, striking a sculpture's pose. Then Jessie would tickle her thigh and poke her in the side to get her to wiggle more. Melissa crumpled into him, her cackle echoing across the water.

"Totally unprofessional," Stacey muttered to herself. "Get a room." Whatever. She figured Jessie was way out of her league anyway. Of course he was into someone sexy like Melissa. But did she really have to watch them flirt all summer long? Or worse. What if they started making out every day like Desiree and Chad. I should quit.

Stacey distracted herself staring toward the far end of the pool where the lavender twilight sky hung above the glowing aqua water, willing the night to be over. She imagined how she might be able to mix those exact colors from the paints Ms. Moreno loaned her.

At 8:55, Jessie announced to the swimmers over the megaphone that it was time to close the pool.

Finally! Stacey thought. She climbed down her tower.

At nine, Melissa, Jessie, and Stacey quickly pulled the pool cover across while Mark flipped off the lights in the water and locked the gates.

Stacey entered the guard shack ahead of the others and was surprised to find the rest of the lifeguard crew had shown up. Tiffany sat on the desk twirling her gum and kicking her feet. Chad and Desiree were snuggled on the couch, his arm around her shoulder with his fingers casually resting on her breast. Stacey stood staring at them, dumbfounded. Desiree's tank top was stretched-thin over her double Ds and her perfectly bouncy chestnut curls brushed against the spaghetti straps. Of all the female guards, she most resembled a Baywatch Babe in her red suit. And Chad couldn't keep his hands off her.

A slow grin spread across Chad's face. "Whatchalookingat Chapman?" He leaned toward Desiree's ear, his eyes locked with Stacey's. "I think Stacey here likes what she sees."

Stacey blushed and turned away, while Tiffany pretended she hadn't heard the exchange. Stacey went to her locker to collect her things.

Mark came through the door from the pool deck. "How's it goin'?" he asked no one in particular in his Joey Tribiani voice. Then he froze, tuning his ears toward the speaker in mock disgust. "Enough of this." He walked to the stereo and turned the dial to change the station.

"I left my Mariah Carey CD on the shelf. Put that on," Desiree told Mark.

"Hell no," he replied. "I have standards."

Melissa and Jessie entered the guard shack. Jessie grabbed his guitar from its resting place against the filing cabinet, and they settled into folding chairs in the corner, where Jessie began tuning the strings of his guitar.

"What's wrong with Mariah Carey?" Tiffany asked.

"What isn't?" Mark snorted. "If I want my ears to bleed, I can press the blow horn button on the megaphone."

"She's gotten like two Grammys and was Billboard's best female artist—twice," Desiree replied, tugging her tank top up over her cleavage. Chad reached over with his free hand and inched it back down.

"That doesn't mean her shrill, chick-flick pop is actually good," Mark said. "It just means she sold a lot of albums because girls like you have no taste. You throw your money away on any crap that promises some guy'll hold your hand and look into your eyes. I bet you like Janet Jackson and Shania Twain, too."

"You're an idiot, Mark." Melissa rolled her eyes. "Guys like you criticize talented women because of their ability to succeed in a man's world while you struggle even to achieve mediocrity."

"Whoa, hold up! I have no problem with successful women," Mark said, settling on a jazz and funk station. "I plan to see Demi Moore's new movie next week."

Desiree scoffed. "You mean the one where she's a stripper?"

"Hell ya!" Chad lifted his hand to high five Mark. "I'm in whenever you go!"

"Pigs!" Tiffany said.

Melissa turned her back to the group, her knees pulled tight against her chest, and focused all her attention on Jessie. He was strumming his own tune, ignoring the music coming from the radio.

With her book and her towel tucked into the bag on her shoulder, and her keys in her hand, Stacey looked around the room. *Isn't anyone going to ask me to stay?* Tiffany and Mark were perched on the desk shoulder to shoulder. Chad and Desiree were cuddled on the couch. And Melissa twirled her long, dark hair while Jessie serenaded her.

Stacey felt like a nuisance fly. Something was about to happen, and she felt like they were waiting for her to leave so whatever it was could begin. She mumbled, "G'night," and headed out the door.

"Night, Stacey!" Tiffany called with a bubbly wave.

No one else spoke.

As the door closed, Stacey glanced through the cashier window back into the guard shack, and half-expected them to be holding their thumb and pointer finger in the shape of an "L" on their foreheads. But they weren't. She wasn't even on their radar. And that felt worse.

The lobby door squeaked loudly as she pushed it open. Stacey dragged herself to the parking lot.

Sitting in her car, she rolled the windows down and slumped over the steering wheel. Jamiroquai pulsed across the dark pool, gentle humming from the glow of the guard shack. Melissa's all too familiar giggle ricocheted across the water. Stacey clenched her teeth then hit her forehead hard against the steering wheel. She did it again. Then once more, before finally turning the key in the ignition.

She drove away in silence.

When she got home, she fell onto her bed and called Gabe. He was half asleep and mumbled about opening at the restaurant for the breakfast shift at six a.m. Her words spilled out in a torrent.

"Whoa, Stace," he groaned, his voice hoarse. "Chill. They just don't know you. They're probably afraid you're a narc or something."

"I really needed this summer to be awesome. Everything about this job totally sucks."

"Show 'em you're down to party."

"Am I?"

"You don't have to get wasted." Gabe yawned. "That's not what I mean. But...be cool."

"I can be cool. I've partied. Kelly and I drank wine coolers with those guys we met in the desert over spring break."

"THAT was dumb. You didn't know anything about those guys. And wine coolers with your cousin isn't cool."

"I went to that party in the field behind Jason's house, too. There was a keg."

"Whatever. That's not the point. Show 'em your chill side. And, uhh…"

"What?"

"I think that Mark guy smokes a lot of weed."

"Probably. He sleeps all the time."

"Must be nice." Gabe yawned loudly. "Listen, I gotta crash. Talk tomorrow?"

Stacey hung up and conjured an image of the crew laughing while they built a pyramid out of beer cans on the diving board. She pictured them inside the guard shack, passing a giant bong around. She could practically hear Chad making fun of her and everyone rolling with laughter.

Stacey shook her head to clear her mind. It didn't work.

She took out her paints and tried to recapture the peace she'd felt in the art lab the night before. She dipped her brush in an old glass of water and mixed the bright green of the glowing pool and the violet of the sky as she'd seen it earlier that evening. Outside her window, a trio of coyotes howled, breaking the silence. She stepped back from her painting of the empty pool landscape. It looked blocky and childish, nothing like she imagined it would. Along with the coyotes, it left Stacey feeling sadder and even more alone. She crumpled the page and dropped it in the trash can beneath her desk.

There was no escape.

She turned out the light and laid beside Murphy on the floor in the dark, feeling pathetic.

Mark and Gabe were right: she needed to chill. She just didn't know how.

At The Plunge the next morning, there was no skunky smell. Only the standard stench of the public locker rooms and office. Jessie's guitar was back in the corner near Bob's desk and the trash can was full of take-out bags. The air felt cool and steam rose off the water when they pulled off the covers. Desiree and Chad were about as enthusiastic as anyone would be cleaning a community pool at eight a.m. in the summer. From what Stacey could tell, it didn't seem like they'd been up late getting high or drunk.

As they divvied up the jobs, no one wanted drain duty, so Chad suggested the three of them play rock, paper, scissors.

Stacey lost.

Desiree and Chad went to hose down the bathrooms; it was only fair, since they got out of drain duty. Bob was in the chemical room adding chlorine. Stacey grabbed a pair of abandoned goggles from the lost and found that looked relatively new, a pair of rubber gloves, and her towel, and headed out to the deep end.

At the side of the pool, she pulled the goggles over her eyes, then stretched, and let her towel fall onto the deck. The rising sun was warm on her back, and her skin tingled as she anticipated the coolness of the water. It was her first time swimming to the bottom of the deep end since she was a kid. Even then she'd barely touched it with her foot and quickly pushed back to the top. She wasn't confident she could even hold her breath long enough to get the drain totally clean.

She curled her toes over the concrete edge above the "15 ft" depth marker tile. Taking a breath, she laid one hand over the other above her head, bent over, and pushed off with her feet. Her fingers broke the smooth surface of the water, and within a fraction of a second her body was submerged in the cool water in the lower part of the deep end. The pressure hurt her ears and she rebounded off the bottom without even touching the drain.

At the surface, Stacey caught her breath. Locating the drain with her eyes, she dove again, letting some air out so it wouldn't hurt. As she reached it, she quickly scraped all ten gloved fingers across its screen to loosen the suction on the pile of waste. The water was foggy through the ill-fitting goggles, and the bubbles she let out made it even harder to know exactly what she was grabbing. But she collected everything she could in her clenched fists and kicked straight back up.

Stacey let out a gasp at the top and took a deep breath. She flipped to her back and kicked backward toward the wall, holding the sludgy debris pile above the water between her gloved hands. Her head bumped into the edge of the gutter. She turned and lifted her hands out, setting their contents on the side of the pool. It looked like mostly hair and Band-Aids, and possibly another rubber glove mixed in with a few leaves. She climbed out, then snatched the pile. She was about to drop it in a nearby trash can when something white fell to the ground.

She stood staring at the used condom, a million thoughts flowing through her mind. *How did it get here? Was it a swimmer's? Or a guard's? Was it really used, or had someone unrolled it to make a water balloon for some stupid reason? Maybe those kids from the night before, trying to impress Jessie. If someone had sex with it, what happened to whatever was inside? Is it in the pool now? Is that a biohazard?*

She cringed. "Gross."

The image of Chad fondling Desiree's breast on the couch the night before flashed across her mind. And Jessie tickling Melissa in the guard tower. Everyone waiting for Stacey to leave. *Was that what they'd been doing? Having sex? All of them?*

Coach Bob came up behind her, whistling like Andy Griffith. Stacey grabbed the condom in her gloved fist, pulled the glove off around it, and dropped it into the trashcan before he could see.

"You need help taking that out to the dumpster?" Bob asked.

"No. I got it." She grabbed the trash bag pull ties and closed the top.

She wrapped the towel around herself, slipped on her flip flops, then pulled the bag from the can, holding the garbage far from her body. The lock rattled against the metal frame of the chain link gate as she pushed it open, then she crossed the empty parking lot, all the while only thinking about the condom and how many of the guards were probably having sex. With one another. In the pool. She wondered if Christian-club Jessie Thomas drank beer, smoked pot, and had sex. Even with his crown of thorns tattoo and WWJD bracelet. Jessie and the cackling, feminist, track-star Melissa. She'd called him "JT" while running her fingers through his wavy blonde hair and Stacey thought she couldn't have hated her more. Until now.

Then she thought about Desiree and Chad's passionate parking lot kiss that first day. The lace panties. They were definitely having sex. A lot.

She was done being the odd man out everywhere she went. It was her turn. She was going to get Jessie to notice her. No matter what she had to do.

Chapter Eight

By mid-June, everyone on The Plunge staff understood their responsibilities, and (for the most part) had stopped complaining about them. Mark was an excellent mentor to the other guards in terms of his mastery at putting in minimal effort without getting in trouble with Bob. They all knew when they could cut corners on certain chores and enjoyed the extra time in the guard shack lounging away from the heat.

In her first two weeks, Stacey discovered favorite shady parking spaces based on the time of her shifts and the quickest routes for picking up fast food. Determined to prove she was *chill* and win over anyone at the pool, she started going on lunch runs for Bob and herself. Eventually Mark and Tiffany accepted her offers, too, and as they ate, she found ways to talk to them about music and movies.

One morning when she brought her CD organizer into the guard shack, Stacey told Mark she agreed with him about Mariah Carey's voice being shrill, and he said she should pick something good to listen to while they cleaned. They were all tired of the Beach Boys. She chose Tom Petty's *Full Moon Fever* album, and everyone seemed to like it. Even Bob, who had strict rules about what played over the loud speakers outside. The next day she chose Oasis, and the day after that The Eagles.

"What's on deck for this morning's tunes?" Chad asked Stacey as he picked up the bucket and trash-grabber from the corner.

"*Singles* soundtrack." She knew the albums made their maintenance duties tolerable, but was even more grateful it had scored her at least a few extra popularity points.

Chad gave her a quizzical look. "I can't think of any specific music in that movie."

"You've been missing out." She selected track four.

"Oh, damn! I love 'Dyslexic Heart.'"

She nodded, hoping it wasn't obvious how proud she felt.

Work at The Plunge could be mind-numbing. Guards had the same daily cleaning tasks, sat in the same two towers, rotated every half hour, hour after hour, day after day. That was how Six Degrees of Kevin Bacon became their favorite game.

"Meryl Streep and Keanu Reeves," Tiffany challenged Stacey one afternoon.

Two minutes passed before Stacey replied: "Keanu Reeves was in *Parenthood* with Diane Wiest. She was in *Footloose* with Kevin Bacon, and he was in *The River Wild* with Meryl Streep. Three degrees of separation."

Whoever had the least separation points at the end of a round won, and Stacey won pretty often.

Bob allowed them their game so long as it didn't interfere with their work. As a baseball coach, he could get on board with anything that resembled a team-building exercise, but he had zero tolerance for people being late or missing their shift without calling ahead.

Despite his warning from Bob at orientation, Jessie was late again less than two weeks into summer. By 12:28 he hadn't arrived for his noon shift. Tiffany called him and woke him up. Considering the distance on a skateboard, the crew commented it was miraculous he managed to get there by one.

Bob was not as impressed. Before the day was over, he phoned everyone on staff. "Be here at 7:30 a.m. tomorrow, in your swimsuit. You will address the issue of punctuality and dependability as a team."

It was still hazy when Bob opened the door Saturday morning and ushered the crew out to the deep end of the pool. He had already removed the cover.

"You will all be treading water for as many minutes as anyone is late this summer," Bob explained. "Because this is the first offense, I won't make you do the full hour that Jessie was late. But be warned that next time it happens, I won't be so lenient. Today it will be the twenty-eight minutes it took before anyone called to find out why he didn't show up."

"Sorry I didn't call sooner, guys!" Tiffany said.

"This is about teamwork, Tiffany. At least you were looking out for your teammate. Now, the timer will start once everyone's in the water. It will be paused if anyone floats. It will be restarted if anyone gets out before 28 minutes are up."

Mark leaned against the tower, rubbing the sleep out of his eyes, like he was all too familiar with this exercise. Stacey wondered how many times over the past three years Mark had been the reason the crew had to tread water, and for how long.

Stacey's arms were wrapped tight across her belly, gripping her T-shirt. She had her red bathing suit on under her shorts and tee but was still uncomfortable wearing only her swimsuit in front of the other lifeguards. Now she had to undress in front of the whole crew. Despite the chill in the air, sweat gathered under her arms and trickled down her ribs. She hoped no one had noticed.

The other guards peeled off their clothes like it was no big deal, then slithered into the water. The longer Stacey waited, the bigger a spectacle she would be.

"Like ripping off a Band-Aid," Stacey muttered to herself.

She held her breath, slipped her shorts off quickly, yanked her T-shirt over her head, then started down the ladder. Only after she was submerged to her shoulders did she finally exhale.

That's when she noticed that the only guard not in the water yet was Melissa. "This is totally unfair, Bob," Melissa protested. "The rest of us should not be held accountable for Jessie's irresponsibility!"

"If you have a problem with the way I run this facility, Melissa, you are free to quit," Bob said, his arms crossed. "Otherwise, get in the water."

Melissa let out an audible gasp, then pursed her lips, pulled off her tank top and climbed in.

Coach Bob stood on the side of the pool like a swim meet official, stopwatch in hand. He waited to say go until Melissa was in the water.

Treading water came naturally to Stacey, after numerous childhood games of Marco Polo. Once the timer began she was able to relax. During lifeguard certification, they had to tread water for ten minutes with their hands on their heads, and Stacey hadn't found it difficult.

Melissa's voice arched over the pool. "I can't *believe* you couldn't show up on time for a noon shift! Seriously?!?" she shrieked.

Jessie rolled his eyes and turned away from her.

Whatever connection Jessie and Melissa had earlier in the week had faded, and it buoyed Stacey's mood.

Chad paddled closer to Jessie. "How long can you keep your hands up, dude?" Chad asked.

"I dunno. Never did more than the ten we had to. You?"

"Me either. Loser buys lunch?"

"You're on!" Jessie said.

"I'm in," Tiffany said.

"Me, too," Stacey chimed in. "I hope you brought plenty of cash."

Desiree and Melissa moved away from the crew, relocating under the diving board where they whispered to one another. Melissa paddled, chin lifted, as she struggled to keep her hair out of the water.

"All right, then," Chad said. The four competitors circled up in the center of the deep end. "Both hands have to stay dry."

"No kicking or knocking into each other, right?" Tiffany asked.

"Right. And no spitting water or splashing," Chad agreed. "Everyone ready?"

They all nodded.

"Go!"

Eight hands popped out of the water.

Stacey was giddy to finally do something with Jessie.

They all eyed one another, making faces and pretending to be fierce.

"I can already taste that Famous Star with cheese," Chad taunted.

"No way. Sweet success smells like orange chicken," Tiffany replied.

As the sun rose above the facility roofline, and birds in nearby trees chirped above the humming of the valves and motor in the equipment room, Coach Bob announced, "Ten minutes down. Eighteen to go."

Mark and Melissa both groaned. Melissa's chin skimmed the water, her bun fully submerged. She scowled at Jessie.

"How 'bout a round of Six Degrees?" Jessie asked.

Stacey smirked. This really was her lucky day. Her arms felt heavy and sore, but she was determined not to stop, and Six Degrees of Kevin Bacon would be a fun distraction.

Tiffany and Chad nodded in agreement, their elbows dripping as they reminded themselves to keep them up.

"Clint Eastwood and River Phoenix," Jesse said.

Stacey was a huge fan of River Phoenix, and her mom loved romance novels, so they'd watched all the movies made from the books she'd read. "River Phoenix was in *Sneakers* with that guy with the glasses who was in *The River Wild* with Kevin Bacon AND Meryl Streep. She was in *The Bridges of Madison County* with Clint Eastwood. Three degrees!" Stacey blurted.

Tiffany's hands slapped the surface of the water. "How'd you…"

"You lost!" Chad shouted at Tiffany. He let his own hands fall, then maneuvered his way to Desiree.

"Dang!" Tiffany said in mock-annoyance.

But Stacey and Jessie kept their hands up, staring into one another's eyes. Stacey pursed her lips with one eyebrow cocked.

Mark moved in closer to the group, and let out a belch that smelled like rotten eggs, hovering above the powerful chemical smell of the chlorine Bob had added that morning.

"Gross!" Desiree and Melissa plugged their noses and struggled to stay afloat beside Chad.

"You guys don't have to keep going," Chad said. "Tiffany's buying lunch."

"Nice job," Jessie told Stacey, ignoring him. "You gonna quit, Chapman?"

Stacey's heart raced. "Nope." *He called me Chapman!*

"Cool. You got a Six Degrees challenge for me?"

"Robin Williams and Chris O'Donnell."

"Who's that?"

"He was in–" Desiree said.

"Don't tell him the names of movies!" Stacey interrupted. "That's cheating!"

"You can't pick someone no one knows." Jessie argued.

Desiree chimed in. "Everyone knows who Chris O'Donnell is!"

"Chad, Mark…help me out. Is Chris O'Donnell an actual actor you've heard of?"

Mark shrugged. "I've heard of him. I don't like any of his shitty movies, but I know who he is."

"Sorry, man," Chad said. "He's pretty famous."

"Has he been in any movies lately?"

"Duh!" Melissa rolled her eyes, doggy paddling. "Like three in the last year."

"Okay…so, I'm the *only* person who doesn't know who this guy is?" Jessie said, gesturing with his hands. He asked Stacey, "Well, what does he look like?"

"Light brown hair, blue eyes," Stacey said. "He's young. Super-cute."

"So he looks like me?"

"Ehhh…" Stacey teased. "Sort of. A paler, preppier version of you."

"Oh my god…" Melissa exhaled behind Stacey.

Jessie nodded, pleased he'd gotten Stacey to admit what she thought of him. "Can you tell me if I'm right if I guess a few movies he's in?"

"Booo." Chad cupped his hand around his mouth. "Loser needs help."

Stacey shrugged. "Sure."

"Was he in *Dead Poets Society*?"

"Uh uh." Stacey shook her head.

"*Hook*?"

"Nope."

"Admit defeat, Jess," Tiffany chimed in. "Stacey's a film genius."

Jessie shook his head intently. "He wasn't in *A Few Good Men* or *Footloose*, right?"

"Right," Stacey said.

"Oh, wait, is he the guy who plays Robin in *Batman?*"

"Yes."

"Geez... Okay. So, he's in that with Val Kilmer. Hmmm..."

Bob started counting down the last five minutes and warned the crew not to stop moving. Everyone but Jessie and Stacey were basically floating in place, fluttering their hands in the water so Bob wouldn't punish them further. Stacey's whole body was aching. Still, she refused to give up or let her hands drop.

"So, Robin Williams was in *Hook* with Dustin Hoffman, who was in *Rain Man* with Tom Cruise, who was in *Top Gun* with Val Kilmer, who was in *Batman* with Chris O'Conner."

"O'Donnell. But what about Kevin Bacon?"

"Shit. Right. Tom Cruise was in *A Few Good Men* with Kevin Bacon, so..."

"Uh huh..."

"But no Hoffman or Kilmer in that. Or Williams or O'Connell."

Stacey laughed. "O'Donnell."

"Can you do it?"

"Robin Williams was in *Hook* with Dustin Hoffman, who was in *Rain Man* with Tom Cruise, who was in *A Few Good Men* with Kevin Bacon and Keifer Southerland, who was in *The Three Musketeers* with Chris O'Donnell. Four degrees."

"I'm impressed," Jessie said.

Stacey was breathless and her cheeks hurt from grinning, but she clasped her hands atop her head, kicking her feet hard beneath her.

"I really thought you'd give up."

"You don't know me very well," Stacey said, looking straight at him. "I don't quit when there's something I want."

Jessie squinted and cocked his head, quizzically.

She lifted both eyebrows and raised her chin in response. The sound of the guards panting around her was drowned out by the beating of her heart. She was flirting, and for the first time the guy she was flirting with knew it.

Bob blew the whistle. Stacey tied with Jessie, both making it all the way to the end with their hands up.

They climbed out of the pool. Stacey's shoulders were on fire and her legs felt like Jello, but she couldn't remember another time she felt so confident. Without grabbing her towel or her clothes, she stood in front of Jessie in her red swimsuit with her hands on her hips, water dripping into a puddle around her feet. "If you ever need a ride so you won't be late again, I can pick you up," she offered.

He smiled. "Thanks, Stace."

"Anytime. Need a ride home today?"

Jessie's eyes scanned the length of her body. When his eyes met her gaze, he nodded. "Sure."

"Hey, Jess," Chad called from the door of the guard shack. "We're getting donuts. Wanna come?"

Jessie's eyes were locked on Stacey's.

"Jessie?" Chad called again.

Stacey stared back at Jessie. She knew she wouldn't have to worry about being invisible anymore.

Chapter Nine

D on't think too much about it," Ms. Moreno instructed. "We're just making marks on a page."

It was Monday night, a week after Stacey attended the first Art Escape, and she and Ms. Moreno were again the only two people in the art lab. An oscillating fan buzzed in the corner, the warm breeze blowing Stacey's fine hair across her cheeks. Her art teacher's tight chocolatey curls were suspended atop her head, anchored with a pencil. Stacey swirled her own hair up, shoving the pointed end of a pencil through. The hair unraveled, and the pencil clanked on the floor. Stacey sheepishly picked it up and pulled her hair to one side.

"The idea of abstract art is to capture the essence of something while letting it take on a life of its own. The feeling comes from the color, the unique brushstrokes. Introducing a new way of seeing and representing something."

Stacey struggled to understand how the squiggly pale pink marks separated by thin white lines would resemble a flower, but she dipped her brush in the rosy hue and touched the tip of her brush to the paper. Imitating her teacher's gestures, she pressed the brush down as she pulled it in a tight curve, and lifted up again toward the end. The C-shape looked more like a pink slug than a petal to her, but she repeated the motion moving outward, adjusting the length and width for each petal so no two were identical, and the petals grew wider and longer as the blossom spread outward.

"Nice!" Ms. Moreno praised.

Stacey leaned back and squinted. "Something's off…"

"Good eye. What do you think it is?"

"It's…too flat, or something."

"Exactly. It's a beautiful color, and your brushstrokes are well executed. But without a change in hue, it has no depth. Light and dark hues create shape. The petals connect at a deeper point in the flower, while the outside edges are in the light."

Stacey looked at the flower Ms. Moreno had set in a beaker between them, and realized that even though she'd accomplished the right shade of peachy pink, the center of the live flower was much darker, and the outside petals were nearly white. She added more magenta and deep yellow to darken her mix, and rewet the edges of her petals near the center of her blossom. Stacey touched the darker color to the inside edges. It spread and faded across the petals.

"Well done, Stacey. That's a perfect bleed."

Stacey rinsed her brush and swiped clean water along the outside edges of the outer petals, dabbing them with a paper towel to remove some color.

"You have great instincts," Ms. Moreno said.

They each added two more blossoms to their paintings, and Stacey studied her trio of pale pink roses fondly.

"So, how exactly are we 'escaping' into these flowers?"

"Abstract art is about escaping reality while revealing universal truth."

Stacey lifted one eyebrow and looked at her florals again. "I don't get it."

Ms. Moreno stood back and squinted, her right forefinger curled over her mauve lips. "Hmmm..."

"What's wrong?"

"They're too perfect, I think," Ms. Moreno said.

Stacey cocked her head, searching for what Ms. Moreno saw. The flowers looked like roses, without being exact replicas. Wasn't that what they were aiming for?

"They're not very interesting to look at," Ms. Moreno said.

Frustration flushed through Stacey. She'd done what she was supposed to, so why hadn't it worked? She looked again, trying to understand what Ms. Moreno meant. Interesting or not, she'd achieved her goal of painting three roses. That should've been enough!

Ms. Moreno dipped a thick paintbrush in clean water and wet the area of her page around the blossoms. The flowers' edges seeped into the water. Ms. Moreno swept the large brush through the paint, making wonky circles and broad strokes of pink around the blossoms. Working quickly, she dropped darker tones in the centers of some, straight yellow in the center of others. She grabbed a smaller brush and mixed blue with the yellow, dropping various tones of green around the pink blobs.

Foliage. Stacey was bewildered how easy it looked.

Just as with the original petals, Ms. Moreno left white spaces between each, but still allowed the leaves and flowers to touch in some spots so the colors would run.

"What do you think?" Ms. Moreno asked.

"It's cool, but…." Stacey tried to avoid grimacing. "It's kinda out of control." The intensity and chaos made Stacey uncomfortable.

"I agree! I love it. That's exactly what the problem was before: it was way too controlled. I needed to let the painting be more free." She pulled the pencil from atop her head, wild curls falling around her face and thin shoulders. "Messy. Natural."

Stacey knit her brow. "I don't think that's what I meant." She looked past her teacher to the stack of palettes slathered with dried paint cluttering Ms. Moreno's desk.

Ms. Moreno shrugged and grinned. "If there was a bush of perfect roses, or a wall covered in paintings of perfect roses, they all would become really boring. A real rose bush is beautiful because of all the stages of blossoming. The ones that stand out are uniquely imperfect. That is the feeling I wanted to capture."

"Is it okay if I don't want to do that on mine?" Stacey could hear the crack in her voice and hoped that Ms. Moreno didn't notice.

"Sure, Stacey. It's your painting! You should do what you want with your work."

They cleaned up the supplies and rinsed out the brushes. Ms. Moreno asked, "Would you like a popsicle? I thought it would be a nice treat."

"Sure."

Ms. Moreno leaned down to the mini fridge beside her desk. As she walked back to Stacey, she pulled open the white pouch, and split the two sticks apart. "I hope you like cherry."

Stacey smiled. "Thanks."

Sitting on the butcher block table across from where their paintings were resting, they let their legs swing beneath them.

"I have so many happy memories of eating these growing up," Ms. Moreno said.

Stacey nodded, licking the length of her popsicle.

"Isn't it funny that you can't imagine popsicles, or remember eating them, without thinking about them dripping?"

"Yeah! That's so true. My mom has pictures of me when I was little with my face and bathing suit stained."

"And I bet you had a huge smile." Ms. Moreno wiped the back of her hand across her chin, a smear of cherry syrup striping her warm brown skin. She left it and continued nibbling.

"Of course."

"Messiness is part of what makes it so wonderful. Usually kids get in trouble for being messy. Plus you have to enjoy it quickly; that's part of the fun. I like teaching art for the same reasons."

"You are like the opposite of my mom. She doesn't like messes. And she never buys popsicles anymore."

"Have you asked why?"

Stacey shook her head. She could feel Ms. Moreno's eyes on her as she slurped the side of her popsicle, but instead focused her attention on their paintings. She could see how Ms. Moreno had achieved the look of a full bush of roses, but each flower was different: a small tight blossom, another large and in full bloom, the third in profile with much darker hues. "I like that darker rose of yours the best."

"Your roses are beautiful also, Stacey."

"Thanks, but I get what you meant. I'm more drawn to your painting."

"That's why your self-portrait won first place, you know."

Suddenly the sweetness in Stacey's belly turned sour. "Huh?"

"So many students submitted beautiful artwork, but yours captured a real sense of what it's like to be a teenage girl. The loneliness. The self-doubt and insecurity. Especially that you had crumpled the page. That spoke volumes."

The only sound for the next minute was Stacey chewing on her popsicle stick. When it cracked and splintered between her teeth, she took it from her mouth and mumbled, "I was mad at you."

"For taking it out of the trash and submitting it?"

"Yeah. It was really embarrassing." She looked down at the broken and stained popsicle stick in her lap.

"I'm sorry. I wish you'd said something. I would have pulled it from the art show."

"I was afraid you'd lower my grade if I said anything."

"I'm sorry you thought that. I only wanted you to know how much I admired your work. I thought it deserved acknowledgement. I should have asked you."

Stacey shrugged.

"Your feelings matter," Ms. Moreno said. "Your feelings are important. No one should punish you for expressing them."

Stacey's jaw twitched. She looked up, feeling angry all over again. Desperate to change the subject, she softened her voice. "Does yours have a joke?"

"My popsicle stick?" Ms. Moreno asked. She turned it over and lifted it to read it under the overhead fluorescent light. "Uh, yeah. 'How is a bad joke like a dull pencil?'"

"It has no point."

"Right." She smiled, then nodded. "What's yours?"

"Why was the artist hauled to jail?"

Ms. Moreno shrugged.

"To face the mosaic."

Ms. Moreno chuckled. "Does it really say that?"

Stacey shook her head and showed her teacher the decimated popsicle stick. "It says 'Why'd the banana' and 'Because it.' I can't read the rest."

"Hmmm… Why'd the banana…split?"

"Because it was in sundae school," Stacey said.

"Because it saw the ice scream." Ms. Moreno lifted her hands to her face and held her mouth in an "O" like the Edvard Munch painting.

"Because it was sick of being bunched up." Stacey squeezed her arms and shoulders together like she was in a confined space.

"Because it was afraid of getting crushed nuts!" Ms. Moreno put her hands over her lap, and Stacey opened her eyes wide in shock.

They both laughed.

"I'm glad you came back tonight," Ms. Moreno said. "I missed painting with you the last week."

"Me too. Thanks, Ms. Moreno."

"You can call me Sage if you want."

Stacey wrinkled her nose. "Uh… no. I can't." She hopped off the table and headed for the door. "But thanks."

"O-kay…," Ms. Moreno said over her shoulder, a fallen expression clouding her face. "One last thing, Stace. Remember, whether we like it or not, everyone's life is messy."

Stacey was taken aback. "Yeah…" *Sure. But not as messy as mine.* "See ya."

Ms. Moreno turned away and walked to her desk.

As Stacey walked to her car she realized she couldn't remember her teacher ever looking sad before. The hot night air was still and insects buzzed in the mustard weed bushes beside the parking spaces. The lightness she had felt after the first time she painted with Ms. Moreno hadn't returned. Everything felt heavier and Stacey wasn't sure she liked it.

Chapter Ten

Y ou never miss the Juvenile Delinquents," Gabe scolded Stacey through the phone. "The Valley College Ska Fest is their biggest show yet. We've looked forward to this for over a month."

"I haven't had a day out of the sun all week," Stacey whined. "It's going to be like a million degrees in that quad."

"Seriously? You sound like an old lady. Who cares if it's hot? SkipTooth is headlining. It's gonna be awesome."

Stacey didn't want Gabe to know the real reason she was bailing: Jessie. Chad and Desiree were going to the beach, and Chad invited Jessie to surf with him. Desiree asked if Stacey wanted to go to keep her company. It was basically a double date, one that could lead to something major with Jessie!

"It starts at two?" Stacey asked reluctantly. Desiree said they were leaving for the beach at eleven, and she'd already picked out her bikini.

"Yeah. I'll even drive. Come on. We haven't hung out all summer."

"Who else is going? Jenny? Kyle? Dan?"

"Not with me. I haven't talked to Jenny since school got out. I don't know if those guys will be there or not. I was looking forward to hanging out with you."

Stacey's chest swelled. Gabe really wanted to be alone with her! Maybe this meant he wouldn't treat her like a kid-sister-best-friend like at the No Doubt show in May. Was Gabe finally realizing they should be more than friends? If there was even the slightest chance this could spark a real relationship, she couldn't resist.

In his best sing-song voice, Gabe said, "We can get Slurpees on the way…"

"Okaaayyy…" Stacey said, grinning. "If there'll be Slurpees, I guess I'll go…"

Stacey hung up and called Desiree to cancel, then put on her Juvenile Delinquents tape and picked out her outfit—a short, red plaid skirt, a white baby-Tee and white knee socks with black, steel-toe Doc Martins. Maybe if she dressed sexy for her date with Gabe, she could finally win him over.

Standing at the full-length mirror on the back of her door, she put on heavy eyeliner, thick mascara, and red lipstick. She swooped her bangs and hair into a perfect pompadour ponytail, and tied a red bandana as a headband. At the No Doubt show in May, she wore jeans, Chucks, and a T-shirt. *Boring!* She envied the strutting Rude Girls with their short skirts, fishnet stockings, and pin-up-style make-up and hair. Today, she wanted Gabe to think she was sexy, like those girls. She looked nothing like herself, not her usual self, anyway. But looking like Stacey Chapman hadn't worked with Gabe so far. *Go big or go home.* This time Gabe would see her as Gwen Stefani skipping toward him, and if that didn't get his attention, she didn't know what would.

Gabe watched her catwalk-stroll out to his car. He affected his voice. "Do-do-do-do. Do-do-do-do."

"Shut up! Stop trying to be Rod Serling! This is not *The Twilight Zone* and you will never be Rod Serling!" Stacey laughed.

"Says you, Gwen Stefani!" he said as Stacey opened his passenger car door. "Seriously, what's up? You went all out."

"It's a ska show, right? So, I'm dressed for success." She pulled the short skirt under her bare thighs, hopeful the dark vinyl wouldn't burn her when she sat. It was still pretty hot, so she slid down to avoid the skin on vinyl contact, then curled her exposed lower back away from the seat.

"You are a total dork. You know that, right?" Gabe asked.

"Um, hmmm…" Despite her awkward position, Stacey batted her eyelashes up at him as she buckled the seatbelt. "Now, I'm ready for that Slurpee whenever you are."

Gabe laughed and shook his head. "You never cease to amaze me, Chapman."

They walked into the Valley College quad right before the Juvenile Delinquents took the stage. Close to two hundred people were standing around waiting for the show to start. Stacey's makeup was melting. It was over a hundred degrees in the sun and there was no shade anywhere near the stage. Sweat pooled under her arms and between her toes in the hot leather boots. She was afraid the hairspray wouldn't hold against the sweat collecting on top of her head. Attempting to preserve the pin-up girl look she'd worked so hard to create, she wandered over to a low wall in the shade, away from the crowd, and sat down. She was not about to let her effort to look cute go to waste in the middle of the mosh pit.

Gabe hesitated ten feet from her, furrowing his eyebrows. "What are you doing?"

"Let's watch from here," she said, grinning at him.

"But we always go up by the stage." He gestured over his shoulder with his thumb.

"I know, but we don't have to, do we? See how nice the shade is?" Imitating Vana White, Stacey splayed her fingers and motioned for him to sit beside her.

"But...Stace..." Gabe looked behind him toward the stage a football field's distance away, then back, torn.

Stacey patted the wall, a sly smile across her bright red lips.

Gabe shook his head. "I'm not sure what's up with you, but I'm here to have fun." He turned and walked toward the stage.

He didn't look back and she didn't follow him.

He slid quickly into the crowd. The music started. By the second song, a circle pit formed, and Stacey scrambled to stand on the wall and search for Gabe. He had joined a bunch of guys skanking. Guys were pulling off their shirts and swinging them around. Gabe was a head taller than the other dancers and his shoulders were heaving as he elbowed, bounced, and shoved his way around the pit as trumpets blared.

He'd done the same thing in May, heading to the front to dance. Although, between every song, he'd made his way back to her side. They'd sing along together to the first few bars of the next song, then he'd run into the pit again. Now she felt miserably alone and wondered where she'd gone wrong.

Several songs in, the lead singer, Martin, announced over the loudspeakers, "We want to thank our Mesa Valley friends who are here today!" The crowd cheered and Gabe pumped his fist in the air. "You guys have supported us since the beginning, coming to our shows and buying our tapes. It's all happening now because of you." A bunch of other hands flew in the air, clapping and making devil horns. Stacey moved toward the edge of the crowd, wanting to find a way to get by Gabe's side.

The audience was jam-packed. No one would let her in. Martin shouted "Skank till you stank, Delinquents!" into the microphone and the crowd went wild. The band launched into their Mesa Valley tribute song and the whole crowd danced along, kicking and swinging their arms.

When the Juvenile Delinquents set ended, Stacey stood back beside the wall, hoping Gabe would at least make eye contact before the next band began. The crowd broke apart. She spotted Gabe, bare chested and red-faced, carrying his T-shirt. She waved at him.

He trotted over, wiping his face with the T-shirt. "Did you hear that tribute? Awesome, right?"

Stacey nodded, afraid to reveal her disappointment about being too far from the stage to really enjoy it.

"You having fun?" he panted.

"Yeah," she lied. "But you must be dying out there." Maybe if he was too hot he would stay with her in the shade?

"It's not so bad," Gabe grinned and shrugged. "It's worth it!" He looked over her shoulder, smiling. Stacey followed his attention to a group of girls behind her, watching Gabe. One girl waved and Gabe quickly nodded hello. His chest expanded as he caught his breath, muscles flexed and skin splotchy from colliding with other bodies.

"Do you know those girls?" Stacey asked, wishing he was paying more attention to her.

"Not really. They said they're friends with Martin, Josh, and the other guys from the Delinquents, too. I'll be right back."

He tucked his shirt into his back pocket and ran over to talk to them. Stacey slumped back down onto the wall, her elbows on her knees and her chin propped on her right hand. *Is he getting their numbers?*

A few minutes later, Gabe walked toward a concession stand, then returned to Stacey with two waters. He handed her one.

"Thanks," she said.

Gabe nodded and gulped down his entire bottle. "Next band's about to start."

Stacey bit her lip. She was afraid he was about to ditch her again. "Looked like you were having fun out there."

"Yeah...I was," he said, tilting his head down to look in her eyes. "But it'd be way more fun if you were out there, too."

Her heart skipped. "It's pretty lonely over here."

He stuck his bottom lip out. "Oh, poor baby. You're lonely...pouting that it's hot...in summer!" Gabe put his arm around her neck and pulled her against his torso. Her stomach fluttered.

"Ew! You're so sweaty!" Stacey squealed, but didn't pull away.

Gabe laughed as he stepped back and put his shirt back on. "If you're done acting insane," he said, "maybe you could suck it up for the next set? We could go over by those speakers." He pointed to the right of the stage. "It'll be loud, but at least they make it kind of shady."

She licked her bottom lip. "Okay. Yeah. That'd be good."

He still wants me with him!

She took a few sips of water and offered the rest to Gabe. He downed the water in one gulp, then took her by the hand and led her to the front of the crowd.

The second band started and Stacey could feel the brass blast and beat of the drums in every bone of her body. She was sure her ears would be ringing for a week, but didn't care. Gabe's smile was infectious. They sang along and bounced to the rhythm, steam rising from the mass of bodies crowded in the cement quad. Her clothes were drenched with sweat, but Gabe was right: it was worth it.

Gabe was drawn back to the pit time and again, and he'd look over, waving for Stacey to join him. She'd shake her head, laughing, then Gabe would rejoin her to sing along and dance for a minute before he'd run off. It felt to Stacey like a game of hide and seek that neither of them was winning, yet they both were still coming out ahead. Every time he ran back to the mosh pit, she tried to make eye contact with anyone in her vicinity, hoping to catch an admiring glance from someone who assumed they were a couple. But the crowd was too caught up in the music to pay her any notice.

When the show ended at five, Stacey's cheeks hurt from smiling, and there was a constant buzzing in her ears. She was exhausted, but happy.

Gabe wiped the sweat from his head with his shirt, then pulled it back on as they headed toward the parking lot. "Glad you came?"

Stacey nodded, her hot feet heavy with every step across the asphalt. "Did you have fun?" She did her best to ignore the blisters on her toes rubbing against the sweaty socks inside her boots.

"Sure," he said. Then he turned toward her, and reached his thumb toward her left eye. "You've...got something..."

Stacey rubbed the area beneath her eyes with the backs of her pointer fingers. Both came away smudged with black.

Gabe cringed. "I think that made it worse."

Stacey wiped in the opposite direction with the backs of both thumbs, and again both hands were smeared with makeup. "Better?"

Gabe curled his lips inside his mouth, stifling his laughter, and shook his head.

She leaned down and looked into a parked car's side mirror. Both eyes had dark stains of black makeup beneath, and swiped toward her temples. The red on her lips was faded, smeared onto her chin and nose, and with dried red flakes poking up from the cracks in her chapped lips. "Geez! I look awful!" Stacey pulled the bandana from her head, and wiped as much of the makeup away as she could. "How long have I looked this bad?"

"Awhile," Gabe laughed.

"Why didn't you tell me sooner?" Stacey elbowed him in the ribs and they continued toward his car. "I can't believe you'd even be seen with me like this!" As they walked she'd catch her reflection in the windows of cars, and pause, trying to fix what she could before hustling to catch up with him again.

"I still don't get why you wore all that makeup and got so dressed up. You knew it was going to be crazy hot."

"I wanted to look cute." Stacey loosened the ponytail and ran the tips of her fingers over her hair to smooth it down, creating sweaty bumps and creases.

"Why?" There was an irritated tone to Gabe's one word question that immediately humiliated her. She'd misread everything.

She stopped walking and looked down at her boots, embarrassed. Her feet were steaming, and her white knee socks, grimy from the dust and sweat, had slid down. She felt as disgusting as they looked.

"Sorry. I didn't mean…," Gabe said, arriving at his car, looking back at her. "It just… surprised me." He unlocked the passenger door and opened it. When she didn't walk over, he went around to the driver's side and climbed in, turning on the AC.

Stacey dragged herself to the car and slumped into the seat. The vinyl burned her legs, but she kept quiet about it. She closed the door and pulled down the passenger mirror. She looked like a clown. She scrubbed vigorously with the bandana. After air blowing from the vents turned from hot to cool, she adjusted them toward her face and took deep breaths. Lifting her arms to fix her hair, she smelled a sour, musky stink, then saw damp, yellow pit stains on her tee and dropped her arms to her sides, horrified. She glanced at Gabe. A smirk crossed his face. *This couldn't possibly get any worse.*

Gabe put on his 1995 Warped Tour cd and pulled his car into the line of cars filing out of the lot.

After a few minutes, she asked, "So, when's the Warped Tour starting?" She knew the answer but hoped a shift in their conversation might turn the evening around.

"In about a week. I may try to go to Carson. It isn't too far."

"It'd be fun to take a road trip. See it someplace cool, like San Diego or San Francisco. Sleep in the car or something."

"Yeah." Gabe rolled his eyes. "Sure."

"Why not?"

"You can't be serious. Driving hundreds of miles and staying overnight? Just the two of us?" He pulled his chin and head back, while staying focused on driving. "You really think our parents would be cool with that?"

"In a year we'll be away at college," she reminded him. "At some point they can't control us or who we choose to spend the night with."

Gabe wrinkled his forehead. He squinted at the road, exhaled loudly, but didn't say anything.

"Is there a reason you wouldn't want to go with *me* in particular?" she whispered.

"Why would you ask me that? You're my best friend. I usually love going to shows with you."

"Usually?"

"Well…today…you were…everything was…different."

She crossed her arms, turned to look out the window, and chewed the inside of her lip. *With Jessie, I might have had a chance.*

The car was quiet until Gabe pulled up in front of her house.

She unbuckled her seatbelt and opened the door without making eye contact. "Thanks for the ride."

"Are you okay?"

Stacey shrugged, looking at the asphalt outside the open door.

"Are you mad at me?"

"What reason would I have to be mad at you? You didn't ruin today," she mumbled. "I did."

"Stace, I didn't say that."

"You didn't have to. I'm going now."

Gabe let out an audible breath.

Stacey closed the door behind her without looking back. She heard his car drive away as she crossed the lawn to the front door.

"Stacey? Is that you?" her mom called after the screen door slammed. She came out from her bedroom with Murphy on her heels and met Stacey in the hallway.

"Why is the air conditioning off?" Stacey whined. "It's *so* hot!"

Her mom looked at her watch. "I thought you and Gabe would be out later."

"Guess not," Stacey said, twisting her mouth to the side and throwing her palms up. "What's for dinner?"

"I'm going out with Aunt Susie. I didn't think you'd be home."

"Great." Stacey blinked slowly then opened her bedroom door. "Have fun," she said, closing it behind her once Murphy was inside. She sat on the side of the bed and kicked off her boots. They thumped against the back of her closet. Then she pulled off her socks, threw them across the room, and grabbed a pillow, curling into the fetal position on her bed.

There was a gentle knock. Her mom opened the door slowly, then walked to the bed. "Are you okay?"

"I'm fine," Stacey said. "It's hot. I'm tired."

Her mom touched Stacey's forehead. "You don't feel hot."

"I said I'm fine."

"I'll close up the house and turn on the air. Maybe rest will help."

"Thanks." Stacey rolled toward the wall, muttering, "Say hi to Aunt Susie for me."

When Stacey woke up, her stomach was grumbling. Her head felt heavy as she rubbed the sleep from her eyes. The light outside her window was bright, but the clock read 7:30. She was still in her clothes from the concert. She pulled herself out of bed, went to the window, and parted the blinds. The brightness overwhelmed her and she squinted against it. Then it hit: it was Sunday—she was expected to open the pool at eight!

She grabbed her swimsuit, then ran to the bathroom to shower.

Stacey rushed into the guard shack right on time and flopped onto the couch, relieved. She opened the NutriGrain bar she'd grabbed at home and ate half in one bite.

"Are you guys as done with the sun as I am?" Desiree asked no one in particular.

Stacey looked up. Desiree was horribly sunburnt. "Ouch!" Stacey jumped up to grab the big bottle of aloe gel they kept in the corner and handed it to Desiree. "Is that from the beach?"

"Yes. But the worst part is I was actually freezing all day. It was kind of overcast, so I didn't even think about sunscreen."

"That really sucks," Stacey said. "I'm sorry. Did you have fun at least?"

Desiree shrugged, squeezing the green goop onto her fiery pink shoulder.

"It was so hot at the concert," Stacey said. "Like 110 or something. When I got home, I slept thirteen hours."

"Lucky!" Desiree retorted. "I couldn't get comfortable all night."

"I never thought I'd say this," Chad chimed in. "But I'd be cool with getting the flu or something if it meant I could stay in bed all day."

"Wouldn't it be awesome if there was a monsoon?" Stacey said, animated. "Or a power outage or something, that shut us down for a few days? Then we could all sleep in."

"Too bad," Bob replied, hunched over the paper, his back to them. "Looks like clear skies and sunshine in the ten-day forecast. Suck it up. Get out there."

They groaned in chorus and grabbed wide-brimmed hats and sunglasses. After they'd finished cleaning the facility, Bob unlocked the door to a waiting crowd of swimmers.

"Here we go," Stacey said, carrying a squirt bottle. She'd gotten in the habit of misting herself in the tower on hot days.

Desiree slathered on sunscreen until her skin looked chalky pink.

"Hey Stacey," Desiree asked over the megaphone, across the pool. "You busy Wednesday night?"

The day was hot and the pool was packed. Patrons lounging in the water looked up toward Stacey awaiting her answer, entertained by the broadcasted discussion.

"What's Wednesday?" Stacey asked. Desiree couldn't be asking her to cover night swim. That was Tuesdays and Thursdays.

The swimmers' heads swiveled back toward Desiree.

"The third of July."

"The Fourth is already this week?"

"Yeah. The pool will be closed," Desiree said.

The group of swimmers collectively moaned.

"We should put up a sign or something."

"We talked about going to the movies. *Independence Day* comes out Wednesday. You wanna go?"

Had Desiree and Chad talked about this? Or maybe they decided at the beach with Jessie? Did he tell them he wants me to go, too? Is this actually a double date?

"Sure," Stacey said cooly over the megaphone, shrugging to hide the jolt of excitement running through her.

Her knee bounced and heel tapped on the white sandpaper-like platform of the deep-end tower as she anticipated how their movie date might go. She considered what to wear, and what not to wear, deciding against anything crazy like her concert outfit. *Chad and Desiree will probably make out the entire night.* She'd have plenty of time to talk to Jessie. *Maybe we'll share popcorn.*

At 9:30, the door to the guard shack flung open. Chad walked out to the pool deck for their rotation.

"Mark says he's in," he yelled to Desiree across the pool on his way to the far tower. "Let's watch some aliens get blown up!"

Mark? Stacey wondered.

"Stacey's in, too. I'll call Tiffany and Melissa," Desiree told him over the megaphone. She collected her sunscreen and towel, and climbed down from the shallow-end tower. She waited at the base, eager for Stacey to shift into her chair so she could get inside and into the shade.

Stacey's heart sank. This would not be a double date. Everyone was invited. She had no idea where Melissa and Jessie's relationship stood, but if it was another night of him tickling her, everyone paired up, and Stacey feeling like the odd man out, she'd prefer to stay home.

"Hey, Chad," Stacey asked, as she got to the bottom of the deep-end tower ladder. Chad was about to climb up. "Are Jessie and Melissa…together?"

"No way! She's so pissed at him."

Stacey grinned. *Game on.* She dove across the deep end.

Chapter Eleven

*I*ndependence Day was the most anticipated movie of the summer and the lifeguard crew was especially excited for an activity in a dark, dry, air-conditioned space, away from the screaming kids at The Plunge. As soon as the pool closed, they piled into Stacey and Chad's cars, but had to wait for Mark to change and lock up. By the time they finally got to the theater, there were only tickets left for the 10:00 p.m. show, and a line was already wrapping around the building.

"We've got four hours to kill," Tiffany said matter-of-factly. She stepped into line, draped her towel across a spot on the sidewalk and sat down.

Desiree and Melissa linked arms and stepped back. "We'll go find food," Desiree said, nodding in the direction of the mall.

"This place is pretty skeezy," Chad said, scanning the parking lot and the people jumping into line around them. "Let's stay in two groups. I'll go with them." He turned toward Mark. "You four good to stay together here?"

Mark nodded. "We're cool." They commenced their elaborate handshake.

Jessie set his towel down. Stacey nodded eagerly. She sat beside Tiffany, grateful for the towel to shield them from the still-hot, grimy sidewalk. They each handed Chad ten dollars, and he went with Desiree and Melissa to the food court in the mall, promising to return with dinner.

Tiffany pulled a pack of UNO cards from her purse. "No cheating this time," she told Mark and Jessie, while passing out the cards.

"Me? A cheater?" Jessie feigned innocence.

"You didn't like that you kept losing," Mark told Tiffany.

"What are you guys talking about?" Stacey asked.

"A couple of weeks ago, when we were playing Uno after work, Jessie kept laying down more cards than he was supposed to each hand, and Mark kept hiding cards under his butt."

The night they hung out after night swim ended, they were playing Uno? Stacey froze in amused shock. *So much for the bong and group orgy.*

"Don't listen to her. She has no proof," Mark responded.

"When you stood up, cards were stuck to your thighs!" Tiffany shook her head and rolled her eyes, chuckling.

"All lies," Jessie said.

Mark gleefully slid a card up the leg of his shorts.

"See!" Tiffany pointed at Mark.

Mark opened his empty hands like a magician and shrugged.

Winking at Jessie, Stacey lifted a card and tucked it under her bra strap. They all laughed.

The four began playing round after loud, ruthless round of Uno, oblivious to the crowd waiting in line. After a few hands, it was obvious no one was going to play fair.

"Uno!" Stacey proudly held her one card up.

"No way!" Mark scoffed. "She's definitely hiding them in her back pocket."

"Am not! You're the cheater, not me!"

"I know how to get the truth out of her." Jessie squeezed Stacey's thigh above her knee. She squealed and wriggled with delight. He grabbed her wrists and held them together with one hand while he reached around to grope her pockets with his free hand.

"Get off her, Jess," Tiffany said, swatting his hands away from Stacey's wrists. "I thought you had smoother moves than that to grab a girl's butt."

Jessie let go, nodding, his eyes locked on Stacey's. "Oh, believe me...I do."

Although she'd secretly loved Jessie's wrestling with her, Stacey was grateful for Tiffany's solidarity. An hour had passed quickly, and her cheeks and stomach hurt from laughing so hard.

"Why aren't they back with the food yet?" Mark demanded, uncovering two cards from beneath the towel. "I'm starving." He dropped his stack of cards onto the discard pile.

Jessie added what was left of his cards to the pile as well. "You should go find them." He leaned back against the stucco wall.

"We can stay and save our spot," Stacey said.

Mark nudged Tiffany with his elbow. "Want to be on my search and rescue team?"

Tiffany nodded and they both stood. "If they come back without us, make them stand in line so you can come find us at Hot Dog on a Stick."

Stacey nodded, scooching back to lean against the wall next to Jessie. Ever since the treading water contest, she felt more relaxed around Jessie: gorgeous, guitar-strumming, skater-boy Jessie, with golden hair and washboard abs. As Mark and Tiffany walked away, Stacey reminded herself to be cool. *No awkward rambling, Chapman.*

She unwrapped a piece of gum and put it in her mouth, then offered Jessie the green Wrigley pack. He took a piece, and Stacey shoved the pack back in her pocket.

Jessie slid over until he was shoulder to shoulder with her, twirling the silver gum wrapper around his finger. "So, how old were you when your parents split up?" he asked.

It took her a second to respond. "Um… I was a baby, actually. You?" She stuttered, confused about the sudden seriousness of the conversation.

"I was nine."

"I'm sorry. I bet that was hard. I don't even remember my parents together."

"Mine weren't ever happy."

"Mine still fight, too, and they've been apart for like 16 years."

Jessie exhaled. "We haven't heard from my mom since she left."

Stacey looked at Jessie, shocked. "You haven't heard from your mom since you were nine?" The idea of a mom being the one to leave seemed unimaginable to her.

Jessie shrugged. "My dad had like three girlfriends—that I knew of—before she left. And he drinks a lot. I guess she got fed up."

Why didn't she take you and your brother with her?

Stacey was afraid there was no good answer. If Jessie had a mom that would walk out the door and leave him and his brother behind, especially with a dad who drank too much, he probably didn't want to talk about her.

"I'm really sorry, Jessie," was all she could think to say. Then, as an afterthought: "Maybe some people aren't meant for monogamy. Or motherhood."

"That's what I think, too. She sends cards every once in awhile, on, like, birthdays or Christmas. Sometimes with money." He shrugged, folding the smoothed gum wrapper into a tiny airplane. "There's never a return address, but the last few times they were postmarked in St. Louis."

"Do you have other family there?"

"Not that I know of." Jessie stared out at the cars in the parking lot. He was close enough that Stacey could smell the chlorine seeping from his pores. "My little brother wouldn't shut up about how he missed her. Once our dad smacked him hard for it. Told him he was too old for that shit. He was twelve." He flung the gum wrapper plane into the gutter. "She clearly didn't love us anyway. After that, we both stopped talking about her."

From the corner of her eye, she could see how angry and hurt he was. She didn't want him to think she didn't care, but she wasn't sure what else to say. They sat, quiet, for a long time, until eventually Jessie started talking about his trip to the beach the weekend before, with Melissa and Chad.

"It totally sucked you bailed on us," Jessie told her. "You'd have had fun."

Stacey's stomach fluttered. "Yeah…I got my days mixed up. I made plans like a month before to go to a concert." She didn't want to mention Gabe, or how badly that day had gone. "When did you learn to surf?"

"Middle school?" He looked at a spot in the sky as if it held the answer. "After skating so long, it was pretty easy. Crashing in water hurts way less than crashing on concrete. Do you surf?"

Stacey shook her head. "I used to boogie board. My dad lives in Orange County. When I visited in summer, my stepmom would take me to the beach. I didn't have any friends there, so sometimes I'd make friends while waiting for waves."

"Chillest people ever, right? Whenever anyone I knew was going to the beach, I always begged to go along."

Stacey nodded. "Do you want to live at the beach someday...like, when you're an adult?"

Jessie shrugged. "For a while. And the mountains. Mostly I wanna go wherever the next ride is." The sun was setting over the parking lot, and the orangey-glow reflected in his eyes. "What about you? You're going to Harvard or Stanford or something, right?"

"I wish. Probably a UC."

"Why not? You're like the smartest in your class."

She rolled her eyes and shook her head.

"Yeah, you are. You know it. Everyone knows it."

Stacey shrugged. "There's a few of us with high GPAs. But being at the top of our class in Mesa Valley doesn't turn heads at Ivy Leagues."

"You do speech and debate, too, though, right? And I'm sure you rocked the SATs."

"Wow. Jessie Thomas, have you been stalking me?"

"Come on. You're like...untouchable."

Stacey's head jerked back. "What's that supposed to mean?"

"I dunno. Maybe that's the wrong word. I mean, you're one of those people we all know will be someone important someday. You're gonna cure cancer or be a hotshot lawyer or president or something. It's obvious. You're way better than most of the people around here."

"Me? Better than...what are you talking about?"

"Until a week ago, I was sure you thought you were better than all of us, too."

Stacey was stunned and her mind raced. *Is he messing with me?* "That's what you really thought?"

Jessie smiled and pushed his shoulder playfully into hers.

"I spent the beginning of summer feeling like a total loser around all of you."

"Dude, seriously? I—"

Melissa's familiar cackle interrupted Jessie.

Stacey looked up to see the other five guards coming around the corner of the theater. No way was she going to continue this conversation in front of everyone. Most of the cars parked by the mall had disappeared while she and Jessie were talking.

She checked her watch. It was 8:30. The inky blue sky disappeared behind the yellow humming glow of the parking lot lights. Tiffany handed Jessie and Stacey each a corndog and Desiree passed them lemonades.

"We found them sitting in the air-conditioned food court," Tiffany said. "I told them it was unfair to keep you guys out here in the heat alone, starving."

"Yeah, don't be too thankful for Tiffany's bleeding heart," Mark said. "Once she sat down she enjoyed the AC too much to leave for an hour."

Stacey's stomach grumbled as the smell of the grease hit her nostrils. She hoped no one else heard. "Thanks." She took a long swig of the cold lemonade.

Jessie dipped his corndog into mustard and bit a third of it off. "I'd have done the same thing," he said, his mouth full.

"Told you," Melissa muttered to Tiffany over her shoulder, her hands in her back pockets. The lace of her padded bra peeked out of her tiny tank top. Stacey sensed the agreement to stay in the mall was more to prevent Melissa from spoiling the night by attacking Jessie. Melissa had refused to make eye contact with Jessie for more than a week and had switched shifts at least twice to avoid him.

"There's more than an hour for them to go inside now if they want," Melissa purred.

"I hear we missed a killer game of Uno," Chad said, ignoring Melissa. He unfolded another towel to sit beside Jessie, and began arranging the cards into a neat pile.

Desiree sat beside Stacey. "What if we played a game no one could cheat at? Like 'Would you Rather?'"

"Absolutely! I'm going first," Mark said.

"Of course you are." Tiffany shook her head and rolled her eyes. "You love coming up with the foulest, most impossible choices."

The seven lifeguards crowded onto the three towels: four girls on one side, the three boys across from them.

"Melissa," Mark began, "would you rather step barefoot into a pile of poop or vomit?"

"Eeewww…" Desiree squealed. "Why?"

Melissa sneered. "Animal or human?"

"Think about it." Mark tapped his temple. "Does it *really* matter?"

Melissa considered, and shook her head. Looking queasy herself, she answered, "Vomit, I guess."

"I knew it," Mark said.

"As if anyone would choose shit." Melissa rolled her eyes. "My turn. Chad, would you rather lose your penis in a freak accident, or keep it but never have sex again for the rest of your life."

Chad shielded his crotch with one hand. "Oh, I need to keep it. I can always find a way." He motioned with his hand and nodded knowingly.

Stacey laughed nervously, checking the faces of people around them to see if anyone heard and was offended. This game always turned raunchy, but she wished it hadn't gotten sexual so fast. She hoped her Would-You-Rather wouldn't be too embarrassing.

Mark wobbled his head at Melissa, mimicking her high-pitched voice. "As if any guy would choose to lose it."

Melissa's perfectly plucked eyebrows lifted as she wobbled her head in return.

The others chuckled.

"Stacey," Chad said. Her heart jumped into her throat. "Would you rather be a virgin forever, or have sex with a different guy every day for the rest of your life?"

Six pairs of eyes were on her. Stacy reminded herself to *be cool*. Her heart was racing, but she grinned and let out an awkward, grunted exhale through her nostrils. She shrugged one shoulder like her choice was a simple one. "Different guys, for sure. I could travel the world finding worthy partners."

Mark whistled his surprise. Chad let out a high-pitched wolf-howl. Tiffany and Desiree said "wow" in unison. Stacey caught Melissa's furrowed brow and narrowed gaze out of the corner of her right eye, but looked directly at Jessie instead. His eyebrows were raised and lips were turned in a coy smile as he nodded.

Stacey liked the approval her mock-confidence was earning her, especially from Jessie. Now she had to one-up Chad's challenge. Her eyes locked on Jessie's, and before she let herself think about it, the words fell out of her mouth. "Jessie, would you rather give up God, girls, or boards."

Stunned, the other guards' eyes grew wide. Stacey could hear her heart beating in her ears, but kept her face relaxed. Even the crowd of strangers around them was hushed in collective astonishment, and everyone's attention was on Jessie.

Without flinching, Jessie stared right back at Stacey. "God would have to go."

After the movie, Stacey and Jessie dropped Tiffany and Mark back at The Plunge at 12:30 a.m. She rapidly blinked to stay awake as she pulled out of the parking lot. She'd bought a large Mountain Dew at the theater, hoping the caffeine would help since she'd opened at the pool fourteen hours earlier. But when she offered to share it and her popcorn with Jessie, she became hyper aware of each bite and sip, afraid he might think she was hogging it all. In the end, she let him have most of it, and now Stacey found it hard to keep her heavy head from bobbing. She concentrated all of her attention on the dashed yellow line in the middle of the winding road.

"That final scene was killer!" Jessie slapped the dashboard excitedly.

Stacey startled. She shook her head and tightened her grip on the steering wheel.

"The Fresh Prince and Cousin Eddie saved the world. Epic!"

"Um hmm…" She rolled the driver's side window down, deeply inhaling the cool, dusty scent of the foothills.

"You know, there's supposed to be a meteor shower this weekend," Jessie said.

"Really?" Stacey yawned. "That's cool."

Jessie put his hand on Stacey's thigh.

Stacey's breath caught. *Wait…what is happening?*

"We should check it out. Friday night?"

Her heart was racing. *He's fully hitting on me!* She bit her lower lip so she wouldn't squeal. "Yeah. Sure!" Her voice cracked. *Stay calm.* She cleared her throat. "Sounds good."

She was thankful Jessie's street was coming up. She needed to contain her excitement long enough for him to get out of the car.

Stacey pulled the Silver Bullet up to the front of Jessie's apartment and put the car in park. She turned to say goodnight, but moved too fast and bumped her knee hard against the emergency brake. He yanked his hand off her thigh.

Please, Stacey... She closed her eyes and rubbed her knee. *Don't ruin this by being a dumbass!*

"You okay?" he asked.

She nodded and looked up. He was staring at her. In the dark car, Jessie's blue eyes looked navy, a glassy sea that caught the headlights reflecting off his apartment windows.

Nervous, Stacey pulled her arms tight around her waist, her hands clenched.

The side of Jessie's mouth lifted into a slight smile. He touched Stacey's cheek gently with his right knuckles. "Relax," he whispered.

She flattened her palms on her thighs, pushing them toward her knees to get the sweat off.

He reached his left fingers up to swipe a long strand of her hair off her forehead and tucked it behind her ear.

Stacey's stomach clenched and she wet her bottom lip. Her mouth filled with saliva in anticipation of a kiss she'd fantasized about hundreds of times. In her dreams, Peter Gabriel's "In Your Eyes" would be playing for this moment.

Sliding his hand behind her neck, Jessie leaned over, and gently tugged for her to lean toward him.

Stiffly, she leaned in and swallowed hard, digging her fingernails into her knees.

Jessie tilted his head to the left, so she tilted hers opposite his. Stacey briefly puckered her lips, then relaxed them. She closed her eyes, then fluttered them open again to make sure his were closed, too.

The smell of popcorn on his hot breath closed the space between them before their lips touched.

Jessie's mouth pressed hard against hers. She felt his full lips. His tongue began to ease her mouth open, so she dropped her jaw open like a fish. Unsure what to do, she barely moved or breathed, letting his tongue caress hers. She could hear her heart pounding in her ears. *Jessie Thomas is kissing me!*

She relaxed her hands as she absorbed the touch and taste of Jessie's mouth. The strength of his hand behind her neck, and the lingering saltiness on their mouths. The wetness of their kiss and roughness of their chapped lips rubbing against one another. She felt tingling that scared and excited her in places she'd never realized had such sensations. She squeezed her legs together tighter.

As Jessie pulled back, he gave her bottom lip the slightest tug between his teeth.

She sat there, her mouth agape, as Jessie set his hand on the passenger door handle.

"Happy Fourth of July, Stacey," Jessie said.

Part of her wanted to grab Jessie's T-shirt with both hands and pull him back, and part of her wanted him to walk away before the shaking she felt inside became visible to him. She smiled meekly.

"G'night." Stacey sat, unblinking, following Jessie with her eyes as he got out and walked to his apartment. At the porch, he nodded back at her one last time before going inside.

As soon as his front door closed, she put the car in reverse. She pulled out of his apartment complex, her left foot bouncing.

When she was finally parked in front of her house, engine off, she sat with the seatbelt still latched and put both hands to her mouth.

Jessie kissed me.

She looked at herself in the rearview mirror. "I have a date with Jessie Thomas!"

PART TWO

In Too Deep

Chapter Twelve

Stacey laid in bed thinking of their kiss the night before. She needed to know as much about Jessie as she could before their date without him finding out. Remembering that Mary Jo was Christian Club president and had invited her in the first place, Stacey dialed her number without hesitation. *We've been friends since kindergarten...sort of. She'll know.* She leaned back against the giant Eeyore she kept on her bed.

"Hey MJ," Stacey said when Mary Jo answered the phone.

"Stacey?" Mary Jo sounded surprised. "What's up?"

"I was just wondering... how well do you know Jessie?"

"Jessie Thomas?"

As if there were a million Jessies in Christian club? "Yeah. Does he go to your church? What can you tell me about him?" Murphy laid her head on Stacey's lap with a contented sigh. She rubbed Murphy's soft ear fur between her fingers, staring up at the rotating ceiling fan.

"I don't really know him. He only came a few times. I'm not sure he goes to church, actually."

"Oh... I thought he was super religious?"

"What makes you think he's 'super religious'? It seemed like he wanted an excuse to play guitar at club meetings. He met *a lot* of girls that way. He didn't lead prayer...ever. Or share his testimony or anything. He didn't even know how to play Christian songs. He sort of strummed along."

Stacey's mind was spinning. "But what about the crown of thorns on his arm?"

"That generic tribal tattoo?" Mary Jo scoffed.

After the call, Stacey sat staring out the window, dumbfounded. *Does that mean he isn't actually a Christian?* She considered all the other assumptions she'd made about Jessie.

Murphy nudged Stacey's hand with her warm, damp nose.

Stacey looked down into her golden retriever's chocolatey eyes. "What if he thought the same things about me?" *I don't know if I'm a Christian either, to be honest.*

Murphy lifted one eyebrow without raising her head from Stacey's lap.

"Was Christian Club Jessie's scam to meet girls?" Stacey asked Murphy.

Stacey laid back on the bed and closed her eyes, remembering their kiss only a few hours before. The way Jessie's hand felt pulling her to him, his teeth tugging her lip. She dragged the tip of her index finger across the chapped skin on her bottom lip. He knew just what to do. She was so awkward. A sick, excited, nervous feeling seeped into her stomach again as she thought of their date. *Seriously? This is exactly what you wanted!*

The phone in Stacey's hand rang. She sat up quickly, hoping she'd somehow willed Jessie to call her. Inhaling, she pressed the on button. "Hello?"

"Hey... Stace." There was a hesitation in Gabe's voice. They hadn't talked since the concert the weekend before.

"Hi, Gabe." She hoped she didn't sound too disappointed. She wasn't ready to tell Gabe about Jessie. "How are you?"

"You still mad at me?"

Stacey sighed. "I wasn't mad. I was...embarrassed. Sorry I was such a poser that day."

"I didn't mean to embarrass you. Did you have fun?"

"The show was good. But...can we forget about the rest of that day?"

"Deal."

"Cool."

"My family's having a big barbecue. My mom said you should come."

Stacey chuckled. "Glad to know *your mom* wants me there."

"Shut up. I called, didn't I?"

"Aww...thanks. Too bad I can't. I have to go to my dad's. Wanna come with me?"

"I've gotta stick around here. Help my parents cook and clean up and stuff. You sure you can't get out of it?"

"My stepmom has been guilt-tripping me since Dad got me the car. But I hate being alone there."

"Sucks. It'd be nice to...hang out, you know?"

Stacey exhaled. "Yeah. Sucks."

"*Cable Guy* came out. Wanna go tomorrow night?" Gabe sounded hopeful.

Shit, Stacey thought. She'd promised him she'd go as soon as it released, and totally forgot. It had already been a couple of weeks. But now she had a date with Jessie to watch the meteor shower. No way would she tell Gabe about that. "I'm sorry! A group of us are going to see *Independence Day* tomorrow." Her voice faltered on the word 'tomorrow.' She spoke faster to avoid tripping on any more of the words. "It's a work thing. Maybe we could see *Cable Guy* Saturday?"

Only a little white lie. Stacey chewed her fingernail.

"Fun for you." His disappointment weighed heavily through the phone. "I close Saturday."

"Then we'll go Sunday. We'll figure it out."

"Yeah." Gabe exhaled. "Gotta go. Call me later?"

"Sure," Stacey replied. "Bye." But Gabe had already dropped the line.

Stacey flopped back on the bed and let the phone roll from her hand. She stared at the ceiling, her head and heart spinning as fast as the fan above her. She'd never lied to Gabe before. She grabbed the roots of her hair with both hands and tugged, groaning, then dragged her hands down her face. She always chose Gabe over everyone else.

But now she had Jessie. All she could think was how she wanted to be kissed by him again. Gabe might never want to kiss her the way Jessie did.

Stacey's feelings about Gabe and Jessie swirled like bold colors on a blank, wet page. When she thought of Gabe, she envisioned her watercolor brush tip thoughtfully easing dark green and steel gray rivers on the page with ribbons of vivid magenta running through them. With Jessie it felt more like wild splatters of bold yellow and navy blue and bright orange.

The combination of the two felt uncomfortable, like looking at Ms. Moreno's abstract roses. Like all her emotions were colliding into one big, undecipherable blob where the colors ran together into a muddy mess.

There was a tap on her bedroom door. Stacey blinked and the watercolor vision was gone. "Come in." She turned her head to the side, glaring at the door as it opened.

"Doodle Bug, you need to hit the road soon." Her mom leaned into the room, holding the door handle and door frame for support. "There's gonna be a lot of traffic. You said Jackie wanted you there by two."

"Ugh… I know…"

"Well, I'm leaving for Aunt Susie's. Later I'll be at that barbecue I told you about, so I won't be here when you get home."

"Who's having a barbecue?"

"A guy I know from work."

"Like…he's a stylist? Or you cut his hair," Stacey sneered, "and he invited you over for the Fourth of July?"

"It's not like that. There's a big group of us. Drive safe, okay? And don't wait up."

The door closed before Stacey could respond. She looked at the digital clock on her nightstand. 11:45. With a two-hour drive ahead of her, and considering she was still unshowered, she was definitely going to be late. *Whatever. This party is for their friends, anyway.*

Stacey scratched beneath Murphy's chin. "I've gotta get through today at Dad's, Murph. But my date with Jessie tomorrow will be the real celebration!"

She went to her closet to find something patriotic to put on.

More than three hours later, Stacey climbed out of her old Honda parallel parked between a brand-new Range Rover and a vintage Rolls Royce, and realized she should have worn something a little nicer. She tugged at the hem of her denim skirt and pulled up on her red spaghetti strap tank to cover her cleavage, looking down quickly to make sure the laces of her white Converse were tied. She locked her car, then laughed at the absurd thought of someone breaking into the Silver Bullet in this neighborhood.

The street in front of her dad's house was jam-packed with cars, so Stacey had to walk a block and a half past perfectly manicured lawns and trimmed hedges before making her way up the long, steep driveway. Nothing in Marina Vista resembled the trailer parks and brown lawns of Mesa Valley. Each mini-mansion she passed was bigger than three of the houses Stacey lived in with her mom.

Lining her dad's driveway were rows of freshly planted flowers in shades of red, white, and deep purple. *Couldn't they just hang up a flag?* The driveway was so crammed with cars, at the top Stacey had to slide sideways between her dad's navy BMW and her stepmother's silver Mercedes.

The ten-foot tall, cut-glass adorned double front door stood ajar, welcoming Stacey and anyone else who happened upon it into their home.

"No flies or strangers in the OC, I guess," Stacey mumbled, combing her fingers through her hair and pulling on her skirt again. The frosty air conditioning blew overhead as she slowly crossed the threshold into the immense marble entryway.

Thanks to the wall of windows across the back of the house, Stacey could see past the white-on-white couches and grand piano in the formal living room, directly into the backyard, where dozens of people mingled around the pool deck with cocktails in hand.

Jackie, Stacey's stepmother, had insisted the giant kidney-shaped swimming pool with multiple waterfalls be visible from every room in the house, and be the centerpiece of attention as soon as guests arrived. On either side of the pool, white tents were set up with tables and buffets. Between the guests, Stacey could see caterers carrying trays of hors d'oeuvres.

Her dad loved being the bartender for his friends. His bar was set up in the shade close to the living room windows, his back turned to her. Guests were smiling and laughing as he animatedly told the group something while shaking a cocktail, sweat drenching the back of his red, white, and blue Hawaiian shirt.

Stacey squeezed her shoulder blades together, steeling herself for the performance she needed to put on for her dad's friends. "It's only a couple of hours. You can do this," she muttered. Her feet wouldn't budge.

"Stacey?" Jackie's voice sliced over clacking footfalls coming from the hall to her right. Stacey turned to see her stepmother coming toward her from the kitchen, her arms outstretched. "I was wondering when you'd finally get here."

Jackie wore crimson stilettos and white cropped pants, with a ruffled red sleeveless blouse tucked in. She fit the role of Orange County country club housewife perfectly. Jackie's long French-manicured acrylic nails gripped Stacey's upper arms and she stuck out her bottom lip in a pout. "You're more than an hour late!"

Not for the first time, Stacey took in the false eyelashes and platinum blonde chignon, wondering what the attraction had ever been between her dad and her own mother. Her mom and Jackie were polar opposites in every way.

Stacey pulled a smile to her lips. "Hi, Jackie." She let Jackie air kiss each of her cheeks. "Sorry. Traffic."

"I wanted you to visit with your dad before the party started. We needed another pair of hands setting up." Jackie sighed, taking Stacey by the elbow and leading her toward the kitchen.

"I accidentally overslept. It was a late night."

Beside the sub-zero, Jackie let go, and Stacey rubbed the spot where she'd been held. In the blue and white Italian mosaic tiled kitchen, three caterers bustled about in white smocks, one at the Viking stove, one arranging slices of meats and cheeses on a platter, and another at the oversized porcelain sink.

From beside a case of Champagne on the edge of the counter, Jackie picked up a large, shining silver bucket, her hands carefully holding the handles to avoid marking the chrome with fingerprints, and pushed it toward Stacey. "Take this ice out to Chuck so he'll know you're here, then come right back. I have a lot more to go out to the buffet." Jackie's voice edged up. "Thanks!"

Stacey turned and rolled her eyes, gripping the metal bucket to her belly, all ten fingers smudging the shiny surface. She smirked, imagining a look of annoyance crossing Jackie's face behind her as she walked away.

Stacey followed the sound of laughter and voices echoing off the surface of the pool through the French doors. The sunny backyard was hedged in by bougainvillea, palm, and citrus trees, designed to feel like a Hawaiian resort. Music played from speakers tucked behind bird of paradise plants. Stacey eyed the buffet table that belonged more at the Four Seasons than at a Fourth of July barbecue. There were chocolate-covered strawberries and a platter of giant shrimp on ice. The fruit and vegetable platters were adorned with a watermelon whale and a zucchini boat sculpture.

"Stacey!" Maureen, her dad's neighbor yelled from beside the bar, her upper arm waving back and forth in conjunction with the hand she flapped above her head. She was heavy set, wearing a royal blue silk muumuu-style dress and a huge brimmed white hat. "Chuck, Stacey's here!" She hit Stacey's dad on the shoulder, the martini in her hand sloshing out in the process.

"My baby girl!" Chuck announced to his friends, his booming voice echoing off the stucco and windows that surrounded his corner bar.

Stacey blushed and dragged her feet around the group. They lifted their drinks up, cheering, as she passed. *Are they all drunk already?* Stacey sidled up to her dad, who took his cigarette from his mouth with his free hand so he could give her a side hug and kiss her on the top of her head. He'd been mixing a bright yellow margarita and as he clenched the cup to her outside shoulder, her arm got damp. Her dad's distinct scent of tobacco and sweat enveloped her and the people awaiting drinks gave a collective, "Awww."

"Jackie asked me to bring you this," Stacey said when he pulled away, holding up the ice bucket, but unsure where to set it. The small bar was jam packed with multiple bottles of every kind and color of liquor imaginable.

Chuck put the cigarette back between his lips, then spoke around it. "Set it back there." He nodded to a small table behind him, covered with stacks of clear plastic cups that were supposed to look like glasses.

Stacey made room and set down the ice bucket, then looked around. She couldn't see anything non-alcoholic to drink.

"Want a virgin daiquiri, Bug?"

"Can I have a soda?"

"Sure. I've got a few in here for mixers," he said, nodding to the corner beside him where a large ice chest was hidden. He stepped out of the way and continued mixing the margarita in his hand, so she could slip past him. Stacey dug through dozens of Heinekens and tonic waters until she finally found a Coke.

"Tell Jackie I'm out of limes, okay Bug?" he asked as she slipped back out from behind the bar.

"Sure." Stacey nodded. She started back to find Jackie as instructed.

"Wait!" Maureen's flushed face blocked Stacey's path to the kitchen. "Tell me all about school!"

"Hi, Maureen. How are you?"

"I'm good. Just back from a week shopping on the Champs-Élysées. You know: my annual trip to Paris with my girls! They would love to see you! It's been far too long. What've you been up to? You're a senior now, right?"

Maureen smelled like a bar, but didn't slur her words in the slightest, and her lipstick was always meticulous. Stacey wanted to ask how she managed that in the heat, while eating and drinking. "Yeah, I'm a senior. I've been lifeguarding."

A thin woman sidled up beside Maureen. "You've been in the sun," she said to Stacey. Her face–pointed like a cat's–was vaguely familiar. Stacey thought she might be one of Jackie's closest friends. "Be careful. You may have that perfect tropical glow now, but...," she said, then leaned in to whisper in Stacey's ear. "You don't want wrinkles!"

Stacey recognized the sickly-sweet wine smell heavy on each breathy word. She raised her eyebrows, but nodded. The woman was at least seventy and looked like she'd gotten more plastic surgery than everyone in Mesa Valley combined.

"Stacey," Jackie called from the back door. "Sorry, Maureen. Liz. I need Stacey's help for a minute."

"Of course!" Maureen called over to her, then turned back to Stacey. "Come talk to me some more once you've finished up, okay doll?"

Stacey smiled and nodded. She walked toward the house, sipping her soda and wondering if it was possible to get drunk off the breath of her dad's friends.

An hour later, Jackie had exhausted her list of tasks for Stacey, and told her to grab a plate of food. Eyeing tables full of strangers, Stacey made a beeline for the diving board when her dad waved her over.

"Stace! Tell us about your summer so far."

Chairs scraped noisily as the group opened a space at the table for Stacey to squeeze in. Jackie instructed a caterer to bring over an extra chair. Stacey set her food down and pulled the rented white folding chair under her. As she was taking her first bite, her father's friends hurled questions at her.

"Where are you lifeguarding?" asked a man Stacey believed was her dad's colleague.

"The community pool," she replied, covering her mouth as she chewed and spoke. "In Mesa Valley."

Jackie's mouth pursed in distaste.

"I bet you make good money. Smart girl," Maureen said. "Where are you applying to college? That's coming up, you know. Hope you're making plans!"

Stacey gritted her teeth behind her forced smile, nodding. *Of course I know it's coming up! I've been working toward this for as long as I can remember.* She swallowed and took a sip of soda to clear her mouth, minding her manners more closely. "Probably Berkeley, USC, Stanford, UCLA…"

"No East Coast schools?" Maureen tsked. Her face turned serious. "The Ivy Leagues are much better than what's available here. Chuck, tell your daughter she needs to look at schools outside of California."

"Oh, Maureen," Chuck said. "Give her a break."

Jackie chimed in. "I'm sure she's considering all her options. Stacey's top of her class. She'll get in wherever she decides to go."

Oh, really? How would you know?

"Stacey," Maureen waved away their indifference. "Listen to me. You should consider applying to at least Brown and Cornell. They'd be lucky to have you. Vassar, too! Far superior universities."

Stacey grinned, blinking. *Are you planning to foot the bill for those, Maureen? Is there anyone who would even take me to visit those schools?*

"She has plenty of time," Chuck told Maureen. He looked across the table at Stacey, grinning with that hazy glint in his eye Stacey knew all too well. "I'm so proud of my little girl," he said, lifting his glass. "To Stacey!"

The group raised their cups to toast her. Stacey held tight to her fake smile and fought the urge to walk away from the table. Lifting her warm can of Coke, she held it steady as ten plastic cocktail cups thunked against it.

After another hour discussing her job and future plans with random strangers, Stacey's self-imposed two hour minimum had long passed, and she was ready to leave. Her dad was occupied with a group of guys and a couple of putters at the corner of the lawn. She didn't want to risk the onslaught of their attention by interrupting him.

"Tell Dad I said bye," Stacey told Jackie, who she found restocking the chocolate covered strawberries at the buffet.

"You're not staying for the fireworks?" Jackie whined.

"I have to be at the pool at eight tomorrow. It's a long drive. Thanks for inviting me." Stacey initiated a generous hug with her stepmother, willing to do whatever she had to do to make it to the exit quickly.

While Stacey navigated two hours of gridlock on three freeways, fireworks danced across the sky. She kept the windows down and the radio off to listen to the booms, pops, and crackles over the whir of cars passing. The sparkling blossoms of color reignited Stacey's excitement, as she imagined her date the next night, holding hands with Jessie under shooting stars.

As she pulled into the driveway, illegal fireworks were still exploding on neighboring streets, but no one on Stacey's block was outside. She locked her car. The scent of smoke mixed with sulfur still lingered in the air. Out of habit, Stacey looked past the chain link fence to ensure the dry brush behind their house wasn't burning. The smell of smoke scared her after too many long fire seasons.

Opening the front door, Stacey realized the air conditioner was running. "Mom?" she called out, then remembered her mom was planning to stay late at the barbecue. Murphy was afraid of fireworks, so her mom wouldn't have taken the dog with her. *No wonder the AC is actually on.* In the past, Murphy had broken screens to escape through open windows during fireworks. Stacey scrunched up her nose at the pungent scent of urine. She flipped on the lights in the living room and found a puddle on the carpet by the back door. The glass was covered in nose and paw marks, like Murphy had been scrambling to open the door.

"Murphy?" Stacey called.

She grabbed several paper towels and tossed them on top of the mess, then looked for Murphy. After checking under the kitchen table and behind the couch, she called out "Murphy" repeatedly, her panic rising when there was no response and the space under her bed was bare. Finally, in the corner of her mom's closet, behind long coats and dresses, Stacey found her dog curled on the floor, panting and shaking.

"Oh, Murph, it's okay." Stacey's voice cracked with relief. She sat on the floor beside the closet and rubbed Murphy's ears and neck.

Murphy whined, backing further into the corner.

"Shhhh… You're okay. I'm sorry you were all alone. I'm here now." Stacey's eyes misted as her dog looked up at her, still too afraid to inch out of the closet. "Come on, girl. You're okay. You can come out now."

Slowly, Murphy staggered to her paws, her legs unsteady, then sat again, shaking, with long dresses draped around her head.

The closet was humid as Stacey leaned in, wrapping Murphy in a hug, and feeling the dog's heart pounding against her own chest. Stacey closed her eyes, inhaling the damp scent of dog breath, and continued to make shushing sounds.

"Arwoooo," Murphy yawned, ending in that high-pitched squeak that sounded more dolphin than dog.

The phone rang on her mom's bedside table and Murphy jolted backward, shaking more frantically. Stacey ignored the ringing and held her mouth next to Murphy's ear, making calming shushing sounds. After the rings stopped, Murphy's panting slowed, and she stood again. Stacey backed out of the closet. Murphy stepped her front paws out, but kept her body close to Stacey's.

"Good girl," Stacey cooed, running her fingers through Murphy's long golden fur. Still trembling and panting, Murphy gently licked Stacey's cheek, then climbed into Stacey's lap, bumping her head against Stacey's temple, as if encouraging Stacey to embrace her again.

Several minutes passed before the fireworks ended.

"Come on." Stacey gently shifted Murphy's weight off her lap, then stood and patted her thigh. "You need some water, sweet girl."

Murphy trotted close beside Stacey's legs and they made their way in tandem down the hall to the kitchen. Stacey filled the dog bowl with fresh water and set it down. Murphy began lapping it up.

Stacey stretched, arching her back. The wall clock read 11:15 and the answering machine was blinking. She clicked play and the familiar robotic voice reverberated off the Formica countertop. "You have two messages. Message one."

Music and a man's laughter erupted from the machine before Stacey heard her mom's voice. "Heyyyy, honeeeey." She was giggly and slurring. "I'm gonna stay here ta-night." *Here? Where's 'here'? Who is this guy?'* "Call Suuu-sie if ya need any-thing," she said loudly over the party, then hung up.

"Lovely." Stacey eyed the mess on the carpet and pressed delete.

"Message deleted," the machine announced. "Final message."

"Uh, hi Stacey." Gabe's voice dragged, sounding irritated. "It's like ten-thirty. I figured you'd be home by now. I've gotta work early tomorrow but I finish at noon. Maybe if you're free before you go out with your work friends we could go to Tower Records or something? Gimme a call."

Stacey bit her bottom lip and hit delete.

"You have no more messages."

Sorry, Gabe.

Chapter Thirteen

A t seven the next morning, Stacey leapt out of bed. She was eager to see Jessie at work and finalize the details of their date. Crunching into her buttered toast, she watched the clock, willing time to move faster. She had a clear vision of their date in her mind: holding hands while lying on the hood of her car, she would wish on a shooting star, then they would kiss. She'd struggled to fall asleep the night before, imagining the details. Now that it was finally morning, all she wanted was to see him again.

I should have offered him a ride, she thought, as she drove, turning from her street onto Jessie's. *It would be too weird to knock on his door now, right?* She drove slowly and saw no signs of life out front. *That would definitely be weird.* Stacey pressed hard on the gas pedal and sped in the direction of the pool. She could pick him up if she saw him skateboarding along the way. She arrived at an empty parking lot at 7:50, wondering if she'd made the right decision.

Within five minutes, Bob's blue Pathfinder pulled into the parking lot followed by Melissa's red convertible Mercedes. *Great. A whole day with Miss Self-Absorbed.* Stacey willed herself to get out of the car. She dragged her feet as Bob unlocked the doors and flipped on the facility lights while Melissa chattered on and on about ASU.

"So, I'll need a few days off to go to orientation weekend in August," she said.

"We'll figure it out," Bob replied, swinging his heavy lanyard of keys as he walked out the back door to the pool and chemical room.

"I call hosing the deck," Melissa announced to Stacey, following Bob out the door.

"Cool," Stacey muttered over her shoulder, her eyes fixed on the clock. She stood beside her locker, hoping to catch Jessie alone.

At exactly eight o'clock, Jessie pulled the front door open slowly, as if it weighed a ton. His eyes were red and his eyelids heavy. Stacey pulled all her hair over one shoulder and leaned against the plywood locker door beside his, staring at him and smiling as he entered the guard shack and crossed the room.

He walked straight to his locker and set his towel and wallet inside without acknowledging her.

"Good morning!" Stacey sang out as he closed the locker door. Her voice came out unusually high and chipper.

Jessie turned toward her, rubbing sleep out of his eyes. He nodded while yawning, but said nothing. He flopped down onto the couch, leaned his head back, drowsy.

Stacey shrunk back.

The door from the pool deck swung open. Bob said, "Off your butts. Time to clean." He held the door open, a garbage bag and trash grabber in his other hand. "Someone must have climbed the fence. They left quite a mess."

"Get out here!" Melissa barked across the pool behind him. "I'm not doing this by myself!"

Jessie leaned his elbows onto his knees and pushed the heels of his palms into his eyes. Stacey chewed the inside of her cheek, then walked out the door, accepting the bag and grabber from Bob's outstretched hands. Melissa watched her, then turned, tossing her ponytail behind her, strutting toward the bleachers with her grabber held aloft like a wand.

Littered beneath the benches were PBR cans, chip bags, candy and ice cream wrappers. In the already hot morning sun, spilled beer and melted chocolate sludge were dried in sticky puddles onto the benches and pool deck. A corner of the shallow-end pool cover was pushed back and it sagged down into the water. More trash hovered at the bottom of the pool, while the rim was lined with black residue and burnt firecracker wicks.

"Who did this?" Stacey asked no one in particular. She reached between the benches to grab a can. It spilled as she pulled it out. The sour smell of beer hit her nose at the same time it splashed off the hot concrete.

Bob and Jessie came up beside her carrying buckets of soapy water.

"Neighbors called the police when they heard fireworks at about 1 a.m." Bob said. "Whoever it was jumped the fence and ran off as the police pulled up." He began scrubbing the bench with a sponge.

Melissa was beneath the bleachers. "Morons!" she bellowed.

"Totally worth it," Jessie muttered as he walked to the edge of the pool. He knelt down to scrub the burn marks.

Stacey squinted in his direction.

"It happens every summer," Bob said. "At some point the city will pony up for motion lights, cameras, and alarms."

"Will somebody turn some music on, please?" Melissa whined.

"Stacey? You're our resident DJ, right?" Bob lifted his eyebrows in her direction.

Stacey dropped her garbage bag and trash grabber. Standing at her locker, she flipped through her CD catalog, but couldn't stop her thoughts from spinning. *Why the hell is Jessie giving me the cold shoulder?*

She flipped past the albums of mellow music and classic rock that Bob approved of.

Does Jessie want to cancel our date? Or did he forget?

Her hand hovered over the Violent Femmes album, all the curse words in "Blister in the Sun" forming a rant in her head. Bob would have a conniption fit if she played that. She popped The Combat Rock CD into the stereo and turned the volume past Bob's red marker line at seven, up to 8.5, the loudest she could get away with.

"Surprising choice, Chapman," Bob said as she rejoined the group. She picked up her trash bag.

Right before the second song ended, Stacey stripped down to her bathing suit. Jessie didn't look up from scrubbing burn marks off the concrete. She dropped her trash bag next to him, then got into the pool. Standing waist deep in the water, she plucked random pieces of garbage from the bottom of the pool with the grabber and dropped them in the bag she'd set next to him.

"Should I Stay or Should I Go" came over the speakers. Stacey started humming.

Jessie lifted his eyes to meet hers. Stacey raised one eyebrow. He smirked and nodded.

Stacey's brain surged with excitement. *Does that mean...we're on?* She flicked water at him.

Jessie locked eyes with her, his smirk fading, and gently shook his head. His blonde locks swept across his lashes. She couldn't tell what he meant.

Over his shoulder, Stacey could see Bob and Melissa's backs were turned. She looked at Jessie again and lifted her hands up, shrugging, as she mouthed "What's up?"

Jessie looked down, focusing his attention on scrubbing the stain.

Stacey turned away, dragging her feet across the shallow end. A million thoughts swam through her head.

Did I do something wrong? Or make too big a deal of our kiss? Maybe there's still time to call Gabe back.

She couldn't care less about cleaning the bottom of the pool, but spent the next thirty minutes making sure it was spotless to avoid looking back at Jessie.

Over the next few hours, as swimmers trickled in, Jessie kept to himself. He barely acknowledged Stacey or Melissa as they shifted between lifeguard chairs. No games. No conversations over the megaphones. No mention of the date she'd been anticipating the past day and a half. Stacey felt her degrees of separation from Jessie growing as the minutes tick toward noon on the large clock above the office window.

The dread of rejection formed a pit in Stacey's stomach. When the morning swim session ended, they cleared the dozen swimmers from the pool, and filed back into the guard shack.

Melissa was perched on the arm of the couch. "I'll take the first shift on lap swim."

Figures. No one's even here.

Standing beside one another at their lockers, Jessie tapped Stacey with his elbow. "Wanna go grab lunch real fast?"

Tongue-tied, Stacey swallowed past the lump in her throat and nodded. She pulled on her shorts and grabbed her keys. "Want anything?" she asked Bob and Melissa.

"No thanks," Bob said.

"Grab me a BRC?" Melissa asked, handing Stacey a $5 bill.

"Sure." Stacey shoved the money into her back pocket and let the door close on Jessie as he trailed behind her.

Jessie and Stacey climbed into the seats of the Silver Bullet, both silent until she pulled out of the parking lot.

Once The Plunge was in the rearview mirror, Jessie reached across and put his hand on Stacey's thigh.

She looked down at his hand, then side-eyed him.

"Thanks for being cool this morning." Jessie leaned his head back on the headrest and gently squeezed her leg. "I don't think we should talk about tonight in front of..."

A sick feeling washed over her. *Melissa?* Stacey repeated, "In front of..." letting the last word drag. When it was clear Jessie wouldn't finish his sentence, she asked, "Who?"

"You know...all the people we work with. Let's keep it on the down-low...for now."

Stacey wrinkled her forehead.

"You're so chill," he said. She could feel him staring and forced a smile. "Not like other girls. I really like you."

She wanted so badly to believe him. But confusion left her mute.

"You *do* still want to go tonight, right?" Jessie asked.

"To watch the shooting stars?"

"Yeah." He leaned toward her ear and she felt his long bangs grazing her neck. "Someplace dark. Quiet. Just us."

Chills ran up Stacey's spine. "Can't wait," she said and flicked the right blinker at the intersection. She was glad to be driving. It helped mask her feuding emotions. "Seems fun."

"Cool," he said.

As they pulled into the taco stand's parking lot, Jessie removed his hand from her leg and leaned back into his seat. Guys with skateboards sat at tables out front, their long shorts belted so low that at least eight inches of their boxers hung out. Jessie went to say hello while Stacey got in line. He high-fived a skinny kid with greasy long hair, laughing and chatting with the group without ever looking in her direction. When Stacey reached the counter, he trotted back to her side. She ordered her food and Melissa's, then Jessie added his order.

The woman behind the register said, "$15.50."

Stacey put her money and Melissa's down on the counter. Jessie didn't move. She looked at him, her eyebrows raised.

"Uh… can you spot me?" Jessie asked, pulling a single dollar bill from his pocket and adding it to the pile. "I forgot to bring cash. Sorry."

"Oh…ummm…I guess." Stacey pulled another five-dollar bill from her wallet.

"Thanks. Pay you back tonight."

"Okay," she said in a monotone as she accepted her change.

"Great!" he said. "Meet you back at the car."

A sour taste crept up from the back of her throat. Stacey was no longer hungry.

Jessie rejoined the group, taking someone's board to jump it over a parking block. He landed in the middle of the parking space a car was pulling into. The driver honked at him, gesturing through his window for Jessie to move. His friends laughed.

Stacey stood against the faux-Alamo wall, her arms crossed, watching him, as she awaited their order, and considered canceling their date.

Back at The Plunge parking lot, after she parked and pulled the emergency brake, Jessie put his hand on hers. "Pick me up at eight?"

Stacey searched his blue eyes, the ocean she'd been lost in two nights before. He looked away, toward the pool. Now she felt lost with him in an entirely different way, yet she couldn't stop herself from nodding. Hoping.

"Stellar!" He put his finger on his lips and whispered, "Our secret." He jumped out of the car and walked ahead of her, back into the main office.

Stacey left her food in her locker and took over Melissa's tower for the second shift of lap swim. Watching the two senior citizens slowly paddle back and forth, she was hit by wave after wave of conflicting thoughts. *He's such an ass. You deserve so much better. He's only avoiding drama with Melissa. What's so wrong with keeping it quiet while we get to know each other?* Closing her eyes, she could feel Jessie's hand on her thigh and recall the taste of his lips on hers from their kiss. But when the afternoon swimmers arrived at one, and he took over her tower to watch the shallow end, he said nothing. Didn't even make eye contact.

Gabe would never ignore me, even in front of his guy friends. She considered blowing off the date. Calling Gabe. She could apologize, go to Tower Records and *Cable Guy*, and make herself forget all about Jessie Thomas.

She looked across the pool at where Jessie sat in the deep end tower. There was a megaphone by her feet. She could pick it up. Tell him something came up.

Jessie stared straight at her, then slid his glasses down his nose. Smiling, he winked at her, then slid the sunglasses back on and turned back toward the diving board.

Stacey felt a flutter in her chest. *This is dumb. I have a date with JESSIE THOMAS! I'm being too sensitive.*

When the pool closed, Stacey planned to offer Jessie a ride home. But as the last family filed out through the locker rooms, he took off on his skateboard in the opposite direction from their neighborhood. *We have a date in three hours, and he doesn't even say goodbye?*

In her car, she pulled out the Violent Femmes album she'd wanted to play that morning. She flipped through to "Kiss Off." With the windows down, navigating all the turns of the winding road back home, she screamed the lyrics, feeling their truth through every inch of her body.

Her mom's minivan was in the driveway when she pulled in. There was a large, white pick-up truck parked on the street that Stacey had never seen before. The front door was closed and she could hear the loud hum of the AC fan on the side of the house. *Mom has company?*

"I'm home," Stacey announced as she opened the front door. She perked up at the smell of sauteed onions and garlic.

Murphy barked once and ran to Stacey, her tail wagging.

"We're in here," her mom called from the kitchen.

Stacey followed Murphy through the living room. The counter was cluttered with the chopping board and large knife set, scraps of carrots, celery, peppers, onions, and garlic strewn about. There was a box of pasta and an open bottle of Chardonnay set atop a folded grocery bag. Stacey's mom leaned against the counter, sipping a glass of wine. A large man was at the stove, his back turned, stirring something.

"Hey, Doodle Bug," her mom said, smiling as Stacey approached. "This is Greg!" She patted Greg's shoulder. "Greg, this is my daughter, Stacey."

The man turned toward Stacey, waving with the spatula and smiling.

"Hi, Stacey. Nice to meet you."

His voice was deep, but not raspy like her dad's. Stacey guessed he wasn't a smoker. He was tall with thick brown hair and a Tom

Selleck mustache. He wore her mother's red-checked apron with white eyelet trim. It framed the collar of his blue dress-shirt, the sleeves rolled up, tucked into jeans with a belt. Stacey had loved to wear that apron when she was little and they baked Christmas cookies, but hadn't seen it in years.

"Hi." Stacey tried to sound friendly. She was taken aback by the entire scene. It was unusual for anyone to prepare a real meal in their house unless it was a holiday, but she couldn't think of a time in her entire life when a man had cooked for them. She rarely even met the men her mom dated.

Greg went back to stirring.

"He's making us dinner!" Her mom beamed as if she'd won the lottery. "Isn't that nice?"

"Smells good. What is it?" Stacey asked, matching her mother's enthusiasm. She hoped to be offered a plateful too, but was afraid she was the odd man out.

"Chicken cacciatore," Greg sang out in a bad Italian accent, then kissed the tips of his left fingers.

"Sounds delicious." Still unsure if her mom's "us" meant the two of them, Stacey asked, "When do we eat? Do I have time to shower?"

"Aren't you going out?" There was a hesitation in her mom's voice.

"Not 'til eight, and we're only hanging out."

"It'll be about twenty minutes," Greg said over his shoulder.

"Cool. I'll be quick," Stacey said, turning to leave.

Out of the corner of her eye, Stacey watched Greg lean down toward her mom. "There's plenty," she thought she heard Greg say before he kissed her mom quickly on the lips.

Stacey's ears burned and she cringed. *Now I'm my mom's third wheel?*

She took her clothes into the bathroom, began to undress, and then locked the door. Greg seemed nice, but it was strange showering with a man in the house.

She re-entered the living room with her hair wrapped in a towel, wearing her Nirvana T-shirt and too-big boxer shorts. The stereo was tuned to smooth jazz. Stacey slowed to survey the scene. The small kitchen table was set for three with placemats, lit candles, dinner and salad plates. The bottle of wine and a basket of sliced bread completed the restaurant ambiance.

The *Twilight Zone* intro echoed through Stacey's mind. She grinned, remembering Gabe repeating that eerie opening to her dozens of times. *Was the last time at the concert, only a week ago?* Since the summer after eighth grade–when they rented videos and marathon-watched every episode they could get their hands on– Gabe had recited those lines to her hundreds of times. She suddenly wanted nothing more than a night watching movies with Gabe.

Not Gabe. Jessie. You have a date with Jessie.

Stacey silently observed her mom and Greg at the stove, their backs turned, standing hip to hip. Her mom's head was leaned against Greg's shoulder, his left arm around her waist. They swayed in rhythm with the melody on the stereo. Stacey felt her face flush and she looked away. She wished she had offered to go get herself fast food. She took the towel off her head and set it on the arm of the couch, running her fingers through her hair before turning back toward the kitchen.

"Need me to do anything?" she asked loudly, hoping to avoid witnessing another kiss if she could.

"We're almost ready," Greg said over his shoulder. He moved his hand from her mom's hip to the pot handle in front of him. "Can you grab the butter, parmesan, salt, and pepper for the table, please?"

Stacey plunked the items down and slumped into her chair, watching her mom and Greg's synchronized movements. Murphy ducked under the table and curled into the space by her feet. Stacey grabbed a piece of bread and buttered it, taking her first bite before either of them sat. Greg pulled his napkin across his lap and began scooping the pasta dish onto each of their plates.

Stacey's mom served herself salad, then passed the bowl to Greg. Her smile lit her face with a peaceful glow, so foreign that she was almost unrecognizable. Her mousy blonde hair fell in soft, natural waves at her shoulders, and the creases in the corners of her eyes offered only sincere joy. Stacey couldn't pinpoint what it was about this guy, but she was grateful her mom wasn't in another pissy mood.

Stacey tucked her feet under Murphy's soft fur, and turned her attention to Greg. "So, what do you do, Greg?"

"I'm an electrician."

"That's cool." Stacey speared a forkful of salad and shoved it in her mouth.

"He's being modest," her mom said, placing her hand on Greg's. "He owns his own business. Does electrical work all over the Inland Empire."

Stacey lifted her eyebrows and nodded while chewing.

"Your mom tells me you're a senior," he said.

Stacey put another large bite in her mouth and continued nodding, adding an "Um, hmm," to be polite, while looking down at her plate. *Please, not another night like dad's house.*

"She's a straight A student. Top of her class. Debate club president."

Stacey swallowed too soon and pulled her lips into a thin line. Her mom hadn't taken a bite, intent on swooning over each of them, as if this was a job interview. Stacey left her fork on the edge of her plate and sat on her hands.

"She also said you've been lifeguarding this summer at the Seventh street pool." Greg cut his chicken without scratching the plate, and carefully balanced his knife on the edge before switching hands, the way Stacey's stepmom, Jackie, always insisted she ought to.

Stacey nodded.

"Sounds like you're a very mature and responsible person. I can see why your mom is so proud of you."

Stacey smiled shyly at her mom. "Thank you."

Her mom picked up her fork and knife and began carefully cutting her chicken into a dainty bite. Stacey followed suit. Her mom let out a groan of satisfaction, and Stacey rolled her eyes. Trying the chicken cacciatore for herself, though, she agreed with the enthusiasm. Even still, she would never dare make that noise in front of a guy her mom was dating, and wished her mom wouldn't either.

"This is really good, Greg," Stacey said before swallowing, then shoveled a much larger bite into her mouth.

"I'm glad you like it. Cooking became a hobby of mine after...my wife died."

Stacey's eyes grew wide. "I'm so sorry," she said, covering her full mouth.

Greg made a small wave with his hand in a practiced way. "It's been... a few years now. MS. I'm glad her suffering is over."

Stacey's mom flared her nostrils like this was exactly the topic she hoped wouldn't come up over dinner. She washed down her bite with a sip of wine.

They sat chewing through what felt like the longest smooth jazz clarinet riff in the history of music. Finally, Greg said, "You know,

Stacey, I have two daughters of my own. They also went to Mesa Valley High. Melody and Melissa."

Stacey froze mid-chew. *No, no, no, no, no.*

"They're older than you, though," he said.

Staring at Greg out of the corner of her eye, Stacey willed him to supply more details quickly, before she choked. She took in his dark hair. His chiseled features. It definitely could be a match.

"Melody recently graduated from Oregon State. And Melissa...," Greg said. Stacey held her breath as he stopped to take a bite. "Melissa is in her third year of college in Colorado."

Thank God. Stacey swallowed her bite without finishing chewing and the large lump slid slowly down her throat. She exhaled her relief, then gulped her water.

"Melody's a cool name," Stacey said, feigning interest. "You must like music."

Greg shrugged. "I play a little bass. Used to pick up gigs here and there before..." He let his words trail off.

Stacey assumed Greg was trying to avoid broaching the off-limits topic for a second time, and she let it drop, avoiding anything more complicated.

He smiled and looked up at her. "Do you play an instrument?"

"No. But I like to go to ska shows." Stacey put the last bite of food in her mouth and set her fork upside down on her plate.

"Stacey's an artist," her mom said.

"I'm really not, Mom." Stacey wiped her mouth and shook her head.

"I saw the aurora borealis on the fridge," Greg said. He wiped his mouth and nodded in the direction of the refrigerator. "Your mom said you painted that a couple of weeks ago?"

Stacey was embarrassed her mom had put her work on the fridge with magnets, as if she was in kindergarten. Before tonight, she felt certain no one would see it. She eyed the opposite corner of the ceiling. "It was a lesson with my old art teacher. No big deal."

"You won first place in that art show," her mom said.

"That was a fluke." Stacey tucked the napkin beneath her plate.

Greg raised his eyebrows and grinned, watching the volley of words pass between them.

"It's beautiful, Greg. She's hiding it in the back of the coat closet." She set her fork and knife on the placemat on either side of her plate and thumbed over her shoulder in a half-hearted attempt to offer. "I can grab it."

"Don't you dare." Stacey's warning came out too harsh. She added a gentle, "Please," to soften the blow, pleading with her mom, widening her eyes.

"Okayyy." Her mom put both hands up in surrender.

Stacey pushed her chair back. "I think I'm gonna finish getting ready, if that's okay?"

Her mom nodded, refilling her glass.

"Thank you for dinner, Greg," Stacey said. "It really was delicious. And nice to meet you."

"You too, Stacey," he said, setting his fork upside down on his plate the same way Stacey had. He looked her in the eyes. "I hope we can do this again soon. You can help clean up next time, but if you don't mind taking those to the sink, I'd appreciate it."

She nodded and set her dishes and silverware in a small pile beside the sink. She was curious how long her mom had dated Greg. He felt both familiar and authoritative in their home already. It was disarming.

Murphy followed Stacey down the hall and jumped up onto her bed.

Stacey's hair was still damp, so she sat on her bed and blew it dry, smooth and straight. She changed into a strappy, lace-edged white tank top and a pair of 501s that made her butt look great. "Look good, feel good," she recited, taking long, slow breaths to calm her nerves as she applied black mascara. She lined her lips with rum raisin and added pink gloss that she hoped shouted soft and kissable. The makeup complimented her tan skin and long, sun-bleached hair.

"I could have been a stand-in for Alicia Silverstone on the 'Crazy' road trip, right Murph?"

Murphy kept her gaze on Stacey with her muzzle on her paws. After a spritz of Guess perfume, Stacey blew a kiss at the dog, and pulled open her bedroom door. "Wish me luck!"

The clock on her nightstand glowed 7:55.

Chapter Fourteen

Jessie strolled to Stacey's car from his apartment, whipping his still wet hair from his eyes. He was back in his basic outfit of board shorts, a wrinkled T-shirt, and a puka-shell necklace.

Way to dress for our date, dude.

Jessie got in the car, grinned, and leaned toward her. Stacey steeled herself for his kiss. Instead, he reached in the back seat, and grabbed her book of CDs.

"We need mood music," he said, flipping through the pages.

"Good idea." Stacey chuckled nervously and pulled the car onto the main road. "So, where do you think the best spot will be to see the meteor shower?"

"You know where Avenue A runs out, turns into a dirt road?"

Stacey nodded.

"If you keep going a half mile or so, past all the fences, there's a clearing that's perfect."

"This car can't really offroad," Stacey said.

"Don't worry. The path's pretty smooth. Trust me. We'll be fine."

About twenty minutes of dusty, bumpy roads, and several Fugees songs later, the livestock fences ended. Stacey stopped and pulled up on the brake. She wasn't comfortable going any further.

"This is good," Jessie said. "Cut the lights."

Stacey turned off the headlights and they were engulfed in total darkness. The final notes of "Killing Me Softly" played, with only the green glow of the digital clock display on the radio illuminating the space around them. Stacey leaned forward to try to look through the windshield, but could only see dried bird poop and dust on the window, and nothing but blackness beyond. Nothing like the shooting stars she'd fantasized. Nothing like the aurora borealis she'd painted.

"Should we get out?" Stacey asked, trying to remember if rattlesnakes came out at night.

Jessie pressed eject on the CD player and placed another disc in the slot. The hiss of the newly spinning disc took hold and Stacey recognized the deep voice moaning "Blue Spanish Sky."

For two days, Stacey had imagined their next kiss would be even more romantic than the first. That there would be build up, holding hands, making a wish on a shooting star, and looking deep into Jessie's eyes before their lips ever touched. Now, the MTV images of Chris Isaak shirtless, dark, and brooding flashed through her mind, tumbling with supermodels in the sand, the sheets, a pool. It was overwhelming. A lump formed in her throat and she scratched at the back of her neck.

She turned to look at Jessie for a clue of what she was supposed to do next. Before she opened her mouth to speak, Jessie leaned over and kissed her. His lips pushed hard. It didn't feel the least bit romantic.

The further she tilted back, the further Jessie pressed into her, bracing himself on the steering wheel. His tongue searched deep in her mouth.

She could hardly breathe. Stacey put both hands on his chest and pushed back gently. She turned her face from his. "Whoa. Slow down." His chest was hot and firm beneath her hands and she kept them in place.

He inched back, sheepish. "I'm sorry…I…" His eyes flashed back and forth between hers, then scanned quickly down to her cleavage. "I can't help myself. I've liked you for so long. Never thought I had a chance."

"A chance? With me?" She searched for a sign he was joking. "At the end of school you thought my name was Stephanie."

He perched on his seat, one hand on her seat back and the other resting on the steering wheel, hovering like he was ready to pounce again. "Nah. I always knew who you were. So smart. So pretty. I had to act like I didn't know how out of my league you were." He grazed her cheek with his right knuckles, gently, like before that first kiss. "I thought for sure you'd turn me down if I ever asked you out."

She shivered as his fingers ran through the strands of her hair that draped over her arm.

He rested his hand on her thigh.

"That's crazy! I've liked you for the longest time." Stacey put her hand on his upper arm. "I was sure you didn't even know I was alive."

"I always had my eye on you. Being alone with you, before the movie…felt like fate." Jessie intertwined his fingers with hers. "Talking to you felt like we were always meant to be."

Who needs shooting stars? Jessie Thomas likes me as much as I like him! This is my wish come true.

Stacey leaned forward to kiss him softly, her left fingers running up his arm, under the edge of his sleeve. Her eyes fluttered closed. Their tongues gently wet each other's lips, and it felt like she'd imagined. *Yes. This. I like it just like this.*

Jessie's hand moved from her thigh to her waist, then slid down to grab ahold of her belt loop, tugging her closer to him. Their knees ran into the emergency brake, and their mouths pushed harder, lips slapping as they joined and pulled apart. Jessie's fingers slid over the curve of her hip, then backward, his whole hand palming her left butt cheek. Stacy flexed it. *Yeah, okay. This is pretty nice, too.*

Jessie let go of her hand. His fingers traveled up her back, the tips running over the nape of her neck and through her hair. His groans of pleasure vibrated from the back of his throat against Stacey's lips and tongue. Their kisses became wetter. Stacey's heart stomped like a racehorse in her chest.

Maybe we should slow down. Keep this from going too far.

She leaned her head back to inhale. To give words to her thoughts.

Jessie's lips moved down her neck like she'd given an invitation.

Her eyes opened wider, staring at the dark ceiling above her.

His tongue grazed her collar bone, his warm breath raising the skin on her chest to gooseflesh. Rushes reverberated through her body. Her breasts and between her legs felt fuller, more tingly, like even the slightest breeze could set off a gasping spasm.

"Jessie, let's–." Her head spun, feeling too heavy to hold up. She put her hand on Jessie's chest again.

He groaned.

She pulled her hand back.

He kissed her, then moved his mouth next to her ear. "Let's move to the back seat," he whispered. His hot breath tickled the inside of her ear. She reached her hand up to wipe it, then smoothed the hairs on the back of her neck.

Her stomach tightened. "Ummm…"

He reached under and pulled the release, sliding the chair forward, then climbed between the two seats, pushing his seat as far forward as possible.

Stacey froze, her left hand gripping the steering wheel. *We're going too fast.*

She glanced in the rearview mirror. Jessie pulled the long blonde bangs from his eyes. *God, he's hot. Don't be a baby, Chapman. You're making out with JESSIE THOMAS!*

He reached between the seats for her right hand. She let him tug her gently toward him. *We've both liked each other for a long time.* Stacey eased her right leg between the seats, then pulled the latch to slide her chair forward. When she maneuvered the rest of her body to the back, Jessie pulled her on top, to straddle him. She could instantly feel his heat through her jeans and she gasped. *This is normal, isn't it?* Her whole body began to shake.

"Shhhh…" He eased his lips up to hers and kissed her gently on the mouth, his hands on either side of her face.

Her shaking slowed and she relaxed into the softness of his lips.

He reached his hands behind his neck and pulled his shirt off over his head.

Wait.

Stacey's shaking intensified. Her hands stretched on her own thighs, wiping her sweaty palms. A picture flashed in her mind from the first day at The Plunge, staring at Jessie's muscular chest, abs, and arms. But now the way he was looking at her, watching her looking at his bare chest, made it impossible to stop.

Jessie lifted her right hand and kissed each of her fingertips, then placed her hand on his breastbone, and his hands on her hips.

"Your heart is thumping," she said.

He slid his right hand over her shirt, over her left breast, and spread his palm across her heart. Her lips fell open.

"So is yours," he said. He slid his left hand behind her neck and pulled her face to his, sucking her bottom lip in his and groping her right breast over her shirt.

Stacey pushed him back. "This is going really fast." *Is this…second base?*

He let his hands drop back to her waist. The spot where her hand rested on his chest felt damp, but she couldn't tell if it was heat radiating from him or if she was sweating. Lifting her palm slowly, Stacey's fingertips and nails grazed the skin on his left pec, and everything about him inflated.

Jessie groaned and pushed his pelvis upward. He was hard. Hot between her legs. Stacey suppressed her own groan.

Slow down, Chapman! She wanted to outline each of the muscles on his chest and abs with her fingertips, memorizing the curves and gaps, so she could sketch and paint him. And she was afraid that even the faintest touch would explode in each of them something that couldn't be controlled.

Jessie leaned his head back, inhaling deeply, his chest spread wide. She bit her bottom lip. Stacey swiped her hand across his chest. Her thumb caught on his nipple before she rested her hand on his bicep. His tattoo of thorns.

The CD switched to "Wicked Game." Jessie leaned forward, one hand on Stacey's neck, pulling her close to kiss again. The fingers on his free hand slipped under her tank top, running the tips of his fingernails up her spine. Stacey shivered, arched her back. Jessie kissed the place her heart threatened to burst out from.

The air in the car was sticky. Sweat beaded on her forehead.

Their mouths met. They eagerly pressed their lips, tongues, and teeth together.

Being on top of him magnified everything she felt between her legs. There was a throbbing through her 501's. She couldn't tell exactly where it was coming from, but hoped it would never end. *This. Keep doing this. God this feels so good. ONLY this. Forever.*

She spread her legs apart wider.

He pushed up harder.

Heat rose between them. The air smelled like their sweat. The windows were fogged up.

Jessie cupped her breasts through her bra. Stacey tensed. He moved his fingers to her back and she relaxed. He wrapped her in an embrace, then unhooked her bra.

A squeak escaped Stacey's open mouth and she started to pull away. Jessie had already looped his fingers over the bra and tank top straps and was pulling them to the sides.

"Wait!" Stacey instinctively crossed her arms over her chest and tilted away.

Jessie eased her hands down by her sides, shaking his head. "Don't cover up," he whispered. "I want to look at you." His breathy request and Chris Isaak's mesmerizing voice braided Stacey's thoughts.

Strange desire. Jessie wants to look at me. Foolish people. Kiss me. Touch me. Lick me.

She let her arms relax.

Jessie eased the straps down. The loose bra and lace trim barely clung to Stacey's breasts.

I should stop him. Never dreamed. I know I should...stop us...both.

Jessie's thumbs edged the lace. Her nipples hardened, muted her brain. Her lips parted. No words fell out.

Chris Isaak sang warnings about a broken heart.

Jessie eased the tank top down. Stacey froze. Her breath trembled.

Jessie's mouth touched her left nipple. Waves of heat rippled into shivers. His tongue was like a pin, piercing her. Struggling to hold on, she gripped Jessie's ribs. She exhaled. Her panties became damp.

Then Jessie's hands were all over her. He cupped her breasts. It felt good. He licked her nipples and it felt so good. His mouth was on her mouth, her hands explored his chest. She ran her fingers down the ridges of his abs. It all felt too good.

Topless is third base, right? Third base is way too fast for a first date.

His slobber was intoxicating, and their heat, and his hands on her. It all felt dangerously good. Her breath was fast and deep.

This is scary and exciting, but maybe it's okay. No more though…more would be way too far.

Jessie grabbed Stacey's back belt loop, and cradled her to him with his other arm. He shifted them both up and over, and before Stacey knew what was happening she was on her back across the seat, with Jessie above her.

A seat belt buckle pressed into her shoulder blade. Her neck was angled oddly against the side armrest.

"Wait." Stacey shifted under him.

Jessie's fingers curled behind the button of her jeans.

"Wait!" A sharp panic struck her chest.

His fingertip grazed inside the top of her panties.

Her breath caught, and she put her hand on his. "Not yet."

Jessie groaned, gripped her backside, pushing his hard groin against the inner seam of her 501s. His slippery chest slid up her abdomen. "You're so hot," he said, grinding into her crotch.

Stacey's hands stuck to his sweaty back. "Let's…I mean…we should…"

Jessie slid off the seat, onto his knees. He took her left breast in one hand and pinched her nipple between two fingers, his mouth wide on her other breast while he rubbed hard on the inner seam of her 501s with his right hand.

She reached to stop him, but clenched her fist and bit her knuckle instead. A wave of heat sped through her.

Jessie smiled up at her triumphantly. Her whole body flushed. Stacey's brain screamed YES! and NO! in a fog of white noise. She struggled to open her eyes, catching only brief glimpses of Jessie's teeth and tongue, his hand on her breast. Water droplets streaked down the steamed window.

Jessie removed his hand and his mouth hovered by her ear. "You liked that."

She moved her hand to his hip. He pushed himself up and her hand slid down to his bare thigh. *No boardshorts?* Her eyes shot open.

Stacey jerked her hand away. "Jessie, where are your..." She was afraid to look down, and willed him to look at her face. She pushed her hands against his chest, but he wasn't making eye contact.

Jessie grabbed her button and zipper in both hands, and tore them apart.

"Jessie, wai–"

Every pleasurable sensation Stacey had felt vanished. She gripped the seat with one hand and the seatbelt above her with the other, trying to pull herself up. She wriggled her hips back. "I want your pants..." Stacey's voice cracked, searching for the next word.

As she scrambled to pull herself upright, Jessie tugged on her jeans in the opposite direction.

"But, I'm not..."

"I want you so bad." He tugged her pants down, pulling her body back under him in the process. "You know you want me, too."

Not like this! "Bu…" Stacey squeaked, her face scrunching. *What would he do if I stopped him? What would happen?*

"I can't wait any longer."

"Jess—sto…" She shifted her shoulders and reached toward her panties. He pulled them quickly below her knees and spread her legs.

Fists clenched, Stacey turned her face away from him.

He braced one arm against the seat. His other hand groped her with rough fingers. It was like being probed by sharp sticks.

She squeezed her mouth and her eyes shut, her fingernails cutting into her palms.

Jessie thrust himself inside her. She felt her skin tear. Her abdomen being thrust apart. A guttural moan erupted from his throat.

A tear slid silently over the bridge of her nose. His hair dragged along her jawline, catching in the trail of another quiet tear.

He inched back and pushed inside again. Each time worse than the last, until she was numb to it. She held her breath. Jessie pushed three, four, five times, then collapsed on top of her.

The seatbelt buckle pressed into her shoulder. She shifted away from his weight.

Jessie exhaled. She felt him slide out. He pushed himself up, then eased her knees together and pushed her legs aside. Slouched into the seat.

Stacey pulled herself upright, watching as he pulled his shorts up.

A lump formed in her throat. *Was there no condom? Oh, God!* She lifted her hips and pulled up her pants. *No, no, no, no, no!* She began shaking again. She struggled with the clasp of her bra and the arm holes of her tank top, sliding an arm through the neck opening, fumbling, watching him out of the corner of her eye.

Jessie's head was pressed against the seat, his eyes closed, shirt crumpled on his lap, like he'd run a marathon.

That was so stupid! I'm an idiot. Oh god! Her stomach violently twisted in on itself.

Jessie's puka-shell necklace glowed green in the dark, reflecting light from the stereo. Stacey fought an urge to rip it off him and smash it against the windshield.

She looked at the clock. 9:15.

As the song changed, Chris Isaak's voice rose again, repeating over and over how trouble was going around.

Stacey reached between the seats and hit the power button on the stereo, but the lyrics wouldn't stop reverberating through her mind. She squeezed her thighs together, hands clasped between them to stop her shaking.

Somewhere in the pitch-black outside, a coyote howled.

She wiped her cheeks. Rubbed under her eyes. She examined her fingers, but couldn't see well enough to tell if they were covered in makeup.

There was another howl, closer, followed by a chorus of yips.

"You hear that?" he asked. Jessie's hand squeaked against the window pane, like he was wiping it to look out. "They caught something. Maybe a rabbit."

She turned her face toward her window, crossing her left arm over her body. *Dumbass rabbit. Serves you right, out here alone.* She put her right pinky nail in her mouth and chewed the tip of it off, blowing the strip into the side of her seat.

Jessie reached over to put his hand on her thigh.

Her eyes popped open. *Is he…?* She looked over.

Jessie's eyes were sleepy, narrow slits. "Ready to go?" His hand dropped back onto the seat. She bit her bottom lip.

Stacey climbed back into the front seat and buckled her seat belt, blinking back the violent emotions ready to rush out of her. She turned the keys in the ignition. She rolled down her window and turned the AC on high to clear the condensation.

Jessie pulled his shirt on, then climbed back up front. He ejected the *Heart Shaped World* disc and popped in the Garbage CD, then buckled his seatbelt and tugged on the front of his boardshorts.

The surround sound of screaming guitars tightened the knots throbbing across Stacey's forehead. She dialed the volume down. She flipped on the headlights, made a U-turn, and drove past the abandoned fields.

For the next twenty minutes, the music was muffled by the pulsating beat in her temple and the crunch of the tires on the dirt road. Stacey glanced at Jessie, asleep, his head bobbing against the passenger side window. *I should open the door so he falls out.*

By the time they reached the main road, she'd gnawed down two more fingernails, and spit them out toward his lap. "Stupid Girl" filled the silence, and even though she knew the song was coming, the words stung. She didn't turn it off.

Stacey pulled the car into his driveway and wrenched up on the emergency brake before they were fully stopped. Jessie's head fell forward, then jerked up. He blinked, then climbed out of the car and leaned his head down through the open door. "That was fun," he yawned. "See ya later, Chapman." He stumbled to his door and went inside without looking back.

Stacey turned off the music. Silent tears fell to her chin all the way back home. It wasn't even ten o'clock when she pulled in the driveway. The house was dark, but Greg's truck was still out front. She dragged the back of her hands across her cheeks. She didn't have the energy to go anywhere else until her mom's date was over. *What if he stayed the night?* She didn't want to imagine what they were doing, or to answer their questions about her "date." She hoped she could slip silently into her room. Be left alone. She turned off the engine.

She pushed open the front door. Murphy was waiting for her and jumped to attention, the tags on her collar clanking. She wagged her tail and licked Stacey's palm, while Stacey closed the heavy door as quietly as she could. From the entryway she could see no one was in the kitchen or living room. Looking down the hall, the door to her mom's bedroom was open.

Her mom's laughter erupted in the backyard followed by a man's deep chuckle. Stacey's eye's adjusted until she could see her mom and Greg reclined in lawn chairs, their backs to the house, looking up at the stars. Their arms on the rests met in the middle, her mom's hand intertwined with Greg's.

They're watching the shooting stars? Unbelievable.

Murphy padded next to Stacey down the hall and into her bedroom. Leaving the lights off, Stacey closed her door without a sound. She pulled the cover from her bed and wrapped it around herself, rolling into a ball on the floor. Murphy licked her cheek, then curled into her. Stacey pulled the blanket tight around her face and ears, blocking out the world, and imagined dissolving into the darkness. Into the silence.

No stars.

No light.

No wishes or dreams.

Just drowning in that inky blackness where maybe, just maybe, nothing about that night existed.

Chapter Fifteen

Stacey laid awake, curled up on the floor, most of the night. Her body felt broken all over, but when she went to the bathroom, she saw she was physically fine.

She heard the front door open and close, followed by the sound of Greg's truck pulling away. She pretended to be asleep when her mom opened the door to her bedroom, the light from the hallway burning through Stacey's raw eyelids. She held them closed until the door clicked shut again.

Stacey searched the popcorn ceiling for answers, debating and hating herself. *You're such a slut. No, sex is totally normal. You made the biggest mistake of your life. Maybe it's not a big deal at all. Don't freak out…yet.*

She considered whether Jessie still liked her, or ever really did. She ran through dozens of things she wanted to say to him, to ask him, and how he might respond. *How many people have you slept with? Please say there WAS a condom that I didn't see?*

The green glow of the digital time on her nightstand taunted her. It was too bright. Too offensive as the minutes and hours ticked by. It was the same glow that was in the car, reflecting off Jessie's stupid puka shell necklace. She unplugged it and threw the clock across the room, into her closet.

"Stacey, it was only sex," she imagined Jessie saying in his dumb, nothings-that-big-of-a-deal voice. *"Chill out." "I'm SOOO into you!" "Everyone does it."*

She bit her pillow to prevent herself from screaming louder than the voices in her head.

As the first morning light glowed outside her window, Stacey felt mentally, physically, and emotionally wrung dry. It was Saturday. She was due to work the morning shift at the pool at eight.

Up and down the street neighbors began mowing lawns as soon as the sun rose, before the heat of the day settled in. The rev of a John Deere motor next door startled her. Stacey didn't think she'd slept at all. She gnawed the nail of her right middle finger until she heard her mom's bedroom door squeak open, followed by the thunk of the front door. Once the minivan puttered away, Stacey untangled herself from her bedspread.

After letting Murphy out, she took several long slow gulps of water from the kitchen faucet, then looked up at the time on the microwave, considering whether it was too late to call in sick. She had thirty minutes to be at the pool and couldn't even muster the energy to come up with a good lie.

She glared at her painting of the aurora borealis on the fridge. Every hope she'd had for her date with Jessie, the magic of wishing on shooting stars with him by her side, felt bogus. Like seeing something so beautiful and magical as the northern lights would ever be possible for her, either. She pulled the watercolor off the fridge and ripped it in half, dropping the two pieces on the Formica countertop, and dragged herself to the bathroom.

She stared for a full minute at her red-rimmed, puffy eyes and swollen, pink nose. Her tank top was stretched, and her right bra strap had slid down her shoulder. Purple pools hung beneath her eyes. Her cheeks and brows were stained with mascara. Looking at her reflection brought on another wave of disgust. She splashed cold water on her cheeks, trying not to look at the mirror, and noticed her good red swimsuit from The Outlet in a damp heap in the shower.

Back in her bedroom, she yanked off her clothes and kicked the pile under her bed. She pulled on the ugly, granny-panty red suit, covering it with the Nirvana T-shirt and boxers that she'd worn for dinner. She slipped into her Birkenstocks and grabbed her keys.

Mark was unlocking the pool's entrance at 8:03 when the Silver Bullet's tires screeched into a front space in the parking lot. Stacey didn't stop fast enough, and her front right tire went up and over the parking block.

"Goddammit!" Stacey hit the steering wheel.

As she reversed, she scraped the underside of her car, and the bumper thumped one final time before she pulled the parking brake.

Mark and Tiffany surveilled the scene, Tiffany covering her mouth with both hands. Mark left the keys hanging in the lock and offered Stacey an amused golf clap.

Stacey turned off the ignition and leaned her head back.

Chad eased out of his blue Chevelle next to her, checking the side of his own vehicle before he leaned down to look under the front of her car. He knocked on Stacey's passenger window, and raised his eyebrows at her. "You okay?" he asked.

Stacey nodded. At least Bob wasn't there to punish her for being late. With this crew, she had a narrow possibility of actually making it through her shift.

Stacey began to reach for the CD case, then remembered it was Jessie who had left it on the floor. The Chris Isaak disc would be in there. And the Fugees. Along with every CD she'd played the past month to impress Jessie. Leaving the case where it was, she locked her car. She wouldn't be the pool's disc jockey. *Not today.*

Inside the main office, Mark sat at the desk rubbing his face and yawning like a yeti. When his glazed eyes caught Stacey's, she thought he looked like she felt.

"Have a rough night, Chapman? Party too hard?" Mark asked.

Stacey blinked slowly at him, but didn't respond.

"Interesting…" Mark said.

"Believe whatever the hell you want." Stacey threw open the door of her locker, and tossed her keys and towel inside. Her sunscreen toppled over, clanging against her whistle. She turned to Tiffany. "Need me to clean the girls' bathroom?"

"You sure? Only if you want to." Tiffany's voice tinkled like a xylophone. "Or I can. Whatever's best for you. I don't mind."

Stacey resented Tiffany's smile. It was too big. Too happy. Stacey peered into her locker for nothing more than an excuse to turn away. "It's fine," she mumbled, kicking off her Birkenstocks and stepping into her flip-flops. "I got it."

Tiffany followed her out the door, gently touching her elbow once they were outside. "Stacey," she said quietly. "Is everything okay?"

Stacey gazed at the bleachers behind Tiffany, avoiding eye contact. "I didn't sleep well."

Tiffany twisted her fingers together. "It looks like you've been crying."

Stacey shrugged and began chewing what little remained of her right thumbnail. She tasted blood.

"We're friends, Stace. If you need anyone to talk to, I'm here."

"Thanks, but I'm fine." Stacey grabbed the hose and dragged it into the girl's locker room. She sprinkled antibacterial powder across the bathroom and changing room's concrete floors, over the dingy honeycomb tiles in the base of the showers.

Are Tiffany and I actually friends? She squeezed the spray nozzle trigger and began hosing out the shower. She'd laughed so hard playing Uno with Tiffany and the guys on Wednesday, waiting in line at the movies. *How was that only three days ago?*

All that happened since the movie night flooded Stacey's mind. Her first kiss with Jessie. Their date that wasn't a date at all. Not knowing for sure how he felt about her. Every possible consequence that still might be.

Stacey felt water pooling around her ankles. She let go of the trigger on the nozzle, the stream of water becoming a drizzle. She could hear the drain in the center of the stalls glugging for air. "You've got to be kidding me."

At the door of the guard shack, Stacey leaned in and told Mark the shower drain was clogged.

Without turning around, Mark pointed at a plunger in the corner.

Stacey pushed the door open all the way. "What am I supposed to do with that?"

Mark turned in his chair. "Just like a toilet." He demonstrated holding the plunger with his hands. "Push down as many times as you have to to get the water to go down."

"What? Really? I don't know how to do that."

"You're a smart girl," he said, turning back to the desk. "You'll figure it out."

"Why the fuck does everyone expect me to figure everything out on my own? What is wrong with you people?" She threw her hands in the air and stomped over to grab the plunger.

Mark mumbled, "Maybe it's because you refuse to ask for help."

"I just did!" She stood in front of him, scowling. "You told me to do it myself!"

"Actually..." Mark turned to look at her. "You didn't ask for help." He lifted his thumb. "First, you announced the problem with the shower drain." He lifted his index finger. "Then, you said you didn't know what to do with a plunger." He lifted his middle finger. "Finally, you said you don't know how to push down on a plunger, which, frankly, I don't believe. But, you didn't ever actually ask for help from anyone." He swiveled back toward the desk. "You never do."

Stacey gawked at him, then shook her head. She threw her left hand up, then slapped her thigh. "Fine. You're right! Will you HELP me, then?"

"I'd be glad to..." Mark turned his chair toward Stacey.

"Ugh...Thank y–"

"...if you ask nicely." Mark stood and crossed his arms.

"Jeez.." Stacey folded her hands in front of her face and affected her voice. "PLEASE Mark, will you f-ing help me?"

"Was that so hard?"

Stacey rolled her eyes.

They walked into the bathroom together and Mark looked around at the painted cinder block walls and ecru partitions. "A lot less tagging in here than the boys' bathroom."

They entered the shower stalls. The water had gone down. "Of course. Now that you made me beg, I don't need help after all."

"Uh...you may not need help with the plunger, but," Mark pointed at the drain, "you do have to clean that out."

Peering more closely, Stacey noticed a clump of hair as thick as a rat's tail trailing out from the drain screen. "THAT," she pointed, "is NOT my problem!"

"Whose problem do you think it is? You offered to clean the bathroom this morning. I heard you."

"That's disgusting. From the beginning you said all we have to do is sprinkle the pink stuff everywhere and hose it out."

"First of all, you should know better by now than to listen to any of the stupid shit I say. Second, this is a WOMEN'S RESTROOM! You'd better be cleaning it more than that or we are going to get shut down by the health department. Bob told everyone as much your first day, when you were all googly-eyed over Jessie."

Stacey's face flushed. "You're such an asshole!" She stormed out of the bathroom.

Mark followed her. "Get over yourself, Stacey and do your damn job. You need to wipe down mirrors and toilet seats, refill toilet paper, empty those bins in the stalls with disgusting girl stuff inside. AND clean the hair out of that drain!"

"Fine." She looked at her feet. "Will you at least show me how?"

"We need a screwdriver, more gloves, and possibly an exorcist," he said.

It turned out the unused plastic utensils that had been piling up in the guard shack all summer came in handy. Once Mark pried the cover off of the drain, they each scraped and scooped out the muck. Stacey paused to look away when the smell and slime of the clog made her stomach turn. Mark gagged, covering his mouth with his elbow.

Thirty minutes later, the water flowed properly with all the shower faucets running.

After washing her hands, Stacey slumped onto the couch, grateful Chad and Tiffany had offered to take the first shifts in the towers.

Mark sat at the desk, accepting money from the swimmers as they entered. Over his shoulder, he said, "For you to be late, and the way you dragged your ass through here, you're sure you don't have Typhoid or something?"

"I'm fine," Stacey said, crossing her arms and looking down at her red, shredded fingers. "Everyone can back off." Her nails were bitten to their quicks. She pushed her left ring finger cuticle between her teeth and started to tug at it.

"You don't seem fine." He perched on the edge of the desk, his arms crossed. "You're cannibalizing your hands and your clothes are filthy."

Stacey pulled her finger from her mouth and tucked it in her armpit. She looked down at her Nirvana T-shirt. It had small holes in the neck and brownish-yellow stains in the pits. The buffalo check boxers were faded and more than three sizes too big.

"Like you're one to talk," she muttered.

"That's different, and you know it. I'm always a slob. You never are."

Stacey pushed herself to standing and pulled open Melissa's locker to use her mirror. Her hair was greasy and her lashes still held clumps of mascara. Wetting her face that morning only made the black shadows around her swollen eyes more prominent.

"Maybe you have a point. But I'm kinda rocking the angry grunge look."

"Nah. You look like an angsty runaway who needs a shower."

Stacey pulled off her T-shirt and boxers, shoving them in her locker, then wrapped her towel around her waist, double rolling it so it would stay put. Grabbing a hair-tie and bottle of SPF 30 from the back of her locker, she combed her fingers through her hair to pull it into a ponytail. Rubbing sunscreen onto her face, Stacey took care to gently swipe a bit beneath her eyes, then used a tissue from the desk to wipe the smeared makeup away with the extra lotion.

She turned toward Mark. "Better?"

"Yeah. Now don't fall asleep up in the chair."

"You're a hypocrite."

"I know. But one of me is already one too many around this place." Mark turned back to the desk and put his feet up.

Stacey headed out for her rotation in the deep-end tower.

As Tiffany climbed down, she told Stacey, "We've got a few overconfident swimmers today."

Stacey nodded. "We always do."

"We need to watch that one especially." Tiffany pointed out a small, skinny boy, about five years old, in a too-large pair of royal blue swim trunks. "He can barely doggy-paddle."

Tiffany moved over to the other tower to watch the shallow end and Chad went inside.

It was only 9:30, but after a night spent crying and too little sleep, then an hour scouring the dark, dingy bathroom, Stacey's head was pounding. The harsh reflection off the water and bright concrete stung Stacey's eyes, even through her sunglasses. The kids' laughter and splashing pierced her eardrums. Her stomach rumbled.

Despite everything, Stacey's internal debates about Jessie still fought for her attention.

Maybe he'll realize he was a jerk and call today.

You're a dumbass if you think he ever really cared about you.

She pulled at a piece of skin on her thumb, slowly tearing it away until it bled.

When Stacey looked up, the little boy Tiffany pointed out was bouncing his way around the shallow end of the pool. She sucked on her injured finger, inspecting it again.

If he comes to see me today, I'll know I overreacted.

She glanced toward the deep end. The sunlight glared off the surface of the water as a little girl in a Minnie Mouse swimsuit walked to the end of the board and jumped off. She swam to the edge. In line next to go off the board were two older boys.

Focusing back on her hands, Stacey picked at another loose cuticle, this time on her right pointer finger.

She heard the thump of the board followed by a splash. Out of the corner of her eye she saw two arms slapping and two feet splashing toward the ladder.

Stacey examined her left hand more closely.

There were splash sounds around the pool, some loud, others not so much, all as familiar to Stacey as her own breath. But when a quieter sound — the sound of a small body hitting water, a figure so petite it didn't bounce the board at all — made its miniscule splash in the deep end, Stacey's ears perked up. The hairs on the back of her neck raised.

She looked at the deep end again. The bright sunlight danced on the surface as a single ripple moved across the top of the water.

Stacey stood and pulled her sunglasses up to try to see better. The reflection of the light was so bright she had to squint. Beneath the ripple, near the bottom, was someone so small she thought maybe she was only looking at the drain itself.

The girl in the Minnie Mouse suit stood on the side of the pool looking down, both hands over her mouth.

Reaching for her whistle, she realized she was so distracted she never put it on that morning. It was buried in her locker. "Tiff!" she shouted at Tiffany's tower.

Tiffany made eye-contact, then jumped to her feet.

Scanning the water again, she realized the body was not coming back up. Stacey tugged on her towel. Double rolled, it barely loosened. She ripped it away harder. The towel fell into a heap on the deck.

Tiffany blew her whistle.

Stacey jumped feet first from her tower, dropping into the deep end two feet from the small child.

Her left arm encircled his tiny chest. She pushed her feet hard against the bottom of the pool.

The two reached the top within a few seconds. Both gasped for air. With the boy tight to her side, Stacey paddled with one arm and scissor-kicked her legs to the ladder.

The small girl stood by the ladder, her face pale.

The boy slowly pulled himself up the rungs. Stacey lifted his waist from behind.

"Braydon, are you okay?" the girl asked, eyes wide with fright as she put her arm around him.

The boy sputtered water and nodded, his lips purple.

"What were you thinking?" Stacey spat as she climbed from the pool. "Where are your parents?"

"I'm sorry! Please don't call my parents!" The sister's voice rose several octaves. "It's my fault. I told him the diving board was fun. Our parents aren't here. We live down the street."

The crying girl trying to comfort her little brother was no more than seven. She didn't know better, and neither did he. Stacey should have been watching, made sure he didn't go off the diving board in the first place. Tiffany had warned her about the boy.

If he'd drowned, it would have been my fault.

Stacey dropped to her knees. "Listen...don't cry, okay?" She cleared her throat, trying to halt the quiver in her own voice, and rested a hand on each of the kids' shoulders. "I'm sorry I got so upset. You're just not ready for the diving board. You've got to be able to get yourself out."

They both nodded sheepishly. "Are we in trouble?" the little girl asked. "Do we have to go home?"

"No," Stacey said. "But stay over on that end, okay?"

The girl held her brother's hand and led him to the shallow end of the pool. They sat on the side and dangled their feet in the water.

Stacey returned to her chair, hands shaking. She left her towel in the puddle where it landed beneath the tower. Looking around the pool, she counted six adults. There were dozens of kids running, splashing, and jumping in the water.

Stacey's ponytail dripped. Water pooled in her seat. She perched on the edge of the chair, terrified not to give her full attention to the water. Ready to jump again if needed. Her suit clung to her. Despite the heat, her thighs were covered in goosebumps.

Tiffany sat back in her own seat, and lifted her megaphone. "Good save."

Stacey tried to smile, but shook her head instead. She sat on her hands and watched the swimmers.

At noon, when morning swim ended, Chad told Stacey to go in and get out of the sun. The water was cleared and no lap swimmers had shown up yet. He offered to watch as the final morning swimmers filed off the deck. She only had one more hour. After lap swim, Stacey was done for the day. It couldn't come soon enough.

Inside the guard shack, Stacey smelled French fries. She was surprised to find a Carl's Jr. bag inside her locker. She hadn't eaten since dinner, and the salty, greasy smell made her salivate. "Where'd this come from?"

Mark smiled at her. "I had Tiffany go on a quick lunch run. Your first rescue warrants a Famous Star, don't you think?"

"I did everything wrong. I wasn't wearing my whistle. I wasn't paying enough attention. I should have stopped him before he even got on the diving board. I didn't use the Shepherd's Crook like you told me to, or brace his neck or anything."

"It's fifteen feet deep; you knew he didn't have a head or neck injury. And he's fine because you got him out quickly." Mark shrugged. "You know what to do next time, right?"

"How did I not realize we're the cheapest babysitting in town?"

"It gets worse as summer wears on. People get sick of their kids. They need a break and drop them off."

Stacey fell onto the couch, pulled three fries from the bag, and shoved them in her mouth. She unwrapped the hamburger. "Where is Tiffany?" she asked, then took a huge bite.

"She's off this afternoon," Mark said with his mouth full. He swigged from his soda. "She brought the food back, then I told her she could head home."

Holding the bite in the side of her cheek, Stacey asked, "Who else is working lap swi–"

Melissa pulled open the lobby door.

Stacey finished chewing and swallowed her bite, wiping her mouth with the back of her hand before Melissa entered the guard shack carrying a Del Taco bag.

"Hey," Melissa said to Mark as she closed the door behind her.

Mark nodded, his mouth full.

Melissa dropped her keys in her locker. "Oh! Hi, Stacey," she purred.

Stacey didn't trust Melissa's enthusiastic greeting. "Hey." She looked at the clock. 12:02. *Only fifty-eight minutes. I can do this.*

Melissa sat on the other end of the couch, turned toward Stacey, her legs crisscrossed beneath her. "How's it goin'?"

Stacey felt like she was under a microscope. "Fine." She used her tongue to clean her teeth while wrapping up the rest of her burger. *I can play this game.* "How are you?" She set the burger in her bag by her feet, grabbing a few fries.

"What's up with you? Did you do anything fun after work yesterday?" Melissa asked, pulling a small burrito from her own bag and folding the wrapping down to expose the top half.

Mark's chair squeaked as he turned. He twisted the straw in the giant soda in his hand, as if tuning into a soap opera.

"Not really." Stacey's eyebrow twitched. She bit the top of the fries off, watching Melissa out of the corner of her eye.

Melissa picked at her burrito. "Seemed like you and Jessie were pretty friendly at the movies the other night."

"I guess…"

"Did you hook up with him?" Melissa snapped.

"Seriously?" Stacey turned her shoulders to face Melissa. "You were here yesterday. He barely said five words to me the whole day."

"Last night Jessie said he was busy." Melissa narrowed her eyes. "I think he was with you."

"Wow." Stacey lifted her eyebrows high. "I thought you and Jessie stopped talking to each other a couple weeks ago."

"That's not the point."

"What *is* your point?"

Melissa shook her head and turned away. She put her feet on the ground and bit into her burrito.

Stacey picked up her bag and started gnawing on another handful of fries.

Chad pulled open the door from the pool deck. "Any lap swimmers yet?" he asked Mark before stepping inside.

Mark shook his head quickly, attention focused on the mounting cat fight.

Chad closed the door behind him and pulled off his sunglasses. He looked at the girls, then back at Mark. "What's going on?"

Both Stacey and Melissa shot warning looks at Chad.

He put up his palms. "Sorry I asked." He backed up, and was opening his locker when the lobby door flew open, followed by a loud squeal.

Desiree ran to pull open the office door. Chad bent his knees and braced himself to catch her. She jumped onto Chad, wrapping her golden legs around his waist. Their mouths opened as if on hinges before they kissed. This public display of affection was over the top, even for them.

Seemingly uninterested in being a spectator, Mark backed his chair up and turned away. He covered his face with his hat as if taking a nap.

Melissa's irritated pout became more pronounced. She dropped her burrito in her bag, then crossed her arms while staring the pair down.

The clock clicked to 12:08. *Longest shift ever.*

"I missed you so much, baby!" Desiree said between slobbery kisses. "I wish my parents would've let you come with us to the river."

"Me too." Chad gripped under her butt. "Worst Fourth of July ever."

Desiree was at the movies Wednesday night. At most she was gone—what--two days? Seriously?

The room felt claustrophobic and a new wave of exhaustion hit Stacey. She grabbed her Carl's Jr. sack and stood.

"Thanks for lunch, Mark. Seems like your afternoon crew is here. Can I head out?"

Mark gave a thumbs up without uncovering his head or turning around. Stacey reached into her locker to grab her keys, then slid along the wall to ease past the couple.

Before leaving, she glanced at the schedule posted on the wall. Jessie, Melissa, and Desiree were supposed to work night swim. *Awesome. Melissa gets Jessie all to herself tonight.*

After she got home, Stacey checked the machine. No messages. She fell into her bed.

It was late afternoon when she rubbed the sleep out of her eyes.

After a long, hot shower, she found a note on the kitchen counter that said her mom was going to Aunt Susie's. "Your room and bathroom are disgusting, and your car is covered in dust. You need to clean them this weekend." In the bottom corner, a sad face was drawn with an arrow pointed to the ripped Northern Lights painting, still sitting where Stacey left it that morning. Stacey dropped both halves along with the note in the trash.

She made a bag of microwave popcorn and put an old recorded tape of *The Princess Bride* in the VCR. She sat on the corduroy couch braiding her damp hair, Murphy's head in her lap. Stacey squinted when Cary Elwes appeared onscreen; he looked a lot like Jessie. She'd fantasized herself as Buttercup with her own farm boy romance since she first saw the movie in sixth grade.

"Hopefully Jessie is in his Dread Pirate Roberts phase, Murph." She offered Murphy a few pieces of popcorn. "What are the chances it'll turn out this was all an act, and Jessie will whisk me away into the sunset?"

Murphy licked the salt off her palm, then sat up, expecting more.

"Okay, okay…" She gave her dog the last handful, then set the bowl in the middle of the coffee table.

As the light outside faded, Stacey considered calling Gabe. *He definitely hates me by now.* He just wanted to go to Tower Records. To see *Cable Guy.* But she blew him off. *He's better off without me.*

"Good thing I have you to hang out with on a Saturday night." She rubbed Murphy's slobber off on the couch cushion.

When the movie ended, Stacey turned off the TV and stared at the blank screen. She still hadn't heard from Jessie. She thought back over her conversation with Melissa. Jessie was working with Melissa at the pool until nine.

"Maybe I shouldn't wait for him to call me," she told Murphy.

In a sleeveless flannel and cutoffs, her braid hanging over her shoulder, Stacey pulled into a dark corner of the parking lot of The Plunge at 8:55.

She sat in her car with the lights off, watching through the chain link fence. The pool lights were still on, and the cover hadn't been pulled over the water yet. Desiree, Chad, Tiffany, and Mark were all in their swimsuits at the deep end. Mark flipped off the diving board. As tall a guy as he was, big gut and all, Stacey was impressed by how well he landed it.

Melissa's small red Mercedes convertible was still in the lot, but she and Jessie weren't on the deck.

When it was clear no one else was coming out of the lobby door, Stacey approached the lobby entrance, staying hidden in the shadows.

The lights in the guard shack and lobby were off. Metallica was blaring on the outside speakers loud enough to cover the squeak of the hinge as she pulled open the door. Stacey tiptoed across the lobby. She was about to pull open the door to the office when she heard voices in the girls' restroom.

No light showed under the door. Stacey inched up to it, listening. The voices echoed, but were muffled by the music. They were definitely male and female, and Stacey recognized the distinct shrillness of the voice that she'd grown to loathe. Melissa. Jessie had to be with her. But Stacey couldn't make out what they were saying. She eased the door open, careful not to let it make a sound, and stood behind the partition.

"What's going on with you and her?" Melissa asked.

"Nothing," Jessie replied.

"It doesn't seem like nothing," she hissed. "Are you *with* her now?"

"No. Why would I be *with* her? I told you: I don't want a girlfriend."

Confident they had no idea anyone else had entered, Stacey peeked around the privacy wall. Beneath a small frosted window in the corner of the cavernous shower stall, a street lamp outside cast an orange glow over them. Jessie was leaning casually against the wall of mint-colored subway tiles, shirtless in his red boardshorts, and Melissa was facing him, her back to Stacey, in a pair of white cotton shorts and her red two piece.

"You were with Stacey last night, weren't you?" she asked.

Jessie shrugged.

Melissa hesitated. "What did you…do?"

"What difference does it make?"

"It matters to me," Melissa sniffed.

"Why?" He leaned forward, and put his hand on Melissa's waist. "You're not mad anymore?" He pulled her body to him. "Do you want to pick up where we left off?"

Melissa locked eyes with him. Stacey swallowed hard. She could feel again what it was like to be wanted by Jessie. To *want* to be wanted by him.

Melissa tilted her chin and let him kiss her. His right hand slid down her waist and reached under the bottom edge of her shorts. His other hand slid up her ribs to her breast.

Stacey's heart was pounding. Her eyes welled.

Jessie turned Melissa to lean her up against the wall. Stacey turned away. The noises they were making were all too familiar. She didn't want to see what was coming next.

Stacey snuck back out the door. In the Silver Bullet, she kept her headlights off, hoping the rest of the crew hadn't noticed her pulling out of the parking lot.

A block away, she pulled into a 7-11 that was notorious for not checking IDs. She bought a large Mr. Pibb, a lighter, and a pack of Marlboro Reds. She'd snuck one of her dad's cigarettes the summer before with Gabe, and could still remember the foggy feeling she got in her head. Maybe that fog would replace the pain in her chest and blur away the image of Jessie with Melissa. Back in her car, she put in her Eagles Unplugged album and lit a cigarette before pulling out of the parking lot.

For the next hour and a half, she drove with the windows down, lighting one cigarette after another. As "The Girl from Yesterday" evolved into "Life in the Fast Lane" on the stereo, Stacey reminded herself that in a year she'd be leaving for college. Mesa Valley would be a distant memory.

Stacey threw her *Heart Shaped World* CD out the window and into a ditch alongside the road. She was finished fantasizing about love. And she was done with Jessie Thomas.

Chapter Sixteen

Stacey woke feeling nauseous. Her mouth was pasty and sour from the Marlboro Reds she'd hidden in the back of her glove compartment. She had Sunday off and was grateful to have no plans.

She lay in bed, knowing she should call Gabe and finally see the movie she'd promised to see weeks before. But she was afraid she would end up telling him about Jessie. She didn't want to lie, but she wasn't ready for him to know the truth.

Instead, her day off was going to be spent eliminating every naively romantic aspect of her life.

"Time to clean up and grow up, Murph." Stacey put her fingers on her throat, her raspy voice surprising them both.

Passing through the living room, she hit eject on the VCR and tucked *The Princess Bride* under her arm. In the kitchen, she filled a forty-four ounce Del Taco cup with Apple Jacks and milk, and poured a glass of orange juice. Grabbing a giant garbage bag, she took everything to her bedroom, called Murphy inside, and closed the door. She hung the garbage bag off the back of her desk chair and dropped the VHS inside.

She changed out the five discs in her CD player to Ace of Base, The Bangles, The Indigo Girls, Hole, and Sinéad O'Connor, then hit shuffle play. She slurped her cereal while surveying the room.

Murphy sat at her feet, eyes following the spoon from the cup to Stacey's mouth and back again.

Stacey ripped the Eternity ad—with its couple rolling in the sand—off the wall, crumpled it into a ball, and tossed it into the garbage bag. *Not real.* She did the same with the *Teen Vogue* and *Tiger Beat* pages she'd taped up over the past year, of floppy-haired River Phoenix and Leonardo DiCaprio, because they looked so much like Jessie. The magazine cutouts of Matthew Fox, Brendan Frasier, and Chris O'Donnell, who each resembled Gabe in different ways, also got torn and tossed.

She removed the clothes she'd kicked under the bed from her date with Jessie, shoving the whole pile into the trash bag. *Never wearing those again.* She rummaged through her drawers, pulling out knee and thigh high socks, plaid skirts, and every tank top with lace trim. *Bye bye baby doll clothes.* She dumped it all into the trash bag along with her Mary Jane platform shoes and most of her stuffed animals.

She went through her entire closet, tossing in every floral and lacy blouse and dress. She lined up her jeans, plain tees, and flannels in color-order from dark to light.

She cleared her academic awards and debate trophies from her dresser, and deposited them inside a shoebox at the top of her closet. She maneuvered the dresser to the opposite wall, and positioned the desk in the dresser's old spot. After changing her sheets, she flipped her sunflower comforter to the solid light blue side.

Stacey looked around. Everything was purged and nudged and rearranged. The space felt clean, smart, and full of possibilities. A blank canvas. And she knew exactly what she needed to create.

In the entryway closet, she dug past the ThighMaster, ski poles, and her self-portrait. As she'd hoped, she found her old hula hoop along with a large ball of oatmeal colored yarn. Three years before, her mom had said the yarn would become a beautiful blanket, but never even completed a scarf. Another abandoned hobby.

From the back of the kitchen junk drawer, she grabbed a box of thumbtacks, a bottle of Elmer's glue, and scissors. She headed back to her bedroom.

Murphy watched from the bed as Stacey dug through the trash bag, pulling out the discarded jeans and every lace-trimmed piece of clothing she had tossed. She started cutting fabric into long, thin strips.

She applied her geometry skills and created a three-foot-diameter denim-framed yarn-web on her wall. A giant dream catcher. Along the bottom half, she hung a dozen loose pieces of creamy-white fabric and lace embellished with concert tickets, college stickers, and movie stubs, cut and manipulated together to look like feathers.

Dragging the garbage bag and scissors to her bathroom, she cleared off her counter and threw away every pale pink and icy blue shade of makeup she owned. She Windexed the mirror and 409'd the counter and sink, then, feeling proud and accomplished, she looked at herself.

There was one last thing that needed to go.

Stacey felt different, but her reflection showed the exact same person, the girl who couldn't tell Jessie no. Her long, straight hair hung heavy and straw-like around her face, sun-bleached, with a mossy, chlorine-green hue at the bottom.

She picked up the scissors, aligned them with her jaw, and began to cut. Each snip gave her a little jolt of excitement as she turned her face to the side and cut toward the nape of her neck. The fine strands fluttered to the floor around her bare feet.

"What the fu–," Stacey's mother shrieked through the open door. Her hand slapped over her mouth.

Startled, Stacey's hand slipped. She side-eyed her mother's reflection as she re-gripped the last lock of hair, and realigned her scissors. "I decided to cut my hair." Snip. Stacey dropped the clump of hair to the floor.

"Are you kidding me? I thought you outgrew cutting your own hair in preschool!"

"It's *my* hair. It'll grow back."

"I mean... yeah... I guess... but Stacey, what the hell is going on with you? You've been in your room all day. You almost never spend time with Gabe anymore. Now this?"

Stacey wrinkled her chin and elongated her neck, turning her face from side to side. "I needed a change. Looks cute, right?"

Her mom rolled her eyes. "I need a glass of wine." She started toward the kitchen.

"Wait! First, can you make sure it's straight in back?" She offered the scissors to her mom.

Stacey's mom looked down at the hair all over the floor and the dull shears Stacey held out for her. "Not here," she sighed. "Meet me in the van in five minutes. I have the salon keys. We'll do this the right way."

By Monday morning, Stacey was ready to face Jessie and Melissa. She was SO over Jessie, and determined not to let whatever their relationship was bother her. There were six weeks of summer to get through before Melissa would leave for ASU. Jessie had said he would do whatever the hell "involves a half-pipe and a guitar." Stacey would begin senior year and start applying to colleges. New Stacey wasn't about to spend any time pouting and miserable about them.

After pulling into her shaded spot in The Plunge parking lot at 7:55, Stacey adjusted the rearview mirror to look at herself. She ran her fingers through her choppy pixie cut, sweeping her long bangs across her forehead so they hung onto her right cheek. Her eyes were rimmed with thick, black waterproof mascara and her eyebrows were perfectly plucked into thin high arches. She applied another coat of dark lip gloss, then fluffed her hair up in the back, and grabbed her case of CDs.

Coach Bob was flipping the lights on. When he saw Stacey he did his signature "wow" whistle, the same one he offered when reading impressive sports highlights in the newspaper. "New 'do?"

Stacey smirked and nodded. "Mind if I put on music?" She held up her *Tragic Kingdom* CD.

"Go for it." Bob gave a thumbs up. "You're the early bird today. What's your first pick?"

"Clean the deck?"

"It's all yours. Mark said you had a rough time with the drain in the bathroom Saturday."

Stacey scrunched her nose. "Yeah, thankfully he helped clear it. That was really gross."

"And you had your first save?"

She shrugged.

"Good job, Chapman." He put his hand up for a high five. "I guess we'll have to keep you around."

Stacey tapped her palm against Bob's, then pushed play on the stereo. She picked up the bucket and trash-grabber and followed him outside. Bob went to the equipment room. No Doubt's "Excuse Me Mr." put a pep in Stacey's step as she headed for the bleachers.

The guard shack door banged open. Jessie carried anti-bacterial powder into the boys' restroom. His face was stern and his head was pulled back like he was annoyed. Melissa came out of the guard shack, equally irritated as she yanked the hose into the girls' bathroom.

Stacey made her way around the deck, taking her time to collect every loose gum wrapper and empty pixie straw, then hosed it off while doing her best to ignore them both.

An hour later, humming along to "Happy Now," Stacey added goggles and a toddler-sized T-shirt to the lost and found box in front of the guard shack.

Jessie and Melissa stomped out of their bathrooms to the left and right, coming straight at her. Stacey backed against the window, out of their way. The heavy industrial doors slammed behind them in unison. Jessie reached for the hose in Melissa's hand. She dropped it at his feet. The trigger hit the ground and squirted water on his shirt.

"Frigid bitch," Jessie muttered.

"Dumb prick." Melissa put her hands on her hips and swung her long, sleek hair over her shoulder.

"What's up, Stace?" Jessie asked, picking up the hose and flashing his smile at her. "I like your haircut. You look so...*different* since Friday. It's kinda hot."

Stacey crossed her arms, glaring at him.

"You, too? What the... Did Melissa say something to you?"

"What makes you think I said anything?" Melissa asked. "Stacey's smart enough to know you're a hit-it-and-quit-it dickhead without my help."

Stacey leaned her head back and shook her head.

"Stacey, it's not like that!" Jessie touched her elbow.

Stacey pulled her arm away. "Don't touch me. Don't ever touch me again."

"What the fuck?" He threw up his hands. "You're both nuts."

Bob stepped out from the chemical room on the far side of the pool. Pointing down into the deep end, he shouted across the water. "One of you needs to clean this drain ASAP. The other two, get up in the towers. We open in three minutes." He turned back to the loud pumps and valves behind him.

"I've got the drain," Melissa said. "Jessie's not good with anything too deep."

"Shut up, Melissa." Jessie stormed toward the deep-end tower.

Melissa walked away, crossing one foot in front of another as if she were on a catwalk. She lifted her right middle finger over her shoulder and sang along with Gwen Stefani's high-pitched chorus.

"All by yourself."

Stacey smirked at Melissa's timing. She grabbed her whistle and megaphone, then climbed into the shallow-end lifeguard tower.

Once Jessie was up in the deep-end chair, Melissa walked to the edge of the board and whistled. "Hey dickhead!" She executed a perfect jack-knife dive.

After dropping the mess from the drain on the side of the pool, Melissa came out of the water slow and sexy like Nicolette Scorsese in *Christmas Vacation.*

"I wouldn't want you to ever forget what you'll be missing," she hollered at him.

Melissa reached her hands back to squeeze out her hair. Her wet suit clung to her breasts as she pushed out her chest, into his direct line of sight. She turned her back to him and bent at the waist, picking up the garbage slowly, her legs long and taut.

"Cock tease," Jessie said into the megaphone. He twisted in his chair until he faced away from Melissa.

Melissa dropped the pile in the trash, then climbed the ladder to Stacey's tower. She stood on the third rung, her mouth close to Stacey's ear and whispered loudly, "Look, we may not be friends, and you don't have to tell me anything. But I want you to know I'm done with Jessie's bullshit. You should be, too."

"You didn't seem done with it Saturday night," Stacey said through gritted teeth. She focused on the first few swimmers set down their belongings on the bleachers.

"Were you here?"

Stacey pursed her lips and nodded.

Melissa sat on the platform facing Stacey. "Well, I don't know what you think you saw, but nothing happened. We were talking, then kind of kissing, and suddenly Jessie dropped his boardshorts in the girls' showers. I was like, 'EW!'" She put her hands up as if repulsed. "Just because Chad and Desiree have sex in the guard shack, the pool–"

Stacey put her palm up between them and closed her eyes. "WAY too much information."

"Anyway, Jessie wasn't taking no for an answer. He wouldn't go to my house to watch a movie because my parents were home. He told me to drive us someplace 'romantic' he knew of where 'we could watch the stars.'" Melissa used air quotes, and rolled her eyes, exhaling. "Such bullshit!"

Stacey raised her eyebrows and nodded. All of this sounded familiar, but she wouldn't give Melissa the satisfaction of admitting it aloud.

"He refuses to have an actual girlfriend. Only wants to hook up and says whatever he has to to get laid."

Stacey's eyes swept across the pool to Jessie, who was watching them.

Melissa followed her gaze. She turned on the platform, scanning Jessie with contempt. "I'm not interested in being any guy's slot machine, especially some poser like Jessie."

Melissa's last sentence hit Stacey with a thud. A slot machine was exactly what she felt like: Jessie's three minutes of fun, then cast aside.

"We need to give everyone a heads up," Melissa said, turning back to Stacey, her chin up. "No decent girl should give him the time of day." Melissa climbed down and went inside the guard shack.

Stacey didn't trust Melissa, but vindication washed over her. She wasn't the only girl who had fallen prey to Jessie's charms. She looked across the pool at him. Suddenly, he wasn't attractive anymore. Not at all.

Everything about Jessie Thomas felt fake. His tattoo and WWJD bracelets were props. The guitar, too. Everything about him was designed to get people to think he was something he wasn't. Even the things he shared about his family felt like they could have been a scam to get Stacey to see him as a victim, instead of what he really was: an insincere, uncaring, selfish prick. OR, as Melissa put it, a "hit-it-and-quit-it dickhead."

Maybe Melissa was right: they should spread the word about him.

"Why should Jessie have all the power?" Stacey muttered to herself. "Who's to say I wasn't the one who 'hit it and quit it?'"

Anyone who ever asked Stacey about Jessie Thomas would hear how very 'unsatisfying' their date was. How he wasn't worth the gamble for *thirty-seconds* of lousy manhandling.

Stacey smiled to herself. Her first real smile in several days. Then she looked across the pool at Jessie and he caught her gaze. She gently shook her head, grinning coyly, and his eyebrows knit together.

Jessie would understand soon enough.

Chapter Seventeen

After work, Stacey stopped by Gabe's house. He deserved an explanation and an apology, in person. They were way past the point of a phone call. She bought an Abba-Zaba and a Mountain Dew, his favorites, and drove by his house on her way home, windows down for the feeble breeze. A block away, she could hear the sound of him playing the drums from his open garage.

Stacey held her peace offering up as she approached Gabe's driveway. He was shirtless and sweating, hitting his drumsticks hard on the kit in a fast, complicated beat. He glanced up, but quickly looked back at his snare drum. Jaw clenched, Gabe struck the drums harder.

Stacey set the snacks on top of Gabe's dad's rusted yellow Malibu and leaned against the door. The car took up half the garage, its hood open and a box of tools resting on the engine.

When the song ended, Gabe set down his drumsticks and wiped his face and chest with a towel without looking up. He turned toward the door to the house, hesitating before finally standing and pulling on his shirt. Still avoiding eye contact, he made his way over to the Malibu, propping himself against the tire-well, his arms crossed.

Stacey swallowed the lump in her throat. "I'm really sorry. I should have called you back."

Gabe nodded, staring at the floor.

"Did you still go to Tower Records on Friday?"

He bit his bottom lip and nodded again.

Stacey moved closer. "I've been a really crappy friend. I'm so sorry, Gabe. How can I make things right?"

"Yeah...you have." Gabe agreed coolly. "Those for me?"

Stacey grabbed the soda and taffy and held them out to him.

"Thanks." Gabe took both treats, then stretched his arms wide, folding Stacey into a bear hug, his long arms fully encircling her shoulders.

She closed her eyes and pressed her cheek against Gabe's collar bone, inhaling the familiar clean scent of Tide laundry soap with a hint of his sweat. When he rested his chin atop her head, Stacey's confident facade began to crumble. *Why did I ever choose Jessie over this?*

Gabe let go and pushed Stacey away to arm's length. He cocked his head and wrinkled his brow. "What inspired this?"

"I wanted to hang out." She shrugged. "You busy?"

Gabe rolled his eyes and the dimple appeared in his left cheek. "I mean the haircut, dumbass." He shook his head.

"I deserve that." Stacey lifted her chin. "Like it?"

"Sure," Gabe replied, taking it in from all the angles. "It's different. Kind of *Mad Love.*"

"I'm cool with that."

"Wanna go up to my room?"

Stacey nodded, then followed Gabe into the kitchen. She was struck with a waft of sauteed onions and browning beef.

Gabe's mom was cooking dinner. "Hey, Stacey! Where've you been?" She had the same dimple in her left cheek as Gabe had. Her brown curly hair was cut short and teased, framing her pink, round face in a chestnut halo.

"Hi, Mrs. Saunders." Stacey stopped beside the counter and folded her hands over the white tiles. "Just…working. Too much, I guess."

"Me too," she said, smiling. "You stayin' for dinner, hun?"

"I don't think so. My mom is expecting me at home. But thanks."

"You're always welcome. Your mom, too. Tell her I said hello."

"Thanks. I will."

Stacey caught up to Gabe on the stairs, and they turned the corner on the landing to go into his bedroom.

Gabe's room was always tidy. Catching him off guard seemed impossible. His twin bed was made so the plaid bedspread lines were straight and aligned with the corners. There were never dirty clothes on the floor. His closet door was closed, and other than a few CD cases set on his desk, nothing was out of place. Stacey hoped she could keep her room that tidy now that she'd dumped so much clutter.

Gabe left the door ajar and set the Abba-Zaba in the drawer of his desk. He twisted the cap off the soda, taking a large swig before putting the lid back on. Stacey sat on his bed, leaving her Birkenstocks on the floor. She shimmied back to lean against the wall.

"What do you want to listen to?" Gabe asked.

"What'd you get Friday?"

"The new Warped Tour album."

"Put that on. Can I see the jacket?"

Gabe pressed play on the stereo. He handed her the jewel case and sat beside her on the bed.

Stacey danced her bare feet along to "Anxiety." "Cool cover-art," she said, outlining the large guitar and the skateboard with her finger. They looked like they were drawn in permanent ink, then water-colored.

"You'll like the Reel Big Fish and Sublime songs, too," he said.

After a few minutes of listening to music, Gabe nudged Stacey with his elbow. "So… when you gonna tell me what's really been going on?"

"What do you mean?" Stacey studied the skater doing an ollie in the bottom right corner.

"Well, first: why'd you ignore my calls?"

Stacey set the jewel case aside, pulled her legs up and crossed them under her. She tucked the short strands of hair behind her ears. "I started spending more time with everyone at the pool, like we talked about."

Gabe nodded. "And…"

"And we all decided to go see *Independence Day*…when it came out…" Stacey looked into his green eyes. "…on Wednesday."

"So, you told me you were busy Friday night for no reason?"

"No. I was afraid to tell you the truth. That I had a date. With Jessie."

"A date?" Gabe scoffed. "That guy doesn't take girls on 'dates.'"

Stacey looked down at the bedspread and picked at a thread. "I know that, now."

"So, what did you do on your date, then?"

Stacey tangled her fingers together in her lap. "He said we were going to watch a meteor shower."

"In your car?" Gabe asked dryly.

Stacey nodded without looking up.

Gabe tilted his head back and searched the ceiling for a minute. Then he leaned toward her. She met his gaze. Gabe's face seemed pained as he clarified. "So... you... and Jessie... You guys had..."

Stacey nodded before the word could come out of his mouth.

"And that was...your first time...right?"

She bit her lip, nodded again.

"Are you...two...together...now?"

Stacey's eyes welled up. Staring blankly out the window, she shook her head.

Gabe ran his hands through his hair and exhaled loudly. "I'm really sorry, Stace. He's a jerk. It shouldn't have been like that."

One silent tear fell down Stacey's cheek. She nodded again and wiped it away. "I'm afraid..." she said quietly, "he didn't use...protection."

Without hesitating, Gabe leaned forward and put his arms around Stacey. "No, no, no, no, no. Goddamnit!" He shook his head as he hugged her. "Fucking douchebag."

Stacey let more tears stream down her cheeks. Gabe knowing somehow helped her feel less alone.

"Have you talked to your mom?"

Stacey pulled away. "I can't! She'd be so pissed."

"Maybe. But she'd understand."

"No. I'm supposed to be smarter than this. Cause no problems. Take care of myself."

Gabe exhaled. "She doesn't expect you to be perfect."

Stacey avoided his gaze. She wiped her cheeks and willed her strong new attitude to return.

"Your mom loves you, Stace. She'd do anything for you."

She knew Gabe was right, but suddenly wanted to end the conversation. She had no intention of ever telling her mom anything.

Stacey bit her lip, nodded, and turned away. It was easier to lie without looking him in the eye. "I'll think about it." She stood and slipped her feet back into her Birkenstocks. "I should go. Thanks for–"

Her unspoken words hung in the air as she walked out of Gabe's bedroom.

"How was your day at the pool?" Stacey's mom asked, staring at her from across the table between bites. Since dating Greg, her mom had made more of an effort to cook real meals and to eat at the table.

"Fine." Stacey leaned over her plate and bit into the soft tortilla, the fajita juices dripping into a puddle.

"Did you say you stopped by Gabe's?"

"Um hmm…" Stacey nodded and chewed, her eyes down.

"How is he? Everything good between you two?"

Stacey chewed the last bite of her tortilla, nodding, and wiped her mouth. "I guess."

Her mom picked at her rice with her fork.

The ticking clock intensified the silence.

Stacey leaned back in her chair and sipped her water. "How was work?"

"Good. Same old blue-hairs coming in for their same wash-and-sets and perms." She took a sip of wine. "It pays the bills. Lord knows I have plenty of those."

"I have the money to give you for the swimsuits. Sorry I didn't pay you back sooner."

"Thanks. That will help." Her mom smiled and their eyes met briefly, then she stabbed several strips of bell peppers and shoved them in her mouth.

Murphy shifted and groaned on the ground by their feet.

"I like the thing you put up on your wall. It's really cool. It's a dream catcher, right?"

Stacey cringed. "Thanks."

"Are you going back to those art classes?"

Stacey shrugged.

"You should. You're really talented."

"No one else was going. She probably isn't doing it anymore."
Especially since it ended so awkwardly last time.

"You never know unless you show up, right?" her mom said.

Stacey looked at the clock. It was after seven. Ms. Moreno might still be there for a while. If she showed up at all anymore. Stacey turned back to her plate, pushing a shriveled tomato through the puddle of sauce with her fork.

Looking over the rim of her glass, her mom said, "I can clean up dinner. You should go."

"I guess I could drive by. See if she's there." Stacey stood and picked up her plate and silverware. "Need anything while I'm out?"

"Nope." Her mom's expression softened. She looked hopeful.

Stacey was surprised to find the high school abuzz with activity.

The lower parking lot had dozens of cars parked near the football field and gym. The golden glow of the gym's lights poured out from the open double-doors, where large fans exhausted the hot air. The floodlights around the track highlighted about seventy boys in full pads and practice jerseys, running drills in small groups around the field.

Stacey drove up to the staff lot behind the art building. Unlike around the athletics department, the rest of the school still felt abandoned. Once again Ms. Moreno's car was the only one in the lot, and hers was the only classroom with lights on.

Stacey stepped around a large fan in the doorway, only to see several more fans blowing around the room, creating a hum that muffled Stacey's footsteps and the buzz of the fluorescent lights.

Paint palettes and paper were set up in the center of the room with mason jars of water. At another large table in the corner, Ms. Moreno's work surface was covered with drawings and paintings of eyes in varying sizes and shapes. Some were pairs, some were singular staring eyes. They all looked up at the art teacher who was intensely focused on the full-page eye she was sketching in pencil on the pad in front of her. Ms. Moreno held her face close to the paper, a deep line between her brows, and a white eraser gripped in her left hand.

Stacey stood beside the watercolor table, avoiding the creepiness of that many eyes looking up without faces. She cleared her throat noisily to be heard above the fans.

Ms. Moreno jerked her head up, and looked over, surprised and confused. When she realized it was Stacey, her face relaxed. "Hi." She set her pencil and eraser down, and stood. "It's good to see you. I wasn't sure if you were coming back."

"Yeah, I've been…a lot was going on. Work. Fourth of July."

"I get it. I'm glad you're here. Your new haircut looks cute."

Stacey rubbed the nape of her neck. "What are you working on?"

"Oh, this is for a class I'm taking. Kinda weird to see so many eyes in one place, right?"

Stacey nodded, her eyebrows high, but remained glued to her spot.

"Don't worry," Ms. Moreno chuckled, crossing the room. "It's not the Art Escape project for tonight. I had something else in mind. Hopefully you'll like it, since you're around the water so much."

"Too much."

"Well, I promise we won't be painting the community pool." Ms. Moreno pulled out the metal stool beside Stacey and sat down. She set pencils, rulers, and paper on the butcher block in front of her and Stacey.

Stacey sat on the stool beside her and grabbed the pencil. "I thought we were doing watercolor."

"We are. But an important part of watercolor is planning out your project, because you can't always paint over something to redo it the way you can with acrylic or oil paints."

"But won't we see the lines?"

"We'll draw really lightly, and we'll only put the lines we absolutely need, that will be covered with dark paint, or where there's a natural line, like a horizon, where two colors will meet and it will be less noticeable. Done well, the pencil can add to the overall composition or completely disappear."

"Okay....What are we drawing?"

"This." Ms. Moreno flipped over an 8x10 photo that had been lying face down.

Stacey groaned. "The National Monument?"

"It's a simple exercise in perspective drawing AND...drum roll, please." Ms. Moreno tapped her hands rhythmically on the table. "Reflections on water."

Stacey pursed her lips and nodded slowly.

"I can see you aren't impressed, but...give it a chance. I took this photo when I chaperoned the Washington D.C. trip last spring. I love how clearly visible the monument and clouds are on the reflecting pool. And it's easy to draw and recreate it with pencil and a ruler."

Stacey tapped her eraser on the table, irritated. "Lucky you." There was a sarcastic lilt to her voice. "This way I get to 'experience' it, too, right? Like the northern lights? I can stay in Mesa Valley forever and just pretend I went places?"

Ms. Moreno's mouth opened, then snapped shut. She eyed Stacey carefully for a moment.

"I'm sorry, Stacey." Ms. Moreno put her pencil down and rotated toward Stacey on her stool. "I didn't mean to... I couldn't have gone on a trip like that growing up, either. It doesn't matter what we paint." She flipped the 8x10 face down on the table. "We don't even have to do this project. Or paint. We can just talk."

Stacey could feel Ms. Moreno's eyes on her, but she refused to look up from the white page on the table. "It's fine. Let's paint it. You're here. I'm here." She picked up the ruler and set it on her page.

Ms. Moreno turned back to the project, but left her hands in her lap.

Stacey huffed, then flipped the photograph back over. Using the ruler, she drew a large rectangle for the reflecting pool on the bottom half of her page, then a taller, skinnier rectangle above it.

Ms. Moreno sat silently, watching Stacey.

Frustrated, Stacey erased her monument, making the top more pointed. When it still didn't look right, she dropped her pencil. "Are you going to help me, or what?"

"It seemed like you wanted to do it by yourself."

"If I wanted to figure it out on my own I wouldn't be here. You said it would be simple. This is too hard."

"It is simple, once you identify your vanishing point."

"What? What's a 'vanishing point'?"

"In this case, the vanishing point is at the far end of the pool, here," Ms. Moreno pointed at the spot near the center of the photograph. "The monument travels upward from there, and the reflecting pool comes from that point toward the viewer. That's why it looks wider at this end, even though you know it's a rectangle in your mind."

Stacey stopped listening. She stared at the water in the image, but saw the little boy she had pulled from the deep end two days before.

"Is that what it's called—the vanishing point—when you can't see what's under the surface because the light is too bright?"

"No. I think that's…refraction?" Ms. Moreno looked up at the ceiling. "It has to do with the angle of the light source. It's more of a physics thing, but I think that's why these reflective images are better in the morning and at night than the middle of the day. The angle of the sun in the sky makes the reflection clearer. Why?"

"The bright sunlight makes it hard to see, sometimes. In the deep-end of the pool."

Ms. Moreno turned on her stool again. "Did something happen?"

"It's no big deal." Stacey shrugged. "A little boy sank to the bottom when he went off the diving board. The sunlight was so bright on the top of the water that it took me a second to know for sure what I was looking at. I got to him in time, but…" Stacey sighed.

"That must have been really scary, Stacey. I'm sorry that happened." Ms. Moreno put her hand on Stacey's.

Stacey pulled away. "Like I said, not a big deal. He's fine."

"I understand." Ms. Moreno studied Stacey a few seconds longer, then lifted the photograph. "Another thing to understand about refraction is that it can affect how deep water appears. See how it looks like this water could be really deep because it looks so dark around the reflection of the white monument?"

Stacey nodded.

"It's actually only about eighteen inches deep on the sides and thirty inches deep in the middle. The way the light refracts makes it appear deeper."

Stacey thought about The Plunge at night, after they turned off the lights inside the pool. How the lights around the pool reflected on the surface of the water, but the pool itself looked like a black abyss.

"Do you want to give it another try?" Ms. Moreno asked, lifting up a blank piece of paper.

Stacey shook her head gently. "Not really." She nodded toward the drawings of eyes. "You're taking a whole class on how to draw eyes?"

Ms. Moreno grinned. "Well, no, but that's a major focus." She snorted. "Dumb joke, I know."

Stacey pinched between her eyes and forced a chuckle.

Ms. Moreno went on. "It's about communicating a whole story with a single picture, through important details."

"How can a single eye tell a whole story?"

"Think about it: we can tell a lot from a person's single eye." She walked over to the table where she'd been working.

When Stacey didn't follow her, Ms. Moreno gestured for Stacey to come across the room.

Once Stacey was by her side, Ms. Moreno continued. "We can tell if they're happy or exhausted. The wrinkles reveal if they're old, or we know they're really young because of how wide and bright the eyes are." She lifted up a pair of round blue eyes that were above the tops of chubby cheeks, with a few short lashes, and set it beside the image she had been working on. The single eye was surrounded by a web of fine lines, the dark lid heavy.

"So, yeah, that's a baby and that's someone who's old. But those are details about a person. You said an eye can tell a whole story."

"Yeah, the eye is the main character. The way they're looking out of it tells a lot about how they feel. Their perspective. The rest of the story is visible in what the eye is looking at, in the reflection of the light on the pupil." Ms. Moreno pointed to the reflection on her full-page eye. Stacey got closer. There was water gathered in the bottom of the eye, like the person was sad, but trying not to cry. In the reflection on the pupil there was a clear image of an old, large knuckled hand being held by a small child's hand.

"Wow! That's amazing."

"Thank you. I've been working on it the past couple weeks. Trying to get it right."

"Do you have a reference photo or something?" Stacey studied the details more closely.

Ms. Moreno shook her head. "Only memory."

Stacey set the pad down. "This is someone you know?"

"Was." She picked up the sketch. "My grandma. She raised me until I was seven. When she died."

"I'm so sorry." Stacey bit her lip.

"It's okay." Ms. Moreno sighed. "It was a long time ago. I want my project to be a tribute to her. How much she did for me."

"It's really beautiful. I'm sure she would have loved it."

Ms. Moreno set the sketch down and looked at the collection of eyes staring back. "Fun fact: the human eye is 98% water. That's why it reflects light so well. It's what gave me the idea for the other project."

"So our eyes really are pools?" Stacey picked up a pair of eyes that looked kind. Gentle. Tired. Like her mother's eyes. "And the reflection can show how deeply someone cares." She set it down again.

Ms. Moreno crossed her arms. "Maybe. It's also easy to be deceived, when someone refuses to look back."

Deceived. Stacey glanced away, pretending a sudden interest in the wall of windows. The night disappeared behind the reflection of the bright classroom.

"Or when everything about a person is too bright and shiny," she mumbled. "Then the darkness reveals the truth." Her voice was barely above a whisper.

"Stacey, is there something going on?" Ms. Moreno leaned against the table. "Anything you need to talk about?"

Stacey shook her head. She had a sudden urge to get far away.

"Cool project," Stacey said, crossing the room. "Creepy, but cool."

"Thanks. D'you want—?"

"I should go." Stacey grabbed her keys from where she'd left them on the butcher block.

"Okay…" Ms. Moreno's voice was thick with disappointment. "I'm glad you came. I'm always here, Stacey. Stay safe."

Stacey maneuvered around the buzzing fan in the doorway, into the dark parking lot. "What a waste," she mumbled to herself.

Backing out, Stacey avoided the gaze of her own reflection in the rearview mirror.

Chapter Eighteen

A week after the Fourth of July, Travis Nielson was throwing a major kegger.

There was at least one party each summer in Mesa Valley that everyone found their way to. This year, everyone was going to Travis Nielson's.

Travis was one of those rich kids who seemed to pass his classes with a smile. He was on the football team and it was training season. The rumor was his parents left on vacation without him. Travis got along with jocks and skaters alike, maybe because he always had weed on him. His house, in the exclusive Hawk Hill neighborhood, sat on five acres that backed up to the foothills, where a party could go on for days before drawing much attention.

"Come with us, Stacey," Desiree pleaded as they pulled the covers onto the pool Tuesday after Night Swim. "It'll be fun. Stay over! Girls' night!" Desiree's family also lived in Hawk Hill. Tiffany and Melissa were staying over, too, so no one would have to drive.

"What about me?" Chad asked, wrapping his arm around Desiree's waist. "Why can't I come?"

"Dude," Mark said. "Let go of her and take hold of that corner. I wanna go home."

"As if my parents would let you sleep over!" Desiree said. "It's not like I won't see you at the party."

"You sure Melissa's okay with me being there?" Stacey was still skeptical about whether Melissa could be trusted.

Mark chuckled. "Don't worry, Chapman. My guess is this won't be a night of Ouija boards and pillow fights."

"That's oddly specific." Stacey smirked at Mark. She pushed the empty covers cart back up against the wall.

"Why does everyone assume I don't know things?" He locked the chemical room door.

Desiree laughed. "I know that episode! You watch *90210*?"

"Don't judge me." Mark feigned insult, moving over to lock the equipment room.

"*Melrose Place* is better. More sex," Chad said.

"You are both idiots." Desiree turned back to Stacey. "Seriously, though, you should totally come. We're gonna get ready at my house. Eat pizza. Walk over together."

Staying at Desiree's would be easier than trying to sneak in at home after midnight. "Um…yeah. I guess so," Stacey said. Maybe this way her mom would never have to find out where she'd been.

"You're going to a sleepover? Tonight?" Her mom poured coffee into a mug before leaving for work Wednesday morning.

"Is that okay? At Desiree's house. She lives on Hillcrest."

"In Hawk Hill?" Her mom looked up, skeptical. "*How* do you know her?"

"She works at the pool. All the girl guards are staying over."

"So, she already graduated. You're…hanging out? Watching movies?" She eyed Stacey suspiciously.

"Is that a bad thing? Me hanging out with more girls?"

"No. Of course not. That's not what I…" She took a breath and started again. "I'm glad you've made more friends. Will Desiree's parents be home? What's their last name?"

"Yeah. I don't know why they wouldn't be." Stacey nodded. "Their last name is Fox."

"Fox…Desiree Fox… Doesn't ring a bell. Well, I…" Her mom looked at the clock. "Shoot, my first client is in fifteen minutes. I've gotta run." She grabbed her purse and keys, then hustled toward the front door. "Have fun," she yelled over her shoulder.

"K. See you tomorrow," Stacey said as the front door closed.

Stacey slurped Cap'n Crunch Berries while packing her overnight bag. She surveyed her closet, searching for a cute outfit for the party. Murphy jumped on the bed and rested her muzzle on the canvas duffle.

Pivoting to add her cropped KROQ tee to the bag, Stacey noticed Murphy's sad expression. Stacey stuck out her bottom lip. "Don't look at me like that, Murph. I'll be back tomorrow."

Murphy whined, wagging her tail, but held her spot on the duffle bag.

Stacey pulled the bag out from under Murphy and set it on the desk. She added boxers and a tank top to sleep in, a sandwich bag full of makeup, her toothbrush, and hairbrush. Before heading out the door, Stacey squished her pillow into the duffle.

She slipped into her flip-flops. "Be a good girl," Stacey said, as she put Murphy on the back porch with a milk bone and a bowl of water.

She threw the duffle bag into the passenger seat of the Silver Bullet and turned the key in the ignition. The radio blared and

Stacey rolled down the windows. She sang along with Stone Temple Pilots about not feeling like herself. *Maybe not me is a little more of what this summer needs.* Stacey released the emergency brake and backed down the driveway.

Coach Bob caught wind of the party. Afternoon swim ended, they pulled the cover over the pool, and were about to head out when Bob came in unannounced. Everyone was grabbing their keys from the lockers when he stopped them.

"I expect you all on time for your shifts tomorrow," he said. He went around the room pointing his finger in their faces and looking each guard in the eyes. "Ready for a long day," he said to Tiffany. "In the hot sun," he told Stacey. "With loud kids," he pointed in Chad's face. "Got it?" he asked Mark.

"We'll behave," Tiffany assured him, then winked conspiratorially at Stacey.

"Yeah," Stacey nodded. "We'll be playing board games and eating popcorn all night in our jammies. Right, Mark?"

Bob shook his head and rolled his eyes.

"Speak for yourself," Chad said. "I'm not opening tomorrow."

"No, but I still need you here—alive and awake—for night swim," Bob reminded him. "Stacey, you're supposed to be here at eight, along with Desiree and Jessie."

"I'll be here with bells on!" Stacey blinked repeatedly, pointing her fingers into the corners of her smile.

"Don't worry," Mark told him. "I'll keep my eye on 'em." He clapped Bob on the shoulder, then followed the other guards out the lobby door, holding it open for Bob.

"That's exactly what worries me," Bob said, turning off the lights. Once the doors were locked and Bob was heading toward the parking lot, he called out to the guards one last time. "Please don't do anything stupid."

Chad waved a shaka out the window of his Chevelle, then peeled out of his parking spot.

Stacey followed Tiffany to Desiree's house, and they parked in tandem behind Melissa's Mercedes. Stacey took her pack of cigarettes and lighter from the glove compartment and added them to her duffle bag before climbing out of the car. She looked up at the house on the hill and her mouth dropped open. Desiree's house was at least twice the size of Stacey's dad's house, ten times the size of her mom's. Stacey hesitated at the mailbox before climbing her way up the three hundred-foot driveway.

"Desiree lives here?" she asked Tiffany. "It looks like a Massachusetts private school!"

"Come on…" Tiffany chuckled, taking Stacey by the elbow. "Her parents are really nice. You'll love them."

The long driveway was shaded by huge oak and pine trees. More trees were scattered around the brick house, their trunks glowing with the light of the sun inching its way closer to the horizon behind them. White roses, and ivy climbed the three-story walls. Giant white columns flanked the front porch. Double-wide shiny black doors were guarded by a three-foot golden fox statue. His stare was menacing as Tiffany reached over his head to push the doorbell.

Desiree pulled open the large front door. "Yeah! You came!" She gave Tiffany a hug, then wrapped her arms around Stacey. "Come in."

Despite the shaded yard and heavy brick outside, the inside of the house was bright white with gold accents and the white marble floor was studded by small black mosaic tiles. Stacey was afraid her filthy shoes might scuff it. The large, oval foyer was surrounded by a winding staircase reminiscent of old Hollywood.

"Leave your shoes in that basket. Otherwise, Belvedere will eat them." Desiree pointed to a large basket on an antique armchair in the corner. "Or you can bring them up to my room. I never let him in there."

Tiffany and Stacey slipped off their sandals.

"Belvedere?" Stacey asked, dropping the shoes into the basket.

"Our dog. He's…" Desiree was cut off by a giant white labrador galloping into the room as if on cue.

"Woof." Belvedere's booming bark echoed across the tile. His tongue lolled out the side of his mouth.

Stacey bent down on one knee to greet him. Belvedere sniffed her, his drool spilling onto her leg as she scratched behind his ears. "You're such a sweet boy."

"Dad, call Belvedere!" Desiree yelled over her shoulder. "He's being all gross and slobbery."

There was a whistle from the far end of the house, and the dog gave Stacey one final lick before he trotted away.

"Come on. Melissa's up in my room"

Having to choose between playing with Belvedere and going upstairs to see Melissa, Stacey would have preferred to be slobbered on by the dog. But she followed Desiree and Tiffany up the white-carpeted stairs, eyeing a giant crystal chandelier that cast sparkles on the surrounding walls. *This place is fancier than a hotel.*

Desiree's room was at the end of the second-floor hallway.

"Look who came!" Desiree announced as they walked through the door.

"Hey," Melissa said without looking up. She was seated on a large pink velvet bench in front of the picture window, her legs stretched in front of her and a magazine propped on her knees. A rerun of the *Real World San Francisco* was muted on the TV, and Sheryl Crow was playing through oversized speakers.

Desiree's room was practically as big as Stacey's entire house. There was a walk-in closet overflowing with clothes and the vanity was covered with perfumes and compacts of blushes and shadows. The attached bathroom had marble floors and a clawfoot tub separate from the shower. *Why does one girl need all this?*

On a large rug at the foot of the bed sat a pile of magazines, ripped apart, cut up, and surrounded by snacks. Tiffany picked up a bag of Cheetos and an Allure magazine, then squished onto the bench by Melissa's feet.

Stacey looked around for her own place to sit. The desk chair was covered in discarded clothes. The bed was king-sized, expertly decorated with a pink, ruffly comforter and throw pillows, straight out of a fairytale, made for a real-life princess. She was afraid she would mess the bed up by sitting on it.

She sat cross-legged on the carpet, then picked up a bag of barbecue potato chips, munching on them while trying to make sense of the removed pages. Someone had used scissors to cut out certain parts of the people pictured, so a Cover Girl ad had Nikki Taylor's mouth removed, and a girl's body was cut from a Calvin Klein ad of a group in their underwear.

Covering the wall between the large TV and full-length mirror, pictures had been taped together and tacked up: Shannon Doherty's eyes and Cindy Crawford's lips and iconic mole met in the middle with an unidentifiable, elfin nose. A black-and-white image of a wispy girl's long legs and body paired with Soleil Moon Fry's head.

The collage reminded Stacey of Ms. Moreno's collection. There were at least a dozen pairs of perfectly appointed eyes plastered on

Desiree's wall. But it seemed like she had isolated all her ideal female features, then scrambled them together into various mismatched, Frankenstein-like characters.

"What are you wearing tonight, Tif?" Desiree called out from her closet.

"This." She shrugged. She'd changed out of her swimsuit at The Plunge, but put on the same cut-off shorts and loose Cal State tee she'd worn all day with a pair of chunky Airwalks. "It's gonna be dark. Everyone's drinking. No one will be paying attention."

"Ugh… yeah, I know!" Desiree came out in a lacy tank and cutoffs. She stood in front of her mirror and clipped her hair up, turning right and left. "But that doesn't really solve my problem."

Stacey leaned back against the bed and ate more chips, wondering what the problem was. *Desiree looks adorable in everything. Super sexy, actually.*

Melissa set down her magazine and joined Desiree at the mirror. Melissa had on a tight cropped tube top. Her miniscule Abercrombie shorts were cut very low on the waist and left nothing to the imagination. If it wasn't for the zipper and belt loops they might as well have been swimsuit bottoms. Her abs and thighs looked professionally sculpted.

"This one's cute, Dez," Melissa said. "But I still think the pink ribbed tank looked awesome on you."

"No way. My bra straps are too big," she said. "I'm tired of waiting for my surgery. Then I can finally go braless and wear tops from Wet Seal."

Stacey looked up. *Surgery?*

"Are you going to the same place Dawn went?" Tiffany asked, picking up a new *Cosmopolitan* magazine and sitting on the end of the bed, her feet dangling beside Stacey.

Dawn Chavez was a year older than they were, two years older than Stacey. She had always been beautiful, athletic, and popular. But when she was the returning Homecoming Queen in the parade the year before, she looked tiny, like she had lost a lot of weight. Stacey overheard guys in chemistry complaining that Dawn had "cut off her boobs."

"Yeah, in September. I don't move into the dorms until the end of the month."

Desiree is getting breast reduction surgery? But she's gorgeous!

"What'd Chad say?" Tiffany asked.

"Ever since that first fight at the beginning of summer, I don't want to talk to him about it. He thinks he can change my mind." She turned sideways and tried tucking in her tank, then untucking it. Pulling it up above her cleavage, then tugging it down again.

"You'll feel like a whole new person when you start college," Melissa said. "I've begged my parents for a nose job, but they keep telling me no way."

"Oh my god, Missy! You *so* don't need a nose job!" Desiree said, looking at Melissa's reflection. "I need my nose fixed way more than you. My mom is a Spanish goddess, but because my dad's Jewish I ended up short, pale, and everything about me is too big and round." She looked back at herself, slumping her shoulders. "I need to marry a plastic surgeon to afford everything I need fixed."

"I wish I had pale skin!" Melissa pulled her cheeks back. "No matter what sunscreen I wear, I toast like a coconut."

"Ugh. Shut up. You look like a Hawaiian Tropic bikini model."

Tiffany barely looked up while Stacey gawked at them. She never would have thought either Melissa or Desiree seriously wanted surgeries. *How can they not see how perfect they are?*

Melissa started applying white eyeliner while Desiree covered her shoulders with sparkle bronzing lotion. Then they each perfectly lined their lips into pouty bows. Tiffany stood next to them, twirling her soft blonde curls with her fingers until they bounced back into place. Melissa's long dark hair hung smooth and straight down her back and Desiree's shoulder length auburn waves floated over her collar bones.

Staring at them from behind, Stacey admired their petite bodies and perfectly primped make-up and hair. If she stood behind them, she'd be a head taller, and her shoulders and hips would be double the width of any of theirs. Their waists were small, and each girl's tiny shorts fit just right, showing off tan thighs without any jiggles or dimples.

Stacey grabbed her duffle bag and went into the bathroom, closing the door behind her. She looked at herself, wondering how she could possibly walk into Travis's party with that flawless trio and not look like a total ogre. And, if anyone asked her about Jessie, she needed to appear believable when she announced he didn't "measure up to her expectations."

Stacey dug through her bag for her mascara and eyeliner, thickly applying both to make her eyes moodier. More mysterious. Instead of the cropped KROQ shirt she had planned to wear, she grabbed the white tank she brought to sleep in, and pulled it over her black bra. It was see-through enough to be obviously intentional. With her Converse, cutoffs and pack of Marlboros in her back pocket, she might pass as edgy. Opening the cabinets, she found hairspray, mousse, and gel, and used all three to transform her choppy bob into a sexy mess.

Stacey came out of the bathroom and the girls stepped back from the mirror to take her in.

"Wow, Stace! You look…dangerous!" Tiffany said, her eyes wide. "In a good way."

"Wait, you need dark red lips!" Desiree said, digging through her makeup bag. She handed the tube to Stacey. "It's a burgundy lip stain, so it won't smear."

Melissa grinned at Stacey in the mirror and nodded. "We'll show Jessie we don't need his loser ass." She picked up the scissors from the floor. "Let me crop that for you."

"No thanks," Stacey said, looking at herself in the mirror. "Your abs are better for flaunting. Besides, I think I cut enough off this week already." She fluffed her hair.

Melissa held the scissors and crossed her arms, turning to watch Stacey apply the red lipstick in the mirror. "You *are* going to help me make Jessie miserable, right? So that every girl ignores him?"

"That's the plan," Stacey said. She rubbed her lips together then puckered them at her own reflection. "When does the fun begin?"

Chapter Nineteen

At eight, the girls walked through the open side gate of Travis Nielson's yard. Melissa led their group like they were headed into battle.

At least two hundred teenagers were gathered around the pool. Stacey recognized most from Mesa Valley High, but no one seemed to know who she was at first glance. The anonymity gave her confidence. She pulled her shoulders back, lifted her chin, and matched her stride to Melissa's.

Chad came running up. He grabbed Desiree around the waist and lifted her. She squealed before letting him take her by the hand to the garage to get a beer. Melissa took Desiree's other hand and followed after them.

"I'm gonna say hi to friends from track," Melissa announced over her shoulder. "I'll be right back. Don't go anywhere!"

Tiffany was stopping every few feet to talk to different recent grads, none of whom knew or cared who Stacey was. She felt like a shadow. At the far end of the pool, a group sat around a fire pit where the stereo and large speakers were set up.

The Mighty Mighty Bosstones' "Impression That I Get" came on. The trumpet bridge blared across the pool. There were only a few people who would play ska music at a party in Mesa Valley, instead of country or alternative rock. Stacey wandered over to see if Gabe or anyone else she knew was in the group by the fire.

In the glow of the flames, she recognized the lead singer of the Juvenile Delinquents, Martin. He wore a newsboy cap and a short-sleeved button-up black shirt with jeans. A few other guys around him were dressed similarly, in long Dickie's shorts held up by studded belts, and white undershirts under unbuttoned plaid shirts. One wore a black T-shirt with a skeleton drinking a martini, and he had a tall mohawk. They all wore long chains draped down their thighs, connected to their wallets. The group of boys were all seniors, and Stacey knew Martin would be friendly if she tried to talk to them.

Stacey waved to Martin as she approached. He nodded, and lifted his Solo cup in greeting. He stepped out of the circle and took a drag of his cigarette, put it out under his shoe, then tucked it into a pocket. He grinned and leaned his hip against the Adirondack chair he'd been sitting in.

Stacey could tell he was trying to figure out who she was. "Hey, Martin. Gabe and I went to your concert a few weeks ago." Recognition registered in his expression. The music was loud, so she raised her voice. "It was great! I can't believe you're playing such big venues now."

"Thanks! Stacey, hi. Wow, you look…different." Martin gave her a side hug. "I totally didn't recognize you. Yeah, the campus ska-fest was pretty cool, right?" He almost shouted. He motioned with his head to the other side of the speakers where they could talk.

Stacey followed him.

Once the music wasn't blaring in their ears, he went on. "I saw Gabe skanking around the pit at the show. That guy is kind of hard to miss. Where were you?"

Stacey blushed, remembering her failed outfit and hiding in the shade. "I was just...off to the side."

"Next time say hello! It calms my nerves up there to be able to focus on friendly faces."

"What? You never seem nervous on stage."

"I'm terrified all the way up until the music starts. Even then, between songs I'm afraid I might embarrass myself. Or the band. I'd never forgive myself if we lost out on a gig because I said something stupid."

"But...you're so good. Everyone loves the Juvenile Delinquents! No way could you mess that up."

"We have plenty of haters, too, like most bands. And nothing lasts forever. I really don't want to be THAT guy who screwed it up for everyone else."

Stacey nodded. She took the pack of cigarettes out of her back pocket and offered Martin one.

"Nah. I'm good. I really shouldn't have even had that one. Since when do you smoke?"

Stacey shrugged. She put a cigarette between her lips and lit it. "What're you drinking?"

"Soda." Martin took a drink from his cup and cocked his head to the side. "You've really changed. So, where's Gabe anyway?"

"I was looking for him. You haven't seen him?"

Martin shook his head. "Not yet."

Stacey took a drag and looked around the firepit. She didn't recognize anyone else from the band. "I hoped the Juvenile Delinquents might play tonight. Where's everyone else?"

"Jimmy and Josh are straight-edge. Not really their scene." He looked around. "Miles and Steve are around here...somewhere...."

Stacey nodded, remembering the first half-dozen times she'd seen the band play in church basements. Jimmy and Josh were also in Christian Club.

The guy in the circle with the mohawk called Martin's name.

Martin lifted his index finger in the wait-a-second signal. "Hey, I'll tell Gabe you're looking for him if I see him. Let's catch up later, 'kay?"

Stacey nodded, about to walk away.

"And, Stacey." Martin stopped her, "It's kinda cheesy to say this, but...well...be true to you."

The second Juvenile Delinquents song on their album. The lyrics played in Stacey's mind: *Don't get stuck in a stranger's life. Authenticity is worth the fight. Be true to you.*

Stacey bit her lip and nodded again. Martin waved over his shoulder and went back to his friends. When he wasn't looking, Stacey put out her cigarette under her shoe. She picked it up and tossed it in a trashcan.

She made her way around the backyard, avoiding eye contact with couples rolling around under the oak trees. Eventually she found Mark by the keg, but Melissa, Desiree, and Chad were nowhere near. Mark was pounding a beer bong, and Stacey watched as the tube emptied down his throat. When he pulled the tube away, foam shot out from between his lips. Everyone shielded their faces.

Mark's red, glassy eyes looked around hazily, eventually settling on Stacey. He smiled. "Staceeeee...How ya doin'?" He let out a long burp, wiped his mouth, and stumbled over to put an arm over her shoulder. "Guys, you know Staaaaceeey Chapp-munn?" he asked his buddies.

"Hey, Mark." Stacey put her arm around his waist to steady him, and hoped he wasn't about to be sick. "Seems like you're having a little too much fun."

"Yoouuu neeeeed a drink!" he said.

The guy at the keg handed her a full cup. She sniffed and sipped, then cringed. "Mark, this is the skunkiest beer on Earth! How did you chug this?"

He grunted and leaned harder on Stacey's shoulder.

"Eeew!"

It was Melissa's familiar squeal. She was about ten feet away and coming straight at Stacey.

"Gross, Stacey! PBR is rank." Melissa took the cup from Stacey's hand and sloshed it toward one of Mark's friends. "Come on. We found Goldschläger. I want you to talk to someone." She looped her arm through Stacey's, pulling her away.

Mark anchored Stacey to her spot. She wriggled her shoulders against his dead weight.

"Hey, Mark?" Stacey snapped her fingers in his face to get his attention. "MARK! I'm gonna go with Melissa. Can you sit down or something, buddy?"

Mark blinked slowly. "I…gonna…lay down." He burped after every word.

Stacey peeled his arm off her shoulder. Mark slumped into a heap on the ground.

Stacey turned to one of the guys Mark had been drinking with. "Can you make sure he doesn't drown in the pool? Or choke on his own vomit?"

"Dude!" The guy looked at Stacey, repulsed. "Don't kill the vibe! Mark's cool. He'll be fine."

"Seriously, Stacey," Melissa said. "You need to loosen up. Come on. I'll get you a drink."

Melissa led Stacey to the far side of the house. A bunch of girls were tightly huddled alongside the home's air conditioning vent. Stacey took in the supermodel prototypes, their tight golden abs nestled behind rolled-down, half-buttoned, high cut Daisy Dukes. Her chest tightened.

Did Desiree cut these girls from the Abercrombie *catalog, too?*

Stacey unlinked from Melissa, and crossed her arms in front of her waist, trying to cover the softness of her belly. She was at least a head taller than all the girls in this crew and felt like a zoo animal as they turned to look up at her. She swallowed hard, but forced a smile.

"Oh, THIS is Stacey? I know you," Heather said. "You were in my physics class, right?"

"Yeah, first period." Stacey nodded too enthusiastically.

Heather turned to another recent grad near her, explaining, "She's like, hella smart. A genius or something."

Several girls scrutinized Stacey, trying to place her. She bit her lip, shaking her head. "Not really."

"Didn't you have long hair though?" Heather asked.

Stacey nodded again, but her eyes were glued to two girls behind Heather, one whispering into the other's ear while they looked her up and down.

Melissa handed Stacey a Solo cup with a small amount of clear, sparkly liquid in it.

Stacey took the cup and downed it. The back of her throat burned. She coughed, surprised. "What the hell is that?" A river of heat ran into her gut.

"You've never had Goldschläger?" Melissa asked, exasperated. The posse around her giggled. "It's the shit! It's got cinnamon in it. A little bit gets you buzzed super fast, so you don't have to drink all those calories. It tastes like Big Red."

Stacey nodded dumbly, adjusting to the heat seeping throughout her body.

Melissa took her cup and poured in double the liquor. "Here. Just sip on this. Avoid the beer. You'll be chill for the rest of the night."

Stacey accepted the cup and smelled the sugary scent. She took a tiny sip and her mouth was flooded with cinnamon fire.

"Melissa said you went out with Jessie," said a girl in the shadows beside Heather.

Stacey gave a small nod, squinting to see who was talking to her. Something about the girl seemed familiar.

"That's Stephanie," Melissa said. "She asked Jessie to Sadie Hawkins."

Stacey recognized Stephanie from Christian Club. She had much longer, cuffed shorts. Her collared shirt covered her waist, and no cleavage was visible.

One of these is not like the others… The *Sesame Street* song played in Stacey's head. *Why is someone like Stephanie even at this party?*

"You're friends with Mary Jo, right?" Stephanie asked Stacey. "And those guys from the Juvenile Delinquents? I'm best friends with Jimmy's older sister, Natalie."

Stacey nodded, taking another sip, her eyes traveling around to all the faces watching her. Some of the most popular girls who had just graduated stood in the circle.

"I met Jessie at Christian Club, so I thought he'd be nice," Stephanie said. "Melissa told me he's actually, like, a total jerk."

"We only hung out a few times," Stacey replied coolly. She sipped the alcohol again, the smell and taste no longer surprising. She lowered her shoulders and she shifted her weight onto her left hip.

Melissa rolled her eyes and made a W with her hands. "Whatever, Stacey! Jessie was super into you. You know it. I could totally tell." She turned back to the other girls, her chin high. "They went out last week. Then he tried to get with me Saturday. He was playing both of us!"

Stacey's head started feeling fuzzy.

"Did you have sex with him?" Heather asked Stacey.

Sweat gathered under Stacey's arms. She tried to look casual. Her whole body felt hot. *It's now or never.* She lifted her chin, attempting to imitate Melissa's confidence. "Yeah. So?" She chugged what was left of the liquid left in her cup.

"See!" Melissa sounded triumphant. "I knew it! The next day the dickhead tried to fuck me in the girl's bathroom!"

"Oh my god!"

"Gross."

"What a jerk!"

"I know, right?" Stacey agreed. She blinked slowly, the faces and voices around her coming in and out of focus.

"As if!" Melissa shrieked.

Stacey looked into her empty cup. *Maybe Melissa's plan is working after all.*

"Jessie never tried anything like that with me." Stephanie sounded embarrassed.

"Did you and Jessie go out with a group?" Melissa asked.

Stephanie nodded.

"That was smart," Melissa said. "He probably didn't have the chance. If he'd gotten you alone, he wouldn't have stopped until he got your clothes off."

The girls around Melissa and Stacey exhaled their disgust and *mm-hmm'd* in agreement.

"Was he any good?" Stacey heard a voice behind her ask.

The entourage of girls grew silent and pulled apart to allow the new girl in.

As Stacey turned to see who was there, a puff of smoke caught her in the face. The smoke cleared, and a devilish smile appeared behind it. Stacey locked eyes with Kristi Carpenter.

Stacey's cheeks drained.

Kristi was a senior varsity cheerleader. She'd been with Jason Temple since freshman year. Everyone knew they had sex. All. The. Time. And Kristi wasn't the least bit shy talking about it. Stacey saw them in the act behind the bleachers during the jaws-of-life drunk-driving presentation. That was the only other time Kristi Carpenter seemed to notice Stacey before Travis Nielson's party.

Stacey's eyes circled the group. Melissa and the girls beside her leaned in, their mouths open, awaiting Stacey's response.

Before she knew what she was doing, Stacey heard herself say the words she'd practiced in the mirror a dozen times. "You mean three-second-Jess and his microscopic prick?" She held up her right hand, her thumb and forefinger pinched.

Melissa appeared victorious as Heather and the other girls around her squealed. All except Stephanie, that is, who looked horrified.

"Let's just say, he's lucky he's cute," Stacey went on, pulling her packet of cigarettes out of her back pocket. She shook a cigarette out of the pack and stuck it between her lips. Lighting it, she lifted a single eyebrow and sucked the smoke in as she said, "But after his pathetic performance," she blew the smoke in Kristi's direction, "I'm not interested in wasting any more time with that puka-shell-poser."

Bingo.

Stephanie walked away, shaking her head. The remaining girls erupted with laughter. Stacey held her cup in front of Melissa for a refill while watching Kristi.

"Who would've guessed Stacey Smartypants was so hard to satisfy?" Kristi said. "Get this girl her drink. Jason knows some guys who might do a better job measuring up for her." Kristi dropped her cigarette onto the lawn and stepped on it.

Melissa poured in a splash more Goldschläger. She held tight to the bottle as Stacey reached for it. "Stace, this stuff is pretty strong." Melissa's face was serious.

"I'm good *Missy*," Stacey said, pulling the bottle away.

Melissa crossed her arms. "Don't expect me to hold your hair later."

Stacey added several ounces to her cup then handed the bottle to Heather. Stacey downed the liquor in a few gulps then dropped the Solo cup on the lawn. "Lead the way, Kristi." She put the cigarette back in her mouth and took another puff.

Several girls Stacey didn't know followed as Kristi guided Stacey toward a group of guys standing near the edge of the pool. Everything around Stacey felt blurry and heavy, like she was walking in sand. Her full attention went to her feet. She could not embarrass herself.

One mistake is all it would take—that's what Martin said.

"You'll never guess what Stacey here just told me," Kristi said, sliding beside Jason.

Jason put his hand in Kristi's back pocket, and bobbed his head up to look at the girls. "Which one's Stacey?" He sounded bored.

Just act cool.

Stacey stepped forward, tucking her left hand in her own back pocket, her cigarette pinched between the fingers of her other hand. She pushed her shoulders back and looked Jason in the eyes.

Kristy laughed. "She said Jessie Thomas is a quick-draw with a tiny dick!"

Jason chuckled.

One of Jason's friends hooted. "Oh, man! That's low!"

The other guys around the group laughed, covering their mouths and shielding their crotches with their free hand.

Stacey flicked her cigarette into the pool and blinked flirtatiously. "Yeah, you boys seem to know how to...swing your bats." She pursed her lips and picked up a cup that looked half full of beer and sniffed it. *Not beer.* Her gaze shifted back to Jason. "But with Jessie's pencil-prick, he's best equipped to score keep a game of mini-golf. And the way he fucks is just about as exciting."

The boys hooted and hollered, half-chortling.

"Oh fuck! Did she say what I think she did?" a boy yelled. Heads swiveled toward the group.

Stacey gulped the contents of the cup like it was water, swallowing back a near upchuck and ignoring the gasoline-like burn in her throat.

"Aren't you in—like—Model UN or some shit?"

Stacey shook her head in slow motion, her eyelids heavy. "Debate...team," she corrected him.

Jason and his friends laughed hard. She wished she hadn't said anything. Her face flushed.

She noticed the joint in Jason's hand.

Jason locked eyes with Stacey. "You give a whole new meaning to 'Easy A,' Stacey!" He took a hit and passed the joint to Kristi.

Kristi sucked at the joint, passed to someone else, then smirked at Stacey.

Stacey felt her stomach turn. The party was starting to spin around her. Everything felt too big. Too loud. She needed to get away. Quickly. Before she humiliated herself.

Stacey lifted her pinky finger and mock-waved goodbye.

The girls behind Stacey giggled and followed her as she strutted away. They elbowed through the crowd. Stacey's ears were ringing. She was certain she was going to vomit. She needed to sit down.

"Wherz Ma-issa?" Stacey hiccupped. She couldn't focus and had no idea who she was even talking to.

"Melissa went over there," one girl said. She pulled Stacey by the arm, easing between groups of people. Stacey bumped them and stumbled. Drinks spilled. Something soaked the left leg of Stacey's shorts.

"Sor-ree," Stacey said. "Scuse me." She did what she could to keep up, despite her desire to lie down. Anywhere.

"Oh. My. God!" One of the girls stopped dead in her tracks.

Stacey ran into her and almost fell backward.

"He's here!" Another girl said.

"He. Who?" Stacey blinked long and slow, then followed her eyes to where the girl pointed. Jessie was on the opposite side of the glowing pool. Someone was talking into Jessie's ear as he glared at her.

Stacey steadied herself on the girl's shoulder. She sucked in her stomach in and stood tall. Stacey grinned at Jessie, then lifted her pinky and waved with it.

The girl beside Stacey lifted her own pinky, and they all laughed as her friends did the same.

Stacey narrowed her eyes and flipped Jessie the middle finger. She tried to step toward him but was wrenched backward.

"Shit! Stacey!"

The girls struggled to keep her upright.

"Stacey! You almost fell in the pool!"

"Let's find Melissa," a girl said.

Another voice added, "She's really trashed."

"I got go Des-i-rey's," Stacey slurred. She put her hand over her mouth.

"What did she say?"

"She's gonna be sick."

Stacey saw an open area in the trees and stumbled toward it. No one followed. Her foot caught in a gopher hole, twisted, and she fell to her knees. Scrambling up, she moaned profanities, but managed to get behind a tree before she vomited. A half-dressed couple backed away from her. She threw up three times, then rested her cheek against the trunk of the tree and wiped her mouth with the back of her hand.

The tree's bark felt sharp on her face. Her ankle hurt. She reached down to rub it and winced.

She pulled herself up and turned to face the house, bracing herself against the tree. She scanned the blurry scene trying to identify a familiar face. The only people she recognized were Kristi Carpenter and Jason Temple.

Maybe Kristi can help me find Melissa.

The noise of the party was gone. A sharp pain pulsed between her temples. Stacey realized she was sitting low to the ground and leaning against something hard on her right. She blinked and saw bricks. Asphalt. Concrete. Lifting her heavy, throbbing head, she looked around. An unfamiliar street with a few cars. She was sitting on a curb. Her legs and hands were dirty. Her ankle ached.

Feeling warmth on her back, Stacey looked left. Gabe was seated beside her. She raised her hand to her pounding head.

"You done?" he asked, pulling his hand away from between her shoulder blades.

"Done?"

"Puking?" Gabe stood. He was glaring at her. "If you're done, we should go."

Stacey looked around. The brick she was leaning on was the edge of a planter. Under ice plants was a foamy puddle. She felt the bile rise in her throat.

"When... did you...get here?" Stacey wished her eyes would focus and her head would stop swaying so the world could stop spinning around it.

"I've been at the party for a couple of hours. You were...busy," he whispered, annoyed.

"Where's... Ma-lissa?" Stacey was hiccupping. She covered her mouth, afraid more vomit was about to come up.

"How the hell would I know?"

"Tiff-ny?" She propped her elbow on the wall and tried to hold her head still with her hands. Her head kept slipping and bobbing. "We're staying at Dez-ray's house."

"It's one o'clock in the morning, Stacey. I didn't see anyone from the pool at the party."

"It's... what time?" She squeezed her eyes hard to get the pain to stop.

"ONE. A.M. You were doing shots and smoking pot with Kristi and Jason and a bunch of their friends when I got here at eleven. Martin called me. I don't see your car. I don't know where Desiree lives. And I'm not about to take you around to knock on doors."

Gabe said a lot of words. It took a minute for Stacey to absorb them. She forced her eyes open and looked up. He had a red mark on his cheek and his lip was bleeding. She reached up as if to touch it but it was too difficult. He leaned away and her hand fell to her side.

"What... hap—ned?"

"You seriously have no idea, do you? Trent-fucking-Severson happened. He had his hands all over you. You were clearly out of it. He never should have… You know what? Never mind. Just get in the car."

Gabe pulled Stacey to her feet, and pain shot through her ankle. Her leg gave out. Gabe caught her like he'd expected it to happen. He wrapped an arm around her waist and held her up, leading her to the passenger side of his car.

"Don't. Puke!" he said, as he shut the door.

Once behind the wheel, Gabe rolled the windows down, and reached across to attach Stacey's seatbelt.

He steered the car away from the curb. With every turn, Stacey felt more nauseous. She rested her face on the side of the window frame, grateful for the air blowing in. She kept her eyes closed and tried to sleep.

The next thing she knew, the car was stopped and the dome light was on.

Stacey lifted her head and opened her eyes. The dashboard clock said 1:35.

Porch lights came on to her right and Stacey squinted to look in that direction. Between long blinks Stacey tried to figure out where she was.

Gabe walking back toward the car.

A lawn.

Behind him was the silhouette of a woman. The woman was pulling something on, wrapping it around her. A bathrobe?

Her mom.

NOT HOME! All that escaped her lips was a moan.

Gabe pulled Stacey out of the car. With her mom's help, they dragged Stacey to the house.

Murphy's loud bark echoed across the porch.

"*Shhh.*" Stacey's mom pulled open the screen door.

As soon as they were inside, Stacey pulled away, hurling herself into the bathroom. She crawled to the toilet, retching up bitter yellow stomach acid. Each heave made her head explode with pain.

Murphy sniffed at Stacey as she gripped the cold porcelain.

"Thank you, Gabe," Stacey heard her mom say.

She heard the front door close, then the sound of the lock sliding in the chain.

Stacey pushed away from the toilet and rested her cheek on the ground. Through the slits of her eyelids, Stacey saw Murphy settle by her feet, alongside the tub. Beyond that, her mom stood in the open doorway, biting her bottom lip.

A moment later, Stacey felt her hand being jostled. She opened her right eye a sliver.

"Take these." Her mom pushed two small pills in her hand. She held a cup of water.

Stacey fumbled the pills onto her tongue. She lifted her face a few inches off the ground. Her mom held the cup to her mouth. Water drooled down Stacey's cheek, but she got enough in her mouth to swallow the pills.

She laid her head back down. "Belv...deer."

"What?"

"Bel-va-deer," she mumbled, her eyes closed.

"Tell me about Belvedere later. I'll be on the couch so I can hear you if you need me."

Stacey felt the puddle of drool on her cheek as darkness spun in her head. She curled her knees up and surrendered to the swirling abyss.

Chapter Twenty

Stacey awoke on the cool tile floor, shivering. She peeled herself off, desperate for water. The cup beside her was on its side and Stacey's shirt was damp.

She pulled herself up on the lip of the vanity. Pain shot from her foot up her shin. She leaned her elbows onto the counter and lifted her foot. The faucet squeaked as she twisted the knob. Water flowed out fast. After several long, thirsty gulps from the spout, she mustered the strength to turn off the water. She pushed herself up to standing.

Looking in the mirror, she saw that her face was pale and splotchy. Ashy makeup was smeared under her eyes, with red lip stain on her left cheek and chin. She grabbed a washcloth and tried to balance on one foot as she scrubbed until her skin felt raw. She pulled the washcloth away. Her mom was by her side, offering a dry towel. Stacey accepted it without looking into her mom's eyes.

"Let me help you to the couch." She draped Stacey's arm over her own shoulder, and gripped around Stacey's waist. They inched their way to the living room.

Stacey fell onto the couch and pulled the blanket over her. The spot was still warm from her mother's body. Stacey rested her head on the soft armrest and stretched her sore ankle to rest on the coffee table. Her mom propped a pillow under her foot. Beneath the filth and grime from the night before, the ankle was swollen and bruised.

"You need these," she said, handing Stacey a warm can of 7-up and two more aspirin.

Stacey popped the pills in her mouth and took a swig from the can. Her mom draped a bag of frozen peas over her ankle, then sat on the couch beside her. The clock on the VCR read seven.

"What time do you have work?" Stacey asked. Her voice was hoarse.

"I called Yvonne from the salon. I told her to reschedule my first few clients. I don't have to be there until eleven."

Stacey nodded.

"You need to call Bob. You're in no condition to work today."

Stacey pushed her fingers into her eyelids and nodded again.

"Are you ready to tell me what's going on?"

Stacey sat silent. Flashes of the night before crashed into each other in her mind. "Can we eat something first?"

Her mom nodded. She crossed to the kitchen and started putting slices of bread in the toaster.

Stacey grabbed the phone next to the couch and dialed 411 to get Bob's home number.

"Hello?" Bob answered, chipper as ever.

"Hey Coach…" She attempted to clear her throat. "It's Stacey."

"Hey Stace. What's up? All okay?"

"Not really." She looked up at her mom who was watching her over her coffee cup. "Sorry, but I'm…I don't think I can come in today."

"Oh," Bob said. After a long silence he exhaled. "I see."

Stacey wasn't sure if he was waiting for her to say more or not. She chewed the inside of her cheek.

"Well, thanks for letting me know. Give me a call later if I need to figure out your shifts for tomorrow also, okay?"

"K… thanks, Coach."

Stacey's mom nodded as she hung up, and turned to butter the toast.

As Stacey sipped her 7-Up, it felt as though needles were piercing her abdomen. She attempted to swallow small bites of bread. Her mouth tasted like an ashtray, but her tongue couldn't taste the food.

"What did you drink?" Her mother stared across the couch at her, her toast finished and plate set aside. Murphy was curled up between them.

"*Gold-slogger*? After that…I'm not sure."

"You mean Goldschläger?"

Stacey shrugged, looking at the crumbs on her lap.

"Planning to do that again?"

Stacey shook her head.

"When did you start smoking?"

Stacey studied her mom's face.

Her mother shook her head ever so slightly. Stacey knew it was her mother's most fed-up way of saying "Don't bother lying anymore."

"I got them over the weekend. But I don't want to smoke anymore, either."

Her mom lifted an eyebrow and nodded. "That's wise."

Stacey leaned forward and set her plate on the coffee table. She put her hand on the back of Murphy's head and rubbed the fur between her fingers.

"You know, I was about your age when I snuck out with a stolen bottle of my parents' gin." Her mom sipped from her coffee mug.

Stacey nodded.

Her mom went on. "I wanted to see my boyfriend. I was afraid he was going to break up with me if I didn't have sex with him. I thought the alcohol would help me get over my nerves. One of the stupidest things I ever did."

Stacey looked at her mom out of the corner of her eye. "What happened?"

"I got really drunk. Lost my virginity to him. He broke up with me anyway. Then, I got grounded for a month, and was sick like you are now."

Stacey bit her lip.

Your mom will understand. Gabe's voice echoed in her head. She closed her eyes and all she could see was him standing over her, angry, his lip bleeding.

"Stacey, none of this is like you. You changed your room, threw away your clothes, cut your hair. Now this. I barely recognize you. Something clearly happened. But I can't help you if you won't talk to me."

Tears began streaming down Stacey's cheeks.

Her mom scooted closer and placed her hand over Stacey's, which was still on Murphy's neck.

"Friday night." Stacey swallowed. "Jessie and I were in my car."

"Jessie, the guy who works with you at the pool?"

Stacey nodded. "It was…my first time."

Her mom's hand squeezed Stacey's. "Did you want to?"

Stacey slowly lifted her shoulders to her ears.

"Did Jessie…" She took a deep breath. "…rape you?"

"I never stopped him."

Her mom exhaled slowly.

"But–" Stacey's voice cracked. "I…don't think… He didn't wear a condom."

Her mom's eyes closed and she squeezed Stacey's hand again. When she opened them, Stacey saw her eyes were wet, and Stacey's tears multiplied.

"Saturday he never called, and I saw him in the bathroom with Melissa. I thought they had sex. That's when I bought the cigarettes."

Her mom sighed. "And the next day you cut your hair."

Stacey nodded and wiped her cheeks.

"Was Jessie the guy Gabe got into a fight with?"

Stacey's crying intensified. "That was another guy. But, I don't remember—" Stacey started to shake. Snot dripped from her nose.

"Shhhh… Calm down. It's okay. Gabe said you were fully clothed. He said the other guy looked a lot worse."

"I said so many things last night that I shouldn't have."

"Drunk people often do." She patted Stacey's outstretched knee with her free hand. "Let's hope people know that, and you haven't done permanent damage."

"I said a lot of things before I was drunk." Stacey's lip quivered as she looked up into her mom's eyes. "I felt so pathetic. And Melissa was mad at Jessie for trying to be with both of us. She said we should let girls know never to trust him. I wanted everyone to think Jessie was the pathetic one, instead of me."

Her mom wrapped her arms around Stacey. "I wish you'd talked to me."

Stacey pushed her forehead into her mom's collarbone as she coughed out the sobs. "I'm so stupid!"

Murphy wriggled out from between them and settled on the carpet beneath the coffee table.

Stacey's mom slid her fingers through Stacey's hair and made shushing sounds. "You did some stupid things. That doesn't make you stupid."

"You must hate me."

"Why would I hate you? All teenagers make mistakes. But I'd be disappointed if you chose to live your life this way. Listen…" Stacey continued to sob. Her mom moved her lips closer to Stacey's ear. "Are you listening?" she whispered

Stacey nodded, trying to catch her breath.

"I may not always like what you do, but I'll always be grateful if you talk to me about it. Okay? We can get through anything together."

Stacey sniffed and choked back tears. She pulled herself upright.

"This is too big for you to deal with alone." Her mom pursed her lips and lowered her head. "We need to take you to a doctor. Figure this whole thing out."

Stacey nodded again, staring at the ribbons of light from the rising sun shining through the window beside the front door..

"Let's get cleaned up, then we'll go, okay?"

Tears continued sliding to Stacey's chin and dripped to her tank top. She exhaled. "Okay." She pushed the blanket aside and was about to stand.

Her mom stopped her. "One more thing: who's *Belvedere*?"

Stacey's brow furrowed. She wiped her chin and cheeks.

"After Gabe brought you home, on the bathroom floor, you said 'Belvedere.'"

"Umm…Belvedere is Desiree's dog."

"So, you really were sleeping over at Desiree's house? What happened to the other girls you were with? Why did Gabe have to bring you home?"

"I lost track of them." Stacey picked at a snag in the corduroy on the arm of the couch. "Melissa tried to tell me to stop drinking, but I didn't listen. Once I was drunk, I don't remember seeing anyone I knew again."

"That's dangerous. You're lucky Gabe was looking out for you. He's a good friend."

"I don't think he wants to be my friend anymore."

"He was pretty upset." Her mom nodded. "He really cares about you."

"Maybe he shouldn't. Not everyone deserves to be forgiven."

"He wouldn't have a fat lip if he didn't care. But you are the only person who can prove to Gabe whether you deserve to be forgiven or not."

By nine o'clock Thursday morning, Stacey and her mom were showered, Stacey's foot was wrapped in an ACE bandage, and they were pulling into the parking lot at Planned Parenthood. It was in an industrial complex a couple of cities away. The entrance and signage faced away from the street. There were no windows, just dark tinted glass doors at the end of a handicap ramp.

Four women in their mid-forties stood outside the building with signs showing enormous fetuses in utero. The signs read "Abortion = Murder" and "Planned Parenthood does the Devil's work." The women chanted, "A person's a person, no matter how small."

Her mom turned off the engine and rotated in her seat. She looked quickly over her shoulder at the protesters, then placed a hand on Stacey's knee. "Whatever happens in there, I love you. You are not stupid or evil. We're here to get information so you can make a choice. Whatever you choose doesn't have to define you. Don't let other people determine how your life turns out."

Stacey nodded, her stomach fluttering. "Can we get this over with?"

Her mom took a deep breath, and they both climbed out of the minivan. Stacey hobbled to the rear bumper where her mom was waiting. She slid an arm around Stacey and helped her cross the lot to the ramp that led to the front door.

"Every life is precious," a woman shouted in her face as Stacey tried to steady herself on the ramp's railing.

Stacey's heart raced. She tried to look away from the signs and the people carrying them.

A woman stood in front of Stacey and her mom, her hands splayed toward the sky, her voice that of a preacher's. "For the Bible tells us in Psalm 139 that God knit us in our mother's womb, and sees us before our body is even formed."

"MOVE!" Stacey's mom growled sharply at the woman, as she supported Stacey's weight with her left arm and reached for the door with her right.

The protestor stepped aside, but began chanting louder, "A person's a person, no matter how small." The others joined in, one voice blasting through a megaphone.

Once inside, Stacey's mom pulled the door closed behind them, muffling the protestors' chants. The waiting room's bright fluorescent lights buzzed and blinked. The linoleum floors and orange plastic chairs reminded Stacey of a classroom. Three women sat in chairs against the wall. Only one was filling out paperwork on a clipboard, but none of them looked up or made eye contact with Stacey or her mom.

Across the room, on top of the reception desk, sat a privacy partition with a narrow window-like opening in front. The partition reached all the way to the acoustic square ceiling, and a call bell sat in front of it on the reception desk.

Stacey and her mother shuffled across to the desk, her mom's work sneakers squeaking loudly. Stacey's mom peeked through the opening, then shook her head. No one was back there.

Stacey lightly tapped the bell.

Behind the reception desk, a door opened with a beep and a click, then closed with a loud thud. A friendly female face appeared, framed by the partition's opening. The receptionist was in her early sixties and wore lavender cartoon cat scrubs. Her fine white hair was twisted up in a bun, her skin almost translucent.

"Good morning. How can I help you?"

The receptionist had put a bit too much pink blush on her cheeks, too much lavender eyeshadow on her lids, but wore no mascara.

"My daughter needs to be tested for pregnancy and STDs. And she'd like to be put on the pill."

The woman's eyelids raised, but her smile never faltered, as she turned her attention to Stacey. "Is that correct? *Would* you like to be put on the pill? *Do* you need those tests?"

Stacey nodded enthusiastically, and squeezed her mom's hand. "Yes. Please."

"Okay, then." The receptionist grabbed a clipboard and a pen and handed them through the opening to Stacey. "You need to fill these out. After you're done, set them here and ring the call bell. A nurse will let you know when someone is available to see you."

"Thank you." Stacey took the clipboard and looked around the room for a place to sit.

"Excuse me, ma'am." Her mom stopped the receptionist who was already headed back toward the door she'd come from. "Can you tell me what all of this is about?" She gestured at the partition.

"Ever since the shootings a little over a year ago, we're extra cautious." The receptionist lowered her voice to a whisper. "There have been bomb threats at facilities all around the country."

Stacey's mom closed her eyes and took a deep breath. "Thank you."

They sat down and Stacey began filling out the forms as her mother mumbled under her breath. "'Every life is precious,' my ass."

Stacey turned to her. "Mom! *Shhh…*"

Her mom put her hands up to make it clear she would stop. Her nostrils flared.

The keypad lock on the door behind the receptionist beeped several times as different nurses emerged and called the names of other women in the waiting room. Finally, a thick Jamaican accent called out Stacey's name.

The nurse was a tall, sturdy Black woman in her thirties, wearing bold scrubs covered in colorful squiggles. She had long, thin braids wrapped into an ornate bun, and her large, serious eyes gave her narrow face a no-nonsense expression.

Stacey's mom stood to go inside with Stacey. The nurse held up her beautifully manicured hand to stop her.

"This about Stacey, an the choices she make for her health, Mother."

Stacey's mom nodded and sat back down.

Stacey swallowed and hobbled her way to the door, where the nurse reached out her hand to help.

The door shut hard behind them. They were in a bright corridor with buttery yellow walls, cheery aqua blue doors, and white tiles intermingled with blue and yellow squares on the floor.

The nurse guided Stacey down the hall. "Miss Clarisse, by the way. We ahead to room three here on the right." She helped Stacey onto the table. The paper crinkled under her as Stacey shifted her weight back. The nurse sat on a rolling chair and opened a manila folder on her lap.

Nurse Clarisse's face softened as she looked at Stacey. "Now, tell me what goin' on, baby gal."

Despite the nurse's kindness, Stacey was exhausted from the night and drained from her conversation with her mom. She felt numb and wanted to do and say whatever she had to so she could put all of this behind her. "Ummm… Friday night, I had sex…for the first time. But he didn't wear a condom."

"The sex, it was consensual?"

Stacey looked at her lap, but nodded.

"Is important that you know, you never have to do a thing you never wanna do." The nurse's voice was serious and her face was somber. "No man, no woman, no parent, teacher, boyfriend, doctor. No one can make you do nothing you no wanna do. An I don't mean just sex. Understand?"

Stacey nodded.

"How you hurt your foot?"

"I was at a party last night. Drinking. I tripped in a gopher hole."

"You was drinking alcohol when you had sex?"

Stacey shook her head.

"What about the boy? He had sex before?"

Stacey nodded. "I think so."

"How many partners him have? You know? Him ever test yet?"

Stacey shrugged.

"You know anything else that might transmit disease? Oral sex? Shared needles?"

Stacey thought of Pedro living with HIV on *The Real World*. Despite taking health class and attending school assemblies about

AIDS, most of what Stacey understood about STDs was from MTV. She shook her head. "Nothing."

The nurse scribbled notes on the paperwork and flipped the page. "Says here you last period was eleven days ago."

Stacey nodded.

The nurse closed the chart and folded her hands on top it. "Sorry, is probably too soon to tell if you pregnant. Too soon too to know if you catch STDs."

Stacey felt her stomach drop.

"We can do tests to be sure, but…you likely need to come back. Most of the test accurate two weeks post encounter. Some twenty-eight days. You can always do a pregnancy test at home end of next week. Come back here for the other tests in a month."

Stacey sucked in her bottom lip, her eyes welling up.

"I know that not what you wanna hear. Sorry, gal. We'll get yuh on the pill today though. Get you some condoms. Do what we can. How that sound?"

Stacey nodded.

"Now, show me you foot, baby gal."

By 9:50, Stacey had provided urine and blood for the various tests. The nurse assured Stacey that her ankle wasn't broken, just twisted, and told her to elevate, ice it, and do minimal physical activity for the next few days. Planned Parenthood would call with test results in a couple of hours, but Stacey should be prepared to test again in a few weeks to be certain she was really in the clear.

Stacey and her mom walked out together, ducking through the picket line.

In the car, Stacey's mom's jaw ticked as she buckled her seatbelt. She glared in the rearview mirror at the women with the signs who were shouting at the van. She held her hand on the horn, startling the women. They jumped backward. The van's tires screeched as she whipped the car out of the parking lot.

While her mom drove, Stacey stared anxiously out the window chewing on her thumbnail. "I'm so sorry."

"This is going to be a long few weeks for us both." After a minute of silence, her mom asked, "Do you think there's any chance Jessie has...would he get tested?"

Stacey shrugged. She never imagined she would be dealing with any of this. She always thought she would be in a relationship and know everything about the person she lost her virginity to. "After everything I said last night, I don't know how I could ever face him again."

"Well, you work together...facing him seems inevitable."

"You'd be surprised. For the first week, I was totally invisible at The Plunge. It's going to be like that again, now. For the rest of summer. I know it. I should just quit."

"Quitting won't make it go away. We always imagine things will be worse than they actually turn out. I think you'll be surprised how understanding people are if you give them a chance."

Stacey pictured Mark spitting foam from the beer bong. The crew hanging out without her. She felt Melissa's glare. Heard Bob's disappointment over the phone.

"I know these people. They have no reason to be nice to me."

"Even still, it's too late in summer to get another job. It's good money. Do you really have anything to lose by waiting a week or two before you decide to quit?"

They stopped in front of Desiree's house. Stacey's mom hugged Stacey again, then waited as Stacey used her spare key to unlock the Silver Bullet.

"Everything's going to be okay. I promise," her mom said.

Stacey put her key in the ignition. *If any of those tests are positive, nothing will ever be okay again.*

PART THREE

Breaking The Surface

Chapter Twenty-One

S tacey was awakened by the phone ringing beside the couch. "Hello?" Her voice was groggy.

"May I speak with Stacey Chapman?"

"This is Stacey." Her heartbeat quickened.

"Stacey, this is Planned Parenthood. Did you visit our office this morning?"

"Yes." She put her left thumbnail between her teeth.

"Your test results are negative. However, I see a note here that Nurse King believes the accuracy of these tests is questionable given the date of your recent exposure. She encourages you to return any time after August 2 to redo the bloodwork. Her note also says to do an at home pregnancy test after July 19. Do you have any questions?"

"No. Thanks."

Stacey called her mom and shared the news, but felt no relief. Her life would be in limbo for at least another eight days. Other than her mom and Murphy, she didn't feel like she had a friend in the world to talk to.

She laid on the couch staring at the ceiling. Snippets of the night before flashed in her mind. She imagined how Gabe felt when he found Trent touching her. How she must have looked at that moment. Waves of disgust pulsed through her as she imagined the places Trent's hands must have roamed on her body. She wondered who threw the first punch.

Stacey wanted to tell Gabe he was right; that talking to her mom was what she should have done from the beginning. To thank him for helping her. She desperately wanted to believe they could be friends again.

She also wanted to tell Melissa she should have stopped drinking, and find out if Mark was okay. Were any of them looking for her when she lost track of them at the party? What exactly did Jessie hear she said about him? Was Bob angry after he warned them to be careful? Who covered her shift? She wanted to apologize to them all.

Mostly she wanted to erase everything about the past week. Make it all go away however she could. That felt impossible.

You'll be surprised how understanding people are if you give them a chance.

Stacey decided to go into the pool office and apologize to Coach Bob, face to face. She had the least amount to lose with him. The worst he could do was fire her. She figured she'd end up quitting anyway, so it wouldn't matter if he did.

It was 12:45 when she hobbled into the guard shack. Mark was asleep on the couch. Melissa and Desiree were sitting together in the shallow-end guard stand, chatting while watching two elderly lap swimmers. Bob looked up from the desk, surprised, and turned off Vince Scully's broadcast of the Dodger game.

"I thought you were out for the day," he said.

"I thought so, too. I'm so sorry about this morning, Coach. I really screwed up last night. It won't happen again. I can work this afternoon, or tonight, if you want me to."

"You can't imagine how surprised I was when you called, Stacey. I figured at least one guard would be irresponsible at that party and call out sick. I just hadn't figured it would be you."

"Who covered my morning shift?" She leaned against the lockers to take the weight off her sore ankle.

"Melissa. She assumed you wouldn't be feeling well. Desiree was scheduled to be here. They told me it was obvious you wouldn't make it to work."

Stacey looked out the window. Embarrassed as she felt, she should thank Melissa for covering for her. She looked down at Mark. "Is he okay?"

"Mark? Yeah. He got dropped off here a while ago, but his shift's not 'til one. Seems okay though. I think everyone's a little worse for wear. Jessie seemed like he had a rough night, too."

Stacey looked at the floor. "What do you mean by 'rough?'" *Had Gabe also punched Jessie?*

"Looked like he hadn't slept. Angry. Or sad. I dunno." Bob nodded at Stacey's foot. "Why is your ankle wrapped up?"

"I twisted it in a gopher hole."

Bob exhaled. "Well. I'm glad you came by. Takes a lot of courage to own up to your mistakes." He leaned back, crossed his ankles on the edge of the desk and folded his hands in his lap. "You should go home and put that ankle up. Ice it. Hopefully it's well-enough tomorrow to come back."

She nodded, ashamed.

"You're a smart kid with a lot of potential," he said. "Don't blow it, okay?"

"Thanks, Coach."

Bob planted his feet on the floor, then turned back to his transistor radio and sports pages.

Lap swim ended and Melissa and Desiree came inside the guard shack.

"Oh, my God, Stacey!" Desiree ran over and threw her arms around Stacey. "Are you okay?"

"We were so worried when you never came back to Desiree's house," Melissa said, her hand on Stacey's upper arm. "What happened?"

Stacey's cheeks flushed. "I'm okay. My friend Gabe took me home."

"You must have been soooo hung over!" Melissa's expression was serious. She eyed Bob, then said under her breath, "I never should have given you that third shot. Or let you out of my sight."

"I heard Jessie had a rough night. What was it like working with him this morning?"

Melissa crossed her arms and smirked. "He had exactly the kind of night he deserved. I never expected you to be so..." she eyed Bob again, "*entertaining.* Anyway, Jessie will be fine. He won't be talking to us anytime soon, but he won't have luck with any other girl, either."

"We need a redo girls-night to talk about *everything,*" Desiree said, taking each of their hands. "Tiffany can come after she gets off from nightswim. Your stuff is still at my house."

"I don't know if I can. Let's just say I wasn't in the best shape when I got home. My mom won't want me staying overnight anywhere or out late for a while."

"We're done at five," Desiree said. "You want to come get your stuff from my house then?"

"Sure." Stacey gestured toward Mark. "He didn't drive last night, did he?"

"Oh, God, no!" Melissa shook her head. "He crashed at his buddy Derek's house. We're taking him to his car near Travis's house after our shift."

"Speaking of which," Bob said. He stood and grabbed the megaphone from atop the filing cabinet. "Plug your ears ladies."

Stacey got her hands to her ears a fraction of a second too late, as Bob pressed the siren on the megaphone.

Mark jolted his head to the side and squeezed his eyes shut.

Into the megaphone, Bob said, "Rise and shine, Sleeping Beauty. It's time to get to work."

"Jesus!" Mark sat up, his eyes still closed with his hands on his temples. "Was that really necessary?"

"Maybe not. But it was fun." Bob grinned like a little boy as he set the megaphone aside.

At 5:30 Thursday evening, Stacey rang the doorbell at Desiree's house. She heard Belvedere's deep bark, followed by the click of the lock. A woman opened the door. She had Desiree's auburn hair and heart-shaped face but was much taller. Her makeup was classic, as was the chignon she'd twisted her hair into. She wore a creamy silk blouse, narrow slacks, and stiletto heels.

Stacey's cut-off shorts, Birkenstocks, and bare face made her feel self-conscious. She tucked her blonde bob behind her ears.

Belvedere immediately snuffled Stacey's hand and thumped his body against her thigh, pushing her sideways a step.

"Hi, Belvedere. Hey Buddy." Stacey petted his ribs while trying to keep his weight off her bum ankle. She looked up. "I'm Stacey. Is Desiree here?"

The woman's face softened. "Yes. She and Melissa are up in her room." She had a thick, musical accent. She motioned at Stacey's foot. "Are you okay to get up there on your own?"

"I can manage. Thanks." Stacey removed her shoes and carried them as she gripped the railing and eased herself up the winding staircase. Each step burned up her shin and the pain radiated throughout her foot. She stopped at the top and caught her breath. *So much for staying off it.*

She knocked on Desiree's bedroom door, and a voice called, "Come in."

Seated on the floor in front of her mirror, her legs crossed, Desiree wore boxers and a tank top, her hair up in a towel like she'd just gotten out of the shower. She had a pair of tweezers and was squinting at her reflection as she plucked between her brows.

"Hey, Stace. Missy's in the shower. She'll be out in a sec."

Stacey sat on the rug and leaned against the end of the bed, reclaiming her spot from the evening before. She set her shoes on the rug beside her, then looked around, confused. The room was spotless. The pile of magazines and snacks were gone, and the clothes had all been put away. The bed looked as if it hadn't been slept in at all, and all of the makeup on the vanity had been cleaned up. "When did you clean your room if you both went to work at eight this morning?"

"Roselba comes every day. My mom's a lawyer. She doesn't have time to clean or shop or cook or anything."

"I want your life," Stacey muttered.

Desiree shrugged and pulled the towel off her head. "It's nice, I guess. But I can't ever find anything." She set the tweezers aside and started to squeeze a small pimple on her chin.

Stacey pursed her mouth and raised her eyebrows. *Maybe you need less stuff.*

The room was quiet and Stacey felt uncomfortable watching Desiree poke at her face. She looked toward the closet, envying the abundance of designer clothes and accessories crammed inside. She heard retching. She tilted her ear in the direction of the bathroom, and heard another retch, followed by a muffled cough.

Stacey looked at Desiree, who either didn't hear or was unphased.

Melissa is throwing up? She didn't seem hungover at The Plunge.

A few seconds later the toilet flushed, followed by the shower being turned off.

When Melissa stepped out of the bathroom, surrounded in steam, she was dragging a wide-toothed comb through her long, wet hair. A towel was wrapped around her body under her arms.

"Hey, Stacey." She smiled, her cheeks flushed.

"Hi. How's it goin'? You feeling okay?"

"Yeah," Melissa scoffed. "Why?"

Desiree turned to watch their exchange.

"I thought I heard you getting sick in there."

Melissa lifted one eyebrow, shaking her head at Stacey like she was crazy. "You should get your hearing checked. I was just taking a shower."

Desiree's jaw clenched before she looked away again.

"My mistake," Stacey mumbled, too exhausted to argue.

Melissa pulled the closet door closed behind her, returning a minute later in baggy pajama pants and an oversized tee. Stacey had never seen Melissa so covered up.

Melissa hung the towel over the back of the desk chair and plunked beside Stacey on the rug. "It's time to spill. What *happened* last night?"

Stacey's cheeks burned.

Desiree scooted over to form a small circle with them on the rug. "Yeah, this afternoon Chad said there was a fight? And your friend basically carried you away."

"Well…" Stacey pulled her knees to her chest and wrapped her arms around them. "I don't exactly…remember."

"Oh, shit!" Desiree put her hand over her mouth. "You blacked out?"

Stacey rubbed her forehead. "I guess so."

"What's the last thing you remember?" Melissa asked.

"I remember talking to Jason and his friends when I walked away from you, then I saw Jessie across the pool. Right after that I twisted my ankle on my way to puke in the orchard. Next thing I knew, I was with Gabe on the curb by his car, and he told me it was one a.m. Did either of you see me in between?"

Desiree began talking rapidly. "Oh my God, Stacey you were…"

Melissa put her palm up in front of Desiree.

Desiree closed her mouth.

"First, those girls were eating out of the palm of your hand last night!" Melissa said. "You were so sassy and confident. They followed you around like groupies."

Stacey nodded, remembering the girls beside her when she first spoke to Jason Temple and his buddies. The ones who kept her from falling in the pool, and imitated her waving at Jessie with her pinky. Her stomach knotted. "Were they freshman?"

"Probably." Melissa shrugged. "Then I heard some baseball players saying you were really flirty. They said you told them 'Jessie screwed as badly as he plays golf'?"

"I think I said his dick is the size of a golf pencil and the way he fucks is about as interesting as a round of mini-golf." Stacey smiled sheepishly.

Melissa snickered. "Genius."

"I like mini-golf," Desiree said defensively.

Stacey closed her eyes and shook her head.

"Anyway, at like eleven, Desiree and I wanted to leave, and went looking for you. We found you with Kristi and Jason. You were sitting on some baseball player's lap smoking a joint. I had no idea you even smoked weed."

"That makes two of us," Stacey said.

Desiree's eyes were wide. "Stacey, you really shouldn't mix alcohol and pot."

"I'll keep that in mind. Was the guy whose lap I was sitting on Trent Severson?"

"Yeah. I think so. His hair is buzzed, but I think that was him," Melissa said. "We asked if you wanted to come with us, but he kind of held you down on his lap. You put your arm around his shoulder and said you'd catch up with us later."

Desiree made an expression like she felt guilty about it. "I thought you must have had something going on with him. You seemed so comfortable. But, we really shouldn't have left you."

Stacey rubbed her eyes with her palms. "It's not your fault. But I never went out with Trent Severson. I liked him way back in fourth grade. Before he started taking steroids and became a cocky asshole. I don't think we've said three words to one another since puberty."

Desiree twisted her lips, then out of the side of her mouth she said, "He didn't seem all that interested in talking last night either."

Stacey grimaced. "I think I remember Jason Temple calling me 'Easy A' all night."

"Ooooph." Melissa scrunched her nose. "He's pretty popular. That'll stick for a while."

"Yeah. Should make senior year interesting. What did Chad tell you about Gabe getting in the fight with Trent?"

Desiree bit her lip and looked at the ceiling. "He said it was like midnight. A bunch of people had left, and he was planning to head home. I guess there was a couch in the garage where Mark had been passed out for awhile. Chad went to check on him. But Mark was already gone, and Chad saw you laying on the couch. Trent was on top of you. Chad was embarrassed he walked in on you guys and was backing away when your friend—Gabe?—pushed past him in the doorway. He ran over to the couch to pull Trent off you."

Stacey groaned.

Desiree continued, "Chad told me that's when he could see you were passed out cold. Gabe tried to wake you up, and Trent pulled him back, then decked him. But Trent was trashed, so he made contact, but didn't really hit him as hard as he could have. Gabe punched Trent two or three times before he hit the floor, knocked out. That's when Gabe pulled you over his shoulder and carried you out."

The girls sat in silence for nearly a minute, the weight of what might have happened if Gabe hadn't shown up hanging in the air around them.

"Gabe's like your knight in shining armor," Melissa said.

Stacey exhaled. "He *was* my best friend."

"What're you gonna do?" Desiree asked.

Stacey shrugged. "Transfer? Drop out? Never show my face in town again? What can I do? I made an ass of myself. Everyone thinks I'm a total slut."

"It'll blow over." Melissa tapped her elbow against Stacey's. "Freshman year I got called fish fingers for like a month after Steve Santos told everyone he fingered me at a party. It was the first time I got drunk, but I wasn't *that drunk*. Steve made the whole thing up.

He was mad because he tried to kiss me and I rejected him. Anyways, I was completely humiliated, but he was more popular than me back then. No one believed it wasn't true."

"How'd you get everyone to stop calling you that?" Stacey asked.

Melissa triumphantly lifted her chin. "I hooked up with his best friend, Casey Anderson, and told *him* to make it stop. Worked great: Casey treated me like a queen for over a year."

"I don't plan to hook up with any of Trent's friends, no matter what he tells everyone about last night."

"I don't think you have to worry about that," Desiree said.

Melissa and Stacey stared back, confused.

"Why?" Stacey asked.

"Because Chad was still there when Trent woke up."

Stacey crossed her legs and leaned forward. "What happened?"

"Chad said Travis came in after the fight, and was totally pissed when Chad told him what he'd walked in on. Travis found a big permanent marker—you know the kind to mark moving boxes with—and wrote RAPIST in all capitals on Trent's forehead. They got a bunch of guys together in the garage, and woke Trent up, telling him that if he ever did anything like that again they'd all beat the shit out of him. And Chad made sure Trent understood if he told anyone anything bad about you, or Gabe, he'd personally tell Coach Bob what happened and get Trent kicked off the baseball team."

"Oh my God!" Stacey wanted to cry with relief. "Chad is my hero!"

Desiree touched Stacey's foot. "We all love you, Stace. No guy should do anything to you when you're drunk. Besides, Chad knew I would've dumped him if he hadn't helped you somehow after everything he saw."

"Next party, we definitely won't let you drink so much," Melissa said. "And we won't leave you alone with any guys unless you specifically tell us the name of the guy you're into."

"Thanks. Really. But there won't be a 'next party.'"

"Well, we've got your back. No matter what," Desiree said. Melissa nodded in agreement.

Tears welled up in Stacey's eyes. "I never thought…you might be some of the best friends I've ever had. Thanks."

"Your friend Gabe deserves a medal," Melissa said.

Stacey hated that her mom was right. It would have been dumb to quit. Maybe it wasn't too late to fix things with Gabe, either.

Stacey rushed home, dropped her duffle bag beside her bed, and dialed Gabe's number.

"Hey." He sounded annoyed.

Her voice quivered, "Hi… Thanks for… bringing me home last night." She twisted her fingers in the phone cord.

"Umm hmm."

"I heard what happened. I feel terrible you had to take care of me like that."

"Yeah…" Gabe exhaled. "It sucked."

"I've done a lot of really stupid things lately."

Gabe didn't respond. Stacey could hear the television in the background.

Is he even listening?

"I'm so sorry, Gabe."

"Okay," he said curtly.

"Are you mad at me?" Stacey asked.

"Am I mad?" Gabe hissed into the phone. "I don't know, Stace. You're not who I thought you were."

Tears fell down Stacey's cheeks. She laid her head on her pillow and tried not to let the emotion sound in her voice. "I'm the same person. I just…screwed up."

"Those people you were hanging out with…the things you were saying about what you did with Jessie… The other night you seemed so upset, but last night you acted like you were bragging. And you got completely trashed. To the point that Trent almost…I had to…."

"You're right," Stacey said, barely audible.

Gabe let out a sigh. "Listen, I'm gonna go. I just need… I think I need time to cool off or something."

"Okay." Stacey's voice cracked. Tears pooled on her pillowcase. "Will you call me tomorrow?"

"I'm going on this hiking trip with my dad and my brother for a few days. Maybe I'll call you when I get back." Gabe hung up without waiting for her to respond.

Stacey let the phone fall from her hand. She curled into her knees, sobbing.

Her mom came in. Without asking what happened, she hung the phone up, then wrapped her body around Stacey's. Murphy laid across their feet as Stacey cried herself to sleep.

Chapter Twenty-Two

The Centennial Olympic Games were beginning July 19th in Atlanta, and it felt like the whole world was excited. The opening ceremonies were expected to be the most viewed event on television since OJ on the 405 in the white Bronco.

To boost attendance at the pool, the City of Mesa Valley announced "Plunge Olympics" events for every morning and afternoon swim session over the span of the Olympic Games.

During their breaks, Stacey and the other lifeguards glued chocolate gold medal coins to yarn necklaces, and Bob made a makeshift medal podium in front of the guard shack, with an Olympic rings flag as the backdrop. The acting manager would be the official judge, and parents could take photos along with the possibility of some ending up in the Sun News.

On July 19th, Tiffany's family hosted an opening ceremonies party and invited the crew over to watch as Muhammad Ali lit the Olympic cauldron and Celine Dion and Gladys Knight sang. Bob sat on the couch with Tiffany's parents as the guards squished onto their living room floor, eating pizza and Red Vines. Stacey and

Jessie sat on opposite sides of the room. He hadn't made eye contact with her or Melissa since the party.

Thousands of people danced across the screen in bizarre red, green, yellow, white, and black costumes like monochromatic munchkins with their coordinated oversized drumkits being wheeled around the stadium. Sheets of Olympic-themed fabric, each longer than a football field, were pulled from the top of the stadium over the audience and down onto the field. The spectacle was unlike anything Stacey had ever seen before.

The crew commiserated with the sweating spectators in the stands in Atlanta, and *ooh*'d and *aah*'d at the giant puppets dancing to Louisiana jazz music. From the couch, Tiffany's mom sang harmony with the Southern Gospel Choir.

About an hour into the show, Mark joked that he felt like he was on an acid trip—or needed to be—to understand what was happening on screen. Eventually he acted like he was going to the bathroom, but slipped quietly out the back door.

As the procession of each country's athletes dragged on, Desiree whined, "Is the rest of the ceremony just national songs and flag waving?"

"Pretty much," Tiffany's dad said.

"Boring." Chad chimed in.

"I'm heading out." Bob stood, looking directly at the guards around the room. "I expect all of you to be on time for your shifts tomorrow. Thank you for having me," he said, as he shook Tiffany's dad's hand. Her mom stood to give Bob a hug.

"Can we turn on the jacuzzi?" Tiffany asked her parents.

"Sure," her mom said. "Can everyone head home by ten, though?"

"Of course," Tiffany said, as she led the crew out back.

Mark was seated on the end of the diving board. There were no visible or pungent signs he'd smoked weed, but his face had relaxed into the jolly and sleepy look they all knew too well.

It was almost seven, and Tiffany's house was high enough on the foothills to watch as the golden glow of the evening sky cast purple shadows over Mesa Valley.

Stacey sat between Melissa and Desiree on the warm concrete with their feet in the jacuzzi. Mark and the other guards made their way over to join them. They sat in a circle, like the glow of the light in the bottom of the swirling water was their crew's version of a bonfire.

Mark took a joint from his pocket and showed it to Tiffany, lifting his eyebrows.

"Okay, but everyone be chill about it," she said, looking over at the house to make sure her parents weren't watching.

Another one? Isn't he already stoned?

Mark lit the joint, took a deep breath, and held it. He offered it to Chad who took a hit before handing it to Desiree. By the end everyone had taken a turn, except Stacey.

"You sure? It'll be totally different than when you were drunk. One or two hits and you'll just feel chill," Chad told her.

Stacey wrinkled her nose and shook her head. "I'm still recovering from last week."

The other guards passed the joint around one more time, and as Jessie exhaled the smoke from his lungs, he stared into the swirling water. "Did you ever want to be an Olympian? Or a pro-athlete?" he asked no one in particular.

"I did," Tiffany said. "I always thought I was *that* good of a swimmer. That I could be a gold medalist." She paused. "Turns out I couldn't even get a scholarship for swimming."

"But Cal State has a team, right?" Melissa asked. "You can still swim when you're there even if you don't have a scholarship."

"Yeah. Sure," Tiffany said. "I might try to play water polo, too. It's just different, you know? I thought I was exceptional. But I turned out to be mediocre."

Tiffany looked so disappointed, Stacey tried to reassure her. "There's no way you're mediocre, Tiffany. You were varsity captain."

Tiffany lifted her eyebrows and bit her lip, staring into the water. "Captains are chosen for attitude, not skill. I rarely came in first place my senior year."

Melissa put her arm around Tiffany and rested her head on her shoulder.

"When I was little, I wanted to be a figure skater." Desiree was talking quickly, and even more high-pitched than usual. "I loved the pretty costumes and thought they were the most talented, beautiful people in the world. I asked for a sparkly, skirted leotard for my fifth birthday, and begged my parents to let me take lessons. I wore that leotard all the time, twirling around my living room, until I outgrew it."

"If you'd been a competitive figure skater, we never would have met," Chad said, pulling Desiree closer to him. "I don't want to imagine my life without you."

"Well, get used to it. When school starts, I'll be in LA and you'll be at CSUSB." Desiree turned her face away when Chad tried to kiss her. "Anyway… It was a pipe dream. Figure skaters are tiny; I'm too top heavy. I never even got skates or took one lesson. Plus, the nearest rink is an hour each way, up the mountain. I would have to have had a nanny who drove me or something. And a private coach. Do homeschool. I don't get how families do that when both parents work."

The other guards nodded and *umm-hummed* their agreement.

"Did you guys hear about the X Games last year?" Jessie asked, still watching the water. The crew shook their heads, but said nothing, and he went on. "It was on the east coast somewhere. It's like the Olympics of misfit sports: skateboarding, bungee jumping, dirt bikes..."

Jessie was smiling at the swirling bubbles like he was seeing something there no one else could see. His blue eyes reflected the green of the water. He wasn't wearing his puka shell necklace anymore. The words "puka-shell-poser" rung in her head, and Stacey's stomach dropped. She wanted more than ever to apologize for how she had hurt him.

"You know," Jessie continued, a hint of bitterness in his voice, "it's a competition for those of us who don't have parents who will pay for uniforms, or take us to any sort of practice."

The crew sat still, silent, eyeing Jessie.

"They're going to have winter X Games this year," Jessie said. "With snowboarding on a half-pipe and everything. I think it's gonna be in the mountains around here somewhere."

"That's cool," Chad said. "I tried snowboarding once. It's fun, but tough. Totally different than skiing. Do you get up to the slopes much?"

"Not really. I always have to catch a ride from someone. Season passes are crazy expensive. I was thinking of getting a job up there this winter. Then I could board whenever I wasn't working. Now that it's getting popular, maybe I could give lessons or something."

"That sounds awesome, man," Chad said.

"I don't know. We'll see," Jessie continued. "I'm just saying, the X Games are the kind of thing I'd want to compete in. Way more than those stuffy sporting events like they have for rich kids in the Olympics."

"I was supposed to have a full ride," Mark said, barely audible. He was laying on the deck beside Jessie, staring up at the sky.

"Where?" Tiffany asked.

"Texas A & M." Mark pulled himself upright and propped his arms behind him. "Football. But I blew out my ACL beginning of my senior year. Ruined me for basketball, too."

Mark was three years ahead of Stacey; he wasn't on her radar when she was a freshman. She'd never realized he had been a talented athlete. "Why couldn't you have surgery?" Stacey asked.

"I did," Mark said, "and twelve months of physical therapy. Spent my senior year on crutches. I was told to play at a community college first. They'd renew my scholarship if I came back to full capacity. I blew it out again my third game back. The pain was a real sonofabitch the second time. No amount of therapy helped. That's when they started me on these." Mark sat all the way up and took a prescription bottle out of his pocket, then shook it.

"What is that?" Desiree asked.

"OxyContin. They're the only thing that really takes the pain away, but it doesn't last." Mark opened the lid and put a pill in his mouth. "They keep upping my dose. Now all I ever want to do is sleep. Without it, it hurts so bad I want to cut off my leg. But I can't ever play sports again, so I might as well be knocked out." He leaned forward to watch the swirling water like Jessie had. "Ever since I dropped out of college, my dad says I'm a loser. He used to sit front row at all my games."

Jessie nodded with his whole body. "Parents fucking suck."

Stacey thought about her mom. She could have gone ballistic when Stacey came home drunk. Or freaked out about unprotected sex. But she didn't. Stacey never planned to tell her dad about any of it, but even if she did, she couldn't imagine him calling her a loser.

"I'm sorry, Mark, but your dad's an asshole," Melissa said. "He shouldn't have said that."

"He's actually not." Mark shook his head. "That's the thing. It's just…I don't know…it's like when I got injured, his dream of watching me play college ball got shattered, too." He looked up at the sky again. "Everything feels fucking pointless, now."

"It's not pointless," Stacey said. "If you go back and finish school, maybe you could still coach or something. You don't really want to keep working at the pool, do you?"

There was a collective groan from the other guards.

"No worthwhile team wants a coach who never played college ball." Mark shrugged and put the bottle back in his pocket. "As for working at the pool, of course it's not forever. But it works for now."

"Bob's gonna be at the pool forever," Desiree said, smiling.

"Bob's a PE teacher. And a baseball coach," Tiffany said defensively. "He has a nice house and supports his family. The pool is just extra money over summer."

"Not bad gigs." Chad laughed, lifting an eyebrow in Desiree's direction. "He gets to work with hot, young chicks in tiny shorts all school year and bathing suits all summer. Sign me up!" He wrapped his arm around Desiree's waist and tickled her side, making her wriggle and squeal.

"Ew…don't be gross! You're talking about Bob!" Desiree pushed him away.

Tiffany asked, "What's that creepy line from *Dazed and Confused*?"

Stacey wrinkled her nose. "You mean that line about the sleezy guy getting older while high school girls stay the same age?"

"Damn right," Mark replied. "That's me!" He elbowed Jessie in the ribs and splashed water toward the girls with his foot.

"You guys are pigs," Melissa said haughtily.

Chad and Mark made snorting noises. Jessie rolled his eyes.

"Seriously, Mark," Stacey interrupted. "You've been on those pills for two years now? Your doctor keeps giving you more, but you're still in pain? And smoking weed? Getting drunk to cope? Why aren't you worried?"

"You can't possibly go on like this for the rest of your life," Tiffany added.

Mark stared across the hot tub at Stacey. "You think I'm a loser stoner?" His face was serious, with deep purple bags under his eyes that she hadn't noticed before. I go to work. I do my job, don't I?"

"Why do we have to have a plan for the rest of our lives?" Chad growled. "Mark's fine! None of us know what's gonna happen tomorrow. Let's just live in the moment."

"That's what I'm saying!" Jessie looked around. "Mark is one of the coolest guys I know. Why does he have to pretend he knows what the rest of his life should look like? Things are working out for him right now."

"Because, dipshits," Melissa hissed, gesturing with her hands. "Mark being a 'cool guy' isn't the same as Mark being happy. Are you happy strung out all the time, Mark?"

"What the fuck is 'happy'?" Mark glared at her. "We're lucky if we get to string a few minutes of happiness together in a day." He shook his head. "My parents genuinely love their jobs. They've been married twenty-five years and still like each other. But they're not 'happy.' So, are you telling me I need to be in pain all the time, and never party, so I can end up with a nine-to-five and kids, but miserable? Fuck that."

Melissa scoffed. "Some of us would prefer not to become bums, mooching off of our parents or the government until we die. We want to make something of ourselves. Doing *that* will make us happy."

"Really, Melissa? Now you're the expert on happiness?" Jessie spat back. "And you're really happy sticking your fingers down your throat every time you eat something fried?"

"SHUT THE FUCK UP!" Melissa shouted. "You don't know what the fuck you're talking about!" she added between clenched teeth.

"You act like your fucking track scholarship, law school, whatever—make you better than me just 'cause I want to skate or 'cause Mark wants to work at the pool. You don't think it's obvious to everyone that you're fucking miserable inside, and you can't be happy without tearing someone else down?"

Melissa had tears running down her cheeks.

"That's enough, Jess," Chad said.

"She gets to publicly humiliate me with her two-faced puppet Stacey, but I can't say anything about her? Fuck off."

Melissa got up and stormed away, Desiree trailing after her, sending waves sloshing across the jacuzzi.

Jessie stood and scowled. "What about you, Stacey?" he said. "Or do you only have something to say when Melissa is feeding you lies to repeat to her groupies?"

Stacey felt sick to her stomach, but she had told herself when the time came she would apologize to Jessie for what she'd said. She swallowed hard and exhaled, looking straight across the water at Jessie's flushed face. "I'm not Melissa's puppet. What you did hurt me. But I shouldn't have lied or spread rumors about you. I'm sorry."

Jessie's eyes narrowed. "Suddenly you have such a change of heart? Now you don't mean what you said and I'm supposed to just forgive you?"

"This isn't 'suddenly.' I've had a really shitty couple of weeks, and it all started with you. It's not like *you* ever apologized. Whether you forgive me or not is up to you."

"Well, this has been the most depressing high EVER," Mark said. "Chad, give me a lift home?"

"Sure, bud," Chad said as the group stood.

Tiffany hugged Stacey goodbye while Jessie grabbed his skateboard from the front porch and started down the hill. Mark climbed into Chad's passenger seat and they headed in the opposite direction from Jessie.

Stacey's car's headlights captured Jessie fading into the distance. There was no moon yet, and this part of the foothills had no streetlights along any of the narrow winding roads. She couldn't imagine just driving past him and letting him skate home to their neighborhood in total darkness. She pulled the Silver Bullet up beside him and rolled down the window.

"I'll give you a ride."

Jessie looked ahead on the road, where it was pitch black for at least a mile. It was after nine and they were five miles from home. He looked back at Stacey, scrutinizing her. "If this is pity, or a plan to humiliate me again, I'd really rather get myself home."

Stacey let out a breath she hadn't realized she was holding. "I meant it when I said I'm sorry. I shouldn't have said that stuff about you at Travis' party. Get in."

Jessie opened the passenger door and sat down. "Why did you?" he asked as he stood his skateboard between his legs and closed the door.

She bit the inside of her cheek. "Because I was hurt. And embarrassed."

"But why? I don't get it. I liked you. I thought you liked me, too. We had fun together."

She pulled away from the curb. "I liked you for a really long time, Jessie. When you finally noticed me, and kissed me, I thought it was because you wanted to be with me. Everything happened so fast. I wasn't ready. Then, when I saw that you were still with Melissa, it crushed me."

"Whoa! I've ALWAYS said I don't want a girlfriend. You should have known that. We were just hooking up."

"Why did you think I would just 'hook up' with anyone? I had zero experience before you."

"No way. You're hot and smart and you went to prom with that varsity basketball guy. Everyone has sex at prom."

Stacey pulled over to the gravel at the side of the road and pulled the emergency brake. The headlights lit the winding, narrow road. She took a breath, then turned to face Jessie. "Are you talking about Ryan Johnson? I did NOT have sex with Ryan. Not EVERYONE has sex after prom, actually."

Jessie rolled his eyes and shook his head, leaning back against the headrest. "He's a starter on the varsity team. Of course you had sex with him."

"Jessie, I *never* liked Ryan, and I was a VIRGIN before I went out with you!"

"Bullshit," Jessie said in a sing-song voice as he stared at the ceiling. "That night at the movies you said you'd screw a different guy every day, and when it was just the two of us you told me 'Maybe some people aren't meant for monogamy.'" He held his palms up as though he'd presented proof that supported his argument.

"We were playing Would You Rather and I was talking about your parents!" Stacey said, exasperation creeping into her voice. "So, because I went to a dance with a guy who wasn't my boyfriend, and I said 'some people aren't meant for monogamy,' you assumed I just wanted to have sex with you, no strings attached?"

"Yeah." He shrugged, his expression genuinely confused. "Chicks always seem to want it, like in movies and stuff."

Stacey cupped her forehead in her palms. "Are you talking about porn, Jessie? That's not real. And what happened between us is *not* what I wanted." Tears stung her eyes and her anger burned in her chest, but Stacey took a slow, deep breath and kept the tears in. She leaned her back against the door. "I was super excited when you asked me to watch the meteor shower and actually thought THAT was what we were going to do and maybe kiss again." Stacey looked at her hands. Her voice grew quiet and shaky. "But…you moved so fast… I'd never done ANY of those things with ANYONE before. I wasn't ready to have sex, but I was embarrassed to say no."

Jessie looked back and forth between Stacey's eyes in the dark car. "No way! Bullshit. You were totally into it. You never told me to stop."

"You ignored me when I said to wait. You never asked if I wanted to; you just shoved your cock in me like some slot machine. Then you barely acknowledged me afterward," Stacey said, her nostrils flaring. "Even if it hadn't been my first time, I know THAT is not what sex is supposed to be like. You used me."

"You never told me you were a virgin, and YOU totally ignored ME after."

"I…what?" She shook her head. "You barely said anything when I dropped you at your house. You never called me the next day, or since."

"Our phone is cut off." Jessie closed his eyes and tilted back. His head banged against the headrest. "Most of the time our electricity, too. My dad never pays the bills."

"That sucks, but it's really no excuse." Stacey clasped her hands in her lap to keep them from shaking. "Melissa also really liked you. Neither of us was interested in JUST hooking up, Jessie." She shifted in her seat and mumbled, "Why didn't you wear a condom?"

"What? You didn't tell me I needed to." Jessie furrowed his brow. "Aren't you on the pill?"

"I'd never had sex and didn't think I was going to be having sex. I wasn't on the pill."

Suddenly Jessie's eyes grew wide. "Are you...?" He glanced at Stacey's stomach then back to her eyes.

"I can't know for sure yet," she whispered. "I hope not."

"Shit!"

Stacey erupted. "Seriously? What the fuck, Jessie?" She hit him with the back of her hand. "This is my fucking life. My body. You did this! You have no right!"

"No! No. I know, Stacey! That's...it's not what I meant. I just..." He reached over and took Stacey's hand. She bristled, but he held tight. "I mean, I hope not, for both of us. I was trying to have fun and NOT think about hard shit. Everything is... so fucked up!"

"Yeah, but I don't have the luxury of *not* thinking about it." Stacey looked out the windshield. "I had to tell my mom, and—." She pulled free from Jessie's hands. "We went to Planned Parenthood. The pregnancy test was negative, but they said it was too early. Same for the STD tests."

Jessie's face dropped. "STDs?"

"Haven't you ever been checked? Seems like you have a lot of unprotected sex."

"Sorry, sorry," he said, his voice small and scared.

She turned back toward the wheel. "I need to take another pregnancy test." She released the parking brake and put the car in drive. "Tomorrow."

Stacey stepped on the gas, eager to get him home and out of her car. "You should go with me to Planned Parenthood and get tested for STDs. Then we can both know if we're totally in the clear."

"Okay, I can do that," Jessie said, looking out the passenger window.

"And stop having sex without a condom." Stacey kept her eyes on the double yellow line to navigate the curves in the road. "And make sure the girl you're with actually says yes, that she wants to do it with you."

"Slow down," Jessie said.

"Exactly," she snapped back. "Take things way slower!"

"No. The car." Jessie strained to see where they were in the darkness. "I think you took a wrong turn."

Stacey clenched her jaw and slowed. Scanning the dark fields around them, she realized he was right. They were far from any neighborhood and hadn't passed a cross-street in awhile.

She began a three point turn on the narrow road. As she was backing up, a coyote trotted across the street in front of her car, then stopped in the middle of her high beams.

Jessie was still looking out the side window and hadn't noticed. "Maybe if we go back—"

"Shhh!" Stacey kept her foot pressed hard on the brake, locking eyes with the coyote.

"Oh…shit…," Jessie whispered.

Head held high, the coyote's calm yellow glare burned through Stacey. It had long, strong copper-colored legs, but the tan-and-black coat was patchy on the animal's side and chest, and part of its right ear was missing. There were deep scars on its narrow, red muzzle. The coyote had been through some violent encounter long before. Despite that, here it was standing firm in front of her car. Unafraid.

"That coyote is a fucking warrior," Jessie muttered.

"I wanna be that brave," Stacey whispered.

The coyote blinked, turned its head, and trotted into the brush. Its fluffy tail was the last thing Stacey saw before it disappeared back into the inky night.

Stacey eased her foot off the gas and straightened the wheel. She'd never felt more certain of where she wanted to go.

Chapter Twenty-Three

Saturday was the first day of the Plunge Olympics and the forecast was for temperatures in the high nineties: a perfect day for families to spend at the pool.

Stacey picked up Jessie on her way into work, since they both had to be there at eight and work through lap swim. "I told my mom not to worry if I wasn't home for a few hours," she said as she turned out of his apartment complex onto the main road. "I'm not sure how long our tests will take at Planned Parenthood. It could be busier on weekends."

"Why do we have to go to *that* place? Can't you just take a test from Thrifty or something to see if you're knocked up?" Jessie asked.

"I mean, yeah, but the clinic's pregnancy tests are more accurate, I think. And what about you getting tested for STDs?" Stacey yawned. She'd been awake for hours in the middle of the night, worrying about what might happen.

Jessie pulled out his wallet. "I really don't think STDs are anything you need to worry about anyway." He put a twenty dollar bill in the cup holder. "Is that enough?"

"You promised me you would get tested. You're acting really weird. Like you're scared of Planned Parenthood or something."

"It's just, after you dropped me off last night, I thought more about it. What if someone we know is there?" He rubbed his wrist where the WWJD bracelet used to be. He hadn't worn it in a while.

At the stoplight, Stacey flicked on her blinker and thought about the Planned Parenthood waiting room. How the women didn't make eye contact with one another. How other women stood outside holding signs and spewing judgments.

"You're worried someone from Christian Club or church will be outside, like part of the protest?"

"No!" He paused, looking out the passenger side window. "Maybe. Aren't you? Don't you think if someone recognizes us they'll assume you're only there to have an..." he lowered his voice to a whisper, "...an a-bor-tion?"

Flashes of conversations whirled through Stacey's mind: Stephanie shaking her head at the party, disgusted, when Stacey talked about having sex with Jessie. Mary Jo warning Stacey about Jessie. Both girls were friends with a lot of the same people that Jessie and Stacey knew from Christian Club.

Ugh! Everyone is probably talking about Jessie and I having sex.

"You have a point." Stacey pulled into The Plunge parking lot and parked in the shade. "I'll go buy a test during my break this morning."

Jessie nodded. "Cool. Thanks." He reached for the door handle.

"Jessie," Stacey stopped him. "You know, if I am pregnant, I'm NOT having a baby. It would ruin my life to have a kid this young. You get that, right?"

Jessie nodded again, sucking in his cheeks. He wouldn't make eye-contact.

"There's no way I'm going through that alone. You would have to go with me."

"Let's hope it doesn't come to that," he said. He grabbed his skateboard and towel, climbed out, and walked ahead of Stacey to the pool entrance.

Bob had put a schedule of Plunge Olympics events up in the pay window and hung American flag bunting over the front door.

"Everyone ready for Games Day? Hopefully we'll get a good turnout. *Sun News* will be here to take pictures, so you all need to act professional. Get this place so spotless you can eat off the floor and do it within one hour," Bob reminded them. "Only use the megaphones for safety purposes and keep the chit chat to a minimum. Focus on your job."

Jessie looked at Stacey, his eyebrows high.

She puffed out her cheeks and exhaled slowly.

If Bob only knew how hard THAT will be.

Melissa rolled her eyes. She picked up a bucket and trash grabber and headed out to the deck without slamming her locker or saying anything to anyone.

Stacey offered to clean the girls' bathroom while Jessie cleaned the boys' bathroom and Melissa hosed the deck. Jessie cleaned the pool drain, and they got all the lane lines in place for the races. They were wiping down the picnic tables and bleacher seats as the first swimmers began lining up outside along the fence.

By the time the pool opened at nine, Melissa and Stacey were in their lifeguard stands, and Jessie was holding a clipboard at the end of the pool where families could sign up for the relay race.

Within half an hour, the entire facility was packed with swimmers. They were required to have three guards watching the water at all times for anything over a hundred people, and by rough estimate it appeared they were pushing their max capacity of two hundred and fifty. Bob was giddy over the enthusiasm the community was showing for The Plunge Olympics and put a sign in the pay window that said "MORNING SWIM SOLD OUT." He called Mark to come in so he could remain available to officiate the races.

As the first race started at ten, twenty families had signed up to compete. With only six lanes total, Bob decided they would need to have four initial races of five relay teams each, then a final race between the four winning teams to place for gold, silver, and bronze. Then they could keep the last lane open for shallow-end swimming during the races and the deep end and diving board would remain open the entire time.

Stacey was blowing her whistle constantly. Dozens of people would turn at the sound while the kid running or throwing something into the water appeared oblivious. Despite using the megaphone, her voice was becoming hoarse. She stood in her tower to get a clearer view of the water, but it didn't help much. There were way too many bodies.

That morning Stacey'd had no appetite for breakfast, but as the mayhem around the pool increased, her hands began to shake. She'd forgotten to bring a snack.

"This Olympics thing is insane," Stacey told Jessie as he took over her tower during rotation. "There's no way I can leave during my break."

"Yeah. I hope it's not like this for the full two weeks," he agreed, looking around at the crowd. "Let's just go to the pharmacy after work, 'kay? On our way home?"

Stacey nodded, then made her way around the deep end to take over Melissa's position in the shallow-end tower.

Melissa climbed down the ladder, scowling. "What the fuck is going on with you two?" she hissed into Stacey's ear.

"Me and Jessie?" Stacey tried to keep her eye on the pool, but felt dizzy and nauseous. She gripped the ladder. "Nothing. I swear."

Kids nearby in the water were splashing each other and shriek-laughing.

"It doesn't seem like nothing. After what he said last night, I thought you would have been more loyal. Told him to go to hell. Instead, you gave him a ride home and a ride to work? Seriously?"

From across the pool, Bob eyed them as he directed the relay teams where they needed to line up for the next race. He held a stopwatch in one hand and gestured to Stacey with the other to wrap it up.

"Melissa, it's really not like that, but can we–"

"Obviously you're not as good of a friend as I thought." Melissa spun around and weaved through the throng of spectators to the guard shack.

"Ugh…." Stacey climbed the ladder to the tower, feeling sick to her stomach. Once settled in the tower, Bob nodded his approval. Her head spun with Melissa's words. She looked across the water at Jessie, then tried to push the thoughts from her mind and focus on the swimmers.

Bob was trying to clear the race lanes again, shouting to swimmers to shuffle over to the one free lane. Adults interested in watching the race stood in the water along the end lane-line, crammed so tight it was difficult to see around and beneath them. Toddlers were jumping into their parents' arms from the edge of the deck. Small kids struggled to stay afloat, paddling around the mass of bodies in water too deep for them. Older kids were diving beneath the surface like dolphins, navigating around and between the feet of spectators.

Stacey's chest tightened at the thought of even one child at the bottom, unnoticed, like the boy she'd rescued a few weeks earlier from the deep end. She waved Mark over.

With his megaphone in hand and a red buoy strapped to his back, Mark motioned for Bob to watch his section. He kept his eyes on the pool as he maneuvered close enough to the foot of Stacey's tower that they could talk.

"What's up?" Mark asked through the megaphone to be heard over the crowd.

Stacey leaned over the railing and shouted down to him, gesturing with her hand. "There's a whole section of the pool in the four-to-six-foot-deep area that I can't see during the races, because of everyone crowding by the lane line. If Bob is timing the races and judging the winner, he can't watch it, either."

"Yeah," Mark yelled back. "We really should clear all the water except the diving board area during races. I'll tell Bob."

Stacey looked across at Bob. He was holding up his stopwatch and a few gold coin necklaces while a newspaper photographer snapped photos, the crowded pool as backdrop.

Jessie's whistle blew. Stacey whipped around to see a kid narrowly miss landing on another in the deep end. She was about to jump when Jessie reprimanded them.

Sweat dripped down her back and under her arms. Stacey shielded her eyes and squinted, scanning her own section of the pool again.

The racers were lined up on their blocks. Bob's starter pistol erupted with a loud crack. Stacey startled. Swimmers dove in. Cheering erupted around the water and pool deck.

Stacey eyed Mark standing on the deck by the section of the pool she was worried about, and he gave her a thumbs up that he had it covered. She surveyed the shallow end, saw kids running and blew her whistle, then shouted, "No running" into the megaphone.

The bathroom doors clanged shut, echoing across the concrete among the screams and claps and splashing. Stacey's heart beat hard as she noticed the next leg of the racers diving in. They splashed across the pool and back. Then another group went.

Mark's voice boomed from the megaphone across the water. A pair of middle schoolers sitting on the top railing at the back of the bleachers were told to climb down.

Suddenly, Bob sounded the bullhorn signaling that the race was over. Swimmers flooded into the open lanes again for a few minutes of free swim before the next race began.

Stacey was struggling to pay attention. She felt woozy. She inched forward, sitting on the edge of her seat, gripping the tower railings.

When Melissa exited the guard shack at 11:30 and took Mark's place in the rotation, she was obviously fuming. Still queasy, Stacey was eager to head inside. Mark handed Melissa his red buoy and megaphone before moving to the deep end tower to take over for Jessie, who in turn made his way to take over for Stacey.

"You okay?" Jessie asked as she climbed unsteadily out of the tower.

"This is just too much. Especially with…EVERYTHING ELSE. My nerves are fried." She dragged herself inside.

Stacey found a smushed Nutri-Grain bar in the back of her locker and ripped the wrapper open. Nibbling on the mealy snack, she filled her empty 44-ounce Del Taco cup with water and gulped half down, before slumping into the couch. Soaking in the coolness of the office and relative quiet, she closed her eyes.

A loud tap at the pay window interrupted her dozing. She blinked her eyes open and recognized one of the pool's regulars at the window. The woman was about eighty, with a round, pale face and a lemon-yellow swim cap pulled over her hair, a strap secured beneath her double chin. Stacey stood and pulled open the pay window.

"Can I help you?" Stacey asked groggily.

"It's so loud out there." The woman's voice was high pitched and shaky." I was afraid you wouldn't hear me."

"Yeah, I'm sorry about that. It's a crazy day."

"I saw in the paper about the Plunge Olympics. It's happening for a couple of weeks, right? Will there still be lap swim?"

"Um, yeah… As far as I know."

"Even today?" the woman asked, eyeing the crowd through the guard shack window.

Stacey leaned back and looked up at the clock on the wall above the window. It was five minutes to twelve. She looked over her shoulder, and could see the winning relay families' silhouettes through the tinted glass, posing for their photos in front of the guard shack, their backs to her. Parents handed Bob their cameras and he juggled the collection while the newspaper photographer clicked pictures and directed the children to hold up their medals and smile.

"I think they're just wrapping up," Stacey said. "I'm sure the pool will be cleared in a few minutes."

"Okay. Can I pay now?" She showed her three quarters, the senior discounted price for an hour of swimming laps.

"Sure." Stacey held out her hand and the woman dropped the quarters in. She put the change in the cash box and pushed the window shut as the elderly woman pulled open the door to the girls locker room.

Stacey picked up her cup, gulping what was left of her water. The photo session had wrapped. She perched on the arm of the couch, watching as Mark and Jessie stood in the towers blowing their whistles, announcing the end of the morning swim session. Bob unlocked the gate, ushering patrons out.

Mark and Jessie climbed down, and along with Melissa, they paced the pool deck encouraging stragglers to climb out and collect their belongings.

Water pooled into a lake at the far end of the deck under the diving blocks, where the relay racers had waited their turns in dripping swimsuits. Bob, Mark, and Jessie trotted around the massive puddles on their way to the guard shack. Melissa took a seat in the tower, and the elderly lap swim woman sat on the edge of the bleachers, removing her orthopedic sandals and housecoat. The woman wore a saggy, faded purple swimsuit that was only a few shades darker than her almost transparent lavender skin.

"Okay!" Bob threw open the door, clapping excitedly, and headed straight for the desk. "That was a great start!"

"Are you kidding me?" Mark stopped in his tracks. "That was a fucking circus!"

Bob turned back, his smile ear to ear. "Come on, Mark! Sure, there are some kinks to iron out, but we haven't had that kind of a turnout here in two decades!"

There was a metal clicking noise at the pay window. All four of them turned to see another regular: a shriveled bald man with leather skin and an arched back. He showed them his quarters, then set them on the counter.

The man was already headed in through the boys locker room when Bob waved at him. Bob grabbed the quarters and dropped them into the cash box. He turned back to Mark, whose arms were crossed and jaw was set. "This many people coming in for two weeks straight could convince the city this place is worthwhile," Bob said. "They might even finally refurbish the pool."

"There's no safe way to run that many races twice a day and keep free swim open at the same time." Mark pointed his thumb at Stacey over his shoulder. "Her rescue the other day was with good visuals on all the swimmers. I don't even want to think about what could have happened today."

"I agree. Safety first!" Bob said. "We will always have at least four guards on duty. We'll shut down the shallow end for the second hour of open swim to conduct the races back-to-back. Jessie, Stacey, can you stay on this afternoon in case we need you?"

They both nodded, but gave one another knowing looks.

"Maybe we can get swim team to open the snack bar?" Jessie suggested.

"Great idea. Mark, can you give their director a call? Tell him they can recruit some new swimmers from the events! Let's get some posters made. List the races and top three swimmers' names with gold, silver, or red stars next to their times."

"I can run to Thrifty and grab the poster supplies," Stacey offered, eyeing Jessie. "I'll get back before Melissa's thirty minutes are even up."

"Yes! Great! Thank you. Jessie, order some pizzas for all of the crew, too. Here," Bob took his wallet from his back pocket and handed them a few twenties. "Get a bunch. I'm going to run to city hall, see if the mayor can be here for our two hundred freestyle this afternoon!"

Stacey slipped into her Birkenstocks, grabbed her keys, and ran out the door behind Bob with just her towel around her waist. They turned out of the parking lot in tandem. As they waited at the first stop light on the boulevard, she peered through Bob's passenger window. He was still beaming.

For a split second, she considered Jessie's concerns, and what the person at Thrifty's checkout counter would think about her buying pregnancy tests. Mesa Valley was a small town, and the only people who would wear a solid red swimsuit were lifeguards at The Plunge. It wouldn't take long to put two and two together and for the rumors to fly. But Stacey needed to know if her symptoms were what she feared, and she needed to know now.

Stacey turned her shoulders sideways to run between the pharmacy's slow moving sliding glass doors, and headed straight for the school supplies. She grabbed three poster boards, a pack of star stickers, extra-large poster letters, and a box of Crayola markers. In the aisle with the pregnancy tests, she grabbed two different brands of double kits and hid them under her arm beneath the supplies.

She piled everything on the front counter and held Bob's and Jessie's cash in her hand.

The cashier was in her late twenties, chewing a huge wad of bubble gum. She scanned the items at a glacial pace, dropping them in a plastic bag while staring at Stacey. "You work at The Plunge? This stuff for that Olympics thing?"

"Um hmm." Stacey bounced on her heels, avoiding eye contact.

"Want these in the bag, too?" the cashier asked, holding up the poster board.

"No. That's okay." Stacey grabbed them, shoving the boards back under her arm, and held the two twenties across the counter.

The last two items–both boxes of pregnancy tests–sat on the counter exposed, and the cashier paused as if intentionally dragging out the process. Stacey's heart raced. She glanced over her shoulder to make sure no one she knew was coming up behind her.

"These yours, too?" the cashier asked.

Stacey gawked at her. "Just ring them up and tell me what I owe you."

The cashier made a spectacle of rolling her eyes and dropping each kit in the bag. "$34.45," she said, the gum smacking while she held out her palm.

Stacey handed her the twenties, then strummed her fingers impatiently on the counter as the cashier counted out her change. She gripped the money in her palm as she ran back out to her car. She turned the Silver Bullet onto the boulevard, grateful only ten minutes had passed since she'd left the pool.

In The Plunge parking lot, she wrapped the pregnancy kits in her towel and carried the bundle with her keys and wallet in her left hand, the plastic Thrifty bag and poster boards in her right.

She ran in the main pool entrance and pulled open the guard shack door, quickly dropping the bag and poster boards inside. "I've REALLY gotta pee," she said, staring at Jessie and backing out toward the bathroom.

"Don't need to know," Mark groaned from the desk chair, rubbing his temples, his feet up and head leaned back.

Jessie nodded his understanding. "I'll take over for Melissa. Come out whenever you're ready."

Stacey slammed the bathroom stall door shut and swung her towel over the narrow opening. She quickly peeled open the boxes and unwrapped all four sticks. She pulled her bathing suit aside and squatted over the toilet, careful to pee on each of the test strips.

She rested the sticks on squares of toilet paper on top of the toilet paper dispenser, then exited the stall. She shoved the boxes deep into the trash can, then washed her hands.

Stacey saw herself in the mirror, but barely recognized the person staring back. Her face was thin, her eyes tired. She ran her damp fingers along the sides of her head, pulling the loose hairs across her forehead and tucking them behind her ears.

"In a few minutes this will all be over," she mumbled to herself, then froze. "Shit!" *How did I not think to bring a watch?*

She scrambled back into the stall to see if anything had happened. Biting the nail of her middle finger, she decided to just wait however long it took until something happened in all four indicator windows. *Jessie will understand.*

She locked the stall door and readjusted the towel over the gap in case anyone came in. *If I count to nine hundred, that would be fifteen minutes. But, it's already been like four minutes, right? So, like 650 would be good? One, two, three, four, five, six....*

A whistle sounded out by the pool. There was a loud splash. A shiver ran up Stacey's spine.

Before she was out of the stall, she heard Mark shouting. She pulled open the heavy exterior bathroom door and ran out. Melissa stood in the doorway of the lifeguard office, her hands over her mouth. Stacey followed Melissa's gaze.

Jessie!

He was face down in the pool in the fifth lane. The water around him was turning red.

BLOOD!

Mark was running to the edge of the pool with the backboard. "Call 9-1-1, NOW!" he shouted.

"Melissa!" Stacey screamed. "Call for an ambulance, Melissa!"

Melissa snapped to attention and turned toward the phone in the guard shack.

Stacey ran out of her Birkenstocks, stopping at the pool's edge at the shallow end, and quickly glanced around the pool, getting her bearings.

The old lady was climbing out at the side ladder. The weathered old man was in the third lane in the deep end of the pool, holding onto the metal rung of the diving block with one hand. His back was turned to Stacey, but his other arm was wrapped around something.

No. Someone. Another swimmer? Is he hurt, too?

Mark entered the water in the deep end where Jessie floated and rushed the backboard to him. "Stacey! I need you."

She dropped into the water at the shallow end and made her way to Mark's side. By the time she got to them, Mark had Jessie face up, and was trying to maneuver the board under him. Blood was rushing from a gash on Jessie's forehead and a split across the top of his nose.

Stacey grabbed the Velcro straps to help Mark attach Jessie to the backboard.

Gripping the handles of the backboard, they rushed to get the board with Jessie's limp body to the edge of the pool in the shallow end.

Melissa was there, waiting.

Mark shouted, "Once he's out, apply pressure to the wound on his head, without putting any on his neck. No pressure on his neck!"

Melissa grabbed a folded yellow striped towel from the deck. Flip-flops and keys fell out of the towel, and landed on the wet concrete.

Mark quickly jumped out of the pool and lifted the head of the backboard. Stacey positioned herself to push it from the water. The muscles in her arms and stomach burned as she tried to keep the board stable while lifting Jessie out.

"Are paramedics coming?" Mark asked, lowering the head of the board to the ground, and getting onto his knees beside Jessie.

"They're on their way." Melissa placed the towel on Jessie's forehead and held it steady with both hands.

Stacey climbed out of the water and knelt opposite Mark.

Mark placed one hand over the other just above Jessie's sternum. He locked his elbows and pushed down. Nothing. He pressed again, harder.

On the third chest compression, Jessie heaved and he coughed up water. Mark and Stacey tilted the board to the side to help Jessie clear the water out.

Jessie's skin had paled. Eyes barely open, his face was covered in blood.

"He's breathing. I've got this," Mark said. "Go check on them."

Stacey ran toward the two men on the other side of the pool.

The bald, elderly man held the other swimmer's face out of the water in the crook of his arm.

Oh my God. NO! Is he…

The body was lifeless. The face was bloated, like an anchored buoy tethered to the body beneath. The eyes were open, unblinking. The lips, visibly blue.

Stacey recognized the drowned man as another regular lap swimmer. "Mark!" she yelled as she reached down and gripped under the bloated man's armpit. The old man let go and moved aside. The blue, swollen face started slipping beneath the water again, and Stacey put a knee down to stop herself from being pulled down along with the dead weight.

Mark swam across the pool at lightning speed.

Within seconds, he was out of the pool at her side. Mark and Stacey each gripped the man's wrists with both hands, trying to pull his bloated body onto the deck between the diving blocks. Stacey grunted as her lower back spasmed. The man's body hung limp and heavy against the side of the pool gutter.

"You take under his arms," Mark told Stacey. "And I'll grab hold of his shorts. Pull back on the count of three. One, two, thre-uuuhhh." Stacey and Mark muscled the body barely up, onto the edge of the deck. "Again. One, two, THREE!" They dragged him back further. Stacey lost her grip, and the man's upper body and head landed with a thump by her feet.

Mark knelt in the deep puddle beside the motionless body. "I'll give compressions. You check for pulse and breathing," he told Stacey.

Stacey fell onto her knees beside him.

Sirens sounded in the distance.

Mark started chest compressions. "One, two, three, four, five…"

Water oozed from the pot-bellied man's dark lips. There was no movement in his body. He didn't cough or flinch. His eyes were vacant.

"Eight, nine, ten…" Mark called out.

Stacey probed the cold, wet neck with her fingers, searching for a pulse. She hovered her cheek over the man's open mouth, listening for breath.

"Anything?" Mark asked, still pressing hard into the man's chest.

Stacey shook her head.

"Breathe!" Mark yelled at her, never ceasing his pumping.

Stacey clamped her fingers over the man's nostrils with her left hand, tilted his chin up with her right. She blew as hard as she could into the man's mouth. It was like blowing against a glass window; the air had nowhere to go.

Stacey tried clearing his windpipe with her finger. Nothing came out.

She blew three more times. "It's not going in!"

Mark took over, trying to blow into the man's mouth. "Fuck!" Mark returned to pressing the man's chest.

Paramedics ran up beside them.

"There's no pulse. We can't get any air in," Stacey said as she scurried out of the way.

"Let's intubate," one paramedic said to the other. While Mark continued pumping the chest, the medics opened their kit and slid a metal device into the man's mouth. They pushed a tube through the device and down his throat.

Stacey stood, frozen in place. The pot-bellied man's body lay completely still as paramedics squeezed the ball pump attached to the tube. His empty eyes stared straight up at the sun.

"We need to move him out of these puddles," a paramedic shouted. "AED STAT!"

Mark continued chest compressions until a third medic arrived with the gurney. The squeaking wheels rushed toward Stacey, and she startled, backing out of the way. The four men lifted the body onto the gurney and rolled it to a dry part of the deck.

Unsure what else to do, Stacey trailed them until they stopped in front of the bleachers.

She looked past the gurney, Mark, and the paramedics, to where the little old lady in the purple suit sat in the bleachers, weeping and watching.

The head paramedic held the AED paddles to the man's chest. The limp body jolted with each shock. There was still no response in his eyes.

They squeezed the ball pump again. The man's bloated face was blue-gray.

Stacey turned away, her hand over her mouth.

Two medics wheeled Jessie across the deck to the open gate and a waiting ambulance.

A large red fire truck pulled away from the curb. It cleared the way to the pool entrance for a second ambulance, its sirens blaring.

Police cars arrived, the lights flashing, and blocked the parking lot entrance.

One officer rushed to stand at the exit.

The ambulance transporting Jessie turned on its lights and siren and rushed out of the parking lot, the officer in the street waving him past oncoming traffic.

Another officer ran up to Melissa, who was standing by the gate.

Melissa talked to the officer, pointing and gesturing. Her hands and forearm were smeared with blood. *Jessie's blood.*

A pizza delivery guy appeared by the gate.

A car screeched to a stop by the police cars. Bob jumped out and ran to the pool gate, abandoning his car in the street.

Stacey turned back to the paramedics. The body.

The medic with the defibrillator paddles stepped back. "That's ten shocks. I'm calling it." He looked at his watch. "Time of death 12:47 p.m."

Mark dropped to sit on the ground beside the gurney, defeated. He anchored his elbows to his knees and held his head in his hands.

Stacey looked away.

Bob put his hand on Melissa's shoulder. She turned into his chest, crying. The officer took notes on a small pad of paper he pulled from his pocket.

On the bottom bench of the bleachers, wrapped in her housecoat, the old woman was crying, her yellow swim cap bobbing up and down. The paramedic pulled a sheet over the drowned swimmer's body.

The remaining ambulance turned off its lights.

The old man with the curved back stood beside the lifeguard tower, giving a statement to a firefighter with a clipboard.

An officer wearing gloves dropped the bloodied yellow striped towel into a plastic bag. He picked up the flip-flops and a set of keys and dropped them in a second bag.

The fireman with the clipboard crouched beside Mark.

The doors of the second ambulance closed, but there were no lights or sirens. It didn't race off.

The police officer with the bags of belongings from beside the pool approached Stacey. "Miss, do you know who these keys belong to?"

Stacey shook her head slowly.

"They were his," a high, shaky voice called out.

Stacey and the officer turned toward the bleachers.

The old woman was standing, holding the railing. "The man who drowned. He always folded his shoes and keys into his towel at the end of his lane."

"Thank you," the officer called over to her. "May I ask you a few questions?"

The elderly woman nodded and sat on the bench.

The officer waved over a firefighter with a first aid kit. "Let him help you get cleaned up," he said to Stacey, "then I'd like to get your statement as well."

Confused, Stacey looked at her hands. They were shaking, but she didn't see blood.

Then she looked down. Blood trickled down her thigh.

Stacey waved off the approaching firefighter and turned toward the bathroom. The door screeched open and closed with a heavy thud behind her. Her eyes adjusted to the dim light. She walked into the stall, staring at the four pregnancy tests resting atop the toilet paper dispenser. They were all positive.

She felt dizzy and caught herself against the stall wall.

Tests scattered to the floor.

She heaved the contents of her stomach into the toilet.

Her abdomen cramped.

With each retch, rivers of blood poured down her inner thighs.

She took a wad of toilet paper and wiped the blood from her legs. She dropped it in the toilet, flushed, then slid down the partition onto the wet concrete floor, and hugged her knees. She started shaking uncontrollably. She gripped her elbows tighter and erupted with tears.

Suddenly, Melissa was kneeling by her side, her arms around Stacey.

Stacey looked into Melissa's blotchy red face. The thought of discussing everything that had just happened made her afraid she would vomit again. She slid her legs out in front of her, and put her arms around Melissa. They sobbed into one another's necks.

As they caught their breath and Melissa pulled away, she noticed the tests on the ground.

"What's—?" Melissa's voice caught as she picked one of the tests up. And another. "Stacey?" She searched Stacey's face for an explanation.

Chapter Twenty-Four

He's stable, but unconscious," Bob told Stacey when she picked up her home phone Sunday morning. "He's broken some vertebrae in his neck, and the ICU doctors aren't sure yet if he's paralyzed, or how extensive the damage might be."

"Can we see him?" Stacey asked, wondering whether visitors were allowed on Sunday morning.

"He's only allowed to have family visiting as long as he's in the ICU."

Stacey wondered whether Jessie's dad was there. Or his little brother. She knew his mom wouldn't be, and probably had no idea about his accident. Did he have any other family? Or was Jessie all alone?

Bob cleared his throat. "We've decided to keep the pool closed through at least the end of the week. The city wants each of us to come in tomorrow for interviews. They're investigating the drowning. And Jessie's accident."

Stacey shivered. She pulled her knees up under her on the couch. "What do they need to know?"

Bob's voice was uneasy. "They mostly want to make sure everything was done the way it should be. If…any of it could have been avoided."

Her stomach jumped to her throat. "What happens if they decide it was someone's fault?"

"You don't need to worry about that, Stacey. You weren't in charge, and you did everything you could to help with both rescues," Bob said. There was something in his tone, though, that made Stacey afraid he wasn't confident all of them would come out of this unscathed.

If they decide my being irresponsible led to Jessie's accident, will I have to report it on every future job application? Will I have to include that in college applications? Stacey felt sharp pain behind her eyes and rubbed her forehead.

Stacey's mom was seated across from her on the couch and mouthed "What's up?" Stacey eyed her nervously, then shooed her off.

"What time do I need to be there?" Stacey asked, chewing on her thumbnail.

"I'm meeting with them at ten. Melissa is at noon. Your interview is at two, then Mark at four. I think they'll schedule the others later this week, since they weren't working when…" Bob's voice trailed off. "The recreation director asked me to have you write down as many details as you can remember. Do it today, while everything is still clear in your mind, and bring it with you. You need to know that your official statement will be a matter of public record. That means journalists, lawyers—anyone interested—has access to it."

Stacey clamped her lips shut until the call ended, then dropped the phone and ran to the bathroom. She threw up the toast and orange juice she'd managed to choke down for breakfast.

"Honey," her mom called from the doorway. "Are you okay? Do you need anything?"

"No," Stacey coughed out. "I'm okay." She changed her pad, flushed the toilet, then washed her hands and splashed water on her face.

The drowned man's purple face and vacant eyes stared back at her every time she closed her eyes. The gashes on Jessie's forehead and nose. All the blood. All night long those visions haunted her. Now she had to write it down, relive it all again, and tell it in detail to some investigator the next day.

Her mom and Murphy were waiting when she returned to the couch. Stacey curled into the fetal position, her body around Murphy's. She rested her head on her mom's knee.

"What did Bob say?" her mom asked.

"Jessie's still unconscious, probably paralyzed," Stacey said, looking up into her mom's eyes. "I have to give a statement about everything that happened yesterday."

"I'm sorry, Bug. I can understand how hard that will be. But I'm not surprised." Her mom ran her fingers through Stacey's hair. "They need to cover their bases in case there's a lawsuit."

"I was supposed to be in the tower when the man drowned. What if they say it was all my fault?"

"No one will say that, Stacey. It could have happened to anyone at any time."

"But…he…Jessie was distracted. We both were." Tears rimmed Stacey's eyes. "What if that's why…?"

Her mom gripped Stacey's shoulder. "Jessie's accident was not your fault! And the city doesn't need to know about any of what was going on between the two of you," she said firmly, then loosened her grip. "It's none of their damn business. Just tell them you had diarrhea or something, and that's why you offered to go to the pharmacy. Why you were in the bathroom. And why Jessie covered for you."

Stacey nodded, then curled her head into Murphy's ribs.

Her mom's hand rested between Stacey's shoulder blades and her voice softened. "Are you still bleeding?"

Stacey nodded. Her tears dampened Murphy's fur beneath her cheek.

"Okay. That's good. We'll take another test again in a few days, but I'm sure this means the stress of everything yesterday ended it...naturally."

Stacey nodded again, then pushed herself upright, tucking her feet under Murphy's paws. "Mom, can I ask you something?"

"Of course."

"I'm so thankful that I've had you to lean on the last few weeks. Truly. But, are you..." Stacey hesitated. "...ashamed of me?"

"God, no! Stacey, why would you think that?" She gripped Stacey's hand.

"Because I'm not the daughter you thought I was. It would make more sense if you *were* ashamed." Stacey shrugged. "I've screwed up so much lately."

"I'm not at all ashamed of you, Bug. You made a few mistakes, that's true. But you're a good person. I'm proud of how you're handling things." Her mom inhaled and exhaled audibly. She picked up her coffee mug and stared into it. "Honestly, I could have done a better job preparing you for all of this. If there's anyone I am ashamed of, it's me."

Stacey's eyes welled up. "You're a really great mom. I'm so sorry I made you feel that way."

Her mom sipped from her mug.

Murphy shifted her weight between them and rested her head on Stacey's feet.

Stacey noticed the wildflowers on the coffee table in one of the pottery vases she'd made in art lab. "Why hasn't Greg been around?" she asked.

Her mom followed her gaze to the flowers. "I told him I needed to take a break for a while."

"Because of me? Greg's a really nice guy. I don't want you to do that."

"I just feel like this is all so much for both you and me to think about. Even before Jessie's accident. I'm drained. I don't have anything to offer anyone else right now."

"What if Greg just wants to help you through it? To be there for you? He said he has two daughters, too. He knows what this is like."

"I mean…" Her mom's eyebrows knit together. "I guess that is basically what he told me. But, Stacey, are you telling me you *want* Greg around?"

"Yeah. I like him," Stacey said. "He makes you happy. At least one of us deserves to be happy right now."

"Are you sure?"

Stacey managed a half-smile. "Call him, Mom. Maybe he can make us dinner tonight."

"Is that a jab at my cooking?" Her mom play-slapped Stacey's knee.

"There's no comparison. It's not a personal attack, it's just a fact."

At two p.m. Monday, Stacey sat at the same conference table where Bob and the recreation director had interviewed her for the job two months before.

A woman about her mom's age, with thick, chocolatey brown hair knotted atop her head, sat across from her, a yellow legal pad and several pens on the table in front of her. She'd hung her gray suit jacket over the back of her chair, and the white sleeveless blouse she wore had damp yellow stains under the arms.

"I'm Sylvia Lopez, legal counsel for the City of Mesa Valley."

The fluorescent lights buzzed above them despite the bright glare from the picture window behind the lawyer.

Stacey wasn't sure if she was supposed to speak. "Nice to meet you?" she said, the words lifting into an unintended question.

"Just to cover a few formalities: every member of the Seventh Street Community Pool will be interviewed. All of the statements will be a matter of public record. While we expect some small discrepancies in each recounting of the events of July 20th, if there is a significant difference in any testimonies we will need to clarify with further inquiries. Do you understand?"

Stacey nodded, biting her upper lip and staring at the lined yellow pad. She pulled the folded sheet of notebook paper from her back pocket.

"As you are the only minor involved in this investigation, I must inform you that your participation in our line of questioning is considered voluntary. Do you agree that you are here of your own volition and not being forced to respond under any duress?"

"Um…okay…I guess so," Stacey said.

"I need a simple yes or no answer, please, Ms. Chapman," the lawyer said, with an exasperated sigh. "Are you participating in this investigation of your own free will?"

"Yes," Stacey said, her pulse quickening.

"May I also have your permission to record our conversation?"

Stacey nodded.

Ms. Lopez eyed her, and flexed her jaw, breathing out of her nostrils.

"Yes," Stacey said.

The lawyer set a small tape recorder on the table between them and clicked it on. She asked Stacey for the spelling of her legal name and her birthdate, then wrote them on the top of the page, along with the time and date of the interview. "Now, Ms. Chapman, let's start with a rough outline of the morning. What time did you arrive? Who was already present and who was scheduled to work?" she asked.

With her mom and Greg's help the night before, Stacey had spent two hours planning what exactly she wanted to say. Starting with the end of morning swim, she'd written extensive notes on who was where at what time. She didn't want to give the impression that anyone was irresponsible when Jessie's accident happened.

Now that she had to give her formal statement, though, she felt sick to her stomach. She hadn't realized they'd want her to talk about the whole day. "Um… Jessie lives near me, so I gave him a ride to the pool. We got there at 7:57, and Bob and Melissa were already there. We all had a lot to do to clean the facility and prepare for The Plunge Olympics events. By nine there was a large crowd waiting to come in."

"You are referring to pool manager Bob Smith and lifeguard Melissa Phillips, correct?"

"Yeah."

"Do you know the maximum pool capacity and do you feel it was adhered to during the morning community event? Or do you have reason to believe it was breached?"

Adhered to? Breached? Stacey shook her head. "Uh, the sign posted by the pool says capacity is 250, and I think it was 'adhered to'. Bob put up a sign that no one else could come in. But what difference does it make? The drowning didn't happen during morning swim. It was after, during lap swim, when there were only three people in the pool."

The woman held her pen between both hands above the legal pad. "Ms. Chapman, your testimony is intended to help us understand ALL of the factors that contributed to the incident in question. Whether there are any patterns of negligence at the Mesa Valley Community Pool, and which—if any—safety precautions were disregarded."

"Okaaayyyy…" Stacey's eyes narrowed at the lawyer. Clearly the woman was trying to bait her into saying something that would get her or another guard in trouble. "Well, we didn't go over capacity. And as soon as it was apparent we would have so many swimmers, Bob called Mark to come in, too."

"Yes. Tell me more about that. You are referring to assistant pool manager Mark Rosenthal, correct?" Ms. Lopez asked, flipping back through her notes from her interviews with Bob and Melissa. "What time was he called? When did he arrive?"

"Uh…yeah, so Bob called Mark right around nine, because there was a huge crowd lined up outside. And Mark got there by about nine-thirty."

"How would you characterize Mark's attentiveness that morning?"

Stacey knit her brows. "What do you mean? Mark was very attentive."

"Mr. Rosenthal wasn't expecting to be working that morning, so the request might have come as a surprise. If he had participated in any late-night activities, or had gotten too little sleep, his ability to perform his job to the fullest extent may have been jeopardized."

Stacey narrowed her eyes again. Now she was certain Ms. Lopez was trying to get her to say Mark was at fault. "Mark was totally focused, and noticed hazards and swimmers breaking rules that the rest of us missed."

"Can you expand on that for me?"

Stacey's nostrils flared as she recounted Mark pacing the deck with the lifeguard buoy, and how he even noticed the middle schoolers at the top of the bleachers. "Mark is a really good lifeguard. From my first day working at the pool, he helped me look for ways to prevent accidents and avoid needing to rescue swimmers."

"I see. Let's move on. What time did the morning events end, and how were the patrons cleared from the facility?"

This was the point where Stacey's notes began. She read from her page. "A few minutes after twelve, Melissa was in the tower and one lap swimmer—a little old lady in a purple swimsuit—was about to get in the water. Bob came into the office, followed by Mark and Jessie."

Stacey went on to explain how Bob and Mark discussed ways to make the next Plunge Olympics events safer, and that Bob asked her and Jessie to stay for the afternoon to be sure enough lifeguards would be working in case they had another huge crowd. She said Jessie and Mark stayed, while she ran to the pharmacy and Bob went to the city offices.

"Is it standard practice for Bob to leave unexpectedly or for a guard who is on the clock to leave the premises?"

The tape recorder wheels groaned and squeaked.

"I mean, sort of. Bob never left without Mark being there, though. And, sometimes one person would leave to get lunch or something during lap swim since there were never very many swimmers. But we wouldn't have gone anywhere if we thought the situation wasn't safe."

The lawyer's pen scratched quickly across the yellow page, writing everything Stacey said word-for-word.

"A moment ago, you said Ms. Phillips took the first lap swim shift. But you were at the end of your break when lap swim began, correct? Shouldn't you have gone out to watch the water instead?"

"Yeah, but not always. If any of us wanted to be done lifeguarding early, we would offer to take the first shift. I just assumed that's why Melissa went straight to the tower."

Ms. Lopez's eyebrows lifted as she wrote. "So, despite that Ms. Phillips was one of three guards on duty, and being paid until one o'clock, she might have been planning to leave before that?"

"Wait! That's not what I said. It's just, sometimes there's no one in the water, and other guards might come in early. So—"

"So, under *those* circumstances, it is protocol that a guard might leave the facility before his or her shift ends."

Stacey sighed heavily. "I guess. Maybe sometimes it happened. But it wasn't 'protocol.' And Melissa and I never talked about it. I have no idea whether that was what she was thinking or not."

"Umm hmmm." Still writing, the lawyer flipped to the next page without slowing a beat. "And after thirty minutes, you were supposed to be up in the tower, correct? Not Jessie Thomas, who had worked much more in the previous two hours than you had. But he covered for you? Can you explain that to me?"

"Well, I...Bob—" Stacey's words caught in her throat. She closed her eyes and reminded herself not to say anything that would get anyone in trouble. Her dry mouth offered no relief as she tried to swallow and start again. "Jessie doesn't drive, so I offered to go get the poster supplies Bob wanted," she said in a raspy voice.

"Do you need a glass of water, Ms. Chapman?"

"Yes, please," Stacey breathed out. As Ms. Lopez walked across the room and poured a glass from a pitcher, Stacey lifted her arms, attempting to air-dry the sweat that had pooled beneath them. She flapped the front of her T-shirt a few times to prevent sweat patches from collecting and dripping down her chest.

The lawyer set the glass on the table in front of Stacey, then picked up her pen. "How long do you believe you were gone on your poster supply errand, Ms. Chapman?"

After several long gulps, Stacey cleared her throat again and answered. "About twenty minutes."

"From the timeline you've given me, wouldn't that still have gotten you back in time to take over for Melissa at 12:30?"

"I got back right at 12:30. But I had to go to the bathroom, so Jessie said he would cover for me until I could come outside."

"I see," she said, looking Stacey in the eyes a second longer than was comfortable before returning to her notes.

Did Melissa say something else in her own testimony? About the tests? She wouldn't have. Would she?

Ms. Lopez went on. "Now, please tell me in as much detail as possible what exactly you remember happening. Begin with the moment Jessie said he would go out to lifeguard on your behalf."

"So, like I said, I went into the bathroom at 12:30, and Jessie went out to take over for Melissa in the tower. There isn't a clock in the bathroom, so I'm guessing it was like 12:35 when I heard a whistle and a splash."

"Can you please clarify which guard tower Jessie was in?" she asked.

"I didn't SEE him in tower two, but that was the tower Melissa was in, and where we always sat during lap swim. It's the one closest to the office and bathrooms, near the middle of the pool."

"Five minutes seems like a long time for a quick bathroom break. Can you explain your assumption?"

Stacey licked her lips before answering. "I was, um…having stomach issues." She clenched her fists in her lap.

"Alright. So at approximately 12:35 you heard a whistle and a splash. Then what happened?"

Stacey lifted her own notes again. The paper shook as she read. "I opened the stall door and started to run out toward the deck. Before I was outside I also heard Mark yelling, but I'm not exactly sure what he said. When I pulled open the outside door, I saw Melissa standing frozen in the office doorway. I looked toward the water, and saw Jessie floating face down, blood pooling around him. I also saw an elderly swimmer at the far end holding onto a diving block, trying to lift something heavy from under the water."

Head still down, writing quickly, the lawyer asked, "Was the 'something heavy' Mr. Henderson?"

"I don't know his name. Is that the name of the man who drowned?"

"The individual who drowned is named Mr. Henry Allen Henderson. But I am clarifying whether it was Mr. Henderson that you saw the man lifting, or something else."

"Sorry. It all happened so fast, and at first I had no idea what I was seeing. Mark was running toward Jessie with a backboard and he yelled 'Call 9-1-1.' Melissa went inside to call, then Mark said he needed my help."

"When did you discover that there was a second victim?"

"After Jessie was breathing, I ran over. That's when I realized it was a drowned swimmer that the old man was trying to hold up."

Ms. Lopez asked, "How did you know he had already drowned at that point? Did this affect your response to offer aid?"

Stacey's heart started racing. "No! I mean, he had to have already drowned, right?" Stacey said, her voice becoming frantic. "When I first saw him, the other swimmer had his head above water, but his—Mr. Henderson's—eyes were open and not blinking. His lips were blue." Stacey started to shake. "But we REALLY did everything we could to help."

What if he WASN'T dead yet when I first went outside? Should I have gone to him first and left Mark to help Jessie on his own? Oh my god.

The lawyer looked up. "Take a moment if you need to, Ms. Chapman. I realize this must have been a very traumatic experience for you. I am only trying to get the details as clear as possible from all of the staff's accounting of the events."

The water in Stacey's glass sloshed as she lifted it to her mouth for another sip. She set the glass down carefully and continued reading from her paper. "The old man was holding Mr. Henderson's face out of the water by the time I got in to help. He appeared to already be dead, so I assisted Mark in backboarding Jessie and getting him safely out of the water before attending to the other victim."

"Okay. Stop there for a moment, please," the lawyer said. "Earlier you mentioned there were three swimmers in the pool. So far you have only accounted for two. Do you know where the third swimmer was when you observed the pool after exiting the restroom?"

"Uh, yeah. The lady in the purple suit." Stacey closed her eyes and tried to think. "She was in the shallow end. Lane one. At the ladder, climbing out, I think. Later I saw her on the bleachers, and she spoke to me and the paramedic."

"Okay, for now let's stay with the moment you first saw the pool. Using whatever measurements are most comfortable to you— inches, feet, meters—please estimate for me the location of Jessie

Thomas floating face-down in the pool, when you first saw him, as it relates to the tower he would have been in, the side of the pool where he was provided CPR, and also his proximity to where you saw Mr. Henderson's body being held up."

"Umm...can I—" Stacey pointed to the extra pens beside the lawyer's notepad. She turned her notes over to the blank side of the paper. She began drawing a blocky, upside-down letter L, and marking locations on top of and around it, including a square she labeled T2 to represent the tower, and six stripes stretching the long arm of the L for the lane lines. As she moved the pen on the page, her nerves began to calm.

"So, if this is the pool, this is where the lifeguard tower Jessie would have been in is located, and this is the deep end where I saw Mr. Henderson in the water." Stacey drew a small circle with an H in it in lane three. "I was standing here, by the guard shack, when I first saw Jessie floating around here in lane five," She drew a circle with a J in it between the tower and the H. "Jessie was about twelve feet from the old man and Mr. Henderson. He was about twenty yards from the shallow end, and less than ten feet from the tower. It looked like Jessie dove in, maybe a little too shallow to try to go under the lane lines, when he hit the bottom."

"Do you know how deep the water is where it looked like Jessie might have dove in?"

"It's three-and-a-half feet deep under the tower." Stacey could visualize the numbers on the wall in her mind. "And six feet at the far end where I saw the old man holding the guy who drowned...Mr. Henderson. So, maybe like...four or four-and-a-half feet deep?"

"Is there appropriate signage in that section of the pool that reflects that it is not safe to dive? Was safe diving depth and procedures part of your training?"

Stacey hesitated as she remembered the numerous times she and other crew members had dived into the water from one tower and swum to the other to cool off, even though they knew it was against the rules. She thought of Jessie's and Mark's tricks off the diving board. Jessie's gainers off the side starting on the first day.

In her mind, Stacey could see the faded silhouettes of divers with diagonal lines over them, painted every few feet on the concrete around all of the shallow end of the pool. *What depth do they end at?*

"Yeah. It's marked, and we follow safe diving procedures," Stacey said. "I think Jessie would have just dived in automatically, though, trying to get to the swimmer quickly and avoid the lane lines, not even thinking."

"Isn't that exactly what your training was for, Ms. Chapman?" the lawyer asked. "So, you would think first about how to most safely protect yourself and the other swimmers if ever the need for a rescue was to arise?"

"Yeah, of course. But Jessie would have wanted to get to the man as fast as he could. And the end of the pool where I saw Mr. Henderson IS deep enough for diving. It's just that Jessie was diving from too high up, and the lane lines were between them, and—"

"How high is the tower?"

"The platform where we stand is, like, five feet high, I think?"

"So, you are saying that from a height of at least five feet above the water's surface Jessie dove into water approximately four feet deep?"

"Yeah. I think so, but...." Stacey squeezed her eyes shut, searching for Ms. Moreno's words. "Sometimes the angle of the sunlight can affect how deep the water looks. Because of... reflection? No. Refraction. The lane lines would have created a vanishing point different from the direction of Mr. Henderson's body, and that would have affected Jessie's perspective. His depth perception would have been off."

The woman looked up at Stacey and squinted her eyes. "Those are very technical terms, Ms. Chapman. Have you discussed this testimony with someone who may have been encouraging you to describe it this way?"

"What? Of course not!" Stacey said defensively. "I took art lessons this summer. Watercolor. And my teacher—Ms. Moreno—taught me about how light and distance and angles can affect perspective. I actually asked her more about it to help me understand why a kid I had to rescue a few weeks ago was hard to see at the bottom of the pool."

The lawyer's face became very stern. "There was another incident with a child needing to be rescued this summer at the facility on Seventh Street?"

Stacey's trembling returned, and her voice lurched into a high pitch. "It was nothing like what happened Saturday with Jessie. It was just a little boy who couldn't swim well. He went off the diving board when he shouldn't have. It was no big deal, I promise. I got him out and he was totally fine."

"Did you also jump from the lifeguard tower for that rescue?"

"Yeah. Of course. From Tower One. But, it's the deep end and I went feet first."

Ms. Lopez made a note in the margin of her paper, then sighed. "Okay, back to the incident on July 20th. You left off when…" she dragged her finger up the page and tapped the spot with her pen. "…you got in the water and decided to respond to Jessie's injuries first. What happened next?"

"I helped Mark get Jessie onto the backboard and out of the pool."

"Can you tell me how exactly you went about back-boarding Mr. Thomas, please?"

Stacey pointed at her drawing while she explained. "By the time I got to Mark, Jessie was face up. I'm not sure how Mark flipped him, but he was getting the backboard under Jessie's shoulders. I helped get the rest of Jessie's body onto the board, and started strapping his ankles and arms in place while Mark secured his head."

"What was Ms. Phillips doing?"

"After she called 9-1-1, Melissa came back to the side of the pool. Mark told her she needed to put pressure on Jessie's head wound once we got him out of the water, so she grabbed a towel sitting on the deck nearby."

"Was Mr. Thomas conscious?"

"Not at first. And he wasn't breathing." Stacey couldn't remember anyone checking for Jessie's pulse, or for breath, but decided not to mention it. "Mark started chest compressions. On the third one, Jessie coughed up the water in his lungs. Mark and I tilted the backboard so he could get the water out."

"Approximately how long were you and Mr. Rosenthal backboarding and providing CPR for Mr. Thomas?" the lawyer asked.

"It wasn't CPR," Stacey said. "Just chest compressions. The backboarding took maybe thirty or forty-five seconds. By the time Jessie was out of the water and breathing again, maybe two minutes had passed."

"And for the two minutes you, Mark and Melissa were attending to Jessie, and another swimmer was in the water, alone, attempting to help Mr. Henderson?"

"Like I said, it seemed like he was already dead. But as soon as I knew Jessie was breathing, I ran as fast as I could to see if there was any way to help Mr. Henderson."

"How was Mr. Henderson taken out of the pool?"

"Well, we only have one backboard, and he didn't appear to have any head or neck injuries, so Mark and I pulled him out under his arms."

"You lifted him out together? How long did it take Mr. Rosenthal to arrive so you both could attend to Mr. Henderson?"

"He swam across, and arrived just after I did."

"But Mr. Rosenthal had been out of the water attending to Mr. Thomas beside the shallow end of the pool, correct?"

"Yes," Stacey said.

"How did Mr. Rosenthal swim across so quickly? Did he also dive across the shallow end?"

Stacey considered this. *How did Mark get there so fast? He must have dived in too, right?* "I didn't see Mark dive, and I don't believe he would have, especially after what happened to Jessie."

"I see." Ms. Lopez scrutinized Stacey for a moment. "You said you and Mark 'pulled' Mr. Henderson from the water. My understanding is Mr. Henderson was a very large man. How were the two of you able to lift him safely out of the water on your own?"

Stacey remembered how the heft of the lifeless body kept sinking back toward the bottom of the pool. "It wasn't easy. We had to brace ourselves with the diving blocks, and loop our arms under his, then slide him along the deck."

"Do you believe this was the safest method for the protection of all those involved?"

"Honestly, I don't know," Stacey said, her voice small. She could hear the sound of the man's head thumping on the deck in her mind. "He needed CPR if there was any chance of saving him. It was our best option at the time."

"How long after Mr. Henderson was pulled from the water did it take before CPR was administered?"

"Mark began chest compressions immediately. I checked for a pulse and breathing. There were neither."

"Was Mr. Henderson provided mouth-to-mouth resuscitation?"

"I attempted mouth-to-mouth after Mark did about fifteen compressions. No air would go in. I tried to clear his airway of any obstruction, then tried giving breath again, still with no success. Then Mark tried, and also could not get air into Mr. Henderson's lungs. That's why the paramedics intubated him."

"In the interim, whenever breaths were unsuccessful–" Ms. Lopez said, but Stacey sternly cut her off.

"—Whenever a breath was not being administered, Mark was pumping Mr. Henderson's chest. Hard. He never stopped, except when he tried to provide breath as well. Even after the paramedics arrived."

Ms. Lopez completed those notes before asking, "How much time passed between the time chest compressions began and when the paramedics arrived, would you say?"

"Maybe ninety seconds?" Stacey said. *How would I know?* "I wasn't looking at the clock."

"Once the paramedics were on the scene, did you remain involved in the resuscitation efforts?"

"No. I told them we couldn't get air into Mr. Henderson's lungs and they said they would intubate. I moved out of the way, and let them take over. Mark kept doing chest compressions while two paramedics inserted the tube and pumped air with a plastic pump. When a third medic arrived, Mark helped as the four of them lifted

Mr. Henderson onto a gurney. He had to be out of the puddles when they used the AED."

"Did you witness the paramedics administering the defibrillation?" the lawyer asked.

"Yeah."

"Were you able to determine if any of their efforts to revive Mr. Henderson were at all successful?"

"It didn't make any difference." Stacey envisioned the vacant eyes staring straight up at the sky. Her voice was barely above a whisper. "Nothing made any difference. He was gone."

For the next twenty minutes, Ms. Lopez asked about the ambulances, fire trucks, police officers and medics on the scene, how long it took them and Bob to arrive, where they entered and exited.

Stacey felt numb as she rubbed her eyes and cheeks, recounting details that couldn't possibly matter. None of it would help Jessie. Or Mr. Henderson.

Nearly two hours passed before the lawyer took a deep breath, then looked Stacey directly in the eyes. "Is there any additional information you think I ought to know, Ms. Chapman? Anything that has not been covered in our conversation? Specifically, are there any factors that might have caused, or could have prevented, the incidents on July 20th? Anything that might have prevented you or other staff from responding quickly, or could have prevented the victims from receiving the best possible care?"

Stacey stared back. She knew at some point the lawyer might have found out about the pregnancy tests. Or someone could have mentioned Mark's pills. His habit of sleeping at work. But it wasn't going to be Stacey who told her.

Stacey said calmly, "Nothing comes to mind."

Ms. Lopez slowly nodded as though contemplating Stacey's words, then pressed stop on the tape recorder. She clicked the end of her pen before setting it down next to her notes. "Thank you for coming in today. If we have any further questions, someone from my office will give you a call."

Stacey stood, and turned, leaving her own notes on the table. As she pulled open the conference room door, her eyes met Mark's.

Mark was seated in the hall. His head was tilted back against the beige wall, and his expression was solemn. His eyes shifted toward the open conference room door, and back to Stacey again. Before Stacey could ask how he was doing, Ms. Lopez called Mark inside.

Chapter Twenty-Five

From city hall, Stacey drove straight to the high school. Her mom was still at work, and after being interrogated for the previous two hours, she didn't want to be alone. When Ms. Moreno arrived Monday evening, Stacey was seated in the shade against the stucco wall outside her classroom, waiting.

"Hi Stacey," Ms. Moreno said, smiling. She approached the door and fumbled with her keys in the lock.

Stacey pulled herself to standing, but couldn't muster a smile.

"Is everything okay?" Ms. Moreno asked.

Stacey shook her head. "Can we go inside?"

"Of course." Ms. Moreno pushed the door open, ushering Stacey into the classroom. The room was warm and stuffy.

"Let me just turn on the fans." Ms. Moreno pulled a fan into the doorway and turned the dial to high.

Dust particles drifted in the beams of sunlight stretching from the top windows across the linoleum floor. Stacey sat on a stool at the butcher block table in the center of the room, while Ms. Moreno turned on the other fans around the art lab. After setting her purse on her desk, she grabbed two cans of soda from her mini fridge and placed them on the butcher block.

"Want a Pepsi? Or a Mr. Pibb?" Ms. Moreno asked as she sat down across from Stacey.

Stacey ran her fingernail inside a deep groove in the tabletop. "I don't know what to do," she said softly.

"Whatever is going on, we can figure it out," the art teacher said.

"I just spent two hours talking about it."

Ms. Moreno leaned forward. "If you don't want to talk to me about it, why are you here? Do you want to paint?"

"No. I don't know. I just can't sit at home worrying. I can't sleep. Every time I close my eyes, all I see is…" Stacey shook her head and looked at the blank wall over her shoulder, and whispered, "…blood."

"What?" Ms. Moreno gasped. "Please, Stacey, look at me. Anything you say can be just between us."

Tears spilled over the swollen pink rims of Stacey's eyes. She sniffed, still avoiding her teacher's gaze. "Everyone already knows."

"Okay. That's okay." Ms. Moreno got up and pulled her stool beside Stacey's. She laid her arm on the table and gently touched Stacey's elbow. "Then there's really nothing to worry about. Talk to me."

Stacey's breath quivered as she tried to get the words out. "Jessie broke his neck. He's in the hospital. A man died in the pool."

Ms. Moreno's hand drifted to her mouth. "Oh no," she whispered.

Stacey's eyes finally met Ms. Moreno's. Her words began flying out frantically. "I'm a terrible person. Jessie and I had sex. Then I spread rumors about him at a party after I saw him with another girl. Now his life is ruined. And it's my fault." She covered her face with her hands, sobbing into them.

"What do you mean it's your fault? How did he get hurt?"

"He wasn't supposed to be lifeguarding!" Stacey's lip trembled. "It was my shift. But…I was taking a pregnancy test in the bathroom, and he covered for me. We both needed to know if I was. I think he was distracted. Then the man was drowning, and Jessie dove in to save him, but it was where the water was too shallow!"

Ms. Moreno stood and put her arms around Stacey. "That is SO much to deal with."

"That's not all!" Stacey lifted her head up, desperate to pour the whole truth out. "I'm a horrible person. I got totally trashed at a party and made out with a guy I barely know. He almost…I…" Stacey's voice was panicked. "…I was unconscious, and my friend Gabe had to punch him to get him off of me, and…"

"Shhhh…" Ms. Moreno sat on her stool and took Stacey's hands between her own. "Let's breathe. It's okay. You're safe."

Stacey's eyes skipped back and forth between Ms. Moreno's. "It's not okay! Nothing is okay! Not anymore!!!"

"You can tell me everything. From the beginning. But, first, let's try to calm down." Ms. Moreno took a long, slow breath in through her nose, and let it out audibly through her mouth.

Stacey shook her head and swallowed hard. She felt sick and sad and angry all at once. Like if she stopped trying to hold herself together she really would fragment into a million pieces.

"You can do this, Stacey. Just breathe in for three, hold it, then out for three. I promise, it will help."

Stacey's lips curled over her front teeth as she slowly pulled air in through her nostrils and held it. Her mouth fell open as she gasped the air out.

"Good. Let's do that again a few more times. Slowly." Ms. Moreno continued demonstrating with her own breaths as Stacey followed her direction.

Stacey slowly relaxed with each breath.

"Okay," Ms. Moreno said. "Now, I'm sure there are so many things running through your mind. And, like I said, I'm here and will listen to everything. But I have an idea that I think will help you stay calm while you talk. It's something I learned to do when I'm stressed that helps me process everything. Wanna try?"

Stacey felt her eyebrows squeeze together, confused. *Art? Now?* "What is it?"

"It's mostly a way to get a mess of thoughts out of my head. Sometimes they're ideas or things I'm confused about, but a lot of the time it's things that are bothering me. Things that upset me so much, I have a hard time letting them go."

"So, this project—whatever it is—helps you let it go?" Stacey wiped her cheek with the back of her hand.

"Yeah, actually. It's worth a shot, right?"

Stacey shrugged. "I guess."

"K. Sit tight." Ms. Moreno said, patting Stacey quickly on the knee.

She pulled several sheets of watercolor paper from a drawer, and a sheet of brown cardstock. She pulled open the art supply closet and rummaged around for a long piece of twine.

At her desk, Ms. Moreno folded the stack of paper in half, cardstock on top, then opened it again. She used an extra-long stapler to bind the pages together along the fold in three places, securing the twine under the center staple atop the cardstock cover. She grabbed a similar-looking booklet from her purse and brought both over to the table, setting them in front of Stacey.

Stacey sat, chewing on her fingers.

"I've never shared my journal with anyone," Ms. Moreno said, holding up the worn booklet, covered in sketches and stickers. "But it will give you an idea of what I'm trying to explain." She started slowly flipping through the pages.

Stacey looked at the jumble of images and words. One page had words in blue written like a sky background behind cotton-candy pink watercolor clouds. Another page had a sketch of a silhouetted couple in a warm glow at the end of a dark forest.

Ms. Moreno stopped at a page covered in dark, charcoal etchings, the face of a screaming child in the center, tearing at her hair. The words "afraid," "alone," and "abandoned" burned through the hellish scene in varying shades of crimson and orange.

She spoke softly. "My first few journals looked a lot like this page. If I awoke in the night, or got in a fight at school, I'd put whatever was frightening me on the page." She closed the journal and tied the twine around it. "Then, once it was locked in here for a while, I could usually go back to sleep, or move on with my day. I was so angry, and my journal helped me stop wanting to hurt someone. Or myself."

"I don't know... I'm really worried about Jessie. How is some journal going to help?"

"You can't do anything to help Jessie right now, Stacey. Only his doctors can. But you said you're not sleeping well and are worried all the time. This will help with that, so hopefully you can be a better friend to him when you do get to see Jessie."

"How many of these journals have you made?" Stacey asked, untying the bundle and flipping through more of the pages.

"Dozens. At first, I'd fill a journal like this in a few days. At the time, I really had no one else to tell all the horrible thoughts in my head. Sometimes I hated what I'd put inside these pages so much, and didn't want anyone to ever see it, so I'd burn it in the fireplace. That was its own kind of catharsis."

Stacey set Ms. Moreno's journal down and picked up the blank booklet. "I don't know what I could possibly put in here that would get all of the horrible things that have happened out of my head."

"You don't have to be able to get them all out at the same time. What if you started with one thing on one page? Just one simple image? Something easy. Maybe something you think of when you consider how all of this difficult stuff started in the first place."

"What if I don't know how to draw it? Or it's really dumb?"

Ms. Moreno set a pencil in front of Stacey. "Who's ever going to see it? Put it on the page so it stops weighing you down. Worst case: burn it after. Remember, it's just a piece of paper." Ms. Moreno lifted her eyebrows knowingly.

Stacey snorted at the cheesy line Ms. Moreno tossed off so often. The art teacher collected paints and watercolor pencils, brushes, a mason jar of water, and a cup full of fine tip markers. By the time the supplies were on the table, Stacey had sketched on her first blank page, and was reaching for a palette, brush, and red and blue paints.

Ms. Moreno sat on her stool beside Stacey and opened her own journal to the next blank page. She grabbed a couple of markers and began writing in the center of the page, her words spiraling outward as she rotated the journal, writing in a circular design. Then she picked up a brush and started filling in the space around the words with ribbons of black, purple, and navy paint.

When Stacey set down her paint brush, Ms. Moreno did as well, and turned to her. "How did that feel?"

"Fine, I guess." Stacey shrugged. "It wasn't anything serious. Just…where everything started. Like you said."

"Do you want to tell me about it?" Ms. Moreno asked.

"It's really dumb."

"You don't have to share it at all. But I meant it when I said that anything you tell me can be just between us." She showed her page to Stacey. "Would you feel more comfortable if I shared what I put down on my page? It's nothing earth shattering, either. Most of my entries are repetitive. Reminders to myself."

Stacey shrugged and nodded. "Maybe."

"I wrote: Whenever my thoughts pull me down, and I feel myself sinking into a pit of my worst fears, the best way to escape is by pulling myself free through art."

Around the edge of the pit of words she'd drawn a grassy field with flowers arranged to spell "Art Escape."

Stacey nodded, then pulled her own journal between them. "You said I should put down something simple. How everything started. This is all I could think of." She pointed to a simple drawing of a cardinal red one-piece swimsuit in the bottom left corner. "I had to buy a red suit when I got the job as a lifeguard. And this," Stacey pointed to several paragraphs of blue text written in the shape of an inverted blocky letter L, "is the community pool. I just wrote about how it felt when I got the job, and how nervous I was to wear a swimsuit in front of the crew. Especially Jessie." She pointed to a small sketch in the bottom right corner. "This is supposed to be the ThighMaster, next to my broken lava lamp from when I was trying to lose weight quickly."

"I like all the details." Ms. Moreno looked Stacey in the eyes again. "How do you feel?"

Stacey chewed the inside of her cheek. "A little better, I guess. I actually found the words flowing through my head as I drew, so it was easier to put them on the page after they drifted around in there for a while."

"That's interesting. Maybe something will pour out of your words that surprises you. Do you want to try to do another page?"

Stacey nodded, and picked up the pencil.

For the next three hours, Stacey poured her thoughts across page after page. One page she covered in music notes. She added a stage with her own face in the corner, painted like a melting clown. Another had the sun setting over the parking lot at the movies with Jessie's gum-wrapper airplane in the gutter. She drew the Silver Bullet in an empty field under a starless sky on one page, and her giant dream catcher beside a pair of scissors on the page opposite. She sketched a tiny golf pencil beside an empty liquor bottle. She painted the Grand Canyon, with Gabe's silhouette on one side and hers on the other. She drew a swirling blue hot tub with a bottle of pills, a pair of ice skates, a gold medal and the words "Future" "Hopes" and "Dreams" spiraling down the drain.

On the last page, Stacey painted the background watery blue with a large red splotch in the center. With a white pen, she wrote a poem over the bloody image. Stacey was surprised how calm she felt as she read her words aloud to Ms. Moreno:

> "I sat in class and dreamed of him,
> The skater with a wicked smile.
> I'd picked up the phone a dozen times
> Too afraid to dial.
> Then out of the blue he said,
> 'We should watch the stars.'
> I didn't know what he really wanted.
> I let it go too far.
>
> I got too high, we dove too deep,
> Burned by the summer sun.

No words could make things right.
No place far enough to drive.
Next thing I know, he's on a stretcher
Lucky to be alive.
How did it get so fucked up?
When did things go so bad?
How did my summer fantasy
Become the worst nightmare I ever had?

I got too high, we dove too deep,
Burned by the summer sun."

"Wow, Stacey." Ms. Moreno had a look of compassion and understanding etched across her face. "I'm so honored you shared all of that with me. This journal is an intense and beautiful expression of your pain. You've experienced a lot this summer."

Stacey nodded. "Doing this unlocked something inside me. Stuff I didn't know what to do with before."

"Yeah, and by the end it all came together into that powerful poem. They way it describes a moment when you get what you want and it's nothing like you thought. Everyone goes through that. I bet you could turn those lines into lyrics for a song."

Stacey shook her head and rolled her eyes. "Now I know you're full of it."

"Totally serious," Ms. Moreno said. She put her hand on the page as if protecting it. "You really have something special here. Sleep on it, but if you ever decide to share it with anyone else, I'm certain they will tell you the same thing. You are so talented, Stacey. It shows whenever you take the feelings you keep locked inside and pour them all out onto a page."

Stacey felt her cheeks warm. She looked down.

Ms. Moreno went on. "It's also clear from everything you've shared that—while Jessie's accident is tragic—what happened at the pool on Saturday was not your fault. Under the circumstances, it could have happened to anyone."

"Maybe you're right," Stacey said, suppressing a yawn. She closed the journal and tied the twine. "Hopefully now I can sleep, at least." Stacey picked up her journal and her keys, her shoulders feeling lighter as she stood. She pushed in her stool and started toward the door.

"Just a sec, Stace." Ms. Moreno caught up to her in the doorway. The breeze of the fan blew over the pair of them as she handed Stacey another journal. "I put a new one together for you while you were working. Just in case something comes up, good or bad, and you want a place to put it down."

"Thank you so much, Ms. Moreno." Before she knew what she was doing, Stacey had wrapped her arms around her art teacher, hugging her tightly. "For everything."

Chapter Twenty-Six

S tacey felt someone rubbing her shoulder and the bedsheet twisting in response.

"Hey Stacey," her mom whispered, "wake up for a sec. There's something I want to talk about before I leave for work."

Stacey rolled over and rubbed the sleep from her eyes. "What time is it?"

"Seven-thirty. I have a client at eight."

Stacey blinked, calculating the hours. She had slept nine-and-a-half straight. She hadn't slept that much in almost a month. She pushed herself up then leaned against the wall, yawning. Murphy jumped on the bed and laid her head in Stacey's lap.

Stacey's mom held the folded newspaper up for Stacey to see. "*The Sun* reported on what happened Saturday. I wondered if you'd want me here when you read it?"

Stacey rubbed Murphy's soft, floppy ear between her fingers. "Is there something in there about who they think is at fault for Jessie's accident?"

"No. It just says there's an ongoing investigation." Her mom bit the side of her lip. "There is a picture of Jessie, though. In the hospital."

Stacey took a deep breath and reached for the paper. "I think I'll be alright. I might look at it after I have some breakfast."

Her mom handed her the paper, then stood and kissed Stacey on the forehead. "I love you, Doodle Bug. I'll see you later."

"I love you too, Mom. Have a good day."

A few minutes later, Stacey sat on the couch with her cup full of Pops!, and the top half of the weekly newspaper's front page visible across her lap. The headline read "From Community Engagement to Catastrophe."

Stacey slurped cereal and took in the two large black-and-white photos. The first was of Bob holding up his stopwatch with the gold-coin necklaces, the crowded pool behind him. The second showed a "POOL CLOSED" poster board sign, hanging crooked on the locked chain link fence, and the empty facility in the background. Mylar balloons, prayer candles, and bouquets of flowers were scattered along the base of the fence. People had written notes on the poster board, messages too small for Stacey to read.

She set the cereal cup aside unfinished and flipped the paper over to read the article.

Jessie's senior yearbook photo smiled up between the columns of text next to a photo of him lying in a hospital bed. There was a large metal halo attached to Jessie's head, and a brace around his shoulders and neck. His forehead was bandaged above stitches on the top of his nose and two black eyes. Stacey chewed the dry skin off her bottom lip.

In the lower right corner was a photo of a much younger Mr. Henderson in a Navy uniform. Despite the thinner cheeks and neck, the solemn look in his eyes was the same Stacey had seen during his many visits to the pool. The photo caption read: "Petty Officer Henry Allen Henderson, 1942. Obituary, pg. 6." He looked like he was about the same age as Jessie at the time the photo was taken.

The article recounted Saturday morning's Plunge Olympics events. "Just the kind of wholesome activity our town needs to be offering," one father was quoted as saying. "For only $6, our family got an experience we'll never forget," a mother told the reporter after "her family won the gold in the family relay race." The article noted that the pool was closed for the remainder of the week, and it was unclear whether the Plunge Olympics would be rescheduled for a later date or when the pool would reopen.

The article included portions of the coroner's initial report: "Mr. Henderson suffered a heart attack while swimming. The cardiac arrest likely contributed to food from his stomach being regurgitated and lodging in his throat. Despite the heroic efforts of the pool staff and paramedics, multiple factors contributed to Mr. Henderson's drowning and subsequent death."

The article went on to describe the aforementioned "heroic" efforts of the staff to save Mr. Henderson, including Jessie's attempt and subsequent tragic accident as a result. It said "Assistant pool manager Mark Rosenthal acted quickly and professionally," and that "First-year lifeguards Stacey Chapman and Melissa Phillips proved to be calm and collected given the severity of the situation." The final paragraph stated that "The investigation into the circumstances involving the drowning and lifeguard's injuries is ongoing." They requested anyone with relevant information to contact city hall.

Stacey was turning the page to read Mr. Henderson's obituary when Murphy sat up. The dog ran to the door, barking excitedly and wagging her tail, just before the doorbell chimed.

Stacey hesitated. She didn't want to open the door wearing only a pair of boxers and a tank top with no bra. But Murphy's enthusiasm assured Stacey the visitor was someone familiar. *Maybe Greg left something behind on Sunday?*

Stacey hollered, "Just a sec!" and wrapped the blanket from the couch around herself, running her fingers through her hair as she walked to the door.

She pulled it open and locked on the gentle, sea green of Gabe's eyes. Murphy stopped barking and nudged the screen with her nose.

"Hi," Stacey said.

"Can I come in?" Gabe asked.

Stacey nodded and pulled the front door open wider.

Gabe pulled the screen open and leaned down to give Murphy a scratch behind the ears. "Hey, Murph. I've missed you." He looked Stacey in the eyes. "I've missed you, too," he said to Stacey, then wrapped his arms around her, resting his chin on her head. "My mom just showed me the *Sun News*. I can't believe it. Why didn't you call me?"

Stacey melted into his arms, closing her eyes and breathing in his familiar scent through his white T-shirt. "You said you needed space."

Gabe tightened his embrace. Stacey's arms expanded around his chest, her face against his heart, rising and falling with his breath. "I'm always here for you, when you need me. No matter what."

Stacey pressed her cheek against his collarbone to wipe her tears away. "Are you on your way to work?" she asked, stepping back, shyly crossing her arms over her braless chest, and wiping her hand across her eyes.

Gabe shook his head. "I told them I was sick. I wanted to be able to hang with you as long as you needed. The pool's closed, right?"

"It is...." Stacey looked over her shoulder and sneered at her living room, where she'd spent so much of the last few weeks curled up pathetically on the couch. "But, could we...maybe go somewhere else to hang out instead?"

"Sure. Anywhere," Gabe said.

His grin was so reassuring, Stacey had to resist an urge to kiss him for always showing up when she needed him the most. "The beach?"

Gabe dug his hands into the front pockets of his jeans, rocking a little on the heels of his Converse. "The beach would be great."

"Could you give me like thirty?" Stacey asked, biting her bottom lip.

"I'll come back." Gabe reached down and gave Murphy another firm pat on her side. "We could take Murphy with us."

Stacey's heart swelled. "She'd love that. Do you have any tennis balls?"

"In the garage. I'll dig 'em out." Gabe's dimple appeared in his right cheek as he backed out. "Don't worry, Murph; I'll be back." The screen slammed shut.

Stacey closed the front door and rested her back against it. "Murphy, we get to go to the beach with Gabe. Mr. Wonderful. I really need your help so I don't screw up today, okay?"

Thirty minutes later, Stacey opened the door to Gabe's three-knuckle knock. He held up a bag from Mr. Crumb's donut shop, a Milk Bone, and two orange juices. "Breakfast?"

"Awesome!" Stacey said, leading Murphy on the leash out the screen door, and closing the front door behind her. "I'll drive."

Stacey had already thrown towels and a small ice chest with snacks in the trunk, covered her back seat with an old blanket, and brought an extra water bowl. She popped her seat forward to let Murphy jump in back. The dog spun around once, sniffing the back seat, before sitting proudly in the center.

Stacey rolled her window down, took the cinnamon twist from the bag, and started backing out of the driveway. "You're the DJ on this road trip," she told Gabe.

He held his bear claw in one hand and grabbed the book of CDs from under the passenger seat with the other. "What do you want to hear?" he asked, munching a too-big bite.

Stacey smirked and put the car in drive. "It's not like Kevin and Bean are taking requests on KROQ." She took a big bite, and imitated him talking with his mouthful. "I said *you're* in charge of the music."

"Don't mock me, jackass." Gabe elbowed her.

Stacey shoved another huge bite in her mouth and said, "Takes one to know one."

By the time she pulled the Silver Bullet onto Mesa Valley Boulevard, Gabe had selected "When I Come Around" by Green Day. They sang along, while Murphy's jowls flapped in the wind, her drool dripping on the side window the full five miles to the freeway.

As Stacey turned onto the onramp, she rolled up the windows and turned on the AC. Murphy curled onto the seat and closed her eyes.

Gabe left the album to play, but turned the volume down. "So, are you ready to talk about the accident at the pool?"

Stacey exhaled. "Yeah. I've actually had to talk about it a lot. I had to give my testimony to a lawyer at city hall yesterday."

"Really? What did they ask?"

"Everything from when I arrived in the morning until the coroner left with the body Saturday afternoon, basically. Plus, the lawyer wanted to know about all of our 'procedures' and 'protocols'." She mock-imitated the lawyer.

"I can't imagine," he said.

"If you read the article, you know what most everyone else knows. It was a crazy morning. Way too many people. And we expected it was going to be a crazy afternoon, too." She used her blinker and looked over her shoulder before moving into the carpool lane. "But Jessie's accident actually happened during lap swim, when it's normally slow and boring. Bob went to city hall. By the time he got back, an ambulance was rushing Jessie to the hospital and a paramedic declared Mr. Henderson's time of death."

Stacey hadn't decided yet how much she wanted to tell Gabe. Now, or ever. He was turned toward her and his undivided attention made her uneasy, but she decided that, like the lawyer, there were things that didn't need to be shared. At least...not yet.

"That sounds terrible, Stace. I wish I'd known sooner. I'm so sorry."

She gripped the steering wheel harder. "You went on a trip." Stacey gave Gabe a small smile as she looked over her right shoulder and made her way to the 91 Freeway interchange. "Tell me about it."

He faced the road. "The Grand Canyon. It was beautiful out there. So quiet. Untouched, you know? No one around for miles. We hiked and camped, carried everything in backpacks, hiked like twelve miles a day."

Gabe rubbed his quads. They peeked out from his black and blue striped boardshorts, and his legs were more tan and more defined than before the trip.

"We'd set up camp next to the Colorado River so we could wash off and have water to cook with. Some nights we just rolled out our sleeping bags and fell asleep staring up at millions of stars."

"Sounds incredible." Stacey sensed that if Gabe asked anyone to watch a meteor shower with him, they would *really* be watching the stars. Gabe always meant everything he said.

"Mom stayed at a condo in Oceanside with her sister. She loved having a two-week break from us."

Gabe flipped through the CD organizer. He ejected *Dookie* and replaced it with *Yellowcard*. He turned the volume dial up until "Ocean Avenue" filled the car. They sang along at the top of their lungs, bouncing in their seats.

Murphy slept peacefully, oblivious to their karaoke session.

An hour-and-a-half later, Stacey turned into the lot a half mile north of the Huntington Pier. Murphy jumped to her feet, caught a glimpse of dogs running on the sand, and started whining and panting, beating the seat back with her tail enthusiastically.

"Alright, alright." Stacey grabbed the end of the leash and opened the car door. Murphy squeezed between the seatbacks and into the driver seat before Stacy's feet were even planted on the asphalt.

"You have me to thank, you know, Murphy," Gabe chided. "Stacey would have left you at home."

Stacey's mouth fell open in mock indignation. "Don't feed my dog your lies."

"She's gonna love me even more when she sees this." He grinned, pulled a tennis ball from his pocket, and waved it above the top of the car.

Stacey scowled playfully at him. "She's loyal to me. She won't fall for your bribery." She held the leash firm against Murphy's pulling as she retrieved the towels from the trunk. "Grab that ice chest."

Murphy's breath was raspy as she tugged against the leash, pulling them toward Dog Beach. Once their feet were on the sand, Stacy unclipped the leash, and Murphy ran happily over to another golden retriever. They wagged their tails like long-lost siblings and sniffed each other in circles. They ran toward the rock wall that was infested with ground squirrels. The dogs barked and dug under the rocks as the squirrels scampered out of sight.

Stacey and Gabe dropped their flip-flops, towels, and ice chest near the rocks, and whistled for Murphy as they made their way to the shore. It was late morning, but there was still a light haze of the marine layer over the water, obscuring the view of Long Beach and Catalina in the distance. They walked along the damp sand, tossing the ball for Murphy every few yards, only for her to abandon the game of fetch in favor of sniffing seaweed.

"I'm so glad we did this," Stacey said, her lungs filling with the cool, damp ocean breeze. "It's been too long."

"Yeah. Me, too." Gabe stopped and turned toward her. "But, to be honest," he said, crossing his arms, "I was afraid we wouldn't ever be able to hang out like this again."

Stacey saw the hurt reflected in his eyes. "We should talk about the night of the party."

Gabe nodded gently, his mouth twisting to one side.

"I made so many mistakes that night," Stacey said, shaking her head and looking him straight in the eye. "This whole summer, really. I've acted like a jerk. And an idiot."

"Umm, hmmm..." Gabe nodded again, his eyebrows high. "Go on."

Stacey play-slapped his bicep. "Shut up. I'm trying to apologize."

He grinned. "I'm not stopping you."

"Can we sit, please?" Stacey pointed at dry sand nearby.

They walked over and sat beside one another, facing the water. Gabe dug his toes under the sand, his elbows resting on his bent knees.

Stacey sat crisscrossed and leaned forward, scooping the warm sand with her hands, feeling the grains slip through her fingers. She kept her eyes on Murphy as she spoke. "What I told you in your room about my night with Jessie was true. I wasn't ready and he didn't use protection. I was so scared and angry, and then embarrassed. I wanted him to hurt as much as I did. But I shouldn't have said any of those things about him at the party. That was awful. I apologized to him and we talked about everything."

Murphy trotted up between them and dropped the ball. Gabe chucked the ball into the white water for her. Murphy happily hopped over the rolling waves and scooped it into her mouth. She swam out a few feet before she returned to where they were seated. Murphy shook the salt water on them, then flopped down by their feet, panting.

Stacey lifted her knees and crossed her arms, resting her elbow on her knees and her chin on her forearm. "The drinking, smoking pot…getting trashed…that was completely stupid. At first, I felt nervous talking to so many people. When Melissa handed me a shot, I was glad to take it. But then it seemed like all those people liked me better when I was drinking and talking dirty, so I kept doing it until even I forgot who I was."

"What people?" Gabe dug his heels deeper in the sand, a pile mounding under his feet. "That's what I can't understand. Did you *want* Trent Stevenson to like you before that night?"

"God no! And I still don't!" Stacey turned toward Gabe, tucking one leg under her. "I can't thank you enough for rescuing me from him. He's a total asshole."

"That's about the nicest thing I would call that guy." Gabe clenched his jaw. A muscle on his cheek twitched.

A loud dog barked behind Stacey and she glanced over to see Murphy still panting, unbothered.

"Did you hear what Travis and his buddies did?"

"The marker on Trent's forehead? I heard." Gabe tossed a seashell toward the water like a mini frisbee. "Fucker got off easy, if you ask me."

"What you did… Gabe, I don't know how to thank you for taking care of me that night." Stacey looked down at her hands, pushing her cuticles back with her thumbnails. "I shouldn't have put myself in that position, and I feel terrible about everything you had to do to take care of me. I wish I could make that whole night go away. Erase it from everyone's memories."

Gabe turned to look at her. "The thing is, Stacey, I've never been that afraid in my whole life."

She could see in his green eyes that it was true. The sound of the waves crashing echoed between them.

He went on. "If Trent had actually hurt you, I think I might have killed him. Part of me wanted to knock on Jessie's door and teach him a lesson, too, after you told me what happened with him. That much anger scares me. After the party, I was so worried about you and so furious with you at the same time. You got yourself into those situations."

"I'm so sorry, Gabe. I wish I never put you through any of that."

He looked back at the water. "Up until this summer, you and me…we always came first with each other. I think I took that for granted. Then something changed. At the concert maybe? I got the sense that the way things had always been between us wasn't good enough for you anymore."

Stacey's stomach knotted. "Our friendship has always mattered to me," she muttered.

"Then what happened?"

She was terrified of how Gabe might respond, but he deserved the truth. "I wanted you to want to be *with* me."

Gabe nodded and looked at his hands. "I kinda thought so."

Stacey's heart sank. "If you hadn't seen the article in the paper, do you think you would have called me?"

Gabe shrugged. "I really don't know. Out there in the desert, I'd made peace with the fact that you were different now and we'd grown apart."

"I'm not different," Stacey said quietly, reaching over to rub Murphy's side. "Not really. I don't want to be the girl I was when I was with Jessie, or at that party, ever again."

"I see that. When it's just us, you're still the old you." Gabe had dug down to the damp sand, and scooped it into his hands, forming a ball. "I've thought about us before, too." He rolled the ball of sand back and forth between his palms. "About us being TOGETHER, I mean. I've thought about it a lot, actually."

"You have? I was sure you never thought of me like that."

"Of course I do. We always had fun together. And you're the kind of person who puts her mind to something and she accomplishes it. Like how one day you just decided you wanted to be a lifeguard. Next thing I knew, you were. I'm sure you'll get into every college you apply to, and be great at whatever job you have someday. That's what I love about you, and that's the kind of person I want to be with. Someday."

Stacey blushed at the compliment, but braced herself. Something else was coming.

The sand ball cracked in half. Gabe dropped it and wiped the sand from his hands. "I don't want to be tied to the person I'm going to spend the rest of my life with now. My parents did that. Fell in love in high school and got married way too young. Now they're talking about separating."

"Oh, my god, Gabe! I'm so sorry. When did this happen?"

"It's been coming for a while. I think my dad's going through a midlife crisis or something. That's not the point. I'm talking about you and me. We're kids, and I just want to let myself be a senior, and then in college, without thinking constantly about when I'm getting married or what my girlfriend will think of everything I do."

"I don't want that, either." Stacey said. A large wave crashed and the ground trembled beneath her.

"Don't you see? Things between you and me are already too intense. If we dated, we'd either break up and I'd lose you forever, or we'd stay together forever and miss out on being young and free. Either way, it wouldn't be good for us, not right now."

Stacey stretched her legs out in front of her and rested back on her elbows, watching the waves. A seagull flew past, dipping down and landing on the water in the distance. "I guess I see that. The chances of us going to the same university are pretty slim. If we're just friends, the distance will be easier."

Murphy stood and stretched, then trotted toward a group of dogs surrounding a man with a frisbee.

"That's the difference between you and me," Gabe said, standing. He brushed the sand off his shorts then offered Stacey a hand to help her up. "I would never say we are 'just friends.'"

Stacey took his hand and let him pull her to her feet. "That's not what I meant."

They headed back in the direction of their towels, the ice chest, and Murphy, who was chasing the frisbee with a German shepherd and a beagle.

Gabe rested his forearm on Stacey's shoulder as they walked. "Right now, I 'just date' people. But you are one of the most important people in my life. I hope you always will be. I love you, Stacey."

Stacey stopped and looked up at him. "I love you too, Gabe." She wrapped her arms around his waist and nestled her head under his chin. "Thank you for always being my very best friend."

Murphy snored the entire ride home. "I swear she's smiling," Gabe said.

"It's the two hotdogs I bought her." Stacey grinned.

"No way. She's happy because she chased MY tennis ball in the surf for more than two hours. You made her walk up and down Main Street twice just to buy two stickers and not share your ice cream with her."

Stacey shook her head. "I told you! Dairy gives her terrible gas. We could die of asphyxiation on the way home!"

"That sunset was great though. I'll give you that."

"Wasn't it?" Stacey sighed. She thought about her art journal. She wanted to paint the sunset they'd seen in it, maybe even write a poem to capture the moment. "Hey, if I tell you something, do you promise not to laugh at me?"

Gabe turned to look directly at her. "You know I can't promise that, Chapman, but I'll do my best."

"Nevermind." Stacey put her elbow on the window frame and rested her cheek in her palm.

"Come on." Gabe tapped Stacey's arm. "I was kidding. You can tell me anything. You know that. But I'll be serious now…" After a beat he patted her knee. "Tell me!"

She looked at him out of the corner of her eye. "Okay. Well, I've been taking art lessons with Ms. Moreno this summer."

"What? You've been going to school?"

"Not really. It's at night. Not like a real class for credits or anything. I just went a few times."

"Oh, that's cool." Gabe shrugged. "So…you're thinking of doing art again?"

"I mean, I always liked it, ever since I was a little kid. But I never thought I could do anything with it, so it seemed like a waste if I wanted to go to a major university."

"But that's changed?" Gabe tilted his head, confused. "You think now there *is* something you want to do with art?"

Stacey smiled. "Yeah…I think so. Last night I was working on something in the art lab for a long time, and by the end Ms. Moreno said something that made me think about my art in a whole new way."

"What way is that?"

"I know it sounds weird, but for the first time ever, instead of thinking about what anyone else said or thought or did, or what I should be or do because of what the rest of the world might think— I just created what I wanted, for me, with no intention of ever showing it to anyone. And it felt *so good*."

"You lost me." Gabe threw up his hands. "So now you want to do art, but never show it to anyone?"

"Not exactly." Stacey laughed. "That's the thing. Once I tuned out all those other people's opinions, I finally made something I'm kind of proud of. Ms. Moreno thinks I might be able to make it into a song."

"I thought you said it was art."

"Yeah, it was, at first. The art led to me writing this poem, and the poem could maybe be a song. I want to do art because I think it maybe opens my mind up to write lyrics. Maybe I want to be a songwriter. Is that totally crazy?"

Gabe's face lit up. "I don't think it's crazy at all. You know more about music than anyone. Can I read it?"

"Yeah." She bit her lip. "I think I want to show it to you when we get back to my house. To see what you think. But you have to promise you won't make fun of me if it's totally lame."

"Stacey, you are one of the smartest, most talented people I know. If you want me to read it, I know it won't be lame. What's the poem called?"

"It's called 'Out of the Blue.'"

Gabe smiled. "I like it already."

Chapter Twenty-Seven

The Plunge reopened a week after Jessie's accident. But everything was different.

Despite how complimentary *The Sun*'s article had been to Mark, he quit working at the pool once the city finished their investigation. None of the staff had seen him since the day of the accident, other than Stacey for the brief moment after her testimony at city hall.

"He needed to move on," Bob said when anyone asked about Mark.

"That bitch lawyer better not have made him think he did something wrong," Melissa said. "Mark's the reason Jessie's still alive."

"For the umpteenth time, I told you," Bob said with exasperation, "she was just doing her job. The investigation determined no one was at fault. The city is closing the facility once summer is over, possibly to renovate or demolish it and build a new pool. Either way, Mark was going to be out of a job and he was ready to move on. I support his decision."

"Seems like he should have at least said goodbye," Desiree muttered.

"Yeah, something's off," Chad said. "We were friends. Friends don't just disappear."

The city canceled the rest of The Plunge Olympics, citing the reduced staff. After the bombing at the Centennial Olympics on Sunday, July 27th, the staff considered the word "Olympics" to be a curse, and forbade anyone from uttering it again at The Plunge. But the damage was done. At most, a dozen swimmers came to the pool on any given day. Often less.

Tiffany was made assistant manager for the remaining few weeks of swim season. That left only four regular guards to work all the open swim morning and afternoon shifts. Lap swim was never reinstated. The new staff safety rules required staff be given extra time to take breaks, eat lunch, and take care of work-related errands.

The following two weeks passed in a haze. Jessie's guitar stood in the corner of the guard shack and Mark's wide-brimmed hat sat atop the filing cabinet, both untouched and collecting dust, like monuments to their absence.

"They're definitely gonna tear this place down. Soon," Chad said on Thursday night as the team pulled the covers over the pool. "Look around, ladies. We are The Plunge's last lifeguards."

"A new facility could be way better, though." Stacey pushed the empty cover cart against the wall. "Imagine how Mesa Valley would benefit from a pool twice this size, with retractable safety covers, vacuums that ran at night, and handicap access."

Tiffany flipped off the pool lights and locked the doors to the pump and chemical rooms. "It would be better, but something like that takes years to build. I learned to swim in this pool. I can't even count the number of races I competed in here as a kid. It's just hard to imagine it not being around anymore."

"What if they turned this place into a skate park?" Desiree asked. "That could be cool."

Chad held open the door to the guard shack for them, and the girls filed inside. "Jess would love that. He partied here enough with his buddies at night, it might as well have been a skate park already."

Stacey remembered the way Jessie reacted to Melissa's conniption fit about the mess on the morning after the Fourth of July. Stacey had suspected it was Jessie and his friends who'd been there drinking and setting off fireworks. "Has anyone talked to any of those guys?" she asked. "I hope Jessie can have regular visitors soon. His skater friends are more like family than his dad is."

"So are we!" Desiree whined, grabbing her keys and towel, then shutting her locker. "It's too quiet around here without Jessie or Mark."

Stacey nodded. "Yeah, we were together practically every day for two months, and then suddenly they aren't here anymore. It's totally bizarre."

"That was the saddest part last year." Tiffany leaned against the desk and looked around, her eyes glassy. "I was like you, Stacey; the only lifeguard still in high school. The whole crew left for college at the end of summer and the only two I ever saw again were Mark and Bob. Now Mark and Jess are gone, and The Plunge might close forever. It feels like losing my home."

Desiree and Stacey enclosed Tiffany in a group hug.

"We won't abandon you, Tiffany," Desiree said. "Even though school starts soon, we'll stay in touch."

"Hope so." Tiffany squeezed each of them around the waist.

"We still need to have our girls' night!" Stacey looked at Desiree. "We need to talk to Melissa. Figure out a time we can do it."

"For sure!" Desiree agreed. "I'll call her when I get home."

"Yeah, yeah, yeah. Come ooon." Chad slumped against the doorframe, his hand on the light switches. "It's late. Let's get out of here."

The girls parted. They turned off the guard shack lights and locked the office doors behind them. The other three stood around Tiffany as she locked the outside door, then they all headed for their cars.

On Friday, August 9th, Stacey's home phone rang at seven thirty in the morning.

"I have good news and bad news," Bob said when she picked up.

Stacey was making toast before work, already dressed in her red swimsuit. "What's the good news?" She slathered butter on the toasted sourdough, cradling the phone between her ear and shoulder.

"Jessie is allowed visitors now. You guys can all go see him."

"That's great!" Then Stacey's stomach dropped, and she braced herself against the counter. "So…what's the bad news?"

"The pool is closing as of today." Bob sighed audibly.

Stacey dropped her knife. It clanged on the linoleum. "Oh…" She thought of Chad and Tiffany's words from the night before. How right they'd been.

Bob went on. "With school starting soon, there aren't enough lifeguards to safely keep The Plunge open. And we haven't had enough swimmers to meet our operating expenses."

"I get it," Stacey said, plucking the knife from the floor.

"I'll be here for a few hours. Come by and grab any belongings you left. After that, anything I come across will be placed in the lost-and-found box outside the gate. Goodwill will stop by and grab the stuff in a few days. Then it's out of my hands."

"Thanks, Coach. Maybe I'll grab Jessie's skateboard and guitar, too. I can drop them at his apartment."

"I'd appreciate that," Bob said quietly.

Stacey hung up and stood still beside the counter.

Her mom bustled into the kitchen, dressed for work. "Who was on the phone?" She grabbed a mug and filled it with coffee.

"Bob. They decided to shut down The Plunge for good. Starting today." Stacey's arms were crossed, and she held the toast near her mouth. Murphy stood at her feet staring upward.

Stacey's mom set the coffee pot back, and leaned against the counter, her mug between both hands. "Wow. What a surprise. Did you have any idea it might happen so soon?"

Stacey took a bite of her toast, chewing as she spoke. "We talked about it. I thought for sure it wouldn't be before Labor Day, though."

"I'm sorry, Doodle Bug. Honestly, it surprised me they ever reopened it after the accident. The facility is so rundown; they've talked about a new pool for years. Seems like what happened was the excuse they needed to find the funding."

Stacey took another bite, and Murphy snuffled up the crumbs as they hit the floor. "Bob also said we can visit Jessie now," Stacey said. "I think I'll call and see if anyone wants to go with me."

"Oh, gosh. That's going to be hard." Her mom grimaced. "Especially for you. You think you're really ready to see him again? After everything?"

"I think so. I feel like I need to, you know?"

"Just don't go alone, okay? It might be really emotional." She leaned over and kissed Stacey's cheek, then grabbed her keys. "I've gotta get to work, but call me if you need to. Love you, Bug." She headed for the front door.

"Love you, too." Stacey dropped the crust of her toast for Murphy. "I guess I should change, huh?" She looked down at her red swimsuit and pulled at the loose, faded fabric.

Murphy gnawed the crust out of the side of her mouth, the tags on her collar clinking.

"After all the drama I created about this thing, it's crazy to think I may never need to wear it again." Stacey pushed away from the counter and dragged her feet back to her bedroom.

Murphy quickly sniffed the floor one last time for any rogue crumbs, then trotted behind Stacey down the hall.

Crossing the parking lot, Stacey could feel the hot asphalt through her cheap flip-flops.

"Good thing no one brought chocolate," Tiffany said. "It would melt before we even got inside." She looped her left arm through Stacey's, her bag of Red Vines crinkling in her left palm.

Stacey held tightly to the seam of the bag of Cool Ranch Doritos she had in her opposite hand, attempting to keep as many chips unbroken as possible in her meager gift. On Stacey's left, Melissa gripped a bottle of Mountain Dew between both hands. The trio led the way to the entrance, followed by Chad and Desiree, his arm around her.

Beads of sweat ran down Stacey's spine. The top of her head burned until the moment they entered the entrance walkway.

"Shade, finally," Desiree gasped.

The Red Hills Hospital's large glass doors swooshed open ahead of them, and they stepped inside the frigid, antiseptic-laden air.

"Thank God!" Melissa put her arms out to let the cool air conditioning envelop her, while Tiffany crossed the lobby to ask the front desk receptionist for the room number.

Noting the security guard's lengthy instructions about lefts and rights down corridors, and the importance of avoiding staff elevators, the group began winding through the building's long empty hallways.

Stacey wrapped her arms around herself and rubbed her purply-gooseflesh, regretting her outfit choice. "It's freezing in here!" she whispered, although there was no one nearby to disturb.

"Suck it up, Chapman," Chad said.

"It's just because it's so hot outside." Melissa bumped her upper arm against Stacey's in encouragement. "You'll get used to it." Their footsteps echoed through the hallways.

Exiting the elevator on the third floor, they were met with muted beeping sounds from various blinking machines and the squeaking wheels of the janitor's garbage bin.

"These rooms are so dark, it's sad. Why are all the curtains drawn?" Stacey whispered.

"Keeps the rooms cool. Bacteria spreads faster when it's too warm," Melissa said.

They arrived at Jessie's room as an orderly was carrying out a still mostly full lunch tray of clear soup, red Jell-o, and apple juice. The small, round woman smiled at them, her crooked teeth adding a familiar charm to her kind face. "'He could use some visitors!"

Jessie's blinds were also drawn, and he gazed blankly at *The Price Is Right* on the snowy screen. A thick, white brace spanned his shoulders and chest. Metal rods ran upward from the brace to a halo around his skull, supporting his neck with screws attached to the sides of his head.

Chad led their group in as Bob Barker announced, "Come on down!" to a clapping TV audience.

Jessie's eyes shifted to see who had entered his room. His body lay still.

"Hi Jessie!" Tiffany waved enthusiastically, living up to her role as The Plunge's pep-commissioner.

They surrounded Jessie like he was a wounded bird. Chad and Desiree stood at his right side, and Tiffany hovered on Jessie's left, while Melissa and Stacey stood at the foot of the bed.

"Hey," Jessie's throat scratched out through his dry lips. He managed a meager grin. His eyes lit up as he took them all in. The scrapes on his forehead had healed to a baby pink, the scar on his nose a fine line, and his skin was pale. Purple moons hung under his eyes, emphasizing his sunken cheeks, and his shaggy blonde hair was dingy with oil.

"We've missed you so much!" Tiffany leaned over the bedrail and gave him a gentle embrace, maneuvering around all the medical devices and apparatuses. She set her Red Vines on a small, beige, wheeled table hovering over Jessie's lap.

The other guards added their offerings to the pile: a colorful array of chips, soda, and candy. Stacey worried Jessie wasn't allowed any of it, based on the untouched tray of liquids that had just been wheeled out, but Jessie smiled dimly at the stash of contraband. "Thanks."

"Looking good, man." Chad gripped the bed-rail with both hands. "Anything worthwhile on TV?"

"Sure," Jessie breathed out. Unable to move his head, he smiled, straining to look Chad in the eyes. "Mexican soap operas."

"I hear those are way sexier than American soaps," Desiree said. "You know, you could totally pass as a hot patient on *General Hospital.*"

The other girls grinned and nodded, chuckling nervously.

"Except those patchy face-pubes make you look like Beavis." Chad brushed a finger against Jessie's chin.

"Shut up, Butthead," Jessie managed.

They all laughed. For a brief moment, the teasing felt almost normal.

Stacey squeezed her arms tighter around herself.

"Stacey, take that blanket," Jessie said. "The one on my feet."

Stacey shook her head and dropped her arms to her sides. "No, no, no. I'm fine."

"You're cold." He sounded sincerely concerned. "Might as well take it. I can't feel anything anyway."

And there it was. The uncomfortable truth. Stacey's eyes misted.

Tiffany went to the window and opened the blinds. "This'll help." She was careful not to let the sunlight shine directly in Jessie's face. "See, it's cheerier in here already."

The heat of the sun immediately warmed the room.

On the nightstand next to Jessie was the newspaper article about the accident. There was also a generic rainbow "Get well soon" greeting card, a bouquet of wilting daisies with mossy green water, and a yellow smiling sun balloon that barely floated. Stacey pointed to crayon-drawn cards taped to the wall behind her, just past the foot of Jessie's bed. "Where did these come from?"

"Bob dropped 'em off." Jessie coughed weakly. "Kids left them at the pool for me."

There were pictures of flowers, hearts, smiley faces and rainbows, and one of a stick figure in red shorts with a gold medal that said, "You're my hero!"

"Those belly flop kids keep coming in, asking about you," Desiree said. "Chad gave one $5 for managing a perfect backflop last night."

"It was epic." Chad beamed. "Never saw a kid so confidently do a backward swan dive like that and never break."

Jessie's grin faded. "Bob said The Plunge is shutting down for good?"

"Maybe not," Tiffany said. "They might just renovate it."

"It hasn't been the same without you." Melissa's words eeked out, releasing a flood of her tears. "I'm so sorry, Jessie!"

Stacey bit her lip and put an arm around Melissa.

"It's not your fault." Jessie's nostrils flexed and his eyes welled up.

Chad looked around at the girls who had all started to weep. "We just hate that this happened to you, Jess. But...you'll be back on your board before you know it."

Jessie focused his gaze on the ceiling, and over a minute passed as tears fell silently down his cheeks.

Melissa's crying intensified. Desiree took her hand and led her out to the hall.

"We should let Jessie rest," Tiffany said, wiping her own tears away.

Chad nodded in agreement, and Tiffany went back to close the blinds again.

Stacey squeezed Jessie's foot, then turned to follow them.

"Stace...wait," Jessie breathed out. "Can we...talk?"

Stacey nodded at Tiffany and Chad. They pulled the door closed behind them. She moved to Jessie's side. She perched carefully on the edge of his bed, and took hold of his left hand, tucking her hair behind her ear.

Jessie took slow breaths with his eyes closed. Stacey assumed he was trying to get his tears to stop. Sitting in the silence alone with him made her uncomfortable.

"I, um, grabbed your guitar when I got my stuff from The Plunge this morning," she rambled, wiping her nose between her fingers. "I have it in my car. Want me to drop it by your apart—"

"Keep it," Jessie said.

"No way! I can just drop it off with your brother or something."

"I can't play anymore. I want you to have it. You love music. You should learn to play. Give my board to Chad."

Hot tears streamed down her cheeks, dripping onto her skin above the scoop neck of her tank top. "This is all my fault," she said quietly.

Jessie furrowed his brow, confused.

"You were guarding because of me. I should have been in that chair." She wiped at the damp splashes on her collarbone, the motion doing nothing to slow the pounding of her heart.

"No, you couldn't be in the tower because of me." Jessie closed his eyes. "That was my fault. Are you…okay?"

Stacey bit her lip and shrugged.

"I mean, are you…pregnant?"

A lump formed in Stacey's throat. She swallowed hard and shook her head.

"Thank God." He closed his eyes again. For a moment they both let the relief wash over them.

Stacey wiped her face with the back of her hand. Jessie stared intensely at her.

"Thank you," he said, searching her eyes, "for saving my life."

"I… I didn't," Stacey mumbled, surprised. "Mark did…"

"I know. But, you did, too. And Melissa."

Stacey nodded.

Two of his fingers twitched against Stacey's palm and her heart leapt. "Your fingers!" She gripped his hand tighter.

"They do that. The doctors say it *might* be a good sign." Jessie sighed, rolling his eyes, then looked at Stacey again. "Where's Mark?"

"I don't know. He quit. None of us has seen or heard from him for more than two weeks."

"Tell Mark to come here."

"But…we don't…"

"Please, Stace…" Jessie seemed weak and tired. "I need to see him."

"Okaaayyy." Stacey wasn't sure how, but didn't want to argue with Jessie in his fragile state.

"Promise me." His fingers twitched again in Stacey's hand.

She looked into Jessie's crystal blue eyes. "I will. I promise."

"Don't worry, Stace. I'm a fucking warrior, just like that coyote. This won't stop me."

Stacey thought of the animal that had stood so proudly in front of them, and nodded. "You are a fucking warrior. Nothing can keep you down." She squeezed his hand.

"Get Melissa?"

"Sure." She squeezed Jessie's hand one last time. Without thinking, she leaned down and kissed his cheek. She tasted the salt from his tears on her lips as she looked one last time into his eyes. Then she let go of his hand and stepped into the hall.

"Melissa," Stacey said, leaving the door open behind her. "Jessie wants to talk to you."

Melissa had calmed and wiped her cheeks. She let go of Desiree's hand and crossed the hall into Jessie's room, closing the door behind her with a gentle click.

Stacey turned to Chad and Tiffany. "Do you have any idea how we might be able to get ahold of Mark?"

"His number was at The Plunge," Tiffany said. "But when I tried calling, no one picked up, and there wasn't a machine."

"Do you think we could find his address in the phone book?" Stacey asked.

Tiffany shook her head. "They're unlisted."

"He took me by his house once," Chad said. "It's near the golf course. I don't totally remember how to get there, but we could drive around until we find it."

"Jessie really wants to talk to him." Stacey gestured over her shoulder. "He made me promise to ask Mark to come visit."

Chad nodded, pulling his keys from his pocket. "Desiree can take my car, and I could go look for Mark with you."

Stacey looked at Desiree. "Do you mind?"

Desiree shook her head. "Not at all. I can take Melissa and Tiffany home."

Tiffany nodded. "When you find Mark, tell him to call me, too."

Chad handed Desiree the keys. "If Jessie's still awake, tell him we went to find Mark for him, okay?"

The girls nodded. Stacey headed for the elevator.

Chad kissed Desiree quickly, then trotted to catch up with Stacey. "Let's go."

Chapter Twenty-Eight

I f you had to bet money on it, what do you think Mark has been doing the last two weeks?" Stacey asked, once they were on the freeway back to Mesa Valley.

Chad rested his elbow on the window frame and ruffled his hair with a sigh. "Getting stoned. Sleeping. Playing video games. You?"

"That's what I'm afraid of, too." Stacey exited the freeway at County Line Road. "After that night by the hot tub, I haven't felt right about those pills Mark takes. But, after all these years working together, don't you think Bob knows about it, too? Wouldn't he be worried?" She turned toward the golf course.

"Bob knows more than he's telling us, I'm sure of it," Chad said. "But Mark's doctors give him those pills. They can't be so bad. And Bob sees injured baseball players all the time."

"Maybe I'm overreacting." Stacey pulled to a stop behind a tow-truck at the signal. "Do you remember if Mark's street is anywhere near the clubhouse? That's the only part of the golf course I know how to get to."

"Because of prom?" Chad asked with a chuckle.

"Yeah," Stacey said shyly, embarrassed.

"Me, too! No one in my family golfs, or could EVER afford to live in a neighborhood like Hawk Hill. I'm still totally blown away by Desiree's place and we've been together for like two years. The one time Mark and I stopped by his house is the only time I've been by the golf course, other than prom." Chad shook his head. "It's not really by the clubhouse, but it was kind of on the way. Just go in that direction. I'll see what looks familiar."

Once the signal turned, Stacey navigated around the tow truck, past the Christmas tree farm and antique mall, then turned down Avenue L. Almost every yard they passed was dry and dusty, enclosed in chain-link fencing. Cars sat atop cinder blocks in what would be lawns if there wasn't a drought, and large dogs were chained to the ancient oak trees that offered shade.

Stacey turned onto Country Club Drive, following a small green golf course sign with an arrow pointing right, and the whole environment was instantly different. "Look at this place," she said.

Large rolling green lawns were divided by hedges, with beautifully manicured flower beds. The cars parked in driveways were buffed to a shine. Rather than the two steps and a railing that led to small stoops on Avenue L, the ranch-style country club tract-homes had wrap-around covered porches shaded by blooming magnolia trees, or large, shiny green palm fans.

Chad pointed to a cul-de-sac to the left. "Turn there. I think it's close to the end on the right."

There were only seven houses on the street, three on each side and one at the end. Mark's big truck came into view, parked in a driveway beside a hedge of cypress trees.

Once she saw the house, Stacey could picture Mark, the former football star, being raised there. The gray house had blue trim and shutters, its brick walkway was lined with red and white rose bushes. It was the kind of home that perfect American families occupy on TV, the kind of families she imagined would have a son recruited to play college football for a renowned team like Texas A&M.

Stacey pulled in beside Mark's truck. She and Chad walked side by side to the front door. The house was dark. Chad tried the doorbell and knocked. There were no sounds of animals or people inside.

"If his truck is here, wouldn't Mark be here, too?" Stacey asked.

"Not necessarily. He's really good about not driving if he plans to get trashed."

They stood in silence for a minute, looking around. A lawn mower buzzed in the distance. "What do we do now?"

Chad shrugged.

They walked back to the car and got inside. Stacey bit her lip, and focused on the dashboard, trying to come up with a plan. "What if we hunt down someone else Mark is friends with? Do you think Travis knows him well enough to have an idea of where he might be?"

"I don't think so." Chad looked out the passenger window at Mark's truck. "Mark is two years older than Travis. I'm pretty sure they only know each other because of football."

Stacey pointed to the handle in front of Chad's knees. "I might have a piece of paper and a pen in the glove compartment. We could leave him a note. We could stick it in the mailbox, or wedge it in the front door?"

Chad spread his knees apart and opened the compartment. He pulled out a stack of stapled sales paperwork. They were sifting through to see what could be sacrificed when there was a knock on the driver's-side window.

Stacey startled, accidentally bumping the car's horn.

A nicely dressed woman in her late sixties stood there patiently with a soft smile.

Stacey rolled her window down.

"Can I help you?" the woman asked.

"We're just trying to find Mark Rosenthal," Chad said, leaning over the emergency brake to be heard over the engine and the loud AC. "We need to talk to him."

"I live next door," the woman said, gesturing over her shoulder to the house at the end of the cul-de-sac. "The Rosenthals are on vacation in Hawaii."

"Oh," Stacey replied, confused. She looked at Chad, who seemed equally surprised. "Don't you think Mark would have mentioned a trip like that coming up at some point this summer?"

Chad threw his hands up.

"But Mark isn't with them," the woman said slowly.

"He's not?" Chad said looking up at her through the open window.

"No." The woman clasped her hands in front of her. "Can I ask, how do you know Mark?"

"We worked together at the pool," Stacey said.

"He's our friend," Chad interjected.

The woman twisted her lips and brought her right hand to her mouth, as if she was contemplating something. "If you're here about drugs, you should leave right now."

"What?" Stacey said. "No! Mark rescued another friend of ours, Jessie, while I was there. Mark saved his life. When we were at the hospital visiting, Jessie said he really needed to talk to Mark, and made me promise I would tell Mark to go see him. That's why we're here."

"I see." The woman nodded and dropped her hands. "Mark's had a rough go of things lately, and we have to be careful about who can see him. If you give me a minute, I can find out if he would like to talk to you. At the very least I can give him your message. What are your names?"

"I'm Stacey and this is Chad." Stacey gestured with her hands. "We don't want to be a problem. We've just been worried about him."

"I'll be right back. He's my grandson, by the way."

She crossed the large lawn between the two houses. Stacey rolled the window back up and looked at Chad. "What the hell?"

Chad pushed his palms into his eye sockets, then smoothed his hands over his hair. "Who knows. At least we found him."

A few minutes later, Mark's grandmother waved from her porch for them to come over.

Stacey's flip-flops sank into the cool, damp lawn and thick blades of grass poked at her feet. There was a richness in the air that smelled green, so different from the chicken manure that permeated Stacey's neighborhood.

Mark's grandmother's house was the mirror image of Mark's, so the front entrances paralleled one another on an angle, with a wide view of the golf course in between the two properties. A golf cart and a large, white Cadillac were parked beside one another in the driveway.

"Do you think they drive the golf cart right over the lawn and down there to that path?" Stacey asked.

Chad nodded, his sandals crunching into the grass with each step. "Someday I want a house in a place like this," he muttered.

"For sure," Stacey agreed. "But not in Mesa Valley."

Mark's grandmother stood beside the wide, shiny wooden front door, and ushered them inside.

The entryway had wood-paneled walls and smelled like Pledge. Every surface that wasn't shiny wood was either sparkling glass or fine upholstery, and there was an entire wall of books in the family room. An older man looked up at them from his seat in the corner where he was reading.

The family room's large picture window lit the room well and gave a clear view of the entire neighborhood. Stacey's car stuck out like a sore thumb beside Mark's truck, and she could see how its presence would have drawn their attention immediately.

"Hi." Stacey waved at the man she assumed was Mark's grandfather. "Sorry to interrupt your afternoon."

The man nodded in reply, but did not wave back. Or smile.

"Follow me," Mark's grandma said. "Mark's in the dining room."

The scent of a delicious meal cooking wafted toward them from the kitchen, offering a warm, comfortable aura to the house.

Mark was seated at the table, clean shaven, with a fresh haircut, a buttoned shirt, and slacks. Without his goatee and wild locks, sprawled on the guard shack's thrift store couch in a stained tee and red trunks, this Mark barely resembled the person Stacey had worked with at The Plunge all summer.

"I'll leave you," his grandmother said. "Pop and I will just be in the other room if you need us, Marky."

Chad and Stacey looked at each other, grinning.

"Marky?" Chad teased under his breath.

They pulled chairs out and sat across from Mark at the table.

"Hey, guys," Mark said, cracking his familiar grin. "Whatcha doin' here?"

"No one was answering your phone," Chad started. "Stacey promised Jess she'd get in touch with you. I offered to help, since I remembered where you lived from that time we…." Chad quickly glanced around, then gestured smoking weed with his middle finger and thumb so the grandparents wouldn't hear.

Mark smiled and nodded. He pushed back until his chair leaned on two legs, his arms crossed.

"Jessie really wants you to go see him at the hospital." Stacey chimed in. "That's why we came to find you. Your grandma saw us sitting in my car in your driveway." Stacey gestured over her shoulder. "She invited us inside."

Mark appeared entertained by their rambling, but offered no explanation.

After several seconds of silence, the only sound coming from a timer ticking in the kitchen, Stacey became annoyed. "Are you okay?"

Mark nodded enthusiastically, but said nothing.

Chad and Stacey stared back at him, expectantly, then at each other, confused.

Stacey tossed her hands up in exasperation. "Well, if you're fine, then why'd you disappear? You didn't even say goodbye."

"Yeah, man, why didn't you answer the phone, or call any of us?"

Mark took a deep breath and dropped the front legs of his chair to the ground. He rubbed his hands on his thighs. "I…went to rehab. I got back Wednesday from two weeks at a place in the desert. I'm seventeen days sober."

"Seriously?" Stacey asked. "Does Bob know?"

"Good for you, man," Chad said.

Mark chuckled. "Thanks. Uh…yeah…Bob knows. But," he rubbed his hand through his now shorter hair, "my parents are really embarrassed by this whole thing. They asked him to respect our privacy and keep it confidential. They're pretending we all went on a last-minute vacation. They dropped me off in the morning and then went straight to the airport and flew to Hawaii. They get back tonight."

"How do you feel?" Stacey asked.

"Pretty good, I think," Mark said. "I mean EVERYTHING hurts, all the time. But I understand now that's normal. I have to keep telling myself the pain is more of a thought than a reality." Mark pulled a pack of gum out of his pocket and unwrapped a piece. He offered the pack to them before setting it on the table. "At least I'm not always half-asleep anymore."

Mark leaned forward, resting his elbows on the table, smoothing the metallic paper between his fingers while he talked. The gesture reminded Stacey of Jessie's gum wrapper airplane that night at the movies. A lifetime ago. Her chest ached.

"There were a bunch of people in my program out there who got addicted to pain meds, like me," Mark continued. "I guess doctors are just starting to understand how the pills make your body believe it's in more pain than it is. It takes awhile for the brain to stop telling your body it hurts so much. I just gotta push through." Mark crumpled the wrapper and dropped it on the table. He leaned back again in his seat, shoving his hands in his pockets. "But, if I'm not asleep and I'm not eating, I'm not sure what to do to distract myself from the pain."

Stacey noticed how Mark's cheeks had filled out, and the purple pools beneath his eyes had puffed into bags.

"That sucks. I'm so sorry. So...what now?" Chad asked. "I'm sure you've heard about The Plunge closing for good?"

"Yeah...I heard." Mark exhaled. "I can't stay around here anyway. It wouldn't be long before I reconnect with the same people I've gotten high with and pills from for years. That won't work."

Stacey nodded.

"I'm gonna try community college again," Mark said. "But I'm going to move in with my uncle in Louisiana. He's been sober twenty-six years, so…he knows." Mark nodded toward the living room. "This is nothing new to my grandparents. Anyway, there's a school out there that has a sports medicine program. I figure maybe I could study that, understand my own injuries and get back into the football sidelines or something. Maybe help injured players not get into a situation like I did."

"That's a great plan, Mark," Stacey said. "You should be proud of yourself."

A stern look of disappointment clouded over Mark's expression. "I'm a long way from being proud of myself. I have a lot to forgive myself for." Mark leaned forward, staring at his clasped hands. "Like Jessie, for starters."

"What do you mean, 'Like Jessie?'" Chad asked.

Mark looked up at the corner of the ceiling, like he was watching a reel of the accident. "The last two weeks, I kept thinking, 'If I'd been sober, how would it have gone differently?' I have no idea if I responded fast enough, or if I did the right things. It's all a fog. He could have died. Mr. Henderson did die." Mark chewed at his nail and spit it out. "If I ruined Jessie's chance to ever walk again because of those stupid pills, I could never forgive myself."

"You saved Jessie's life, Mark. He knows that," Stacey said. "It's what he wants to tell you. He wants to thank you."

Mark's face softened as he absorbed Stacey's words.

Chad added, "Yeah, man. Jess broke his neck when he hit the bottom. That wasn't your fault. And you were the only one strong enough to get him back-boarded and out of the water so fast. Maybe Bob could have done that, but maybe not."

"Bob had his own distractions. We all did." Stacey nodded. "I'm really glad you're sober. It's the best thing you can do for yourself. But that day you didn't act like you were high. You did everything you could possibly do to save Jessie and Mr. Henderson. That's what I told that lawyer, and I meant it. You were a hero."

Mark's eyes misted over, but he stubbornly shook his head. "You did just as much as I did. If I'd acted sooner...been more aware of what was happening..." Tears rolled down his cheeks and he angrily wiped them away. "...maybe Mr. Henderson would still be alive."

"He was already dead when Jessie dove in, Mark," Stacey said quietly. "No one could have saved Mr. Henderson."

Mark looked at Chad for confirmation.

Chad nodded. "It's true. There was nothing anyone could have done."

Mark closed his eyes and the tears stopped. He wiped his face before opening them again.

The timer chimed in the kitchen. Mark's grandma shuffled past them and pulled open the oven. "Don't mind me, Marky."

"We should go," Stacey said to Chad. She stood and pulled the keys from her pocket. "Thank you for having us," she called out toward the kitchen. "We're gonna head out. We don't want to interrupt your dinner."

"Okay, dear," his grandma called back. "Thanks for coming by."

Chad stood and pushed in his chair. He walked around the table and clapped Mark on the shoulder. "I'm gonna miss hanging with you. Keep in touch, okay?"

Mark stood and gave Chad a pat on the back.

Stacey waited for them to part then spread her arms wide to give Mark a hug. "Go see Jessie, okay? And call Tiffany."

Mark let go of their embrace and stepped back, saluting her. "Yes ma'am. I promise I won't leave without saying goodbye." He set his hand on Stacey's shoulder and looked in her eyes. "You're a damn fine lifeguard, Chapman. We made a good team."

Stacey sighed. "I learned from the best."

Chapter Twenty-Nine

A re we done yet?" Gabe whined, leaning against the counter at Miller's Outpost.

Stacey looked through her shopping bags, mumbling to herself. "Dickies, Levis, tank tops, flannel shirts. Yeah, I think that's good for now. What time does the movie start?"

Gabe looked at his watch. "Thirty minutes."

"Perfect. We'll have time to get candy and popcorn."

"You know, when you said you'd finally take me to see *Cable Guy*, I didn't think you'd make me go shopping with you first, then only spring for the dollar theater, cheapskate."

"What difference does it make?" Stacey juggled the bags in her hand, looking for her keys.

"It's the principle of the thing." Gabe pushed open the glass door and held it open for Stacey.

Stacey handed him the bags, then pried open her purse continuing to dig for her keys while they crossed the parking lot to the Silver Bullet. "Will it make you feel better if I also buy your snacks?" Keys in hand, she popped open the trunk.

Gabe set the bags inside, then closed the hatch. "I want nachos. Not popcorn. A large Mountain Dew and a Butterfinger."

Stacey climbed in behind the wheel and turned the keys in the ignition, turning the AC on high. "It's hard to believe school is starting the day after tomorrow."

Gabe closed the passenger door and buckled his seatbelt. "I'm bummed we won't have any classes together."

"At least our lockers are close." Stacey backed out, then put the car in drive. "And we got spaces in the senior lot next to each other." She turned out onto the road.

"I was thinking of designing mine with a solid blue background, my white home jersey in the center. That way it has something for basketball with my name, and '13,' my lucky number."

"You mean my birthdate?" Stacey grinned.

"Mere coincidence. What are you painting in your spot?"

"It'll look like the *Tragic Kingdom* album cover, with 'Have No Doubt' across the top 'Stacey Chapman parks here!' at the bottom. There'll be a rude girl with short yellow hair dancing in blue Docs holding a red lifeguard buoy. I'm going to put a black-and-white checked border around the whole thing."

Gabe laughed and shook his head. "You never cease to amaze me, Chapman. Ms. Moreno should give you extra credit now that you switched into advanced art."

Stacey shrugged. "Painting makes me happy. And while I'm painting, I go into this zone where the lyrics just sort of come to me."

He drummed the dashboard. "Yeah. You've got a new song for band practice tomorrow night, right?"

"Seems weird to call it band practice when I've only learned two chords."

"That's all most punk bands play anyway, and you've gotta start somewhere. How else are we gonna record your songs and open for The Juvenile Delinquents in January?"

Stacey blushed and scrunched up her nose. "Do you really think the songs are that good?"

"I told you they are! Martin said if we didn't want to play them ourselves, the Juvenile Delinquents will. 'Out of the Blue,' 'In Too Deep' and 'Warrior' are his favorites. But I still think 'Absorbed' is the best. It's what we have to call the band, and our first album. It's perfect."

Stacey nodded. "Did I tell you about the lyrics I was working on last night? It's about that night at Travis's party. Kind of a 'fuck you' to Trent and Jason."

"Really? That's hard core." Gabe chuckled. He slid his arm between the chair and her back to rest his hand on her left shoulder, watching her out of the side of his eye. "What's it called?"

Stacey glanced at the dimple in his cheek, then caught his gaze, lifted her eyebrows and smiled. "Easy A."

Acknowledgements

This book would not exist without Sarah Cray and Let's Make Art (LMA). In 2020, without a career, and after eight loved ones died over six years, I tried to find some peace during pandemic lockdowns and protests. A social media ad changed my life. I followed LMA's free online watercolor tutorials while I sat at a little desk in our cold garage. As my interest in painting grew, my creative spirit–the part of me that had been buried in grief–was reborn. By May of 2021, I'd applied to grad school for an MA in literature and writing. By the end of 2022, I'd graduated and written my first draft of this novel. Sarah, Ms. Moreno may sound a lot like you, but I hope it's evident no character could ever measure up to the person you are. Thank you for being the art teacher I never knew I always needed.

I also want to thank Joey Garcia. When we met at the San Francisco Writers Conference in February 2023, I knew she was the author coach who could make my goals possible. Joey helped me find Stacey's deeper story by tapping into that passion for watercolor that had started it all. She encouraged me to paint the story in my mind, then put it on the page. And she reminded me to write like I'm talking to a friend, which is what Joey quickly became. Thank you, Joey, for helping me accomplish the tasks necessary to become an author, fulfill responsibilities that I hadn't understood, and for keeping me on track to make this dream a reality, even while life demanded my attention and time for other things.

To all my friends and family, thank you for reminding me this was what you always knew I could do. To those who read drafts, asked about my progress, and promised to be the first to buy this book when it finally came out, thank you for being the audience I knew was out there for *Absorbed*. Thank you for understanding when I sacrificed our time together to meet a deadline. Thank you for helping me create a buzz around this book, to share it with books clubs, schedule book signings, and find opportunities to introduce Stacey's story to readers who will cherish it.

And to all the people I grew up around, who may recognize elements of this book as familiar, I want to acknowledge that because of our shared history, you all were instrumental in my telling Stacey's story. Although Mesa Valley is a fictional place, if you grew up with me, it may feel a bit like our hometown. Each character is a mosaic of individuals I have fond memories of from high school and college, with one exception. The lead singer of the Juvenile Delinquents in *Absorbed* is intended to closely resemble my friend and classmate Martin Arretche. Martin was an inspiration from the very beginning, making his music dreams come true, and he was taken too soon from this earth. Before he died, I told him I wanted to base a character on him, and by doing so I hope a bit of his spirit will always live on in Mesa Valley.

Also, Murphy Brown really was the coolest, sweetest female golden retriever, who we got just before my 16th birthday, and who died days before she turned seven. Murphy deserved to be memorialized as Stacey's loyal companion, just as she had been mine.

Finally, to all the musicians and artists referenced throughout this book, and to the infinite others I had to cut for length, your work is the reason why this story came to me. Your songs are the ones we dance and fall in love to, the music that comforts us as we grieve, and your lyrics convince us to be stronger, fight harder, and dream bigger.

BOOK
CLUB
FAVORITE

READING
GUIDE

Topics and Questions for Discussion

Part 1, "Wading In"

1. Setting and Relevance

How does the 1996 rural Southern California setting in *Absorbed* impact the story? Do you think the book's setting in the nineties makes it more or less relevant to readers today? How does the setting connect with your own experiences, or remind you of a particular time in your life?

2. Music and Personal Connection

Music is a key part of Stacey's journey in the book. Is there a song or album from the nineties that has had a significant impact on you? Maybe a song that helped you get through a tough time, or reminds you of a particular moment in your life? How does the music in *Absorbed* resonate with you? Do any lyrics stand out to you, or bring back memories of your own experiences?

3. Stacey's Art Classes with Ms. Moreno

Stacey uses her summer art classes with Ms. Moreno as an escape from her emotional turmoil. Through these classes, she starts to understand herself and her goals more clearly. How does art help Stacey cope with her struggles? Have you ever found art or other forms of creativity to be therapeutic?

Part 2, "In Too Deep"

4. Sexual Consent and Responsibility

On their date, Stacey is caught in a difficult situation where she wasn't prepared to have sex, and Jesse doesn't use a condom. How do you think society's expectations of males and females around sexual consent and responsibility differ? Has this changed over time? Can you relate to Stacey's feelings of frustration and confusion, especially as she navigates these issues at a young age?

5. The Rabbit and the Coyote

After Stacey and Jessie's sexual encounter, Stacey imagines a lone rabbit being attacked by coyotes for its ignorance. Later, she sees a scarred coyote standing proudly, unafraid of her car. What do the rabbit and coyote symbolize in these scenes? How do these animals reflect Stacey's view of herself or her relationship with Jessie?

6. Mark's Perspective

Mark seems less concerned about how others perceive him compared to the other pool staff. Why do you think that is? How does his attitude affect his relationship with Stacey, especially when he gives her advice about asking for help? Do you think his perspective will change over the course of the story?

7. Stacey and Sharon's Relationship

In the beginning, Stacey focuses a lot on her appearance, while her mom, Sharon, is consumed with the challenges of being a single mother. They often clash and push each other away, but after the party Stacey turns to her mom for support. What do you think changed in their relationship? Have you ever experienced a shift in your own relationship with a parent, child, or close family member? What caused that change?

Part 3, "Breaking the Surface"

8. Stacey and Gabe's Friendship

Stacey and Gabe share a deep friendship, but Stacey hopes for something more, which causes tension between them. In the end, Gabe values their friendship and doesn't want to risk losing it over a teenage romance. Can you relate to the idea of choosing a friendship over a romantic relationship? Have you ever been in a situation where you valued a friendship so much that you were hesitant to let it evolve into something else?

9. Teenagers and Responsibility

In *Absorbed*, Stacey and her fellow lifeguards are properly trained but still experience a traumatic incident that has life-changing consequences. The city investigation requires them to testify about their roles and the pool's procedures. How do you feel about the level of responsibility placed on teenagers in high-pressure jobs like lifeguarding? Do you think teens are often asked to handle situations beyond their years? How does this compare to your own experiences with responsibility at a young age, either in work or other areas of life?

10. **Identity and Confidence**

By the end of the novel, Stacey has discovered a passion for art and songwriting, which helps her embrace a new sense of confidence. Has there been a time in your own life when discovering a talent or passion gave you a boost of confidence? How did it change the way you saw yourself? Did it affect your willingness to take risks?

About the Author

Jaime Townzen is a Southern California-based writer and professional artist. Jaime met her best friend and the love of her life, Patrick, in college when they bonded over a mutual love of music. They married in 2002, and have two daughters. When Jaime's not in her studio, she can be found at the beach with her dogs or listening to live music with her family and friends.

Connect with Jaime Townzen

https://jaimetownzen.com

https://www.facebook.com/jaime.townzen

https://www.instagram.com/jaimegetscreative

https://www.tiktok.com/@jaimegetscreative